BU

D0498179

DATE DUE

MY BOYFRIEND IS A MONSTER

I Love Him to Pieces

OR

MY DATE IS DEAD WEIGHT

OR

HE ONLY LOVES ME FOR MY BRAINS

EVONNE TSANG

Illustrated by JANINA GÖRRISSEN

GRAPHIC UNIVERSE™ · MINNEAPOLIS · NEW YORK

STORY BY
EVONNE TSANG

ILLUSTRATIONS BY
JANINA GÖRRISSEN
ADDITIONAL INKS BY MARIA VILLAR

LETTERING AND COVER COLORING BY
ELDON COWGUR

Copyright © 2011 by Lerner Publishing Group, Inc.

Graphic Universe™ is a trademark of Lerner Publishing Group, Inc.

Graphic Universe™
A division of Lerner Publishing Group, Inc.
241 First Avenue North
Minneapolis, MN 55401 U.S.A.

Website address: www.lernerbooks.com

Library of Congress Cataloging-in-Publication Data

Tsang, Evonne.
    I love him to pieces / by Evonne Tsang ; illustrated by Janina Görrissen.
        p.   cm. — (My boyfriend is a monster ; #01)
    ISBN: 978-0-7613-6004-9 (lib. bdg. : alk. paper)
    1. Graphic novels. [1. Graphic novels. 2. Interpersonal relations—Fiction. 3. Zombies—Fiction.
4. High schools—Fiction. 5. Schools—Fiction. 6. Chinese Americans—Fiction. 7. Saint Petersburg
(Fla.)—Fiction. 8. Horror stories.] I. Görrissen, Janina, ill. II. Title.
    PZ7.7.T8Ial 2011
    741.5'973—dc22   2010030774

Manufactured in the United States of America
1 – DP – 12/31/10

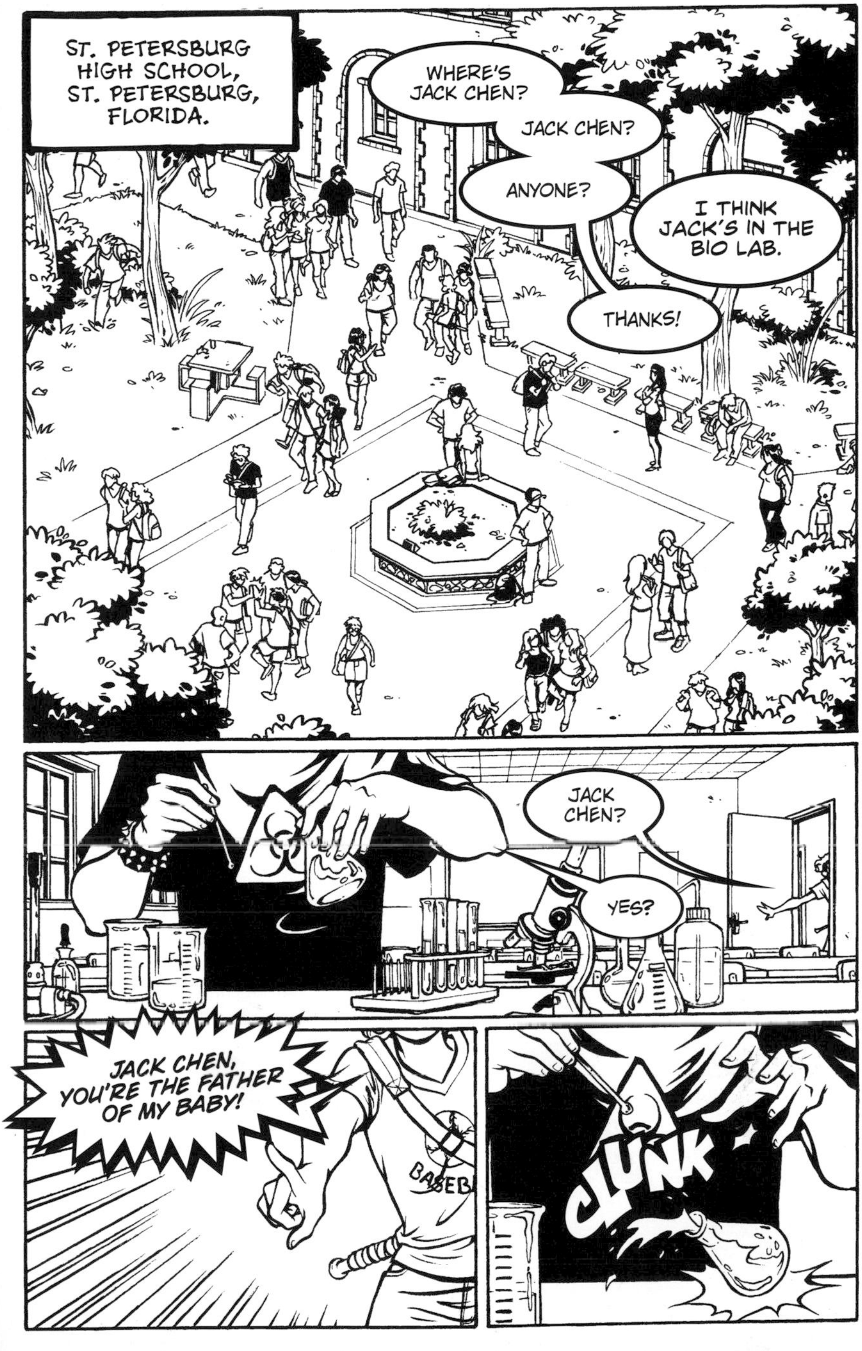
ST. PETERSBURG HIGH SCHOOL, ST. PETERSBURG, FLORIDA.
WHERE'S JACK CHEN?
JACK CHEN?
ANYONE?
I THINK JACK'S IN THE BIO LAB.
THANKS!
JACK CHEN?
YES?
JACK CHEN, YOU'RE THE FATHER OF MY BABY!
CLUNK

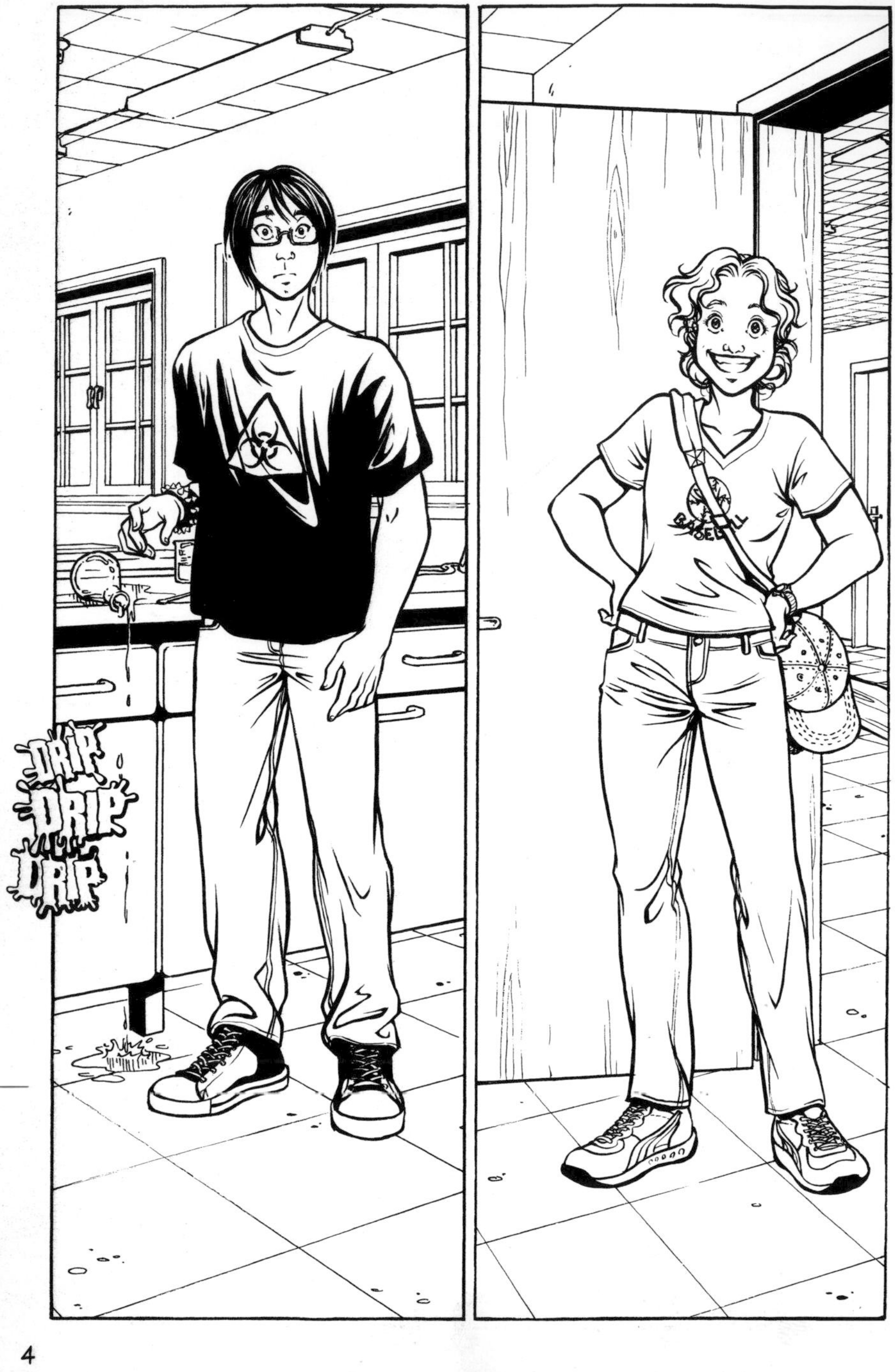
DRIP
DRIP
DRIP

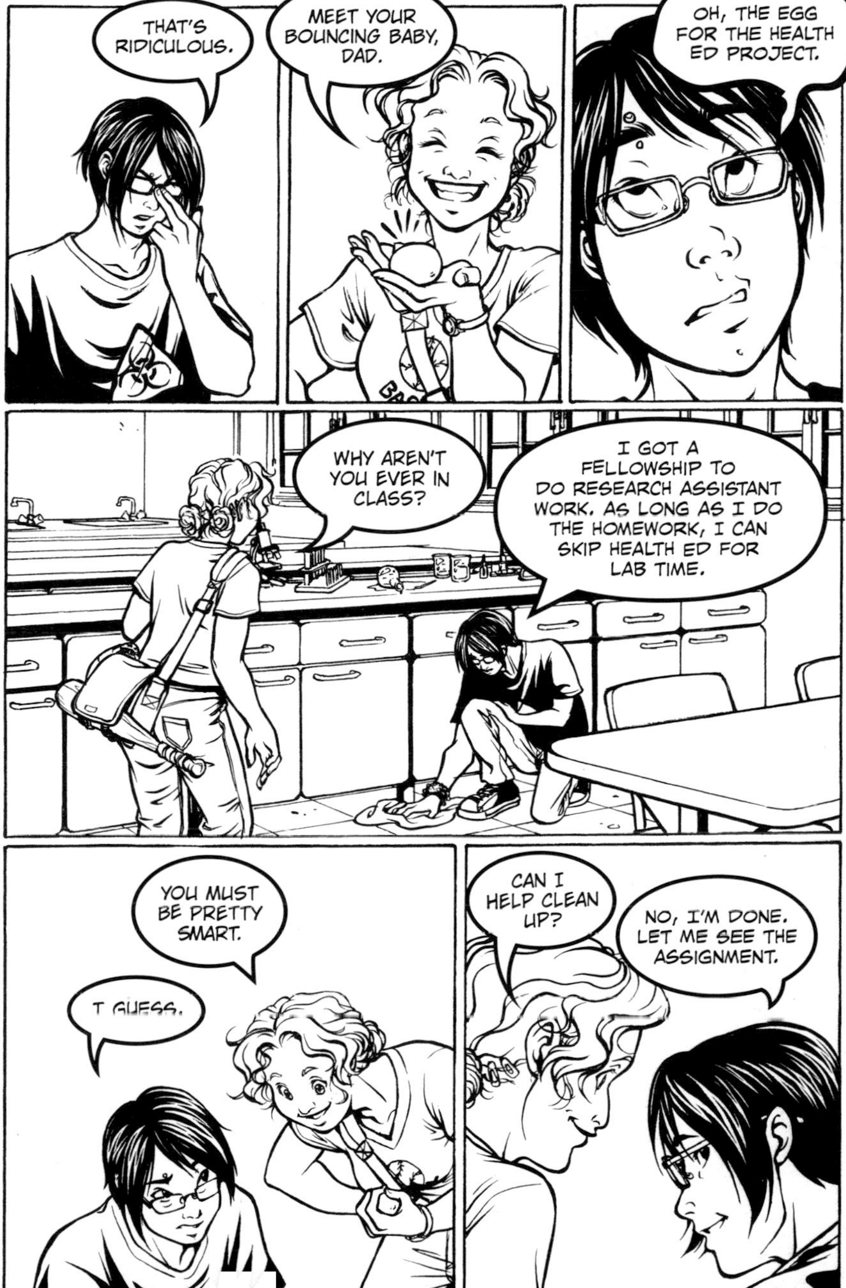
THAT'S RIDICULOUS.
MEET YOUR BOUNCING BABY, DAD.
OH, THE EGG FOR THE HEALTH ED PROJECT.
WHY AREN'T YOU EVER IN CLASS?
I GOT A FELLOWSHIP TO DO RESEARCH ASSISTANT WORK. AS LONG AS I DO THE HOMEWORK, I CAN SKIP HEALTH ED FOR LAB TIME.
YOU MUST BE PRETTY SMART.
I GUESS.
CAN I HELP CLEAN UP?
NO, I'M DONE. LET ME SEE THE ASSIGNMENT.

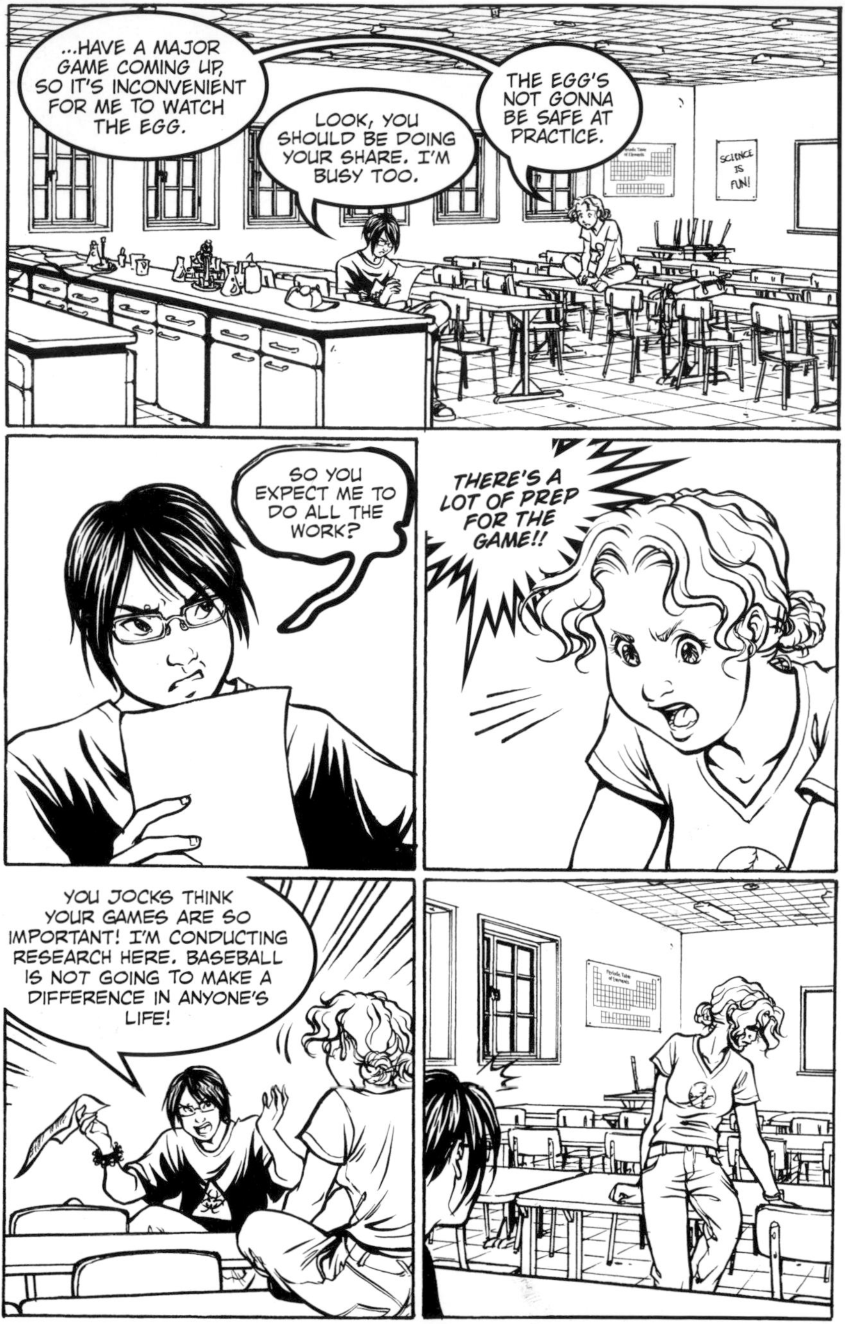
...HAVE A MAJOR GAME COMING UP, SO IT'S INCONVENIENT FOR ME TO WATCH THE EGG.
LOOK, YOU SHOULD BE DOING YOUR SHARE. I'M BUSY TOO.
THE EGG'S NOT GONNA BE SAFE AT PRACTICE.
SCIENCE IS FUN!
SO YOU EXPECT ME TO DO ALL THE WORK?
THERE'S A LOT OF PREP FOR THE GAME!!
YOU JOCKS THINK YOUR GAMES ARE SO IMPORTANT! I'M CONDUCTING RESEARCH HERE. BASEBALL IS NOT GOING TO MAKE A DIFFERENCE IN ANYONE'S LIFE!

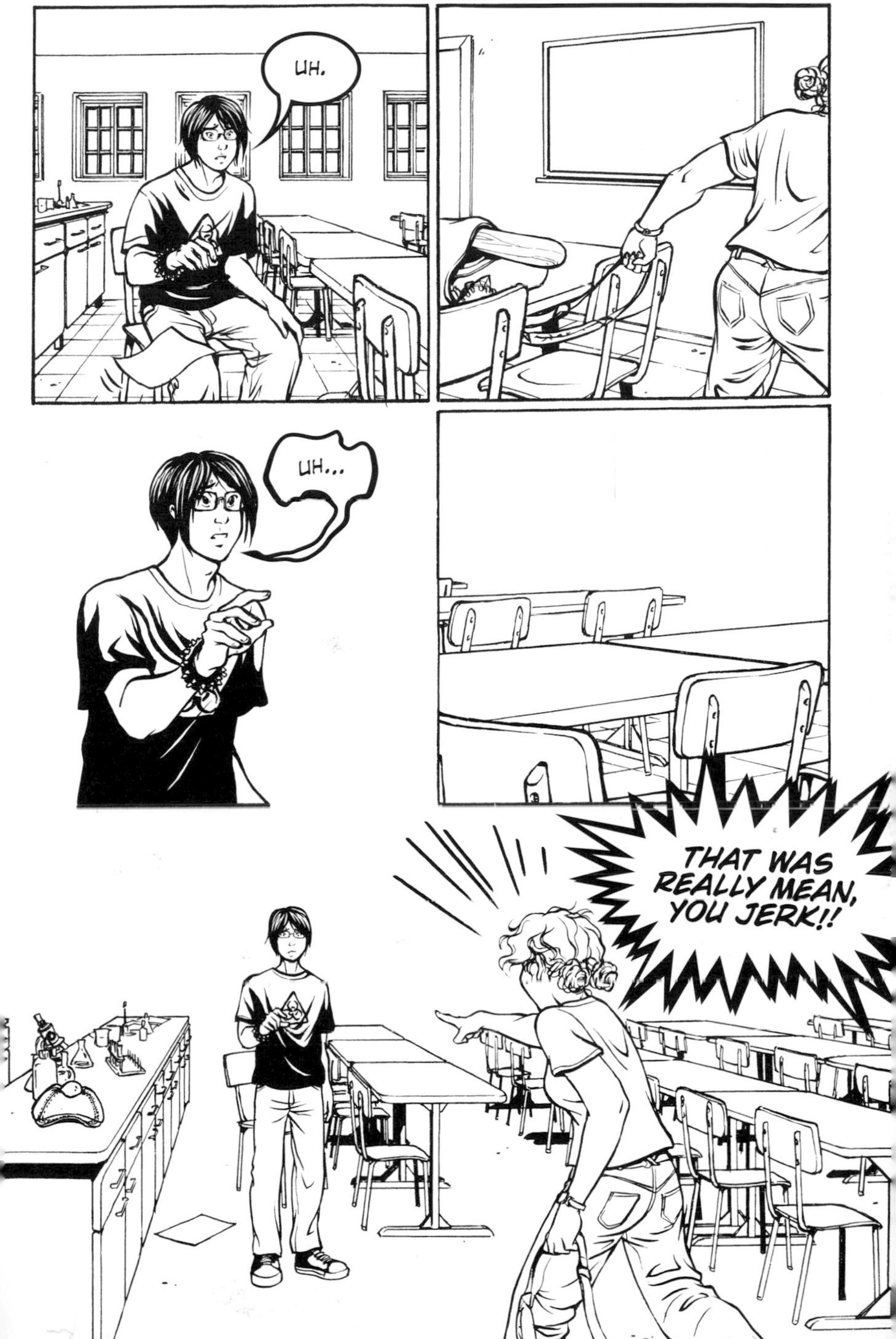
UH.
UH...
THAT WAS REALLY MEAN, YOU JERK!!

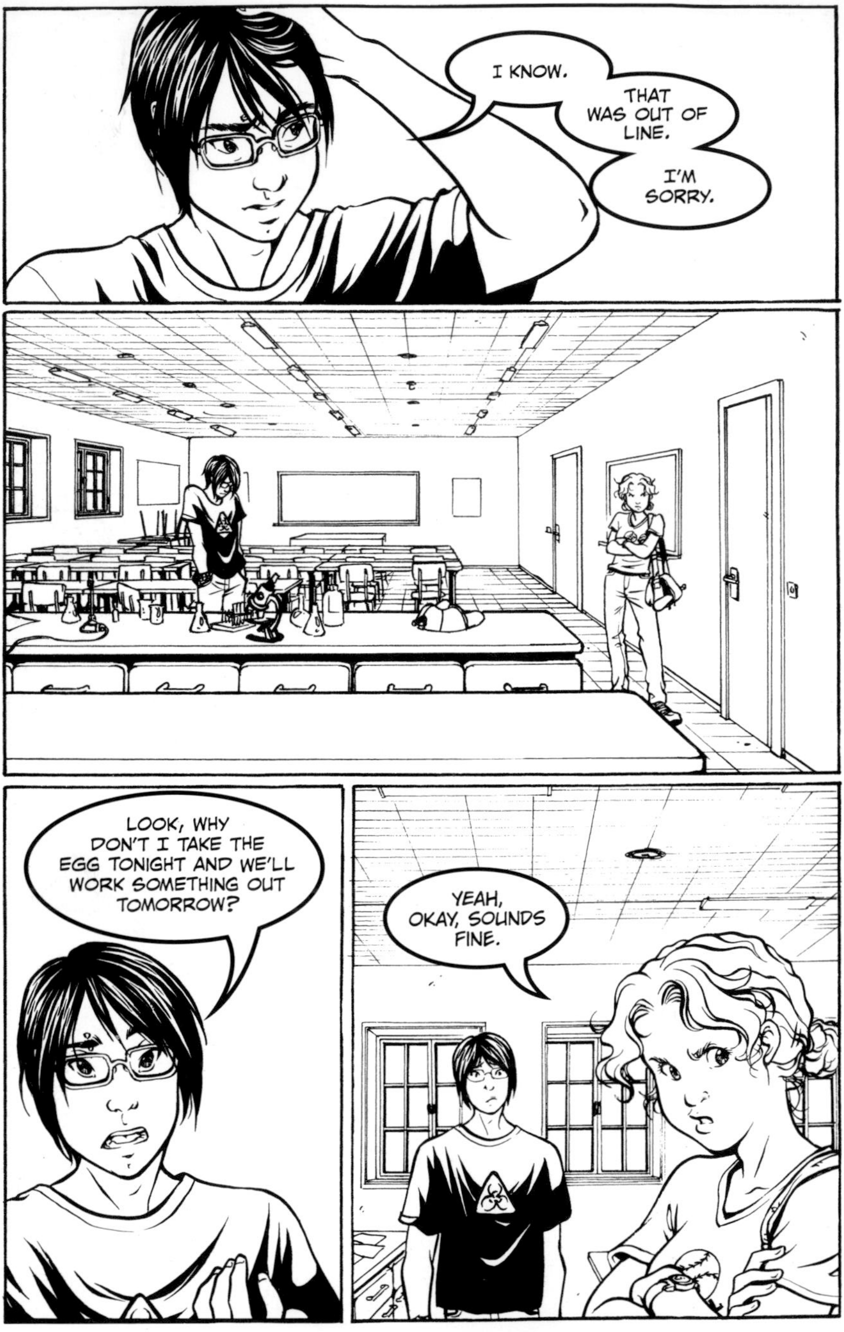
I KNOW.
THAT WAS OUT OF LINE.
I'M SORRY.
LOOK, WHY DON'T I TAKE THE EGG TONIGHT AND WE'LL WORK SOMETHING OUT TOMORROW?
YEAH, OKAY, SOUNDS FINE.

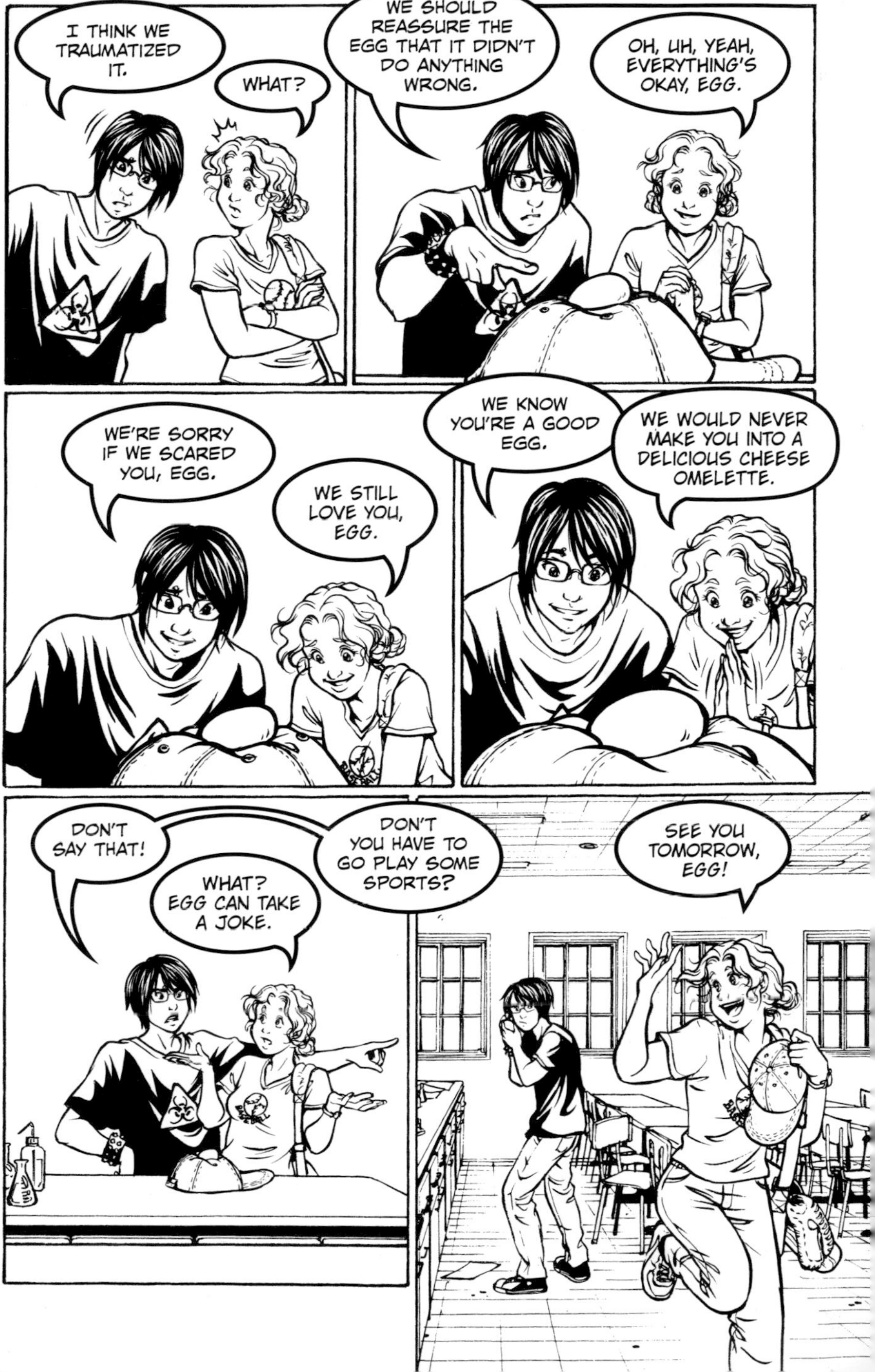
I THINK WE TRAUMATIZED IT.
WHAT?
WE SHOULD REASSURE THE EGG THAT IT DIDN'T DO ANYTHING WRONG.
OH, UH, YEAH, EVERYTHING'S OKAY, EGG.
WE'RE SORRY IF WE SCARED YOU, EGG.
WE STILL LOVE YOU, EGG.
WE KNOW YOU'RE A GOOD EGG.
WE WOULD NEVER MAKE YOU INTO A DELICIOUS CHEESE OMELETTE.
DON'T SAY THAT!
WHAT? EGG CAN TAKE A JOKE.
DON'T YOU HAVE TO GO PLAY SOME SPORTS?
SEE YOU TOMORROW, EGG!

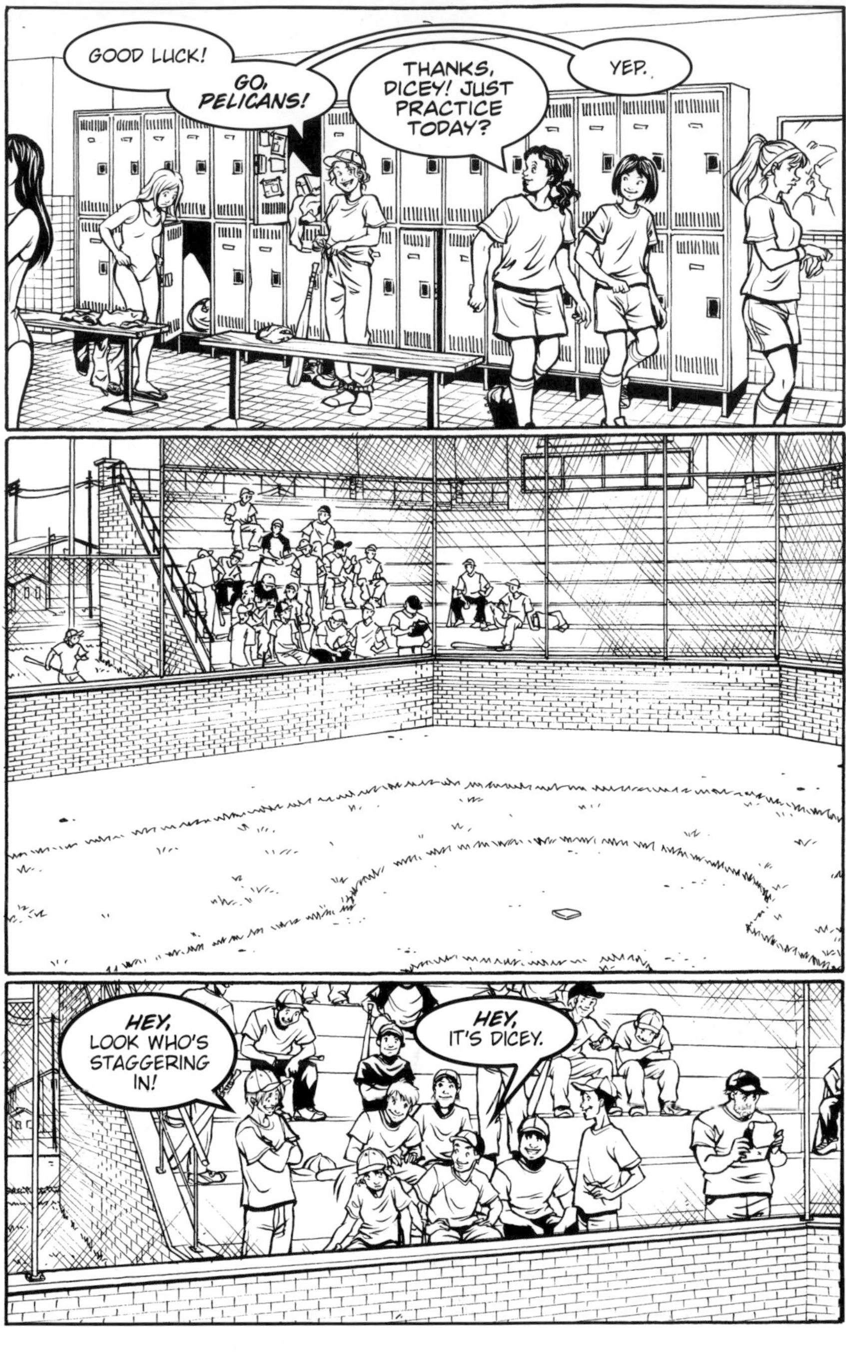
GOOD LUCK!
GO, PELICANS!
THANKS, DICEY! JUST PRACTICE TODAY?
YEP.
HEY, LOOK WHO'S STAGGERING IN!
HEY, IT'S DICEY.

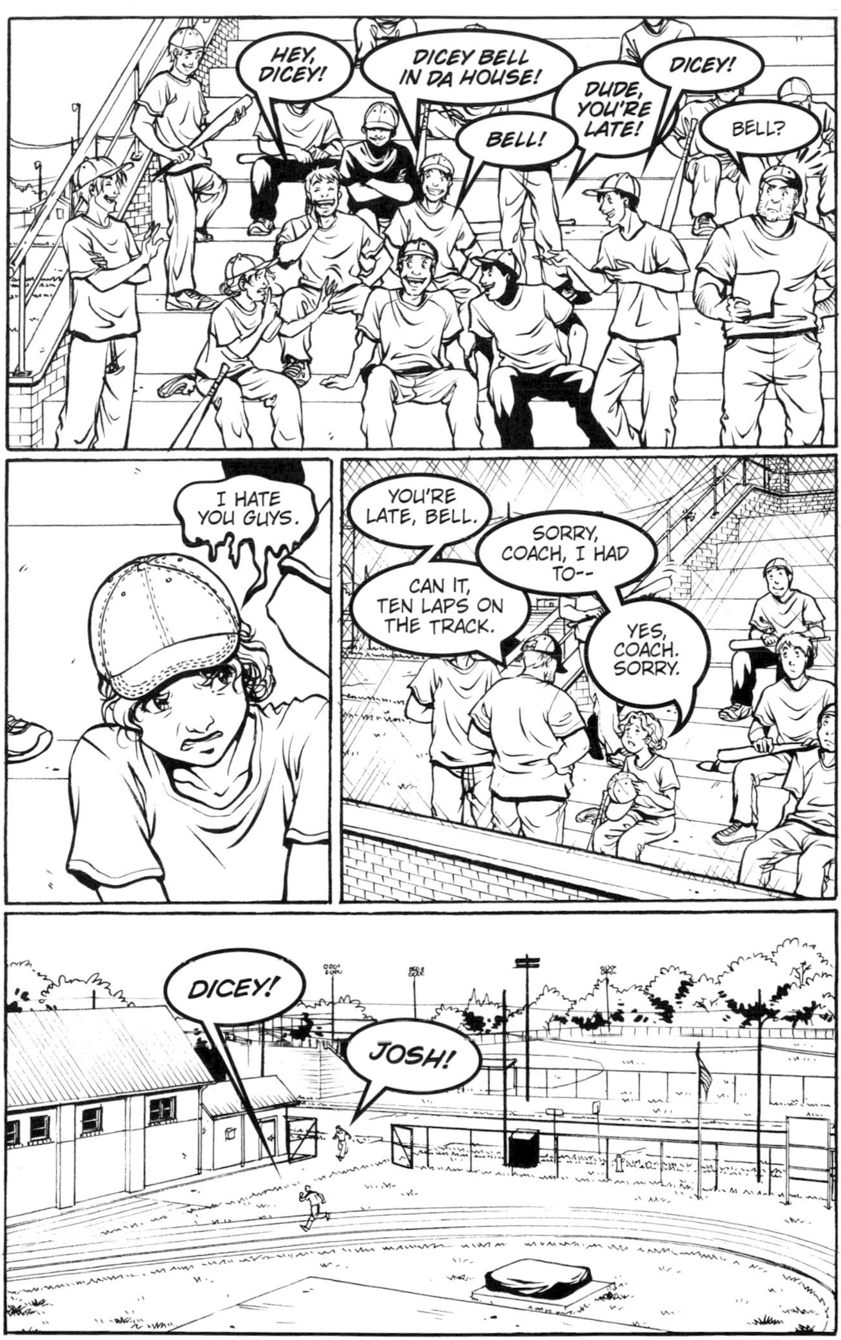
HEY, DICEY!
DICEY BELL IN DA HOUSE!
BELL!
DUDE, YOU'RE LATE!
DICEY!
BELL?
I HATE YOU GUYS.
YOU'RE LATE, BELL.
SORRY, COACH, I HAD TO--
CAN IT, TEN LAPS ON THE TRACK.
YES, COACH. SORRY.
DICEY!
JOSH!

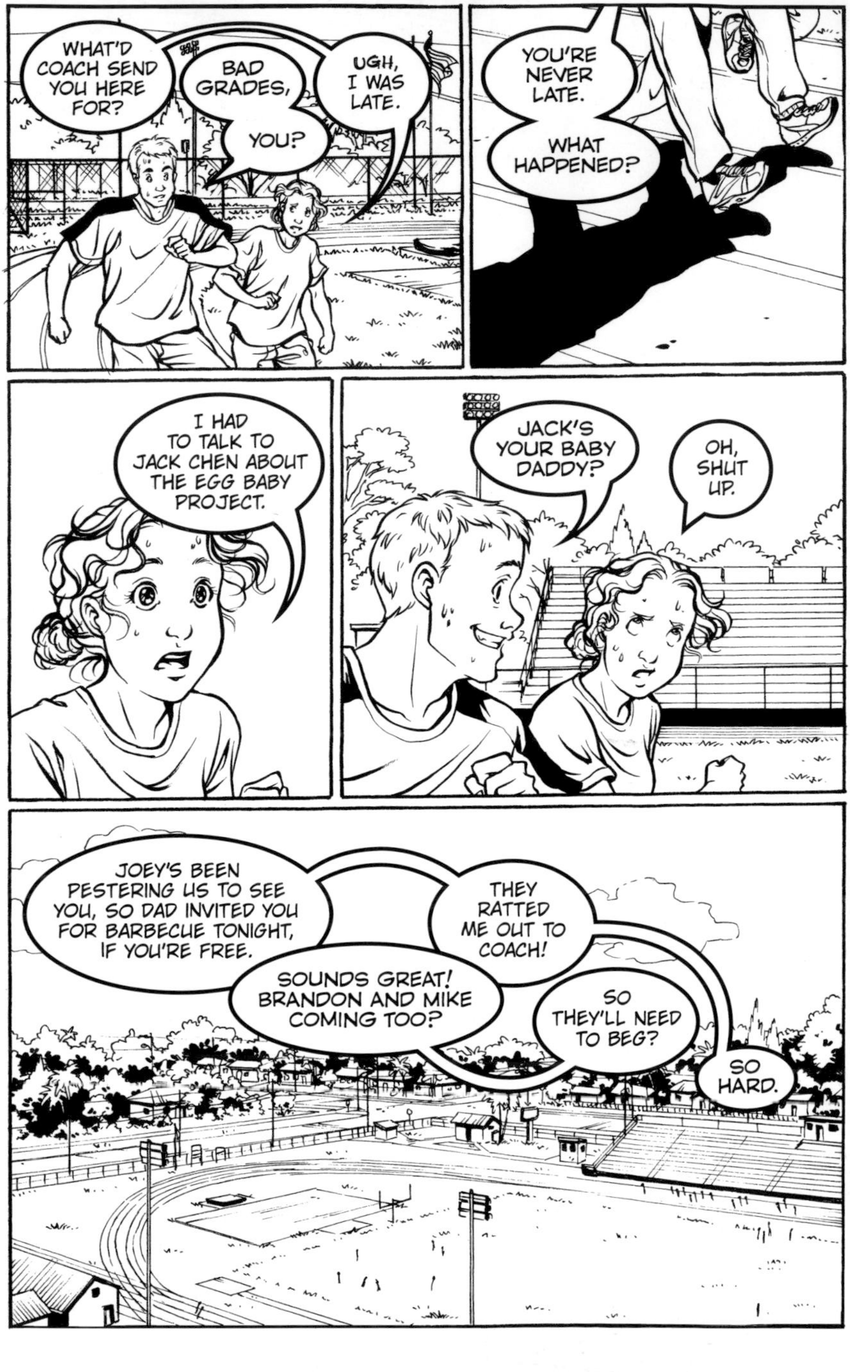
WHAT'D COACH SEND YOU HERE FOR?
BAD GRADES,
YOU?
UGH, I WAS LATE.
YOU'RE NEVER LATE.
WHAT HAPPENED?
I HAD TO TALK TO JACK CHEN ABOUT THE EGG BABY PROJECT.
JACK'S YOUR BABY DADDY?
OH, SHUT UP.
JOEY'S BEEN PESTERING US TO SEE YOU, SO DAD INVITED YOU FOR BARBECUE TONIGHT, IF YOU'RE FREE.
SOUNDS GREAT! BRANDON AND MIKE COMING TOO?
THEY RATTED ME OUT TO COACH!
SO THEY'LL NEED TO BEG?
SO HARD.

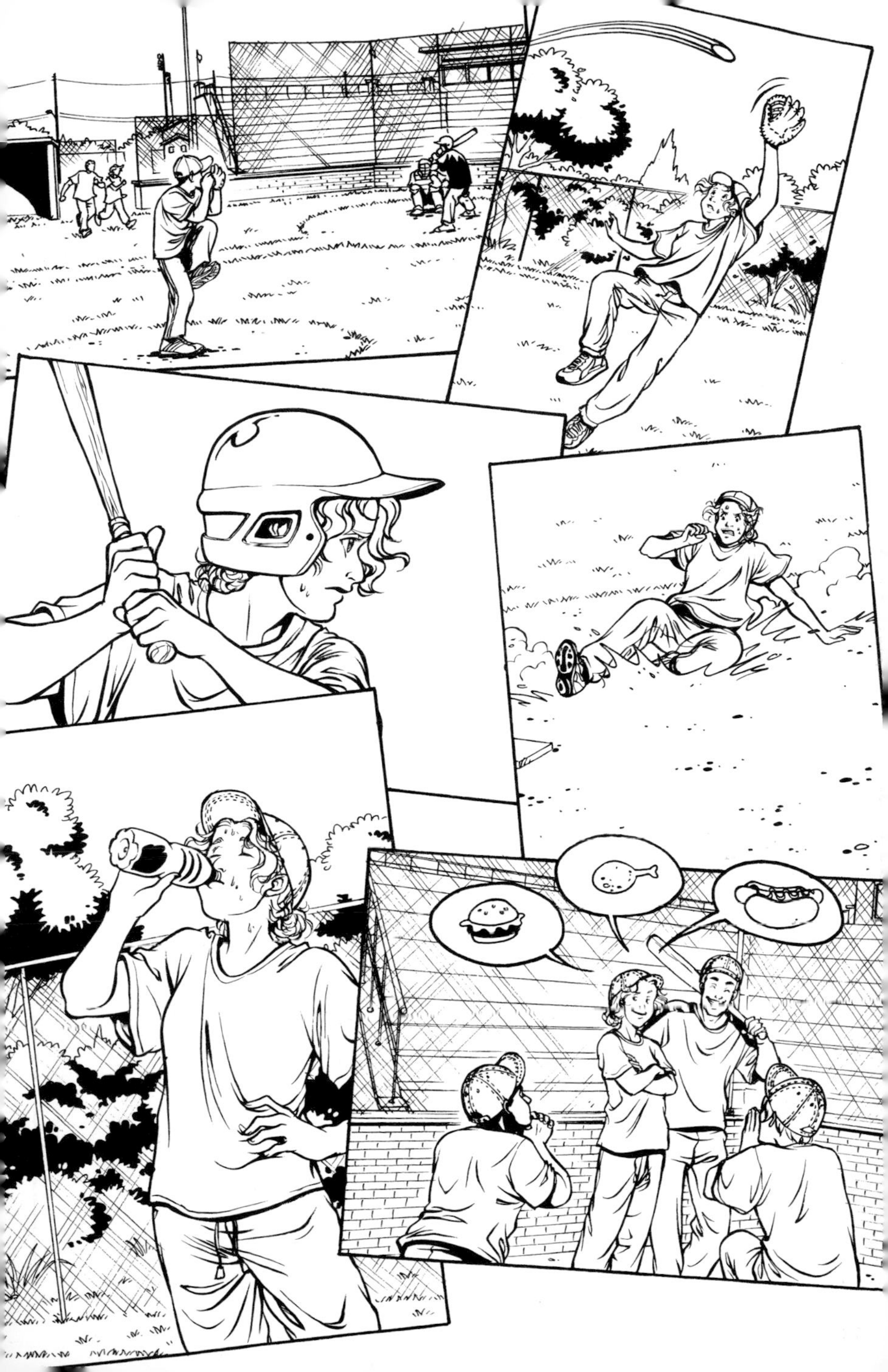

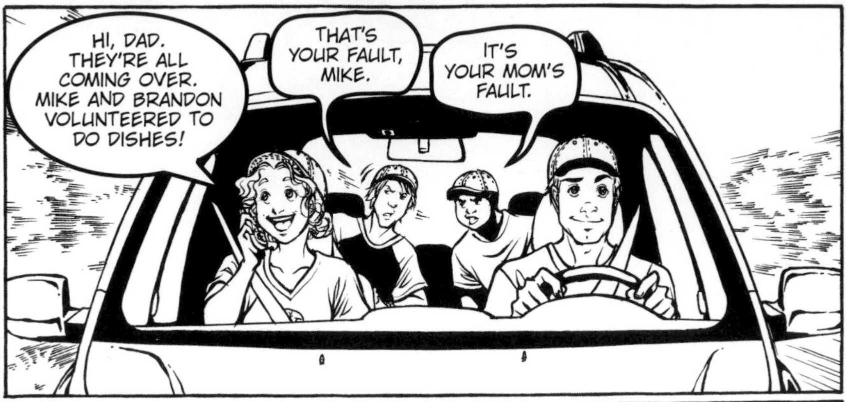
HI, DAD. THEY'RE ALL COMING OVER. MIKE AND BRANDON VOLUNTEERED TO DO DISHES!
THAT'S YOUR FAULT, MIKE.
IT'S YOUR MOM'S FAULT.

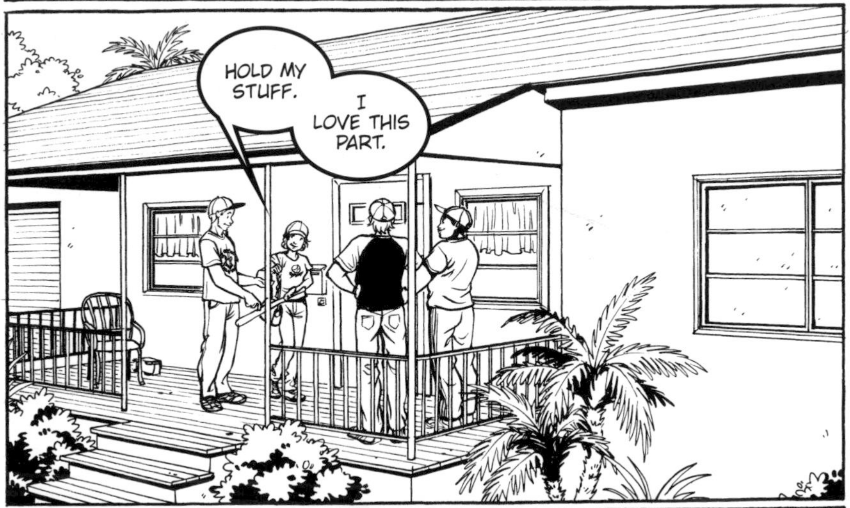
HOLD MY STUFF.
I LOVE THIS PART.

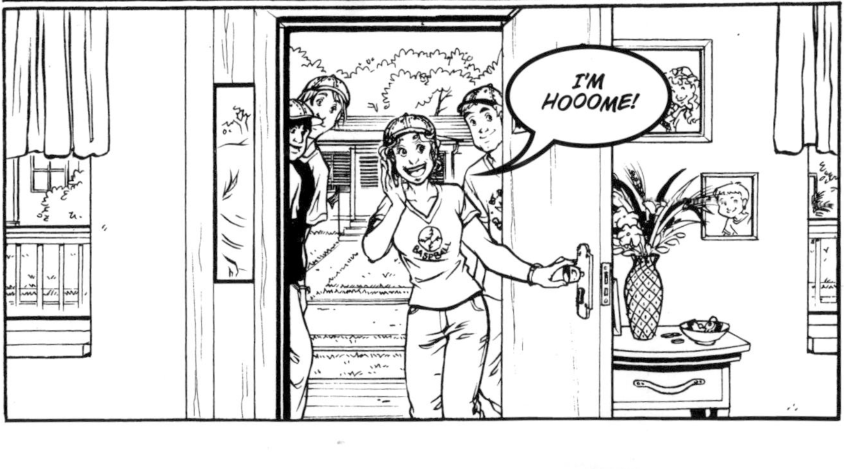
I'M HOOOME!

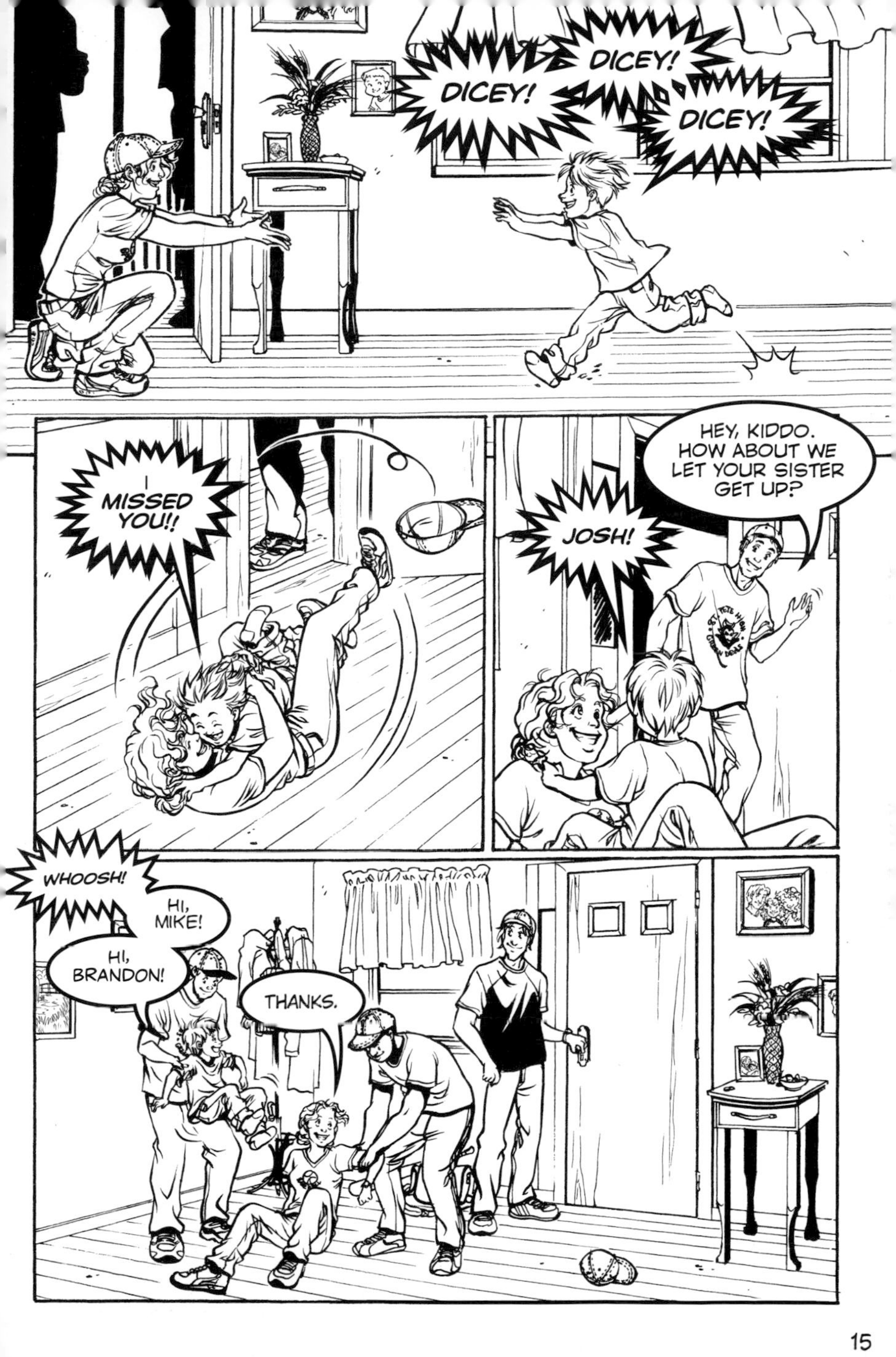
DICEY!
DICEY!
DICEY!
I MISSED YOU!!
JOSH!
HEY, KIDDO. HOW ABOUT WE LET YOUR SISTER GET UP?
WHOOSH!
HI, MIKE!
HI, BRANDON!
THANKS.

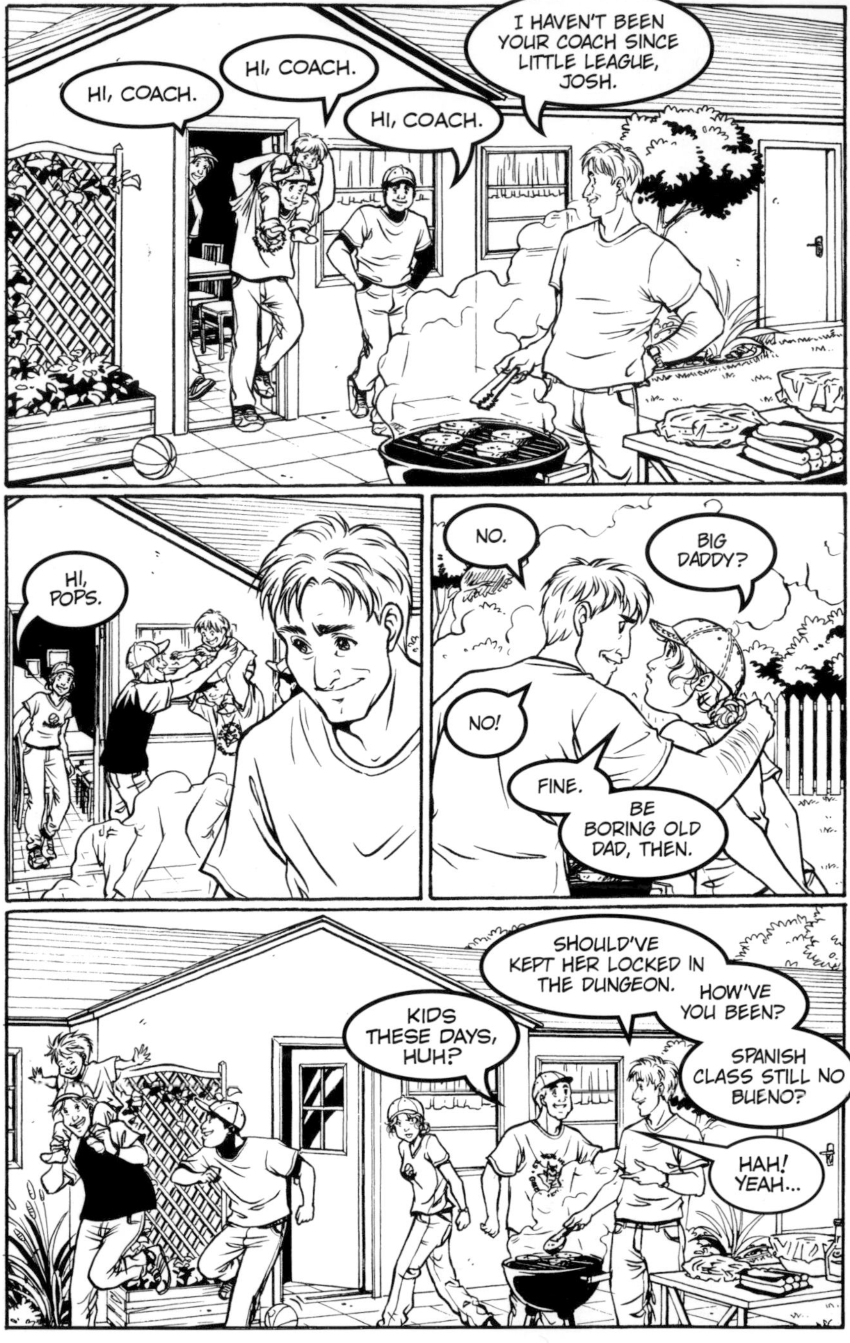
HI, COACH.
HI, COACH.
HI, COACH.
I HAVEN'T BEEN YOUR COACH SINCE LITTLE LEAGUE, JOSH.
HI, POPS.
NO.
BIG DADDY?
NO!
FINE.
BE BORING OLD DAD, THEN.
KIDS THESE DAYS, HUH?
SHOULD'VE KEPT HER LOCKED IN THE DUNGEON.
HOW'VE YOU BEEN?
SPANISH CLASS STILL NO BUENO?
HAH! YEAH...

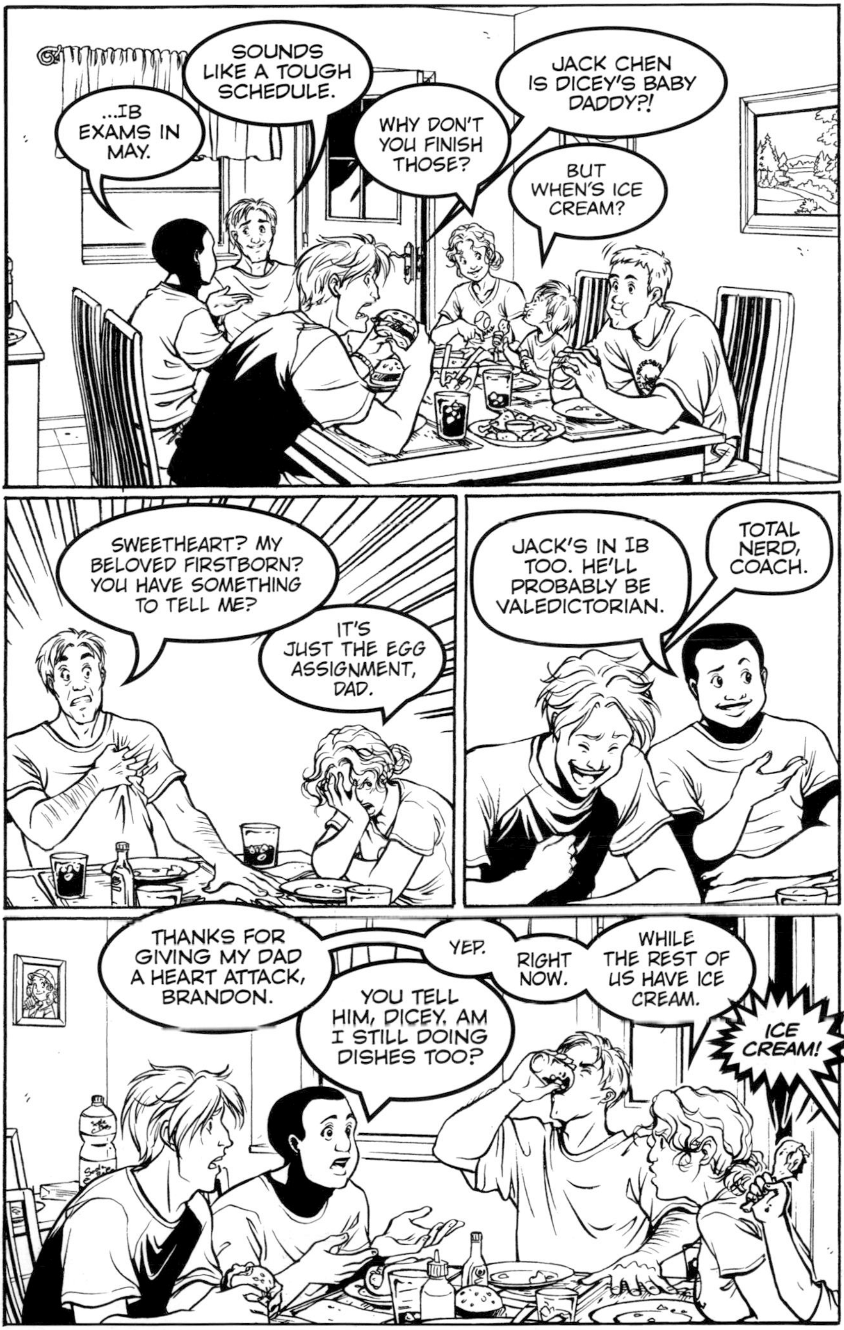
...IB EXAMS IN MAY.
SOUNDS LIKE A TOUGH SCHEDULE.
WHY DON'T YOU FINISH THOSE?
JACK CHEN IS DICEY'S BABY DADDY?!
BUT WHEN'S ICE CREAM?
SWEETHEART? MY BELOVED FIRSTBORN? YOU HAVE SOMETHING TO TELL ME?
IT'S JUST THE EGG ASSIGNMENT, DAD.
JACK'S IN IB TOO. HE'LL PROBABLY BE VALEDICTORIAN.
TOTAL NERD, COACH.
THANKS FOR GIVING MY DAD A HEART ATTACK, BRANDON.
YEP.
YOU TELL HIM, DICEY. AM I STILL DOING DISHES TOO?
RIGHT NOW.
WHILE THE REST OF US HAVE ICE CREAM.
ICE CREAM!

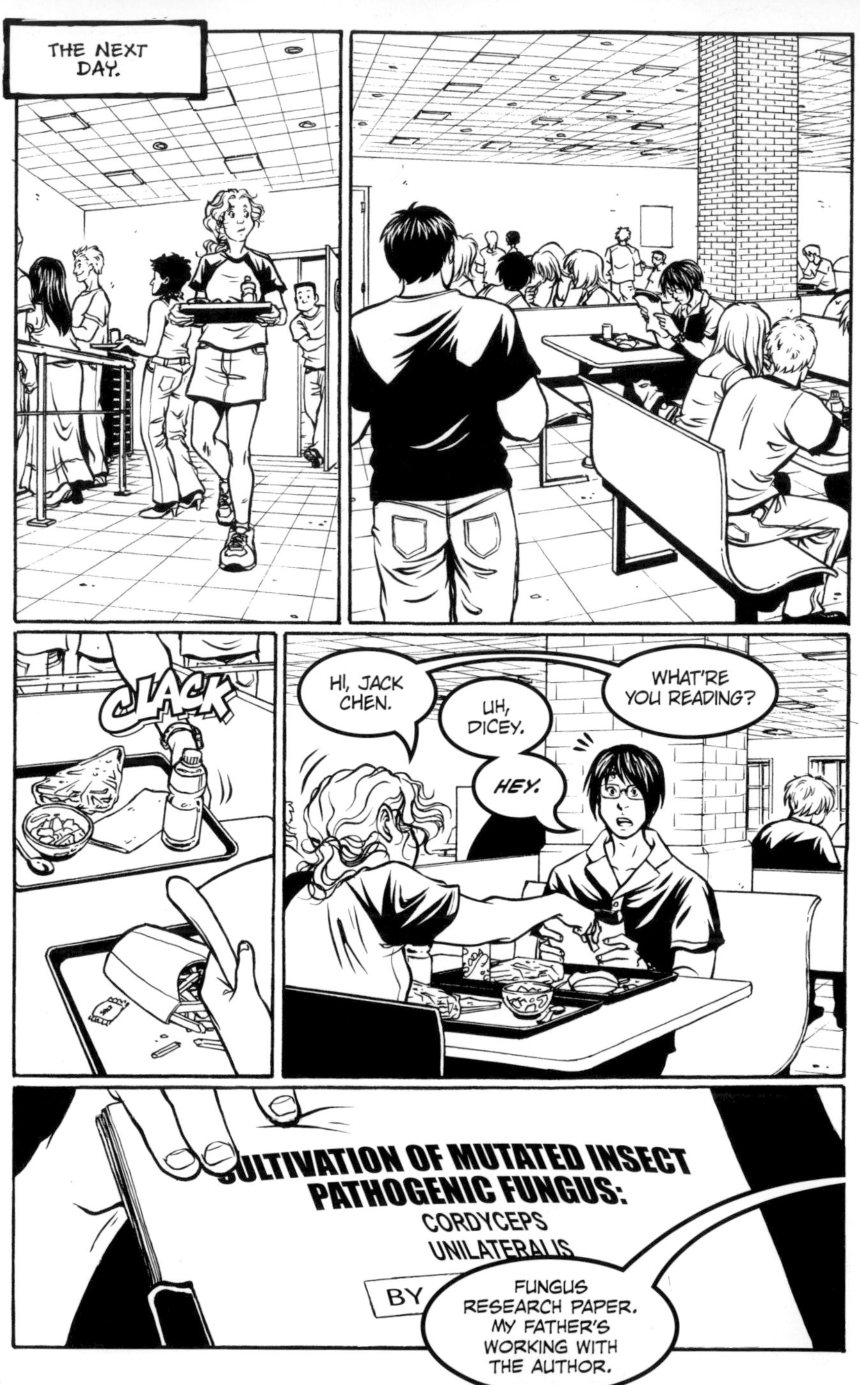
THE NEXT DAY.
CLACK
HI, JACK CHEN.
UH, DICEY.
HEY.
WHAT'RE YOU READING?
CULTIVATION OF MUTATED INSECT PATHOGENIC FUNGUS:
CORDYCEPS UNILATERALIS
BY
FUNGUS RESEARCH PAPER. MY FATHER'S WORKING WITH THE AUTHOR.

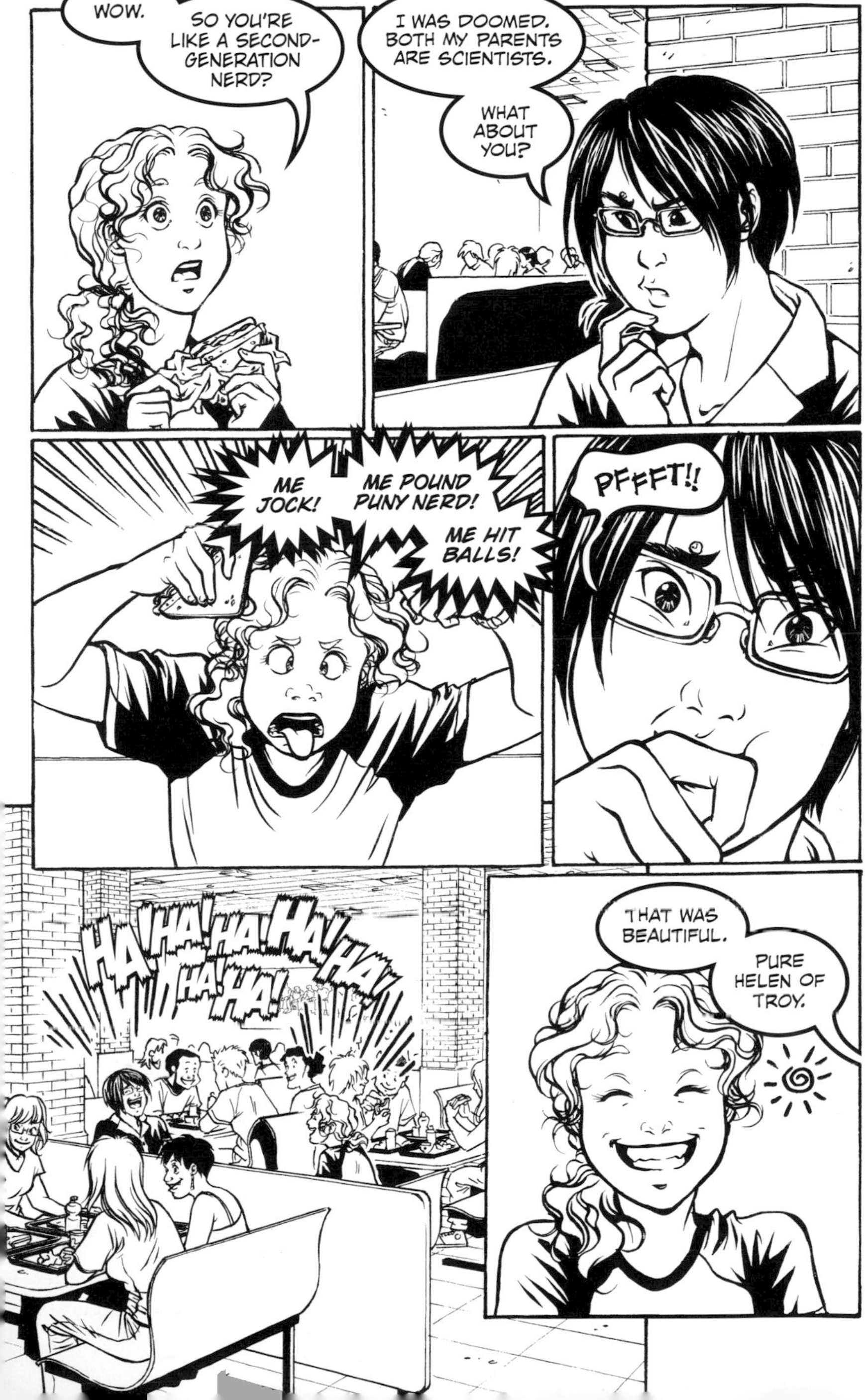
WOW.
SO YOU'RE LIKE A SECOND-GENERATION NERD?
I WAS DOOMED. BOTH MY PARENTS ARE SCIENTISTS.
WHAT ABOUT YOU?
ME JOCK!
ME POUND PUNY NERD!
ME HIT BALLS!
PFFFT!!
HA! HA! HA! HA! HA! HA! HA! HA!
THAT WAS BEAUTIFUL.
PURE HELEN OF TROY.

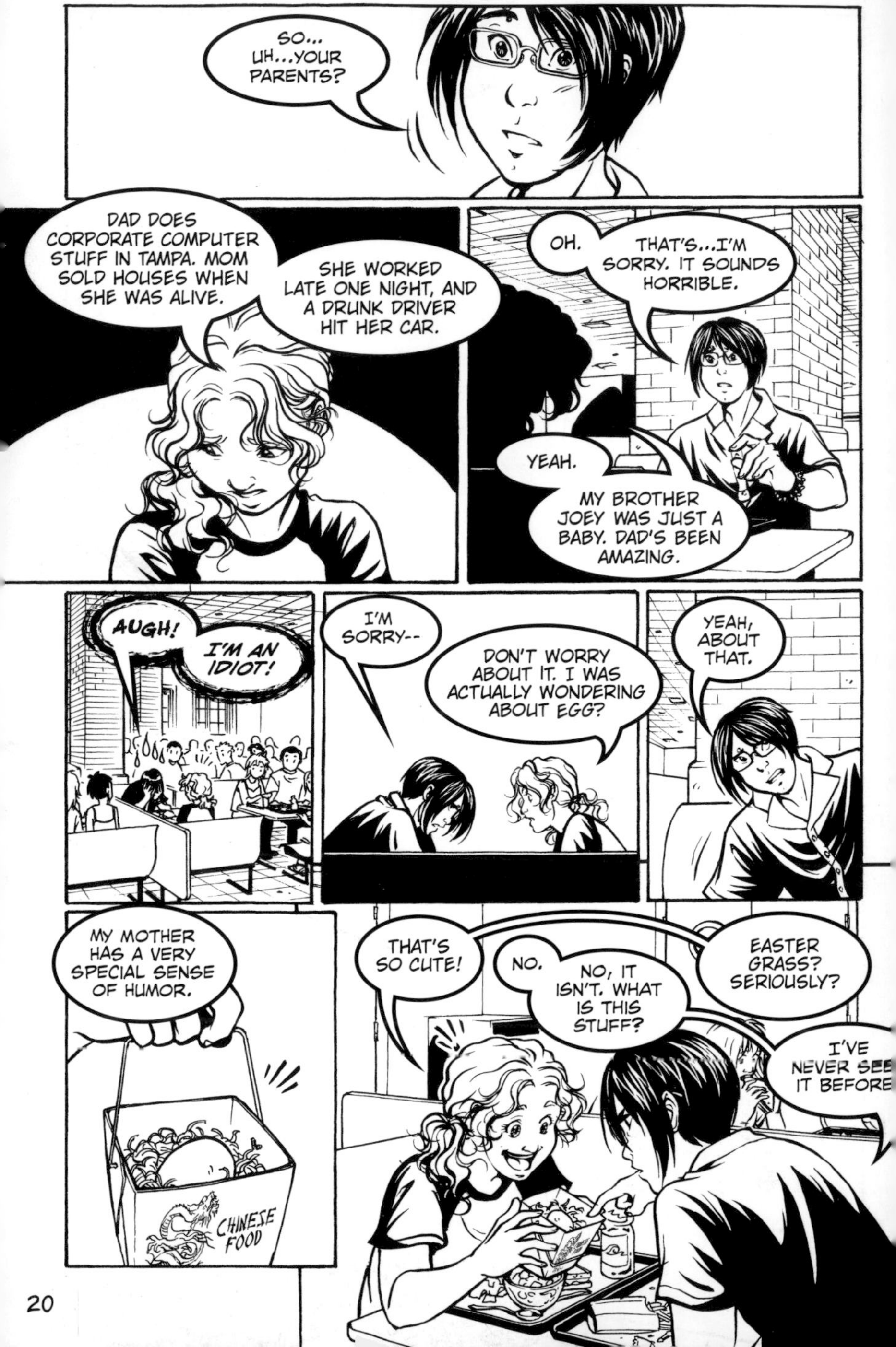

SO... UH...YOUR PARENTS?
DAD DOES CORPORATE COMPUTER STUFF IN TAMPA. MOM SOLD HOUSES WHEN SHE WAS ALIVE.
SHE WORKED LATE ONE NIGHT, AND A DRUNK DRIVER HIT HER CAR.
OH.
THAT'S...I'M SORRY. IT SOUNDS HORRIBLE.
YEAH.
MY BROTHER JOEY WAS JUST A BABY. DAD'S BEEN AMAZING.
AUGH!
I'M AN IDIOT!
I'M SORRY--
DON'T WORRY ABOUT IT. I WAS ACTUALLY WONDERING ABOUT EGG?
YEAH, ABOUT THAT.
MY MOTHER HAS A VERY SPECIAL SENSE OF HUMOR.
CHINESE FOOD
THAT'S SO CUTE!
NO.
NO, IT ISN'T. WHAT IS THIS STUFF?
EASTER GRASS? SERIOUSLY?
I'VE NEVER SEE IT BEFORE

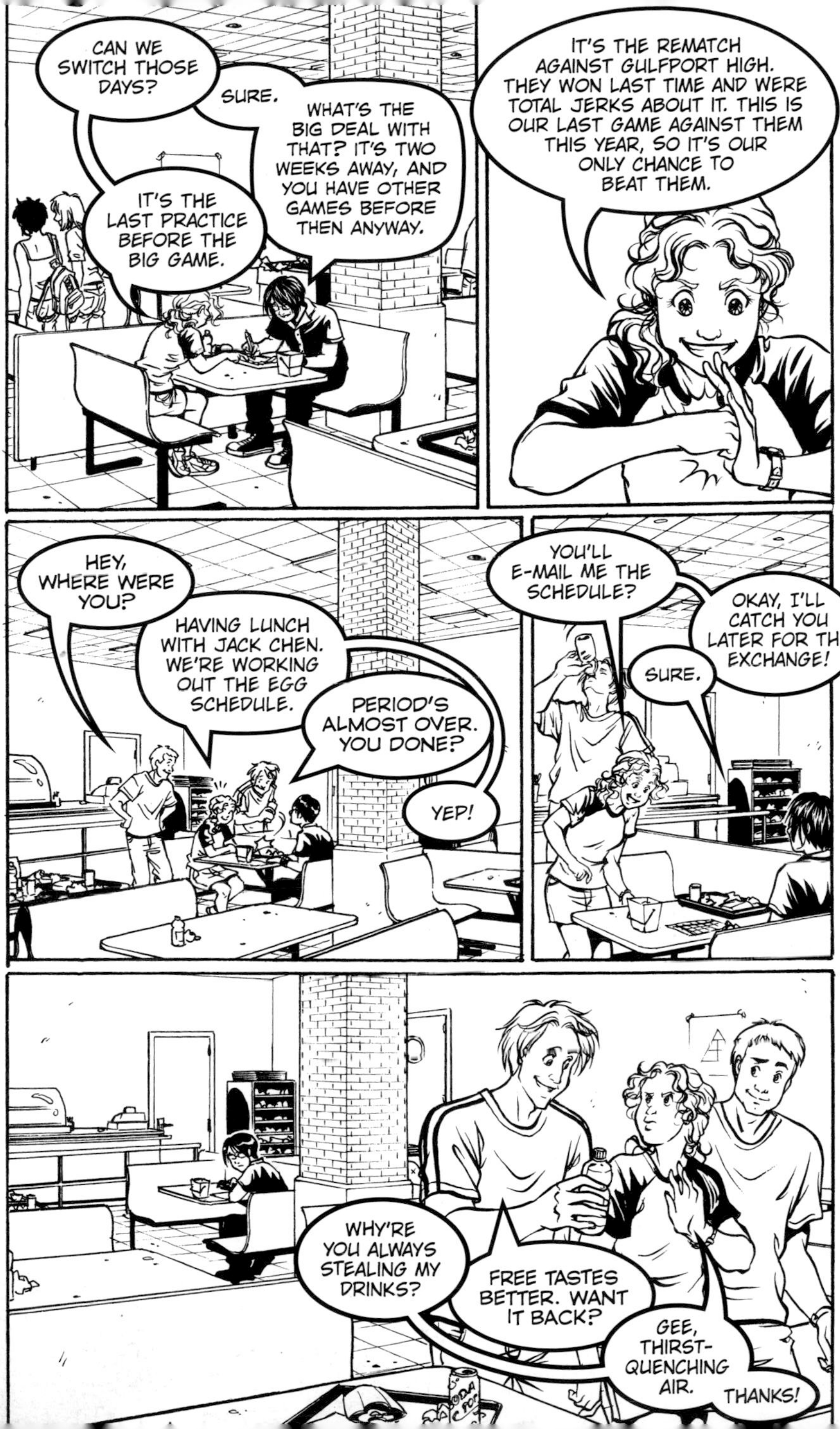
CAN WE SWITCH THOSE DAYS?
SURE.
IT'S THE LAST PRACTICE BEFORE THE BIG GAME.
WHAT'S THE BIG DEAL WITH THAT? IT'S TWO WEEKS AWAY, AND YOU HAVE OTHER GAMES BEFORE THEN ANYWAY.
IT'S THE REMATCH AGAINST GULFPORT HIGH. THEY WON LAST TIME AND WERE TOTAL JERKS ABOUT IT. THIS IS OUR LAST GAME AGAINST THEM THIS YEAR, SO IT'S OUR ONLY CHANCE TO BEAT THEM.
HEY, WHERE WERE YOU?
HAVING LUNCH WITH JACK CHEN. WE'RE WORKING OUT THE EGG SCHEDULE.
PERIOD'S ALMOST OVER. YOU DONE?
YEP!
YOU'LL E-MAIL ME THE SCHEDULE?
SURE.
OKAY, I'LL CATCH YOU LATER FOR THE EXCHANGE!
WHY'RE YOU ALWAYS STEALING MY DRINKS?
FREE TASTES BETTER. WANT IT BACK?
GEE, THIRST-QUENCHING AIR.
THANKS!

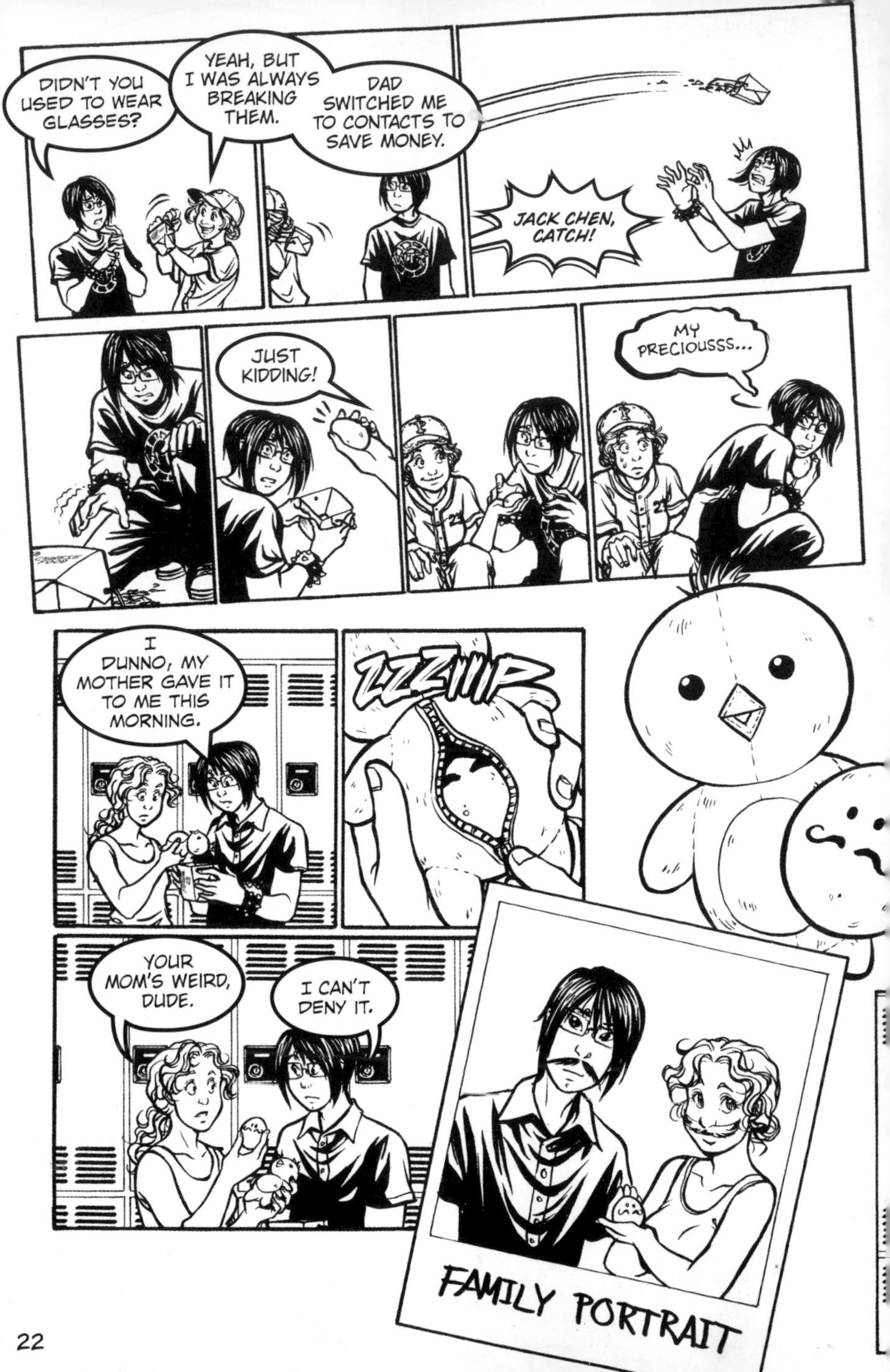
DIDN'T YOU USED TO WEAR GLASSES?
YEAH, BUT I WAS ALWAYS BREAKING THEM.
DAD SWITCHED ME TO CONTACTS TO SAVE MONEY.
JACK CHEN, CATCH!
CHINESE FOOD
JUST KIDDING!
MY PRECIOUSSS...
I DUNNO, MY MOTHER GAVE IT TO ME THIS MORNING.
ZZZIIIP
YOUR MOM'S WEIRD, DUDE.
I CAN'T DENY IT.
FAMILY PORTRAIT

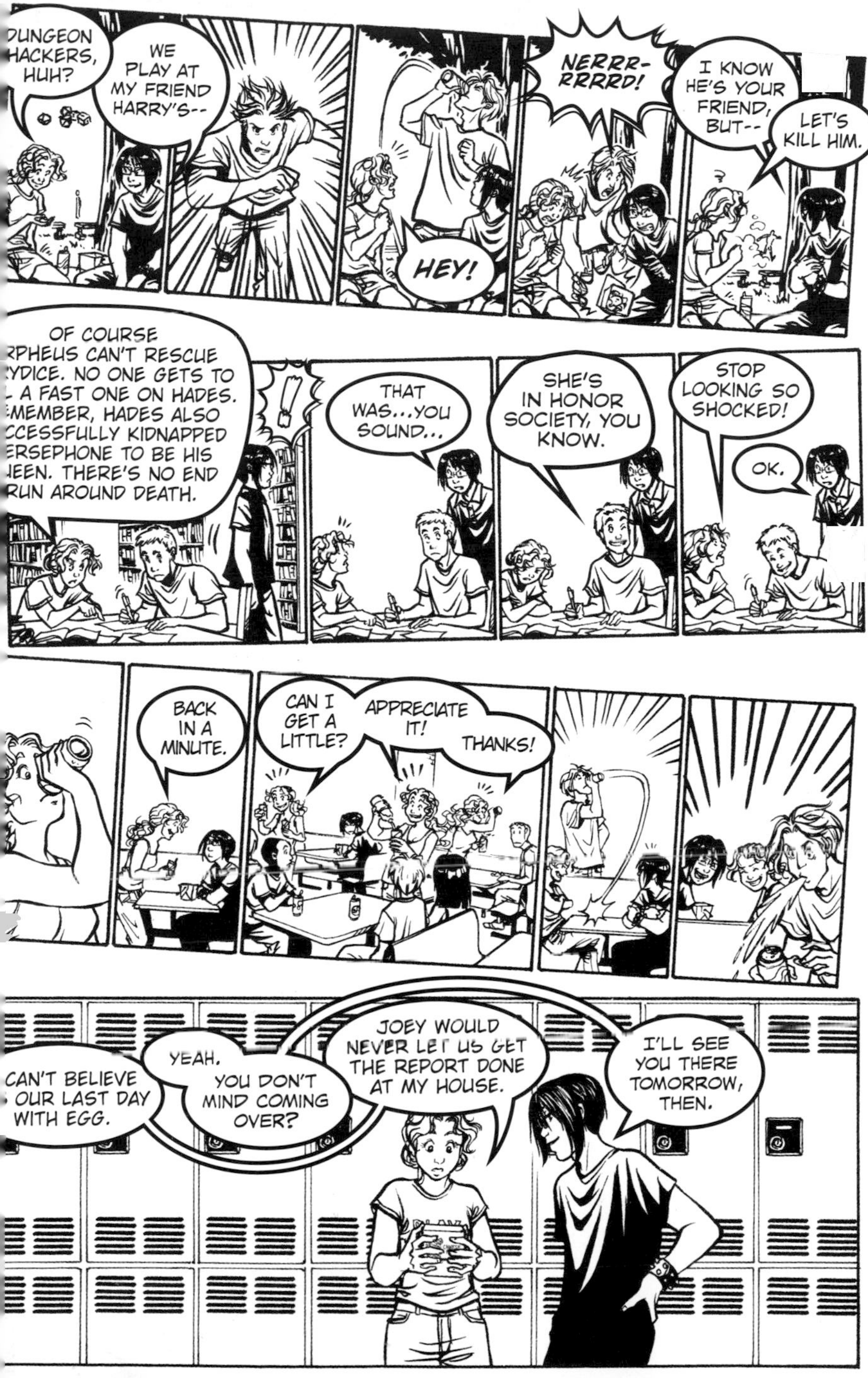

DUNGEON HACKERS, HUH?
WE PLAY AT MY FRIEND HARRY'S--
HEY!
NERRRR-RRRRD!
I KNOW HE'S YOUR FRIEND, BUT--
LET'S KILL HIM.
OF COURSE RPHEUS CAN'T RESCUE YDICE. NO ONE GETS TO L A FAST ONE ON HADES. EMEMBER, HADES ALSO CCESSFULLY KIDNAPPED ERSEPHONE TO BE HIS UEEN. THERE'S NO END RUN AROUND DEATH.
!
THAT WAS...YOU SOUND...
SHE'S IN HONOR SOCIETY, YOU KNOW.
STOP LOOKING SO SHOCKED!
OK.
BACK IN A MINUTE.
CAN I GET A LITTLE?
APPRECIATE IT!
THANKS!
CAN'T BELIEVE OUR LAST DAY WITH EGG.
YEAH.
YOU DON'T MIND COMING OVER?
JOEY WOULD NEVER LET US GET THE REPORT DONE AT MY HOUSE.
I'LL SEE YOU THERE TOMORROW, THEN.

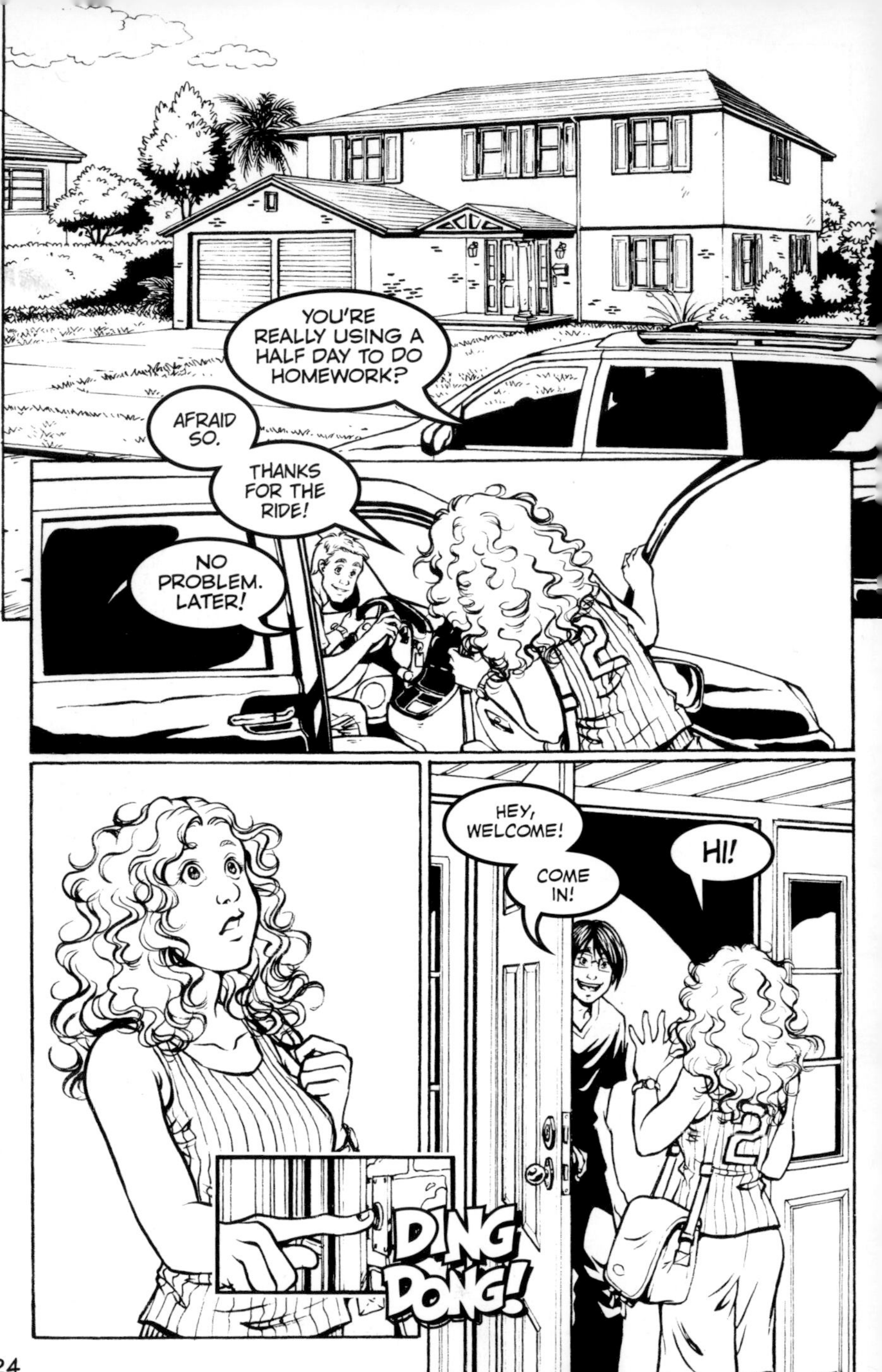
YOU'RE REALLY USING A HALF DAY TO DO HOMEWORK?
AFRAID SO.
THANKS FOR THE RIDE!
NO PROBLEM. LATER!
HEY, WELCOME!
COME IN!
HI!
DING DONG!

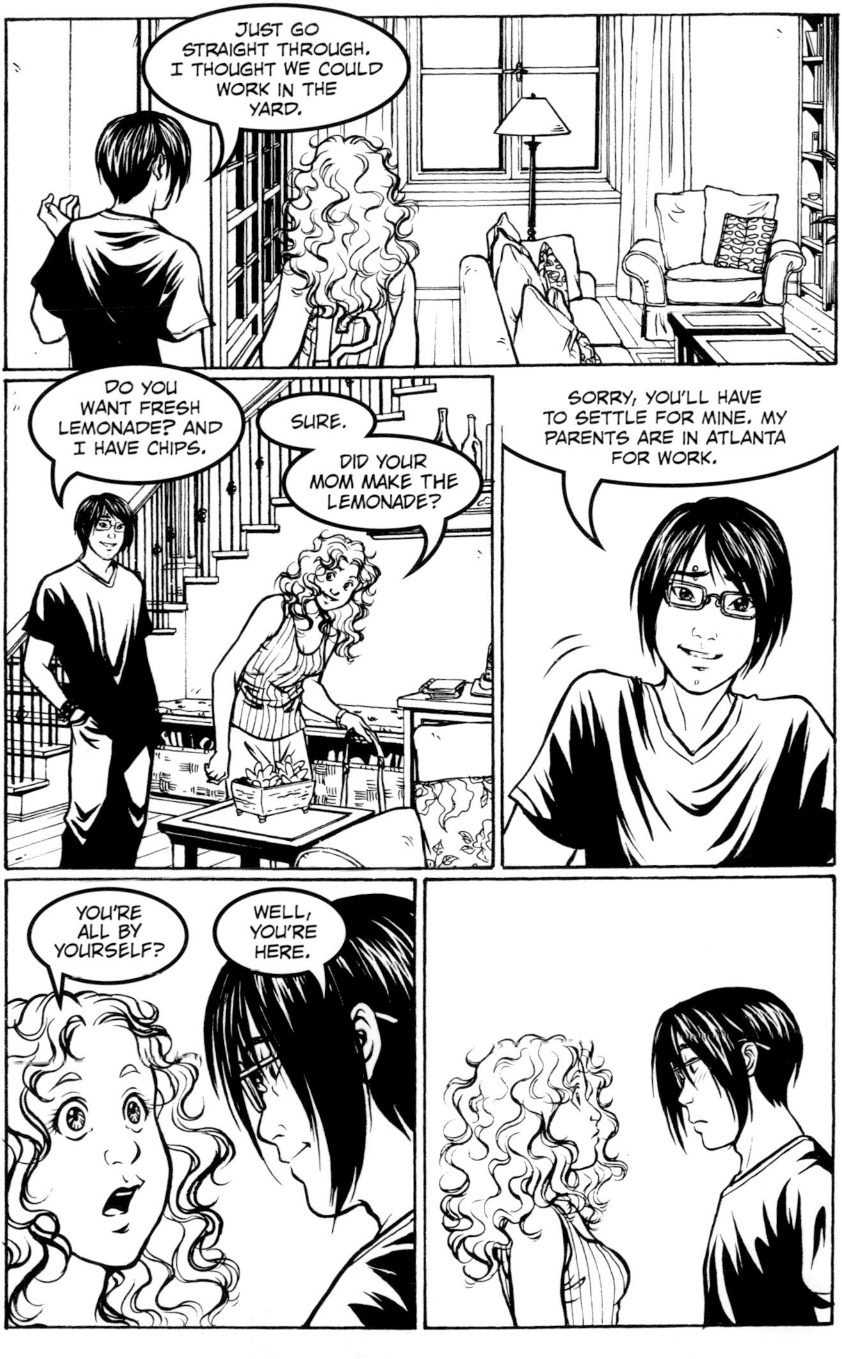
JUST GO STRAIGHT THROUGH. I THOUGHT WE COULD WORK IN THE YARD.
DO YOU WANT FRESH LEMONADE? AND I HAVE CHIPS.
SURE.
DID YOUR MOM MAKE THE LEMONADE?
SORRY, YOU'LL HAVE TO SETTLE FOR MINE. MY PARENTS ARE IN ATLANTA FOR WORK.
YOU'RE ALL BY YOURSELF?
WELL, YOU'RE HERE.

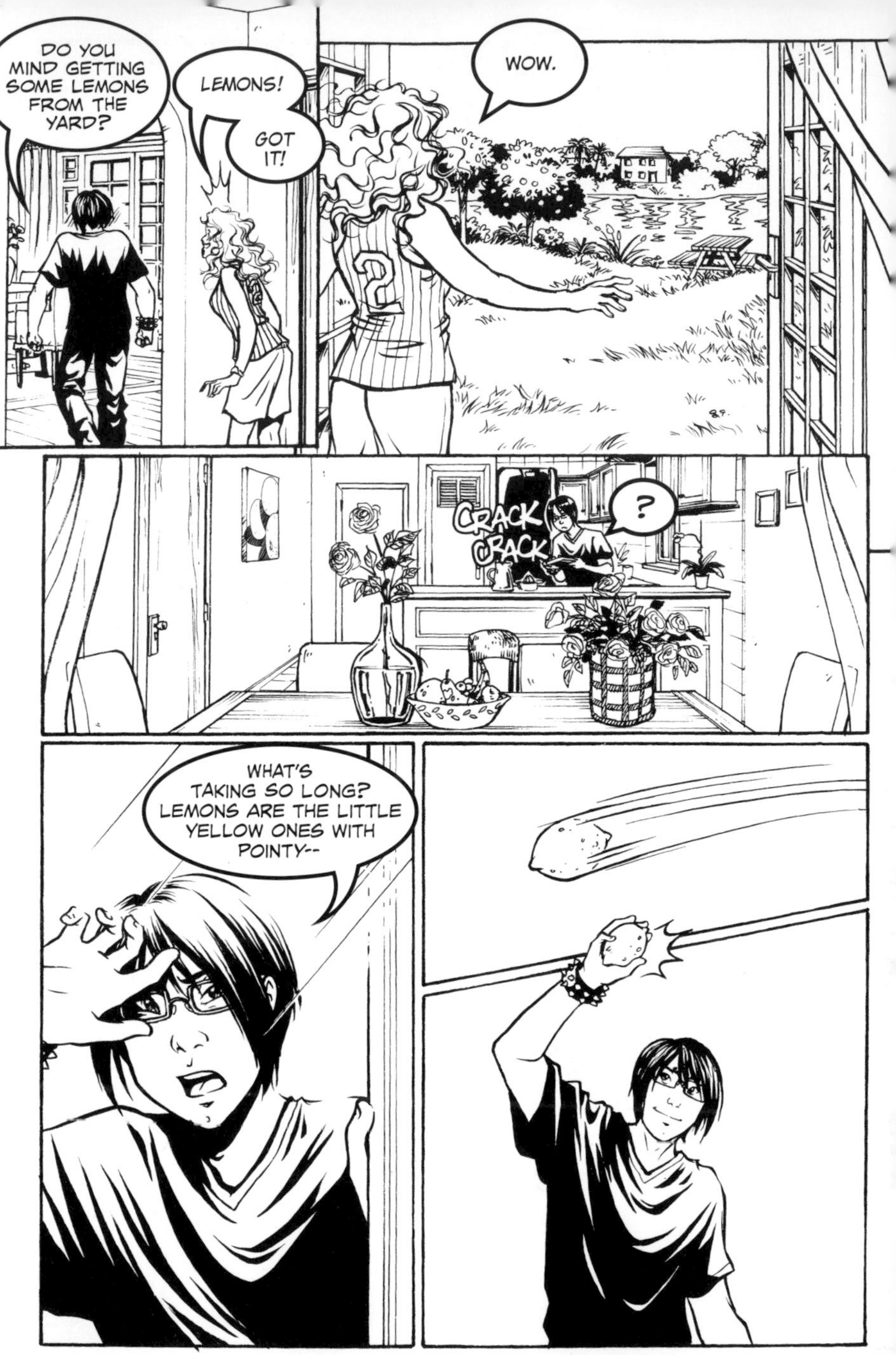

DO YOU MIND GETTING SOME LEMONS FROM THE YARD?
LEMONS!
GOT IT!
WOW.
CRACK
CRACK
?
WHAT'S TAKING SO LONG? LEMONS ARE THE LITTLE YELLOW ONES WITH POINTY--

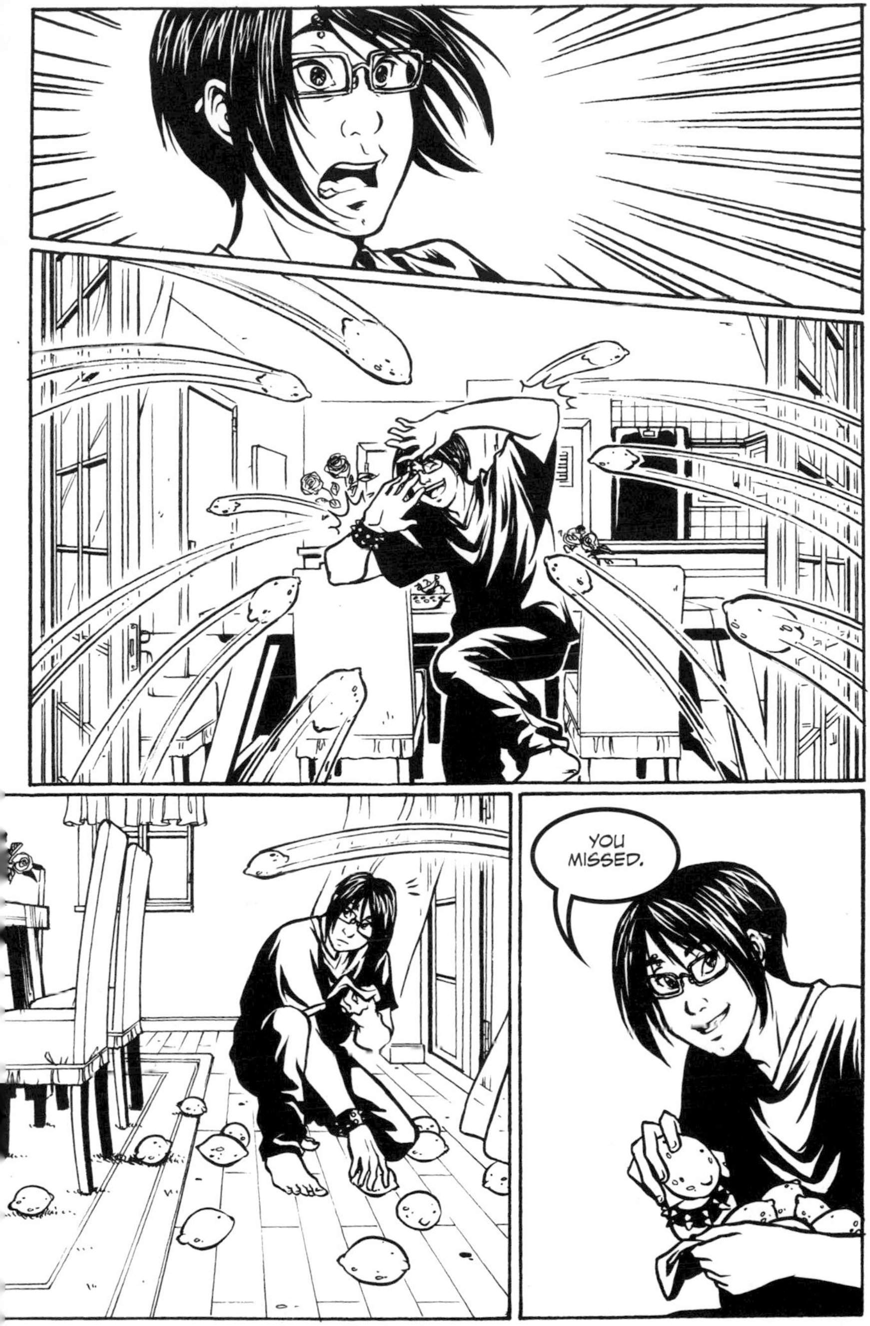
YOU MISSED.

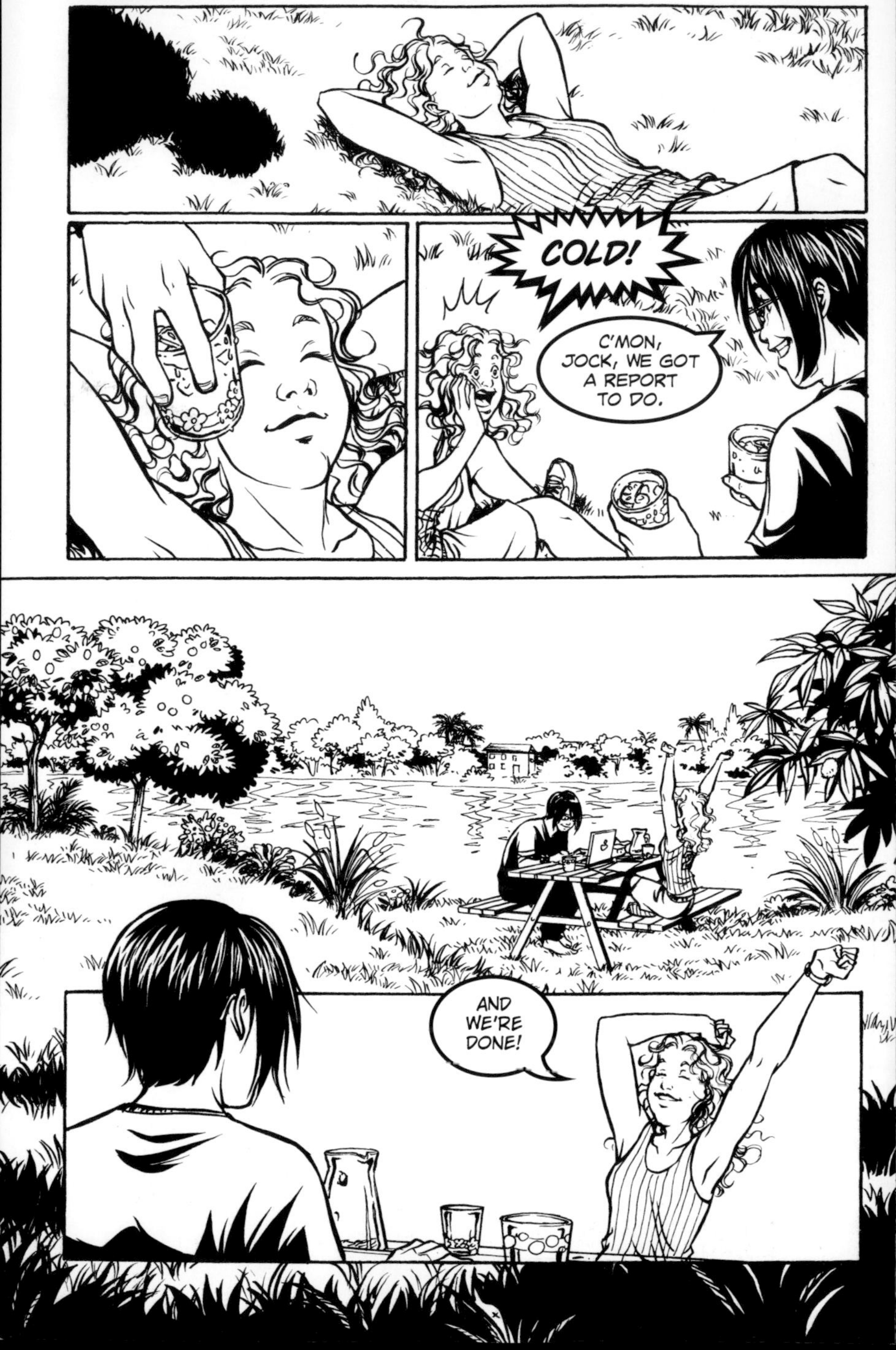
COLD!
C'MON, JOCK, WE GOT A REPORT TO DO.
AND WE'RE DONE!

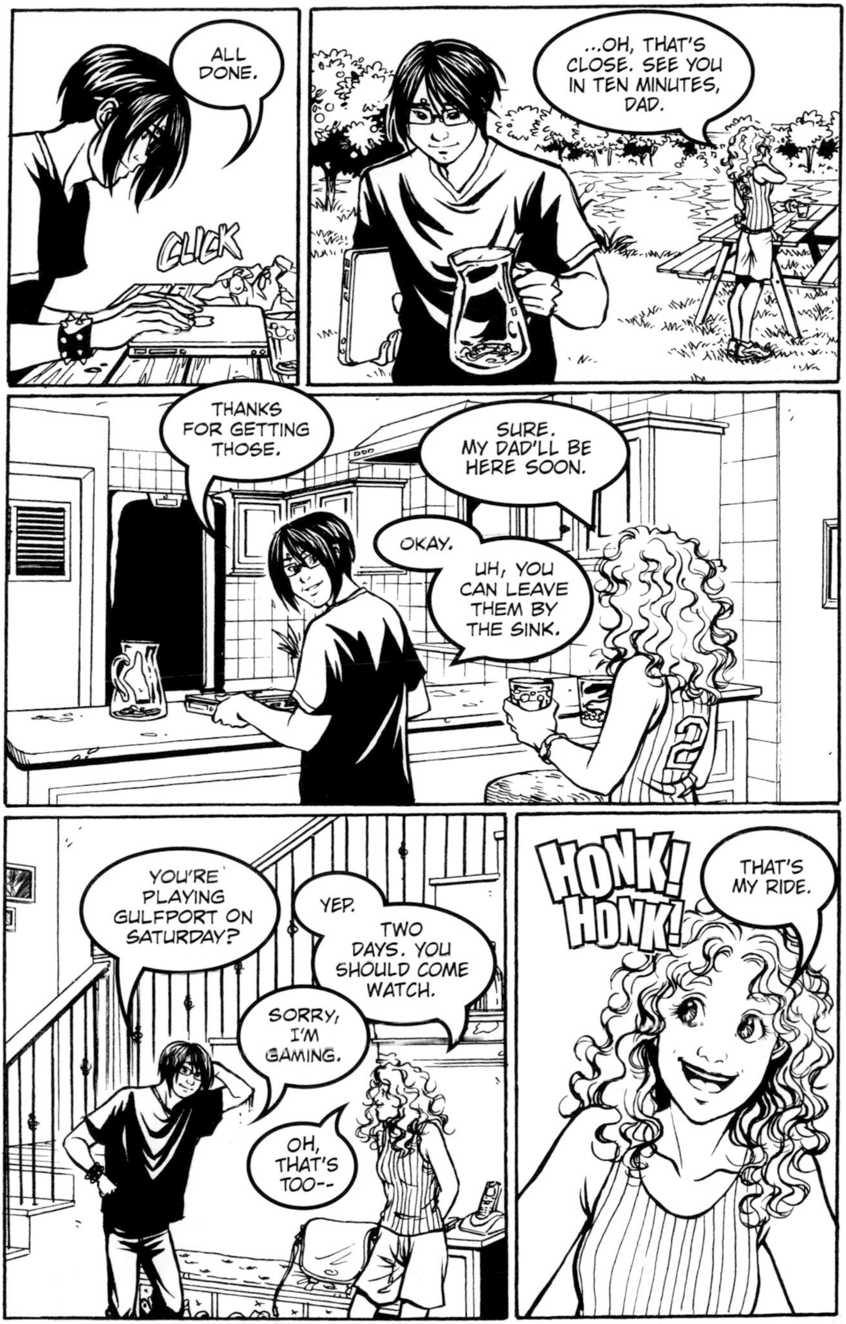
ALL DONE.
CLICK
...OH, THAT'S CLOSE. SEE YOU IN TEN MINUTES, DAD.
THANKS FOR GETTING THOSE.
SURE. MY DAD'LL BE HERE SOON.
OKAY.
UH, YOU CAN LEAVE THEM BY THE SINK.
YOU'RE PLAYING GULFPORT ON SATURDAY?
YEP.
TWO DAYS. YOU SHOULD COME WATCH.
SORRY, I'M GAMING.
OH, THAT'S TOO--
HONK! HONK!
THAT'S MY RIDE.

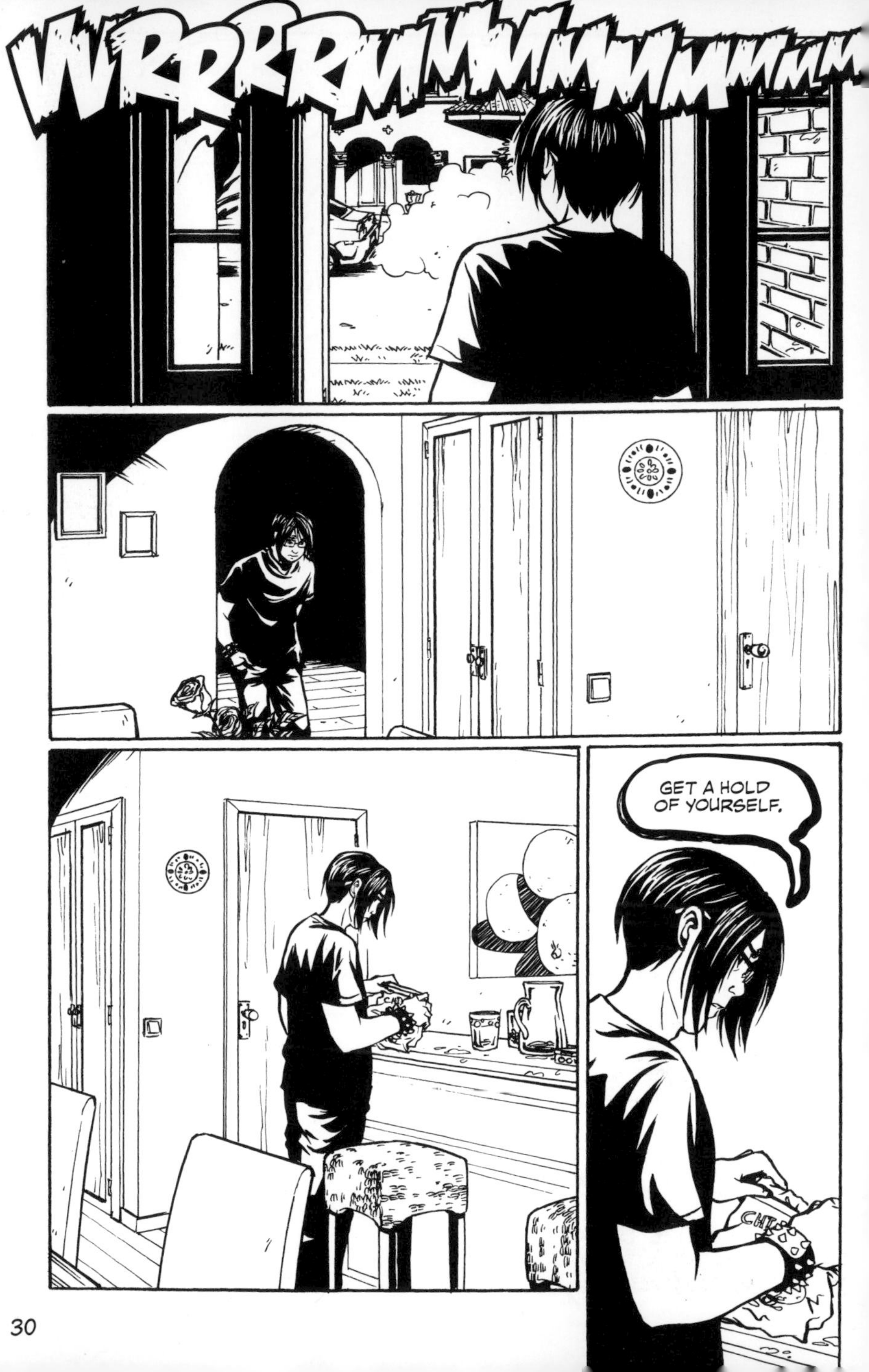
WRRRRMMMMMMMMMMMM
GET A HOLD OF YOURSELF.

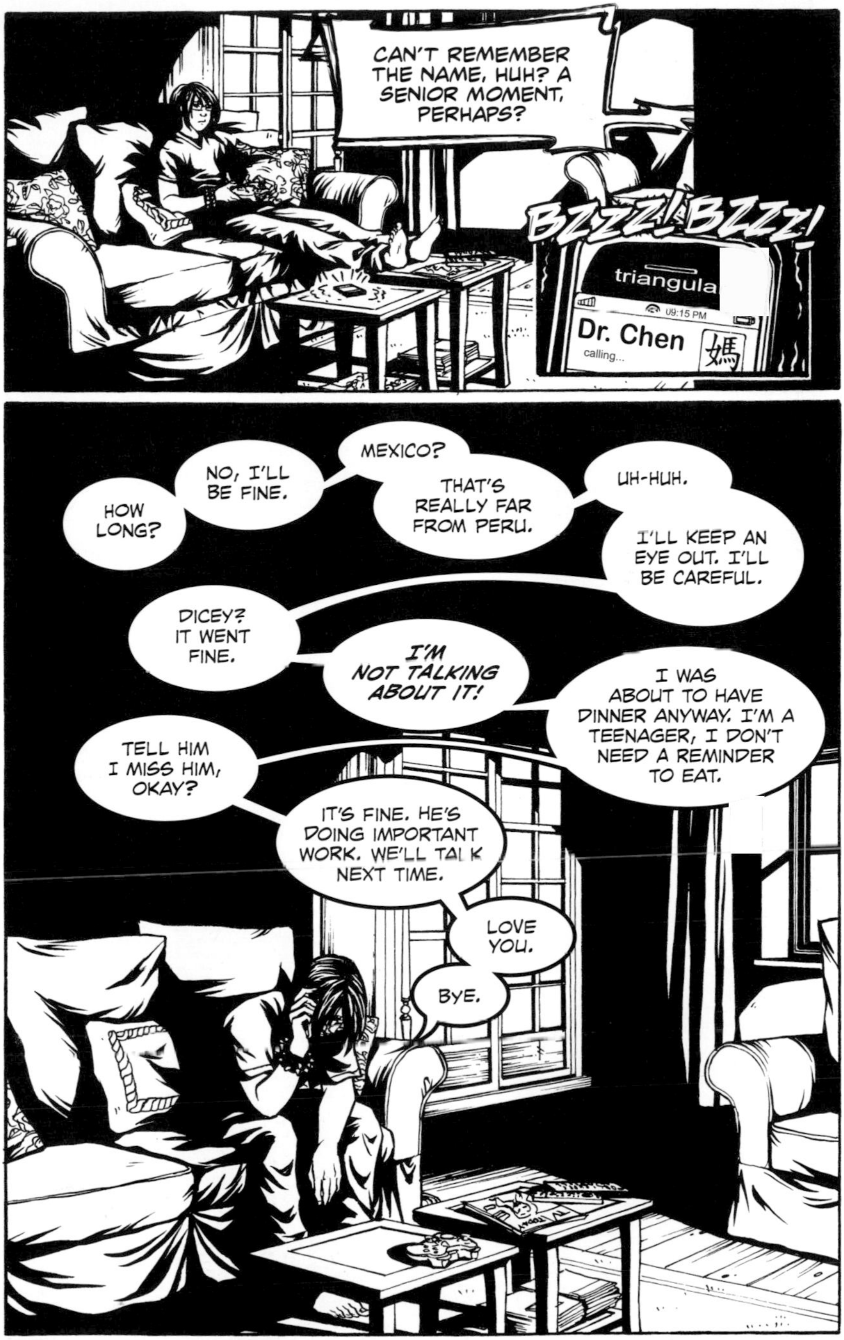
CAN'T REMEMBER THE NAME, HUH? A SENIOR MOMENT, PERHAPS?
BZZZ! BZZZ!
triangula
09:15 PM
Dr. Chen
calling...
媽
HOW LONG?
NO, I'LL BE FINE.
MEXICO?
THAT'S REALLY FAR FROM PERU.
UH-HUH.
I'LL KEEP AN EYE OUT. I'LL BE CAREFUL.
DICEY? IT WENT FINE.
I'M NOT TALKING ABOUT IT!
I WAS ABOUT TO HAVE DINNER ANYWAY. I'M A TEENAGER, I DON'T NEED A REMINDER TO EAT.
TELL HIM I MISS HIM, OKAY?
IT'S FINE. HE'S DOING IMPORTANT WORK. WE'LL TALK NEXT TIME.
LOVE YOU.
BYE.

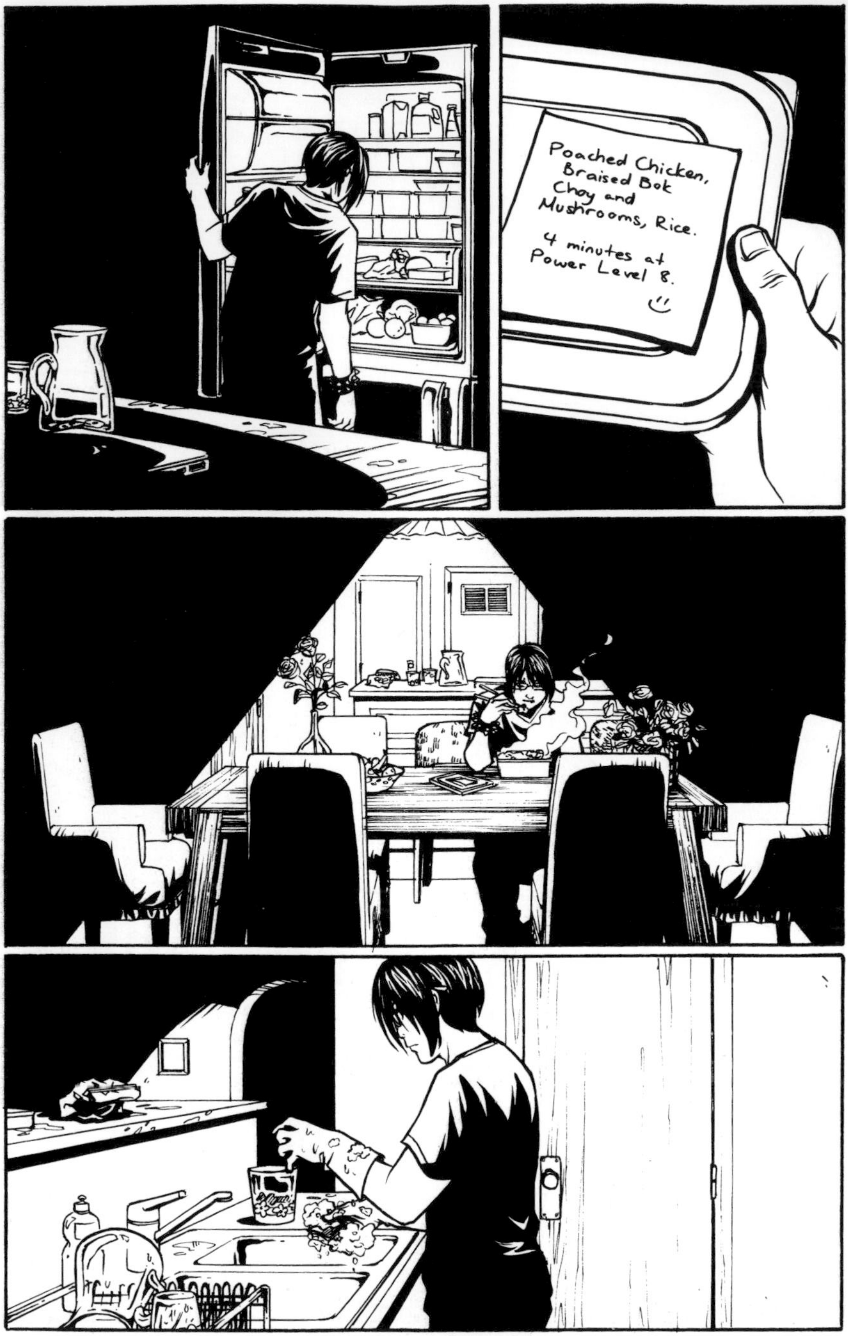
Poached Chicken, Braised Bok Choy and Mushrooms, Rice.
4 minutes at Power Level 8.

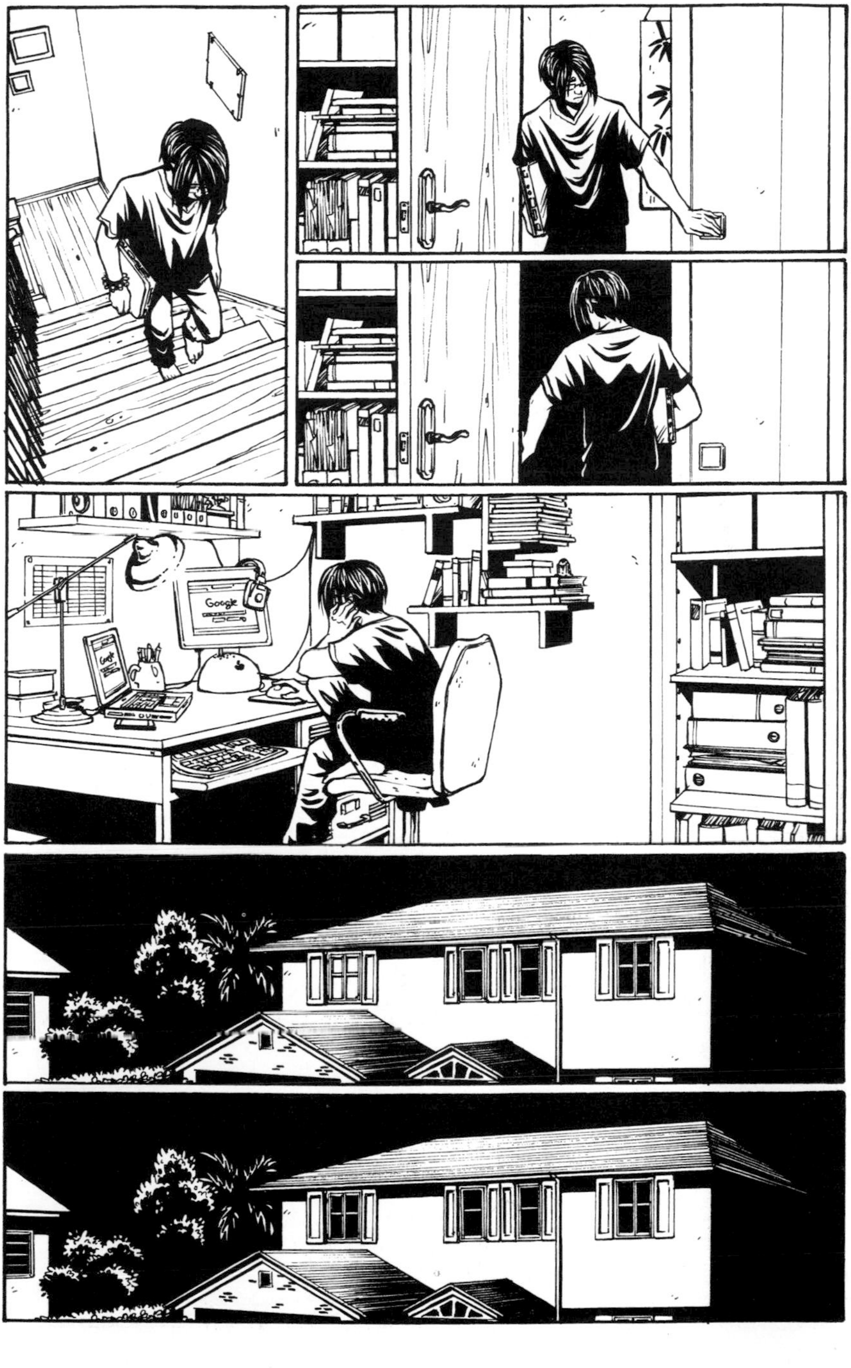
Google

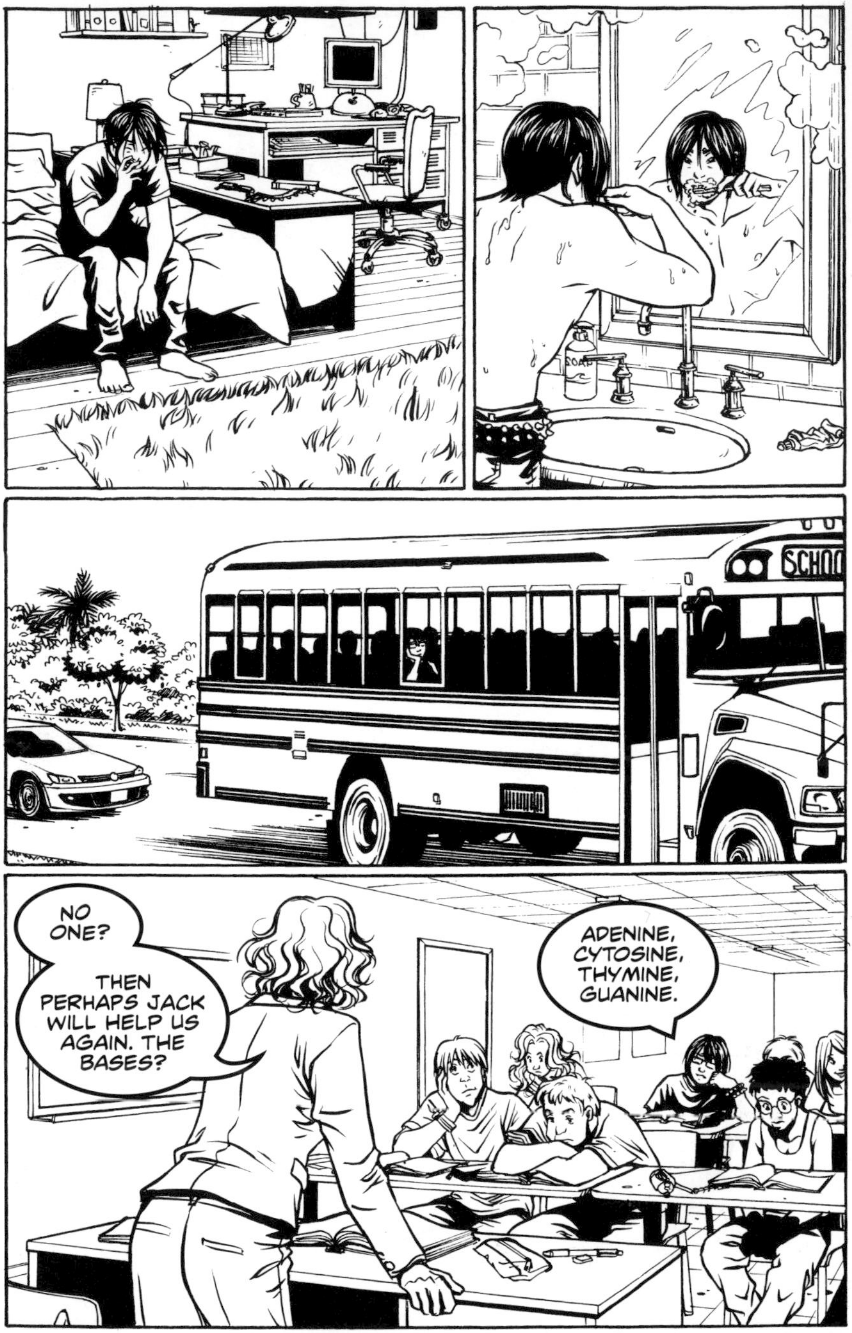
SCHOO
SOAP
NO ONE?
THEN PERHAPS JACK WILL HELP US AGAIN. THE BASES?
ADENINE, CYTOSINE, THYMINE, GUANINE.

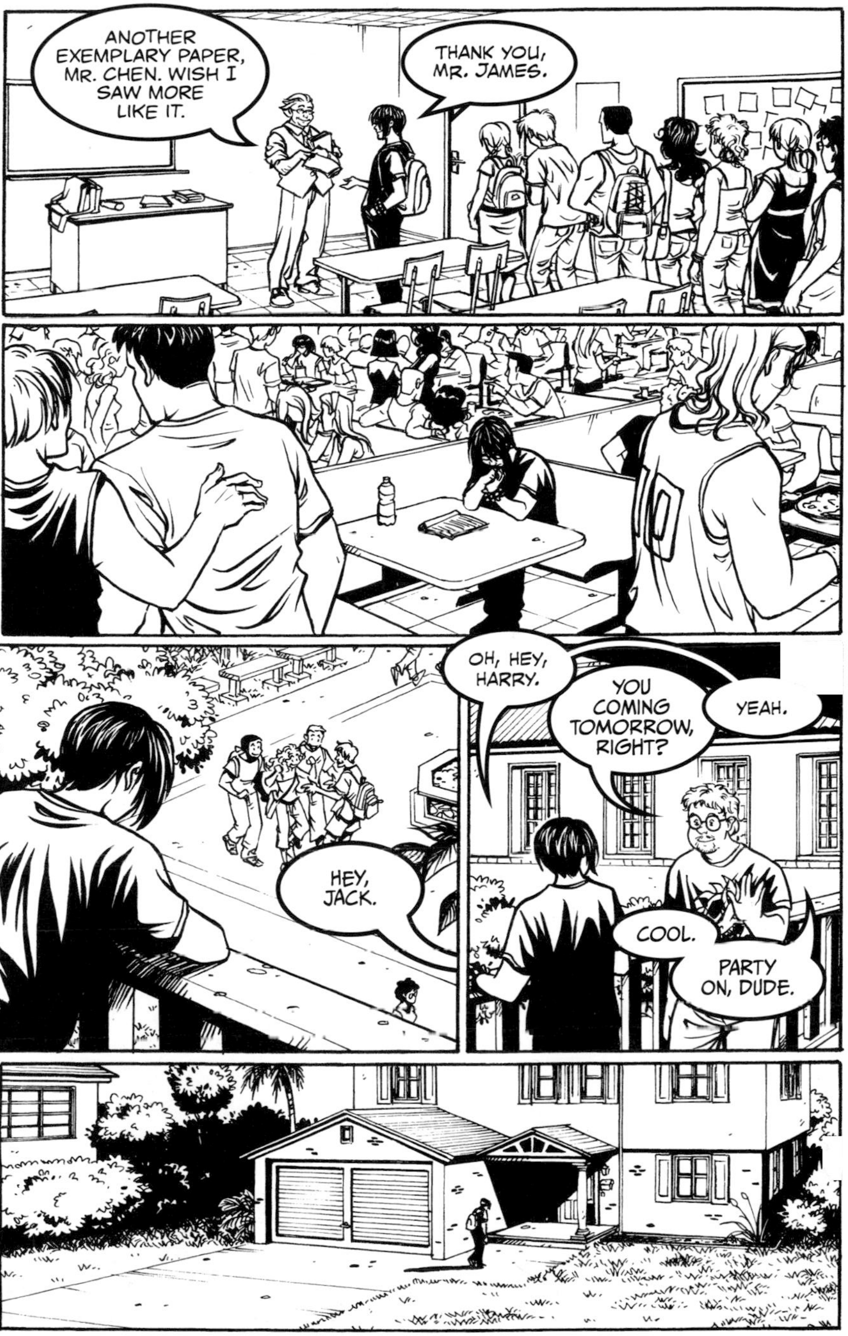
ANOTHER EXEMPLARY PAPER, MR. CHEN. WISH I SAW MORE LIKE IT.
THANK YOU, MR. JAMES.
HEY, JACK.
OH, HEY, HARRY.
YOU COMING TOMORROW, RIGHT?
YEAH.
COOL.
PARTY ON, DUDE.

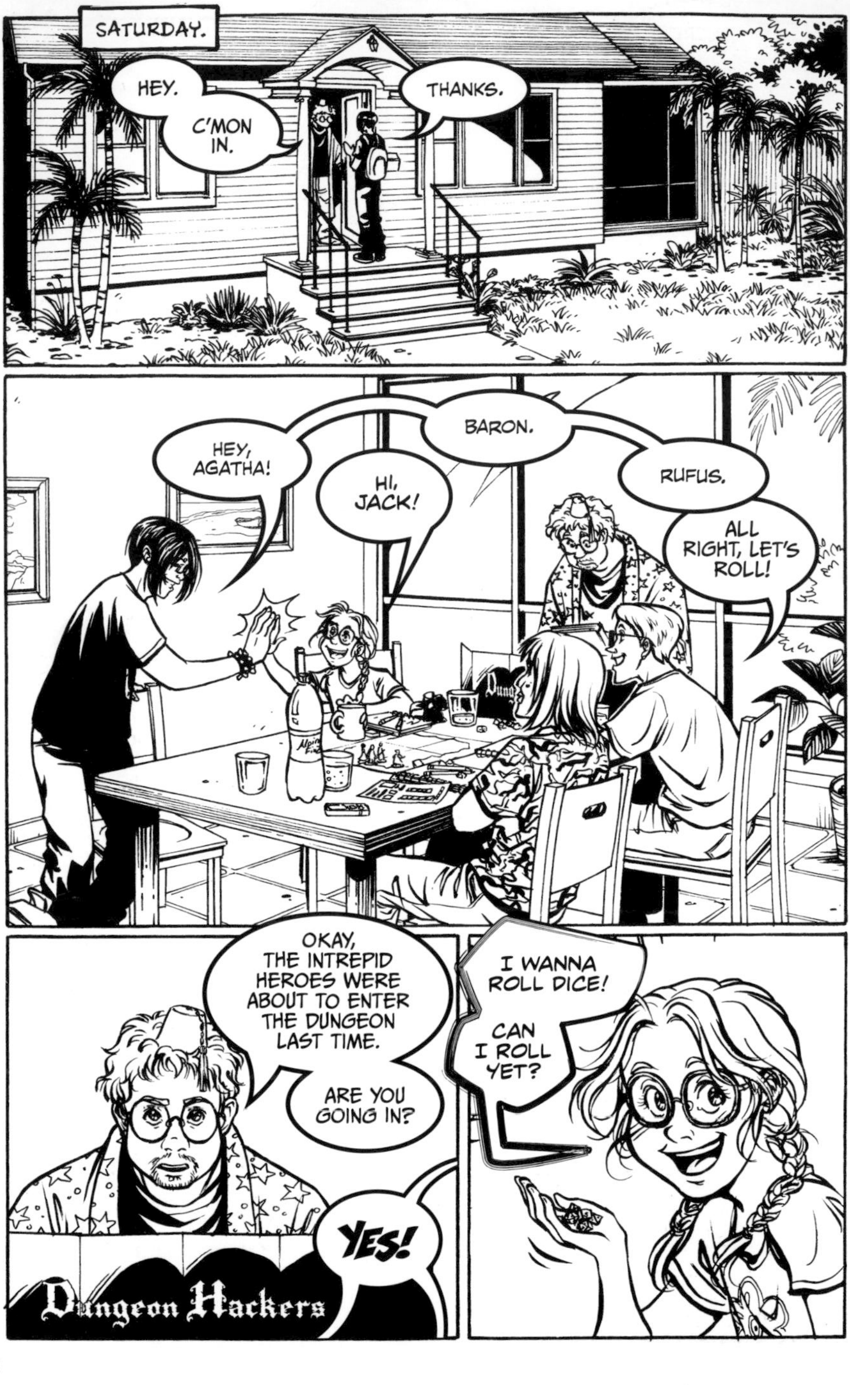
SATURDAY.
HEY.
C'MON IN.
THANKS.
HEY, AGATHA!
BARON.
HI, JACK!
RUFUS.
ALL RIGHT, LET'S ROLL!
OKAY, THE INTREPID HEROES WERE ABOUT TO ENTER THE DUNGEON LAST TIME.
ARE YOU GOING IN?
YES!
Dungeon Hackers
I WANNA ROLL DICE!
CAN I ROLL YET?

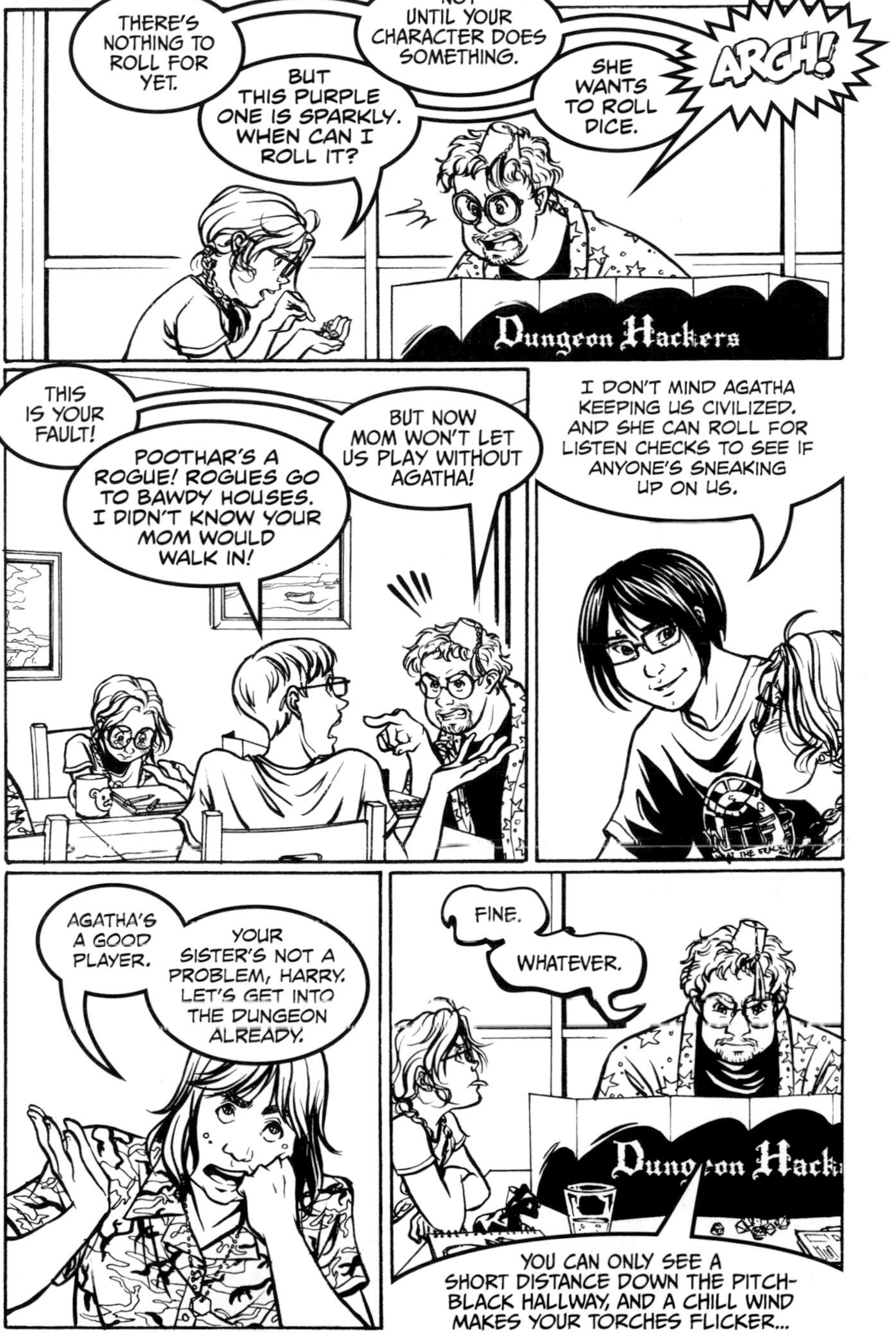
THERE'S NOTHING TO ROLL FOR YET.
NOT UNTIL YOUR CHARACTER DOES SOMETHING.
BUT THIS PURPLE ONE IS SPARKLY. WHEN CAN I ROLL IT?
SHE WANTS TO ROLL DICE.
ARGH!
Dungeon Hackers
THIS IS YOUR FAULT!
POOTHAR'S A ROGUE! ROGUES GO TO BAWDY HOUSES. I DIDN'T KNOW YOUR MOM WOULD WALK IN!
BUT NOW MOM WON'T LET US PLAY WITHOUT AGATHA!
I DON'T MIND AGATHA KEEPING US CIVILIZED. AND SHE CAN ROLL FOR LISTEN CHECKS TO SEE IF ANYONE'S SNEAKING UP ON US.
AGATHA'S A GOOD PLAYER.
YOUR SISTER'S NOT A PROBLEM, HARRY. LET'S GET INTO THE DUNGEON ALREADY.
FINE.
WHATEVER.
YOU CAN ONLY SEE A SHORT DISTANCE DOWN THE PITCH-BLACK HALLWAY, AND A CHILL WIND MAKES YOUR TORCHES FLICKER...

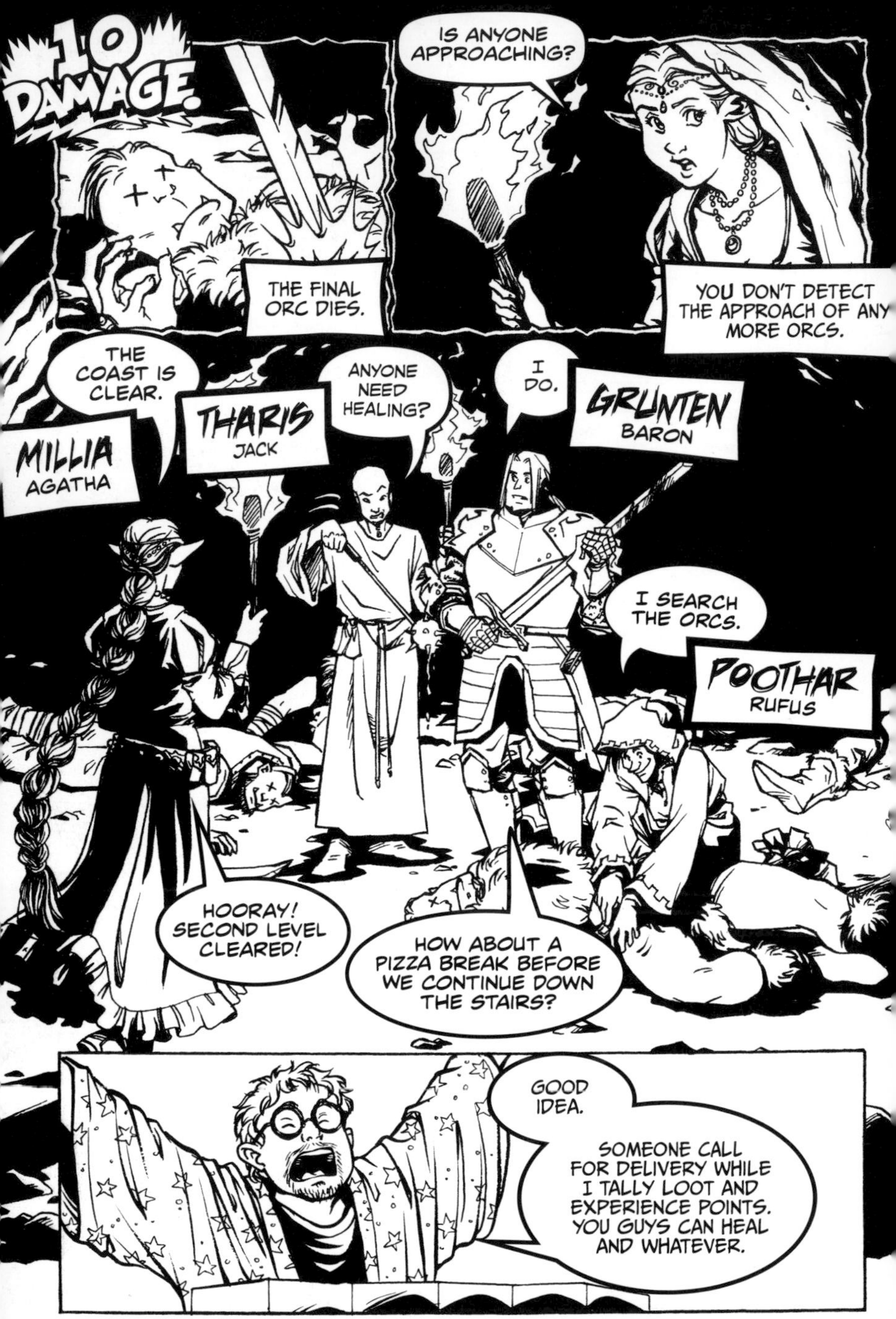
10 DAMAGE.
THE FINAL ORC DIES.
IS ANYONE APPROACHING?
YOU DON'T DETECT THE APPROACH OF ANY MORE ORCS.
THE COAST IS CLEAR.
MILLIA
AGATHA
THARIS
JACK
ANYONE NEED HEALING?
I DO.
GRUNTEN
BARON
I SEARCH THE ORCS.
POOTHAR
RUFUS
HOORAY! SECOND LEVEL CLEARED!
HOW ABOUT A PIZZA BREAK BEFORE WE CONTINUE DOWN THE STAIRS?
GOOD IDEA.
SOMEONE CALL FOR DELIVERY WHILE I TALLY LOOT AND EXPERIENCE POINTS. YOU GUYS CAN HEAL AND WHATEVER.

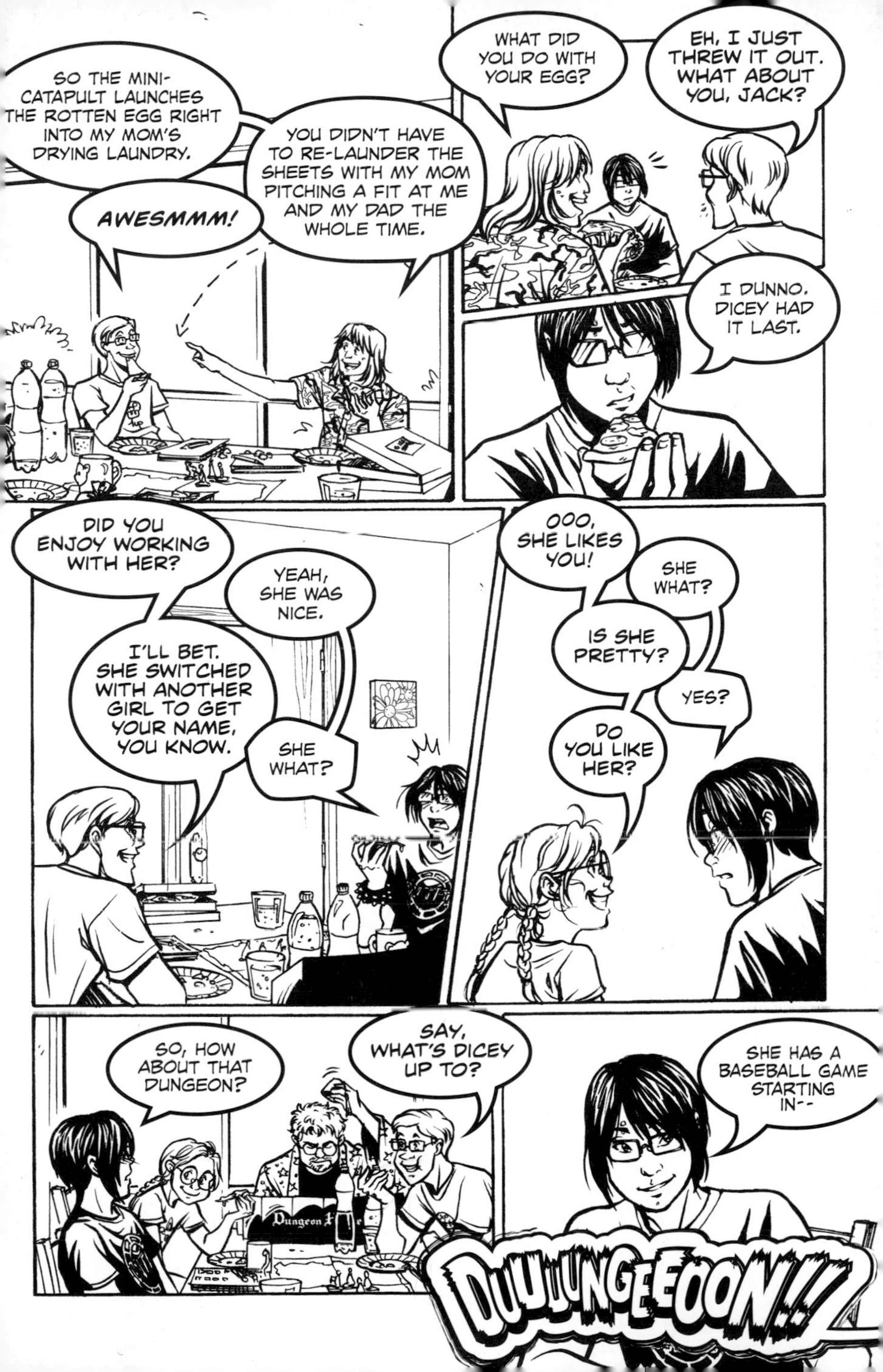

SO THE MINI-CATAPULT LAUNCHES THE ROTTEN EGG RIGHT INTO MY MOM'S DRYING LAUNDRY.
AWESMMM!
YOU DIDN'T HAVE TO RE-LAUNDER THE SHEETS WITH MY MOM PITCHING A FIT AT ME AND MY DAD THE WHOLE TIME.
WHAT DID YOU DO WITH YOUR EGG?
EH, I JUST THREW IT OUT. WHAT ABOUT YOU, JACK?
I DUNNO. DICEY HAD IT LAST.
DID YOU ENJOY WORKING WITH HER?
YEAH, SHE WAS NICE.
I'LL BET. SHE SWITCHED WITH ANOTHER GIRL TO GET YOUR NAME, YOU KNOW.
SHE WHAT?
OOO, SHE LIKES YOU!
SHE WHAT?
IS SHE PRETTY?
YES?
DO YOU LIKE HER?
SO, HOW ABOUT THAT DUNGEON?
SAY, WHAT'S DICEY UP TO?
SHE HAS A BASEBALL GAME STARTING IN--
DUUUUNGEEOON!!

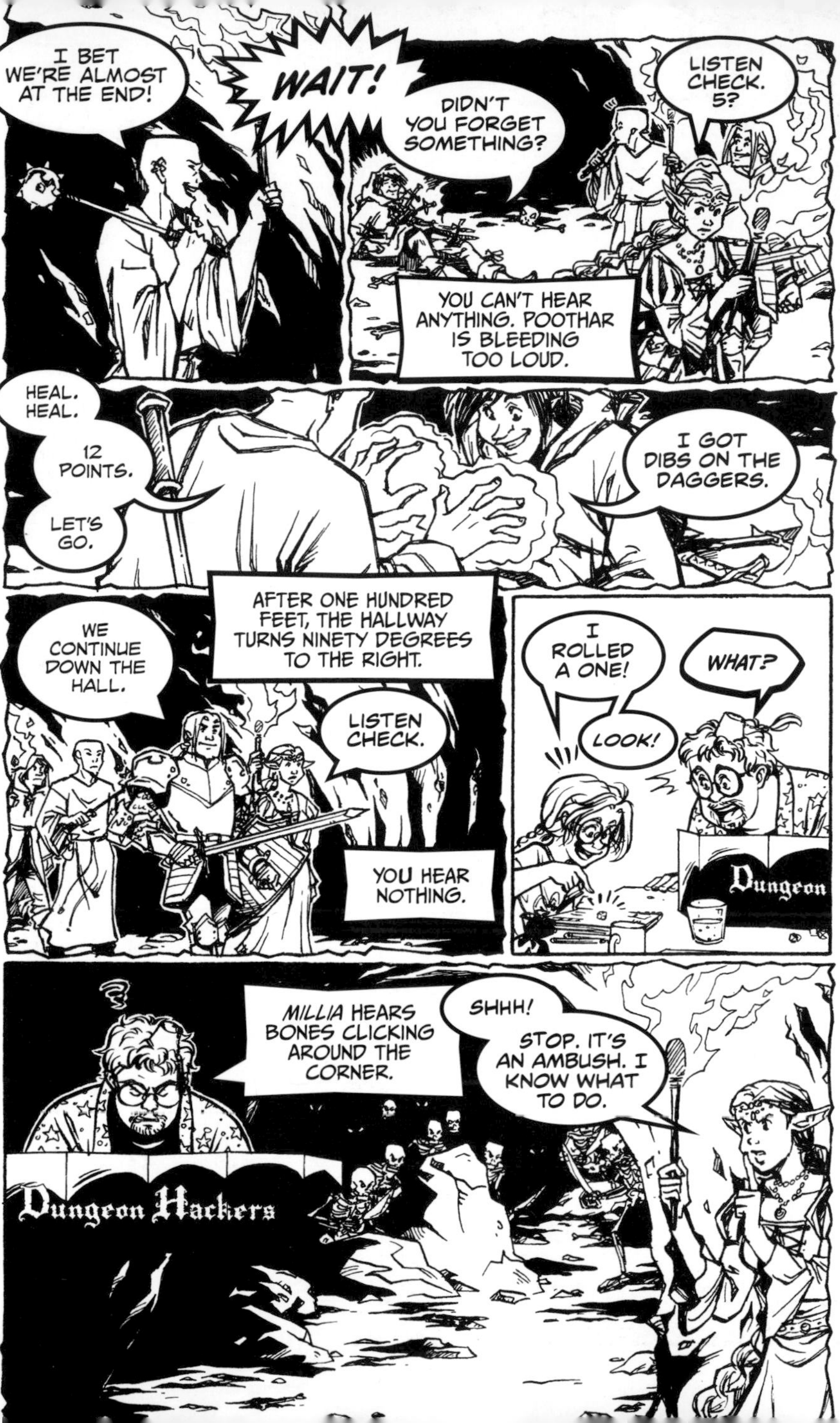
I BET WE'RE ALMOST AT THE END!
WAIT!
DIDN'T YOU FORGET SOMETHING?
LISTEN CHECK. 5?
YOU CAN'T HEAR ANYTHING. POOTHAR IS BLEEDING TOO LOUD.
HEAL. HEAL.
12 POINTS.
LET'S GO.
I GOT DIBS ON THE DAGGERS.
WE CONTINUE DOWN THE HALL.
AFTER ONE HUNDRED FEET, THE HALLWAY TURNS NINETY DEGREES TO THE RIGHT.
LISTEN CHECK.
YOU HEAR NOTHING.
I ROLLED A ONE!
LOOK!
WHAT?
Dungeon
MILLIA HEARS BONES CLICKING AROUND THE CORNER.
SHHH!
STOP. IT'S AN AMBUSH. I KNOW WHAT TO DO.
Dungeon Hackers

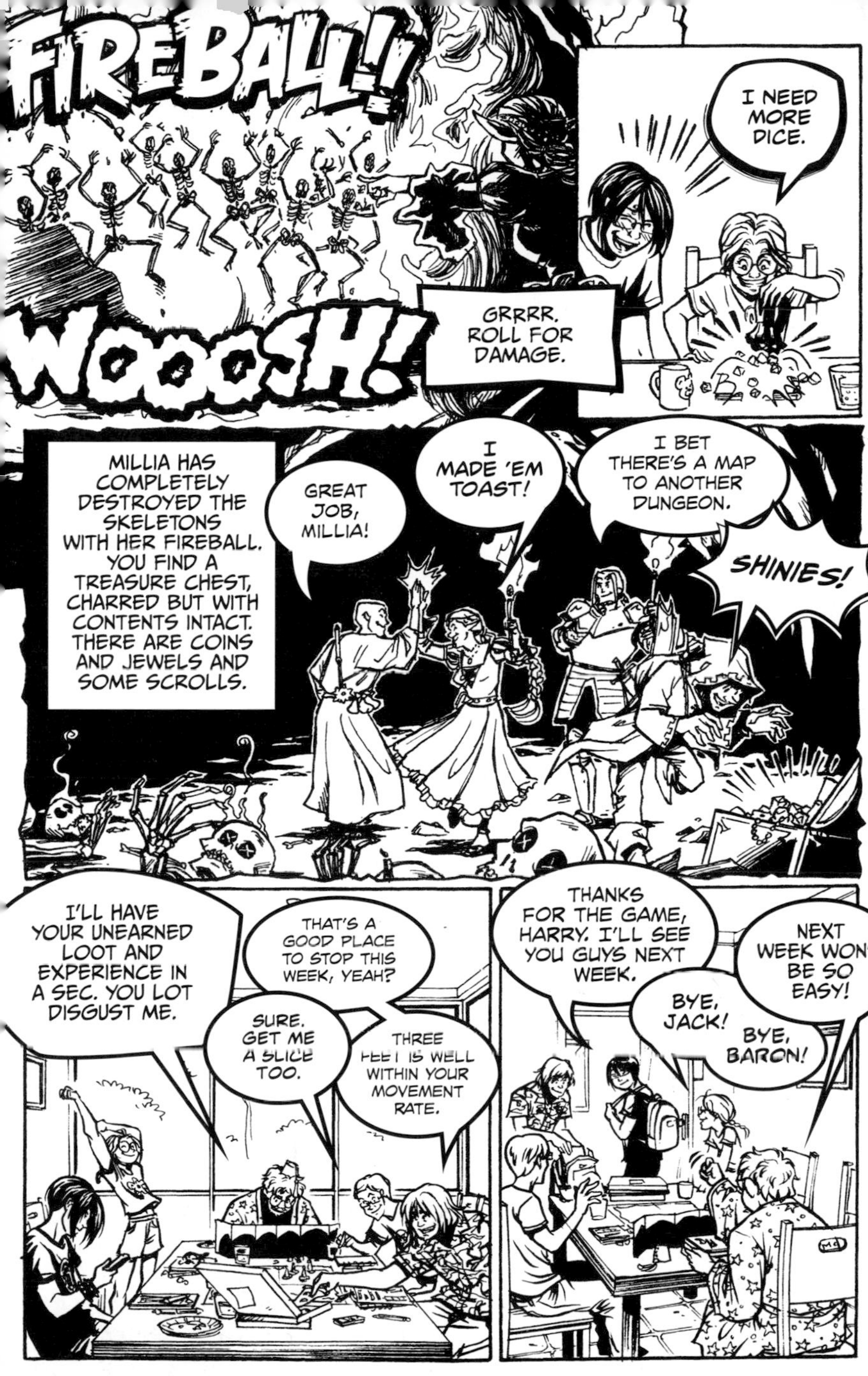
FIREBALL!!
WOOOSH!
GRRRR. ROLL FOR DAMAGE.
I NEED MORE DICE.
MILLIA HAS COMPLETELY DESTROYED THE SKELETONS WITH HER FIREBALL. YOU FIND A TREASURE CHEST, CHARRED BUT WITH CONTENTS INTACT. THERE ARE COINS AND JEWELS AND SOME SCROLLS.
GREAT JOB, MILLIA!
I MADE 'EM TOAST!
I BET THERE'S A MAP TO ANOTHER DUNGEON.
SHINIES!
I'LL HAVE YOUR UNEARNED LOOT AND EXPERIENCE IN A SEC. YOU LOT DISGUST ME.
THAT'S A GOOD PLACE TO STOP THIS WEEK, YEAH?
SURE. GET ME A SLICE TOO.
THREE FEET IS WELL WITHIN YOUR MOVEMENT RATE.
THANKS FOR THE GAME, HARRY. I'LL SEE YOU GUYS NEXT WEEK.
NEXT WEEK WON'T BE SO EASY!
BYE, JACK!
BYE, BARON!

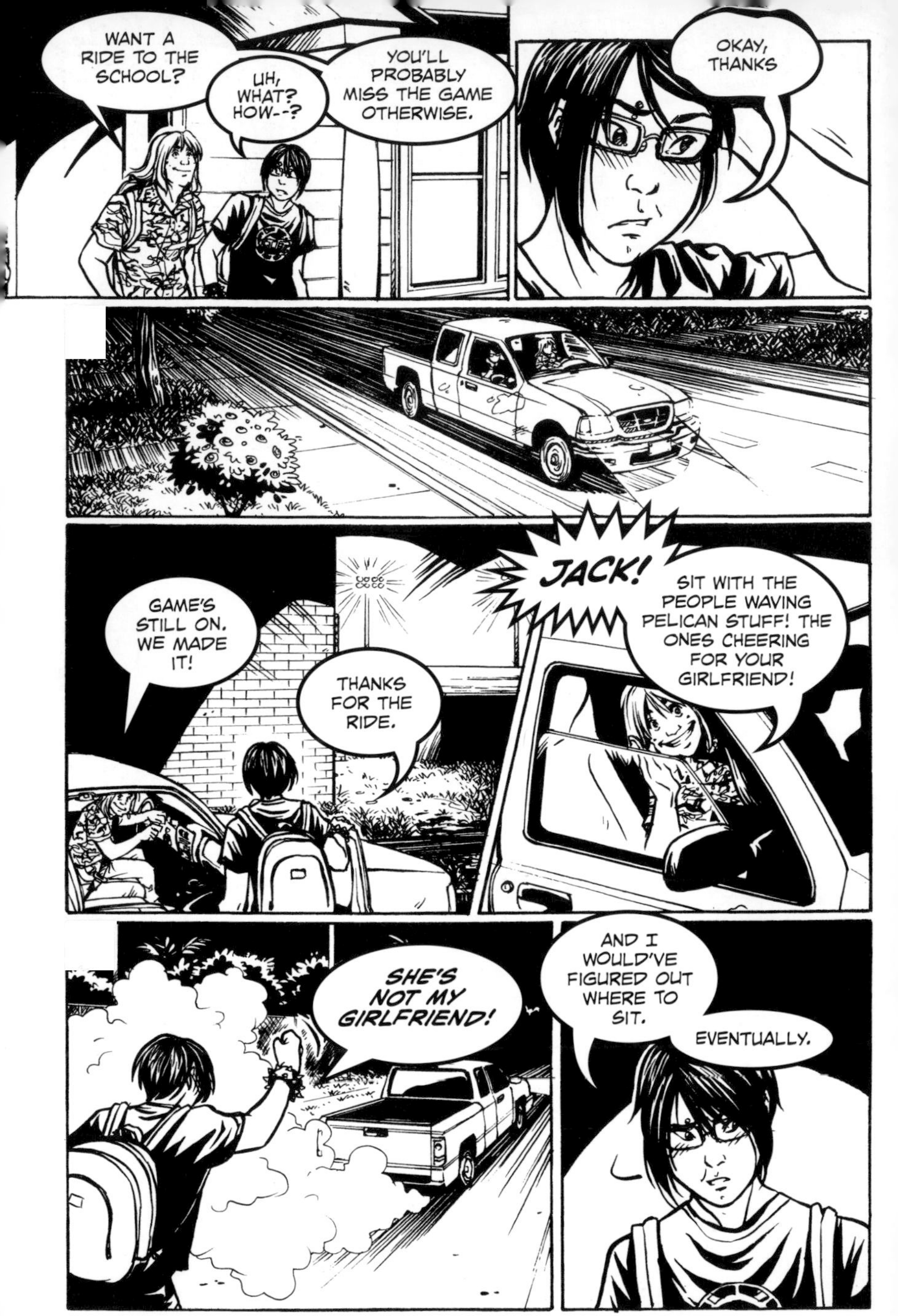

WANT A RIDE TO THE SCHOOL?
UH, WHAT? HOW--?
YOU'LL PROBABLY MISS THE GAME OTHERWISE.
OKAY, THANKS
GAME'S STILL ON. WE MADE IT!
THANKS FOR THE RIDE.
JACK!
SIT WITH THE PEOPLE WAVING PELICAN STUFF! THE ONES CHEERING FOR YOUR GIRLFRIEND!
SHE'S NOT MY GIRLFRIEND!
AND I WOULD'VE FIGURED OUT WHERE TO SIT.
EVENTUALLY.

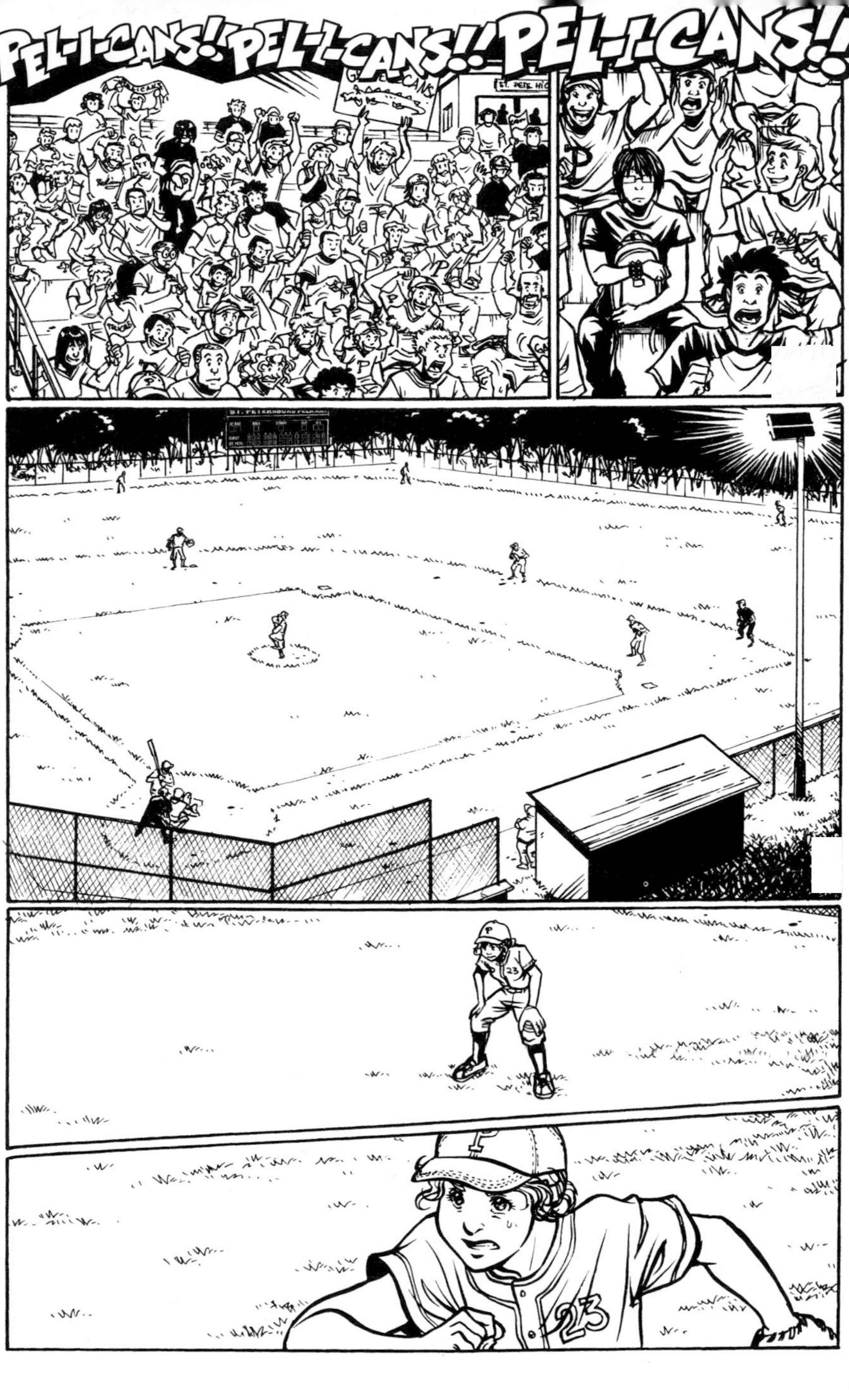
PEL-I-CANS!! PEL-I-CANS!! PEL-I-CANS!!

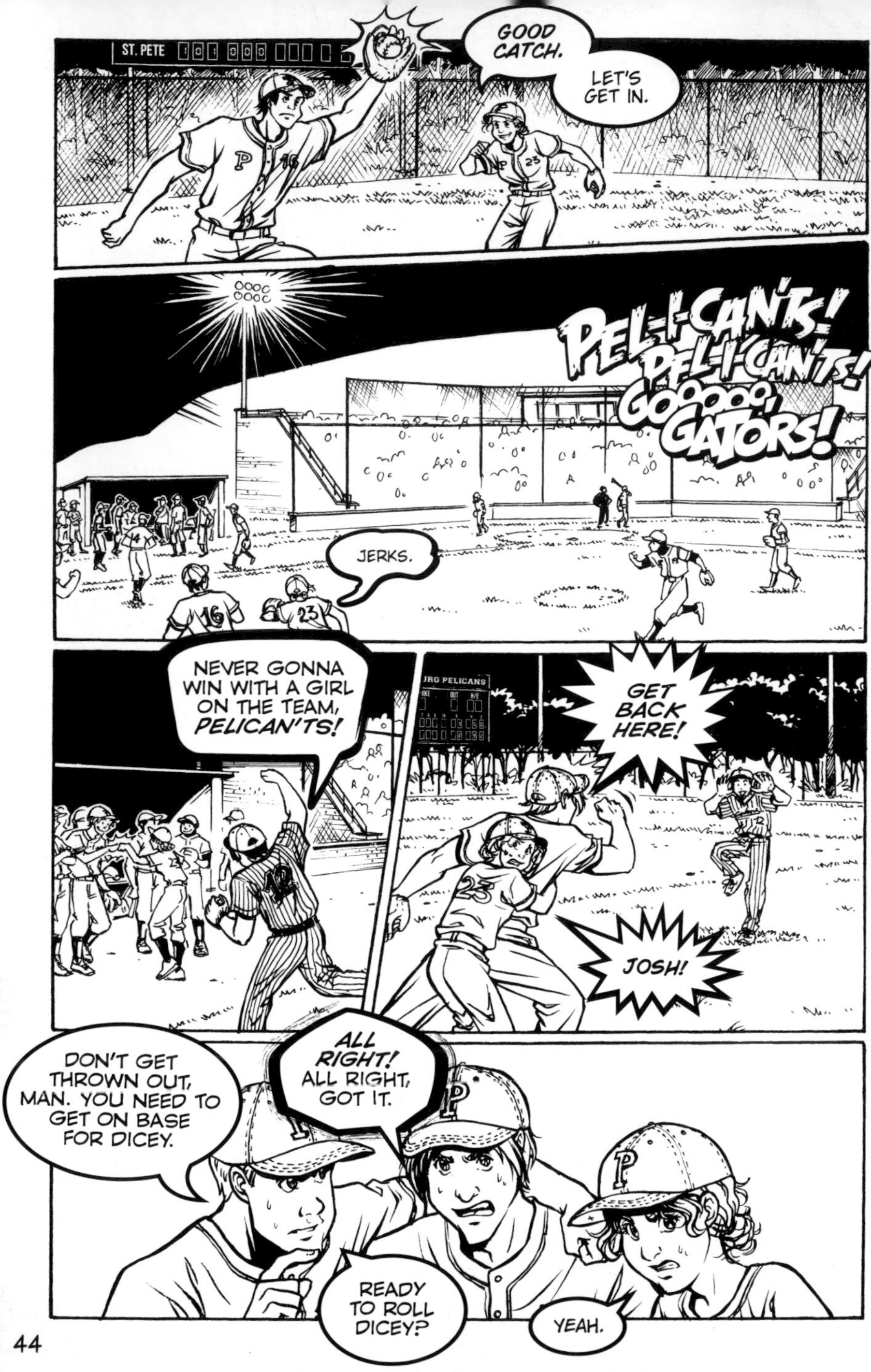
ST. PETE
GOOD CATCH.
LET'S GET IN.
PEL-I-CAN'TS! PEL-I-CAN'TS! GOOOOO, GATORS!
JERKS.
NEVER GONNA WIN WITH A GIRL ON THE TEAM, *PELICAN'TS!*
GET BACK HERE!
JOSH!
DON'T GET THROWN OUT, MAN. YOU NEED TO GET ON BASE FOR DICEY.
ALL RIGHT! ALL RIGHT, GOT IT.
READY TO ROLL DICEY?
YEAH.

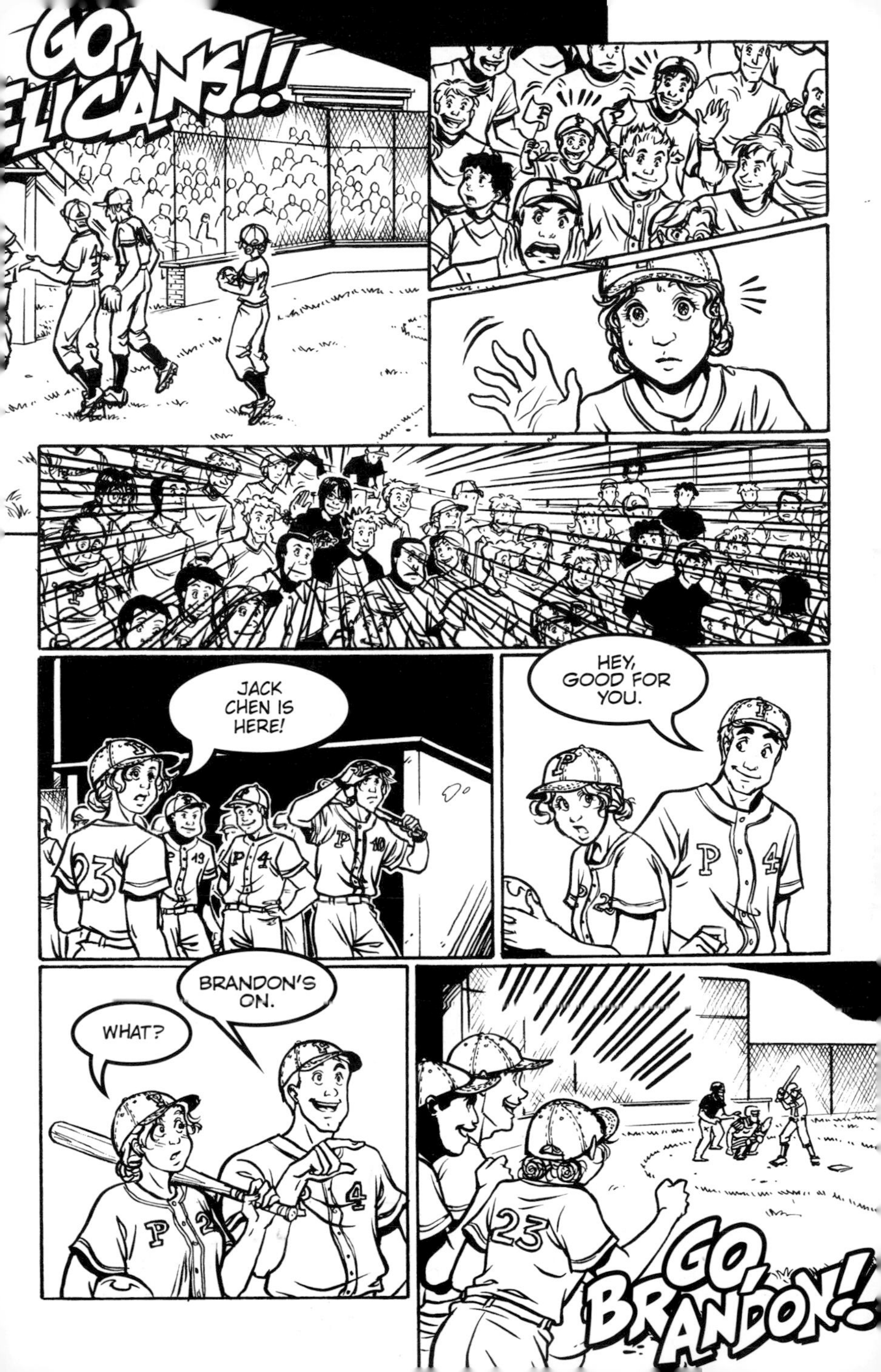
GO, ELICANS!!
JACK CHEN IS HERE!
HEY, GOOD FOR YOU.
WHAT?
BRANDON'S ON.
GO, BRANDON!

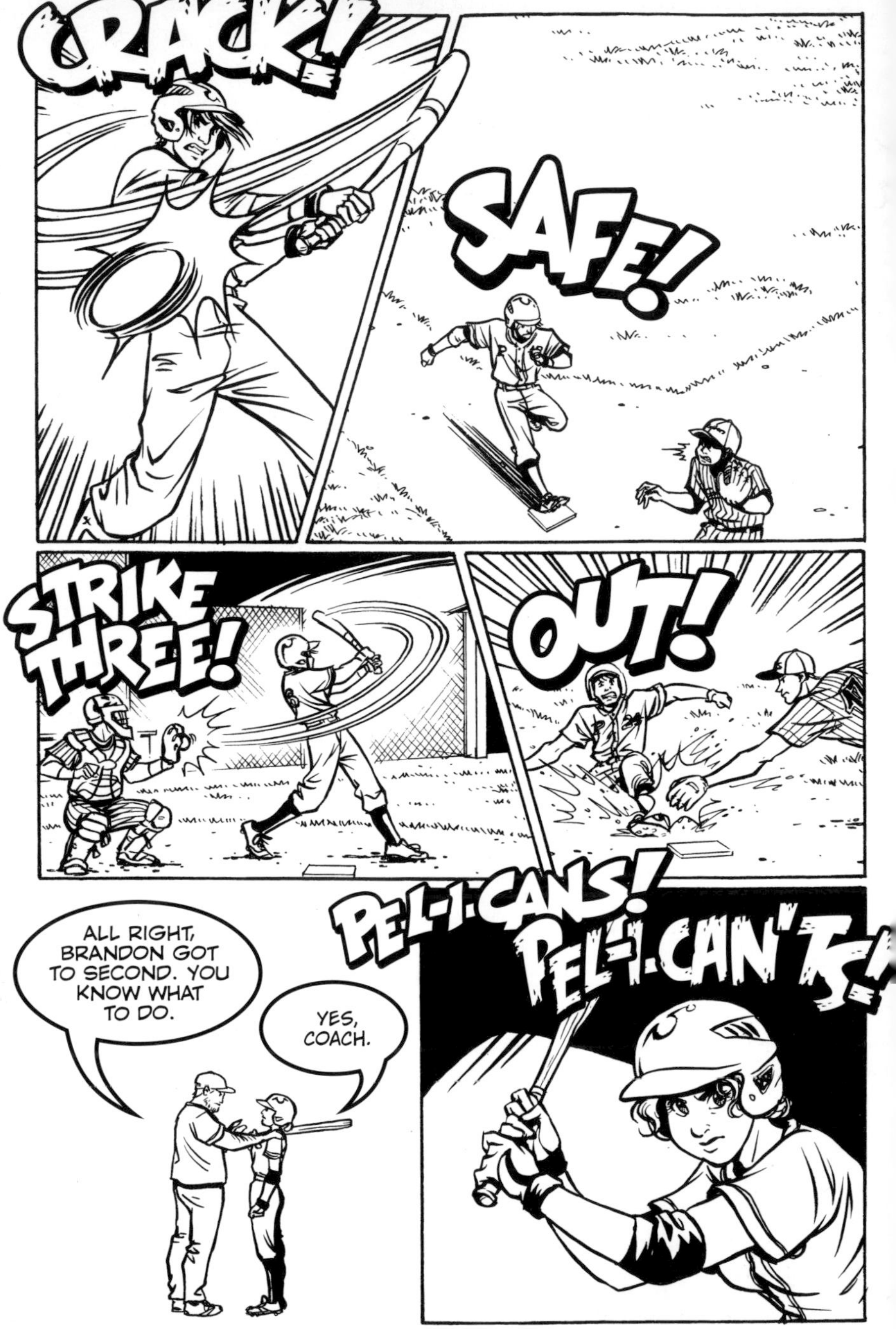
CRACK!
SAFE!
STRIKE THREE!
OUT!
ALL RIGHT, BRANDON GOT TO SECOND. YOU KNOW WHAT TO DO.
YES, COACH.
PEL-I-CANS! PEL-I-CAN'TS!

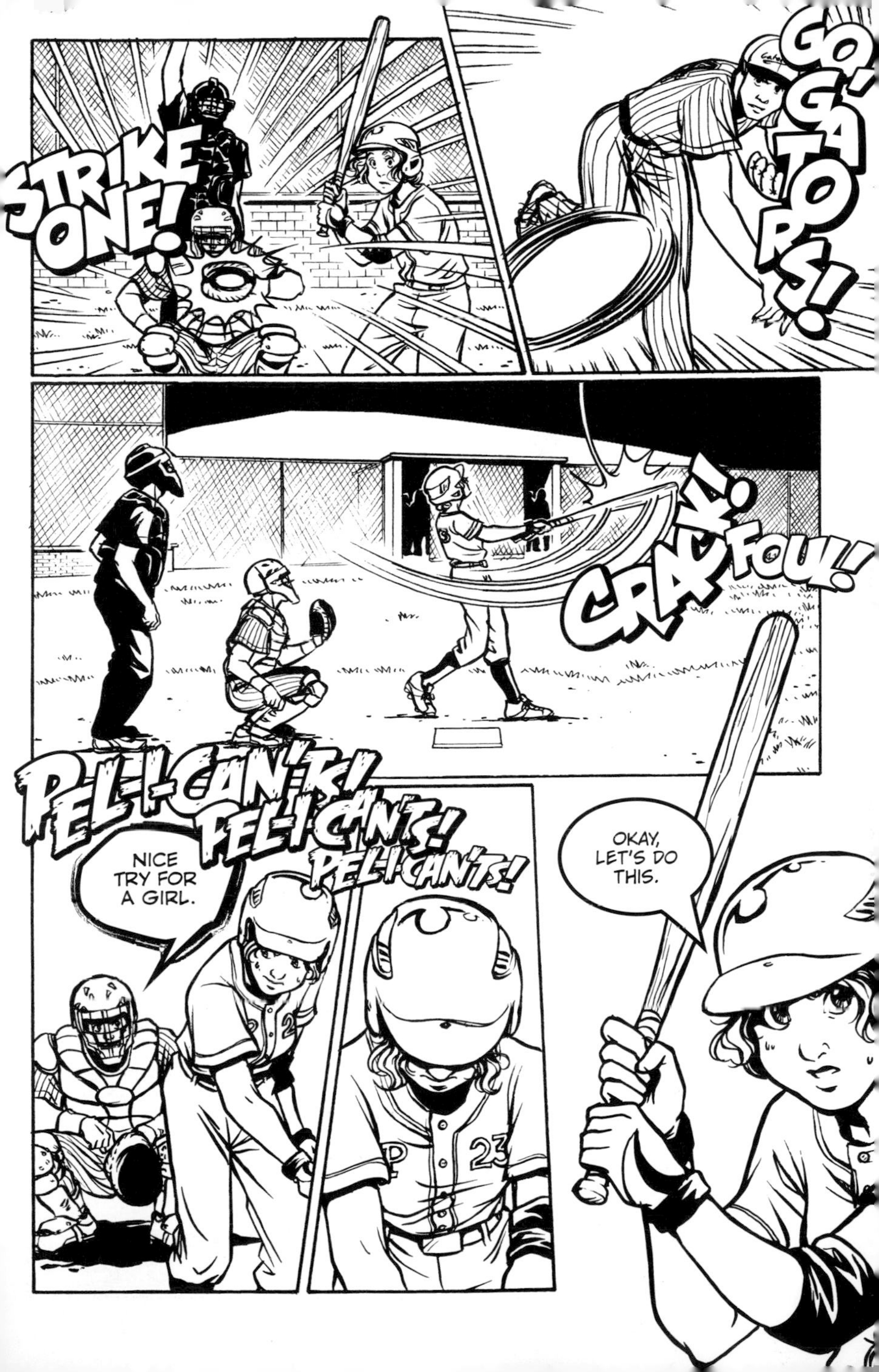
STRIKE ONE!
GO, GA-TORS!
CRACK!
FOUL!
PEL-I-CAN'TS! PEL-I-CAN'TS! PEL-I-CAN'TS!
NICE TRY FOR A GIRL.
OKAY, LET'S DO THIS.

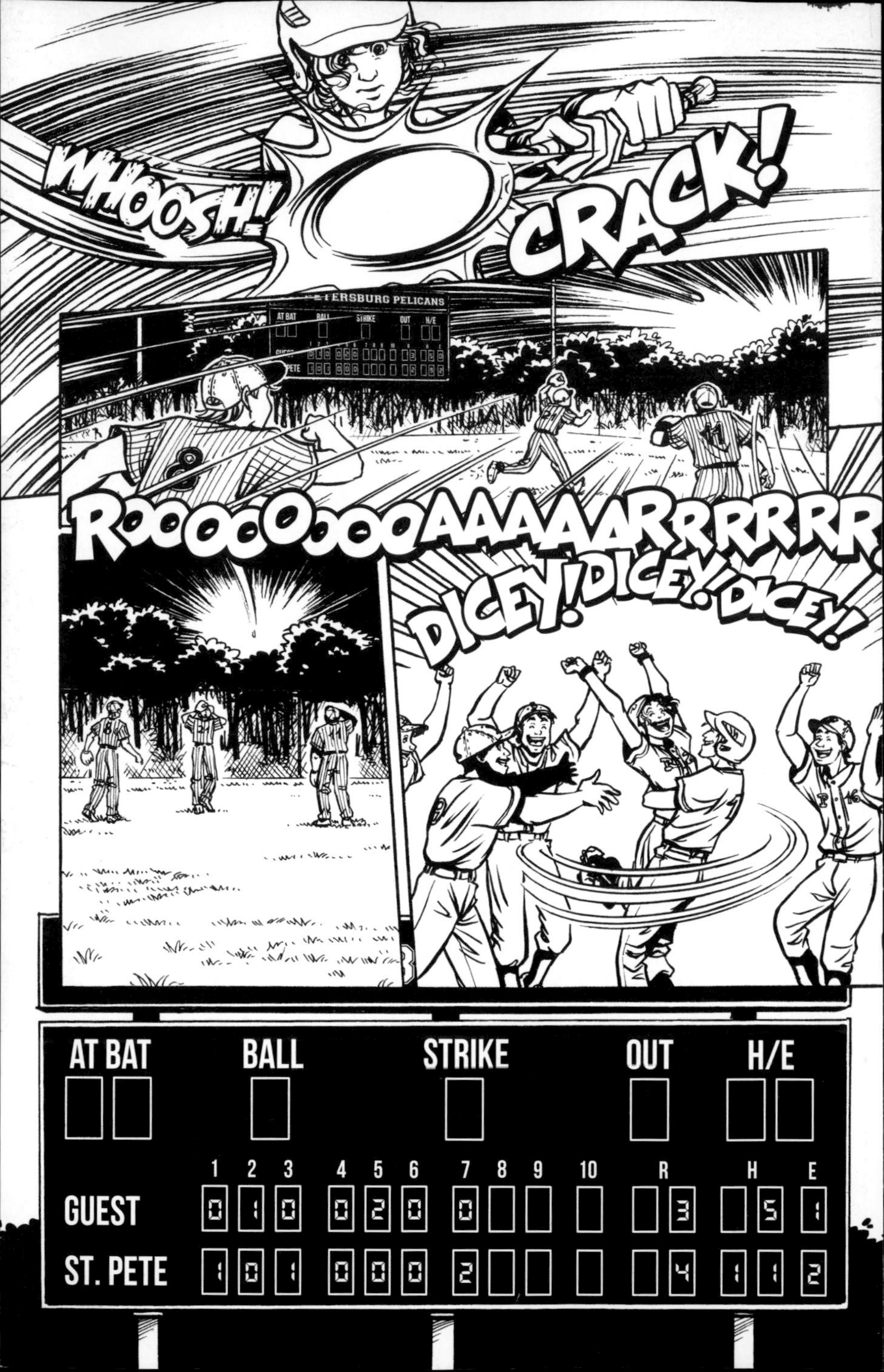
WHOOSH!
CRACK!
...ERSBURG PELICANS
ROOOOOOOOOAAAAARRRRRR
DICEY! DICEY! DICEY!
AT BAT
BALL
STRIKE
OUT
H/E
1 2 3 4 5 6 7 8 9 10 R H E
GUEST 0 1 0 0 2 0 0 3 5 1
ST. PETE 1 0 1 0 0 0 2 4 11 2

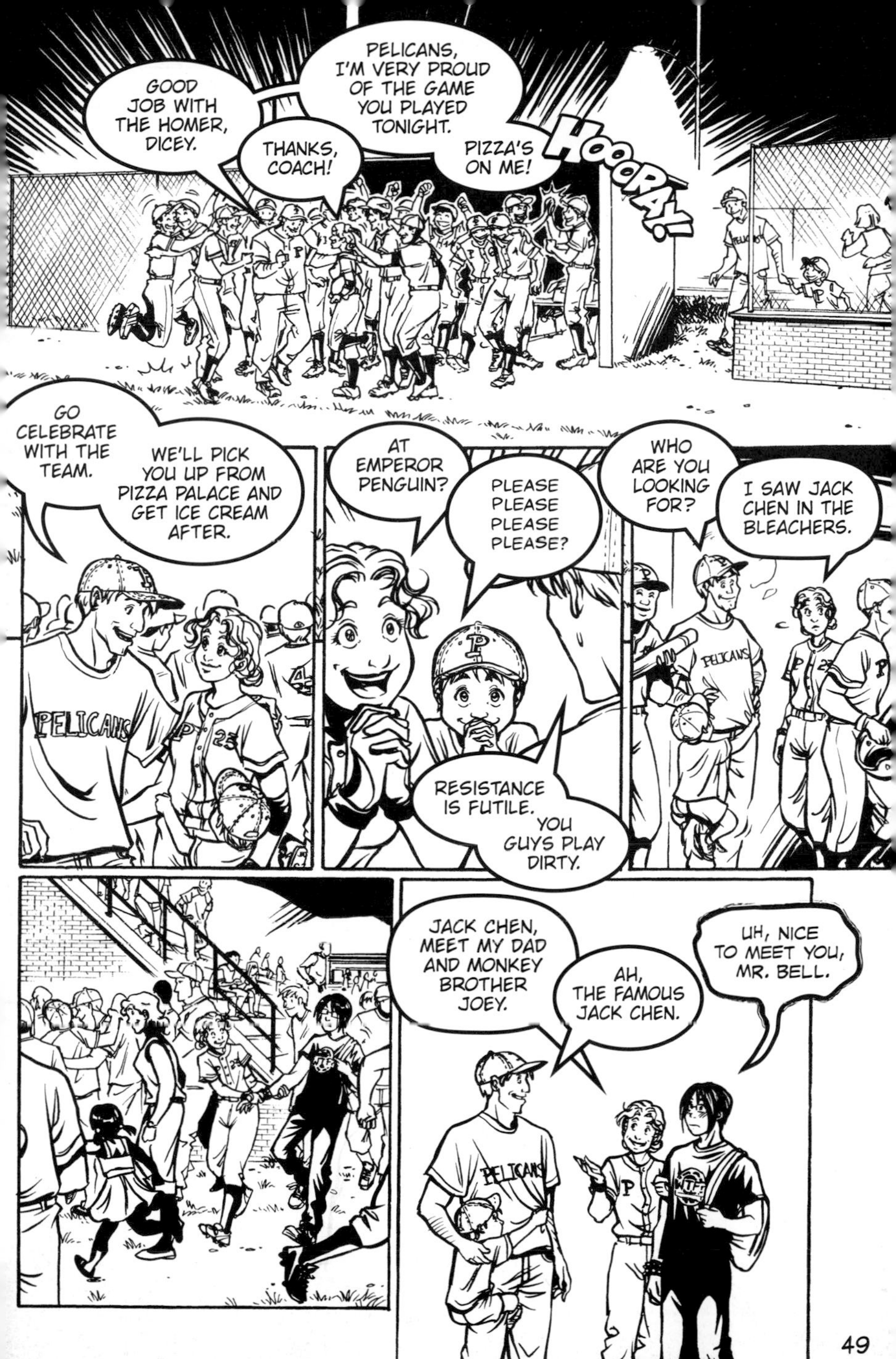
GOOD JOB WITH THE HOMER, DICEY.
PELICANS, I'M VERY PROUD OF THE GAME YOU PLAYED TONIGHT.
THANKS, COACH!
PIZZA'S ON ME!
HOORAY!
GO CELEBRATE WITH THE TEAM.
WE'LL PICK YOU UP FROM PIZZA PALACE AND GET ICE CREAM AFTER.
AT EMPEROR PENGUIN?
PLEASE PLEASE PLEASE PLEASE?
RESISTANCE IS FUTILE.
YOU GUYS PLAY DIRTY.
WHO ARE YOU LOOKING FOR?
I SAW JACK CHEN IN THE BLEACHERS.
JACK CHEN, MEET MY DAD AND MONKEY BROTHER JOEY.
AH, THE FAMOUS JACK CHEN.
UH, NICE TO MEET YOU, MR. BELL.

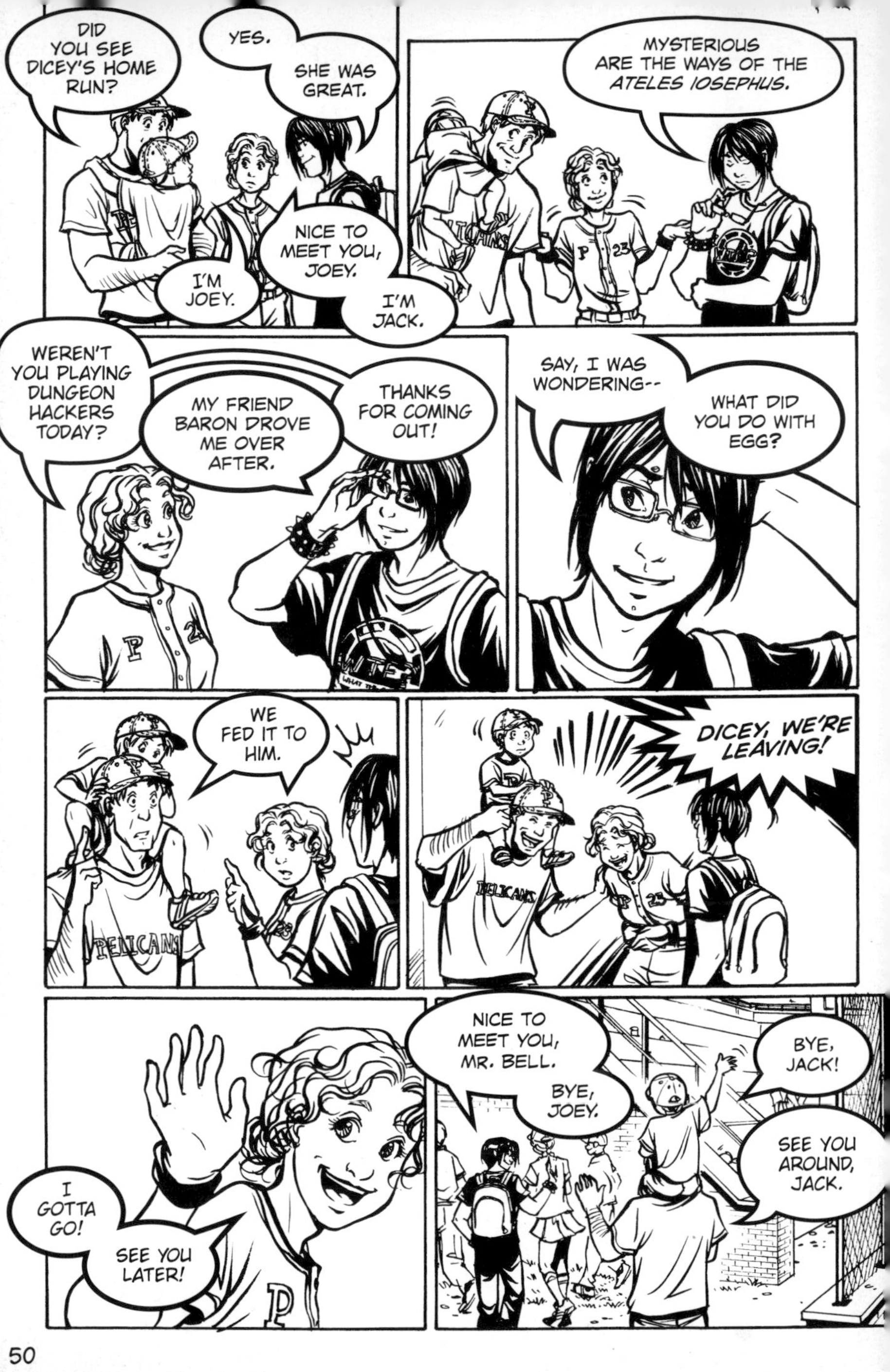
DID YOU SEE DICEY'S HOME RUN?
YES.
SHE WAS GREAT.
I'M JOEY.
NICE TO MEET YOU, JOEY.
I'M JACK.
MYSTERIOUS ARE THE WAYS OF THE *ATELES IOSEPHUS.*
WEREN'T YOU PLAYING DUNGEON HACKERS TODAY?
MY FRIEND BARON DROVE ME OVER AFTER.
THANKS FOR COMING OUT!
SAY, I WAS WONDERING--
WHAT DID YOU DO WITH EGG?
WE FED IT TO HIM.
DICEY, WE'RE LEAVING!
I GOTTA GO!
SEE YOU LATER!
NICE TO MEET YOU, MR. BELL.
BYE, JOEY.
BYE, JACK!
SEE YOU AROUND, JACK.

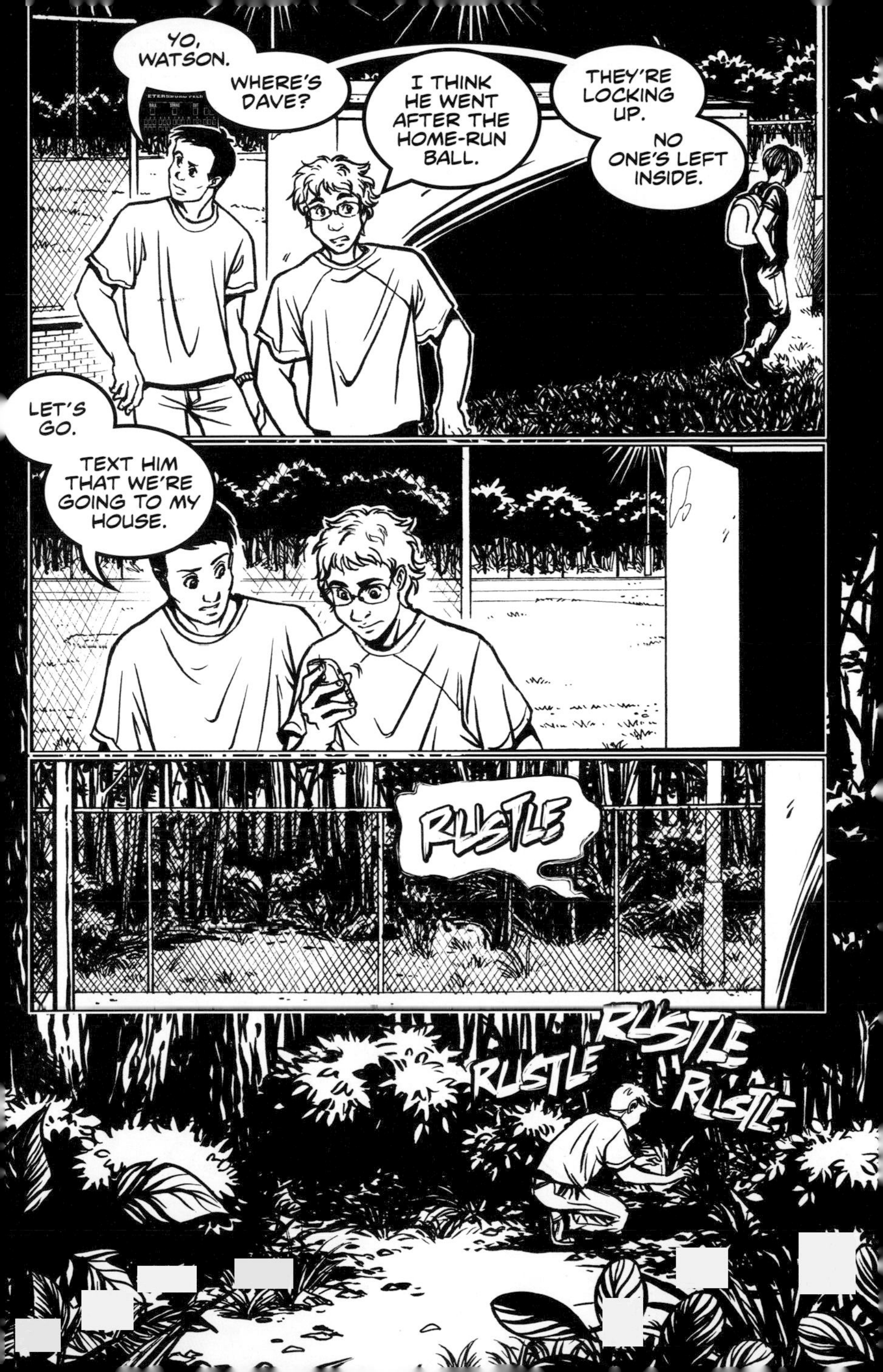
YO, WATSON.
WHERE'S DAVE?
I THINK HE WENT AFTER THE HOME-RUN BALL.
THEY'RE LOCKING UP.
NO ONE'S LEFT INSIDE.
LET'S GO.
TEXT HIM THAT WE'RE GOING TO MY HOUSE.
RUSTLE
RUSTLE
RUSTLE
RUSTLE

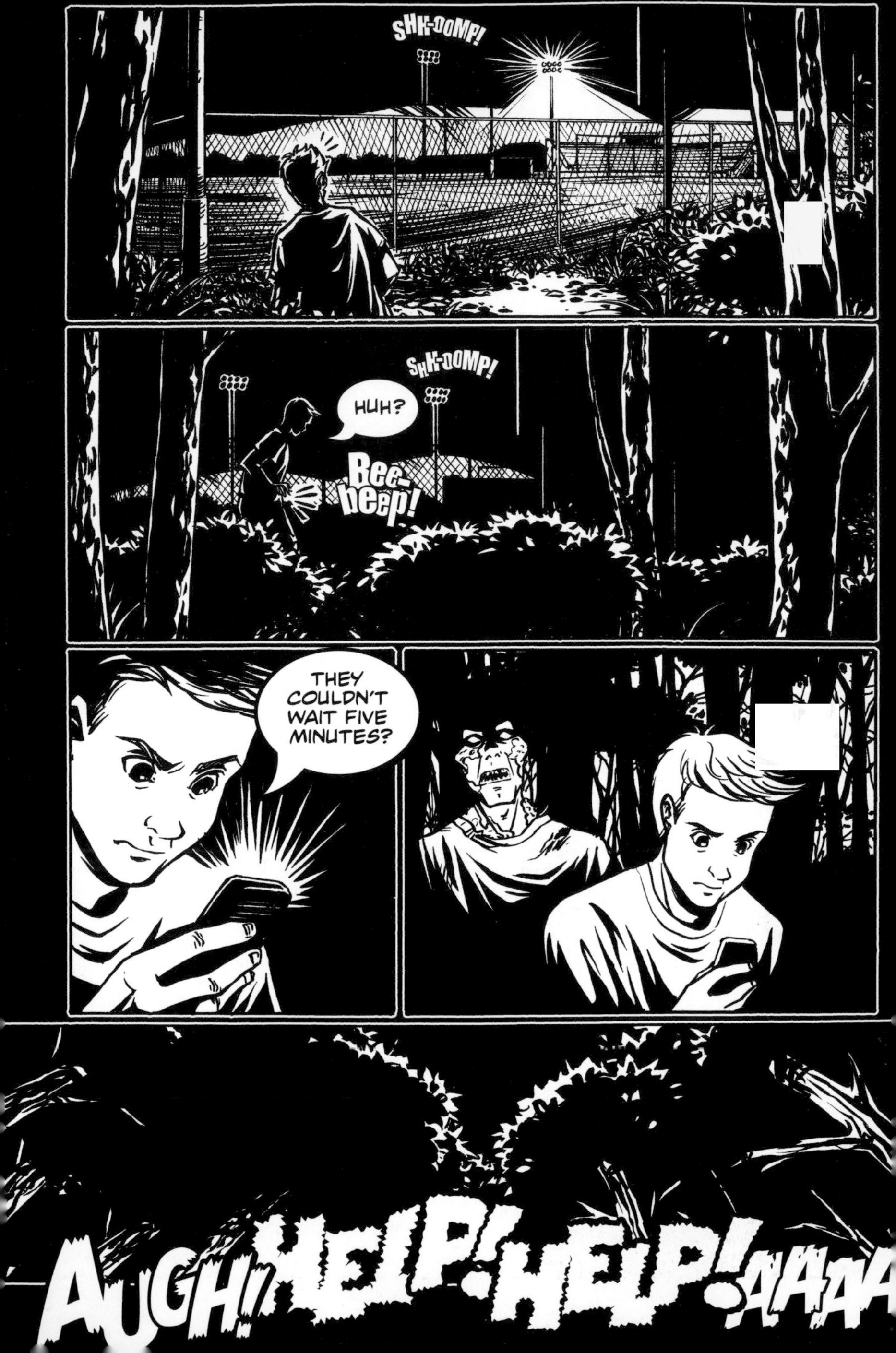
SHH-OOMP!
SHH-OOMP!
HUH?
Bee-beep!
THEY COULDN'T WAIT FIVE MINUTES?
AUGH! HELP! HELP! AAAA

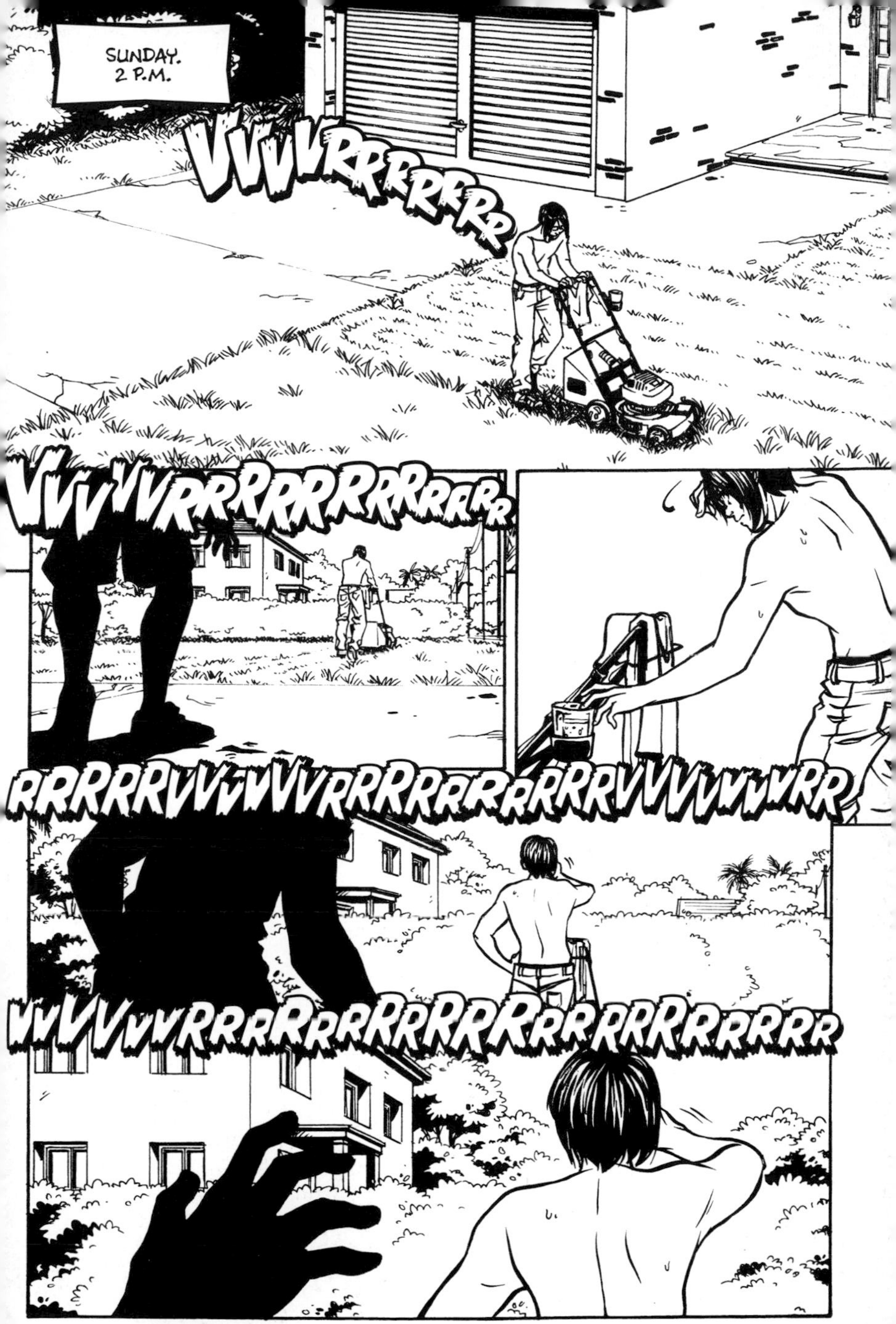

SUNDAY.
2 P.M.
VVVVRRRRRRR
VVVVVRRRRRRRRRRR
RRRRRVVVVVVRRRRRRRRRRVVVVVVVRR
VVVVVVRRRRRRRRRRRRRRRRRRRRR

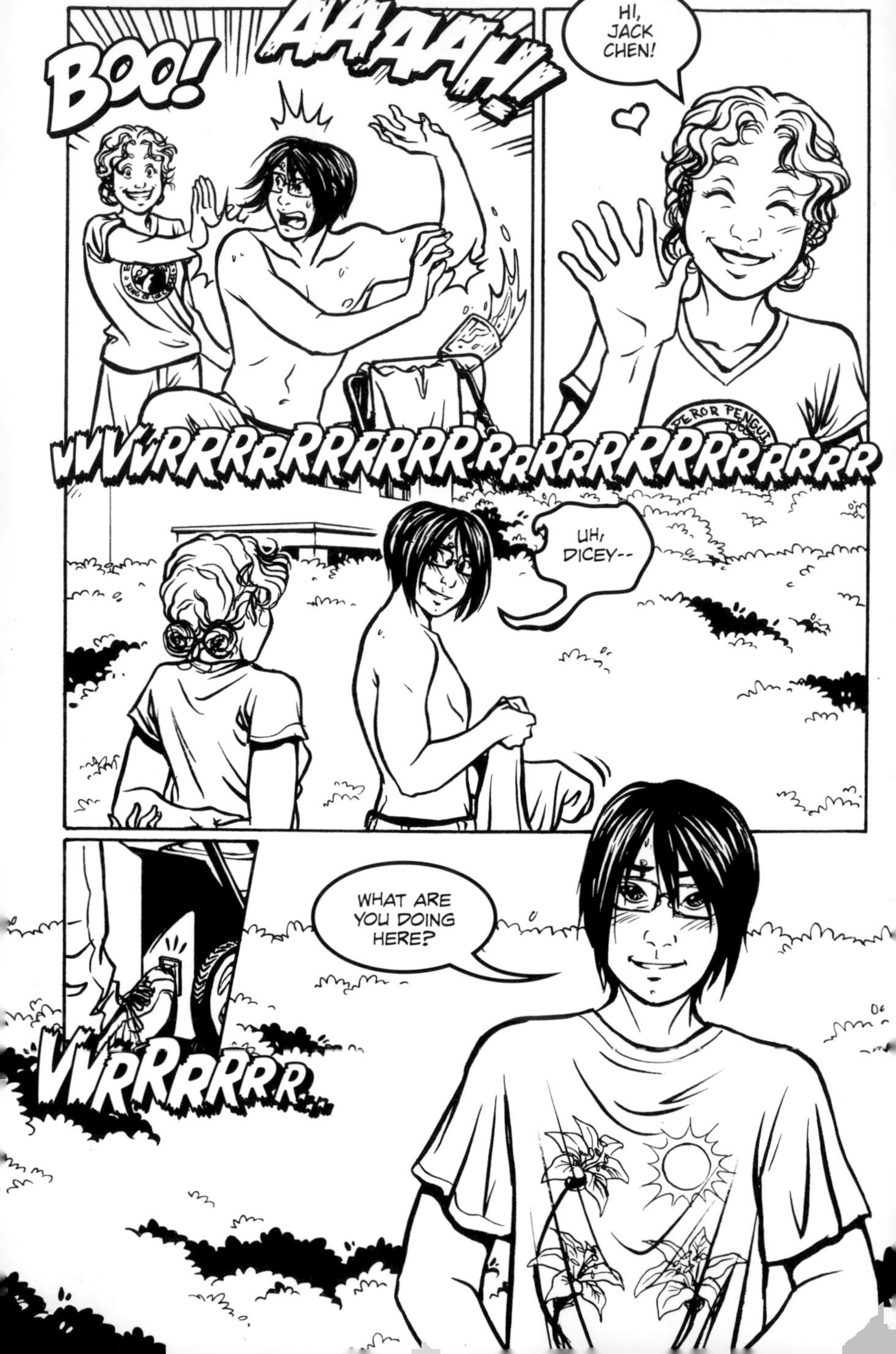
BOO!
AAAAAH!!
HI, JACK CHEN!
VVVVRRRRRRRRRRRRRRRRRRRRRRRRR
UH, DICEY--
WHAT ARE YOU DOING HERE?
VVRRRRRR...

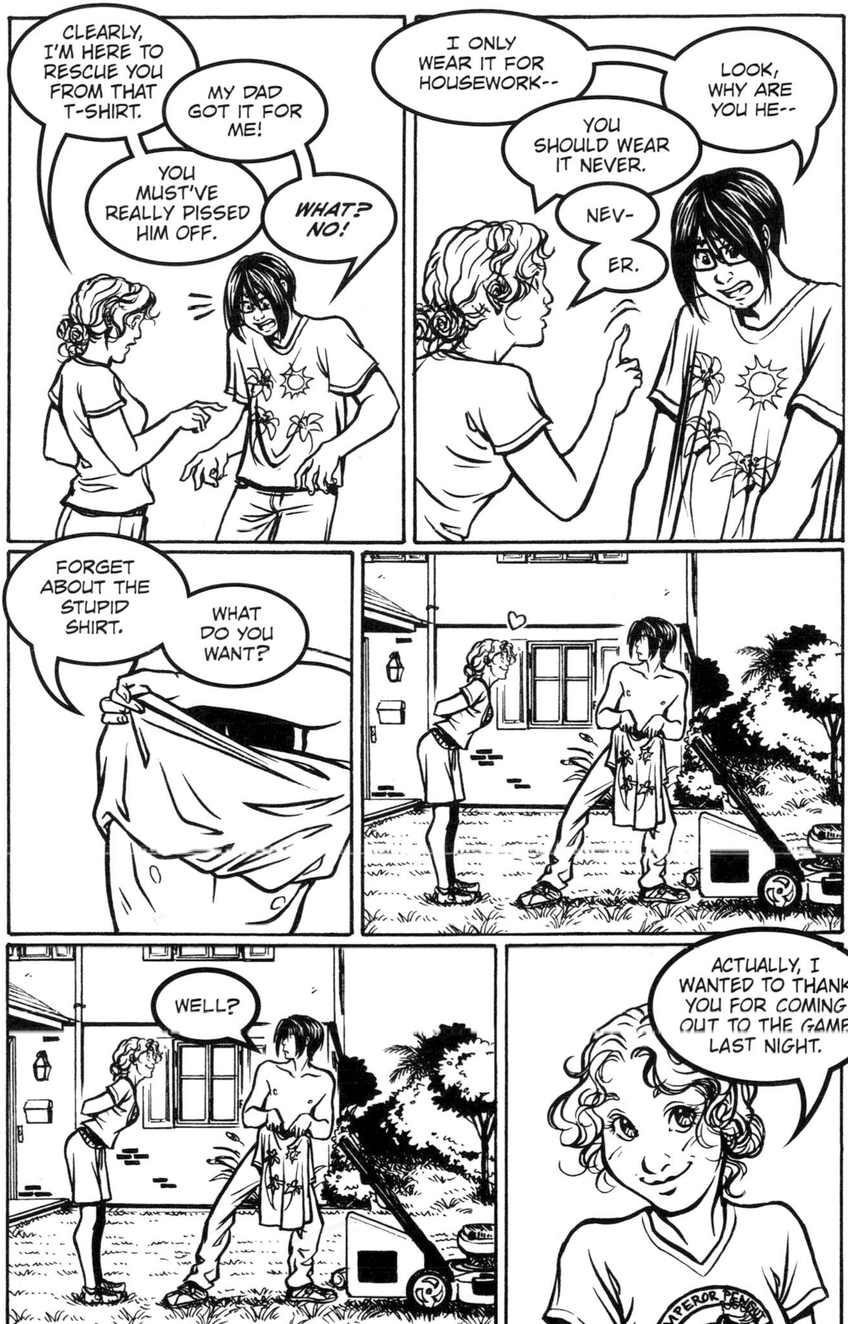

CLEARLY, I'M HERE TO RESCUE YOU FROM THAT T-SHIRT.
MY DAD GOT IT FOR ME!
YOU MUST'VE REALLY PISSED HIM OFF.
WHAT? NO!
I ONLY WEAR IT FOR HOUSEWORK--
LOOK, WHY ARE YOU HE--
YOU SHOULD WEAR IT NEVER.
NEV-
ER.
FORGET ABOUT THE STUPID SHIRT.
WHAT DO YOU WANT?
WELL?
ACTUALLY, I WANTED TO THANK YOU FOR COMING OUT TO THE GAME LAST NIGHT.

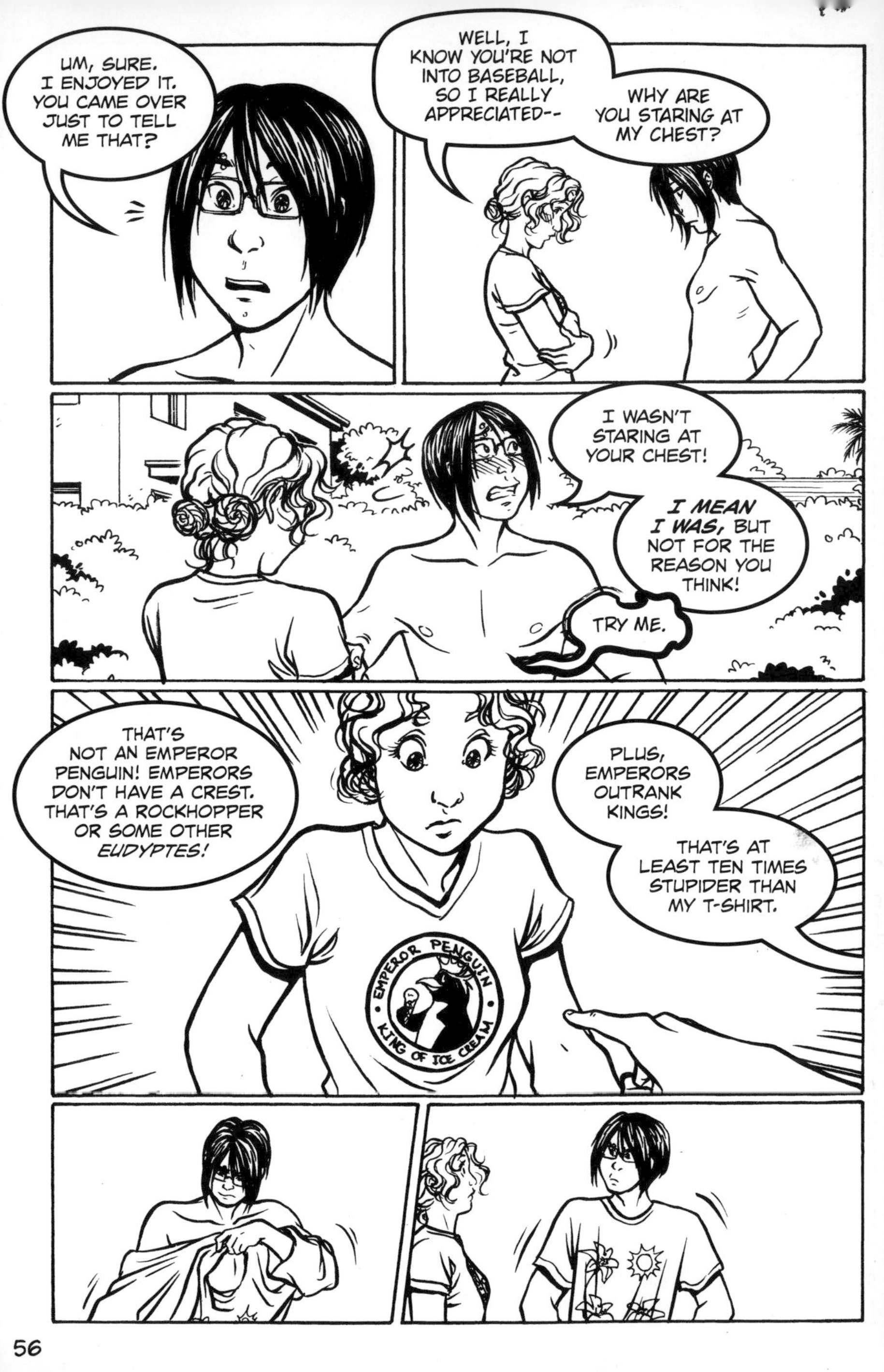
UM, SURE. I ENJOYED IT. YOU CAME OVER JUST TO TELL ME THAT?
WELL, I KNOW YOU'RE NOT INTO BASEBALL, SO I REALLY APPRECIATED--
WHY ARE YOU STARING AT MY CHEST?
I WASN'T STARING AT YOUR CHEST!
I MEAN I WAS, BUT NOT FOR THE REASON YOU THINK!
TRY ME.
THAT'S NOT AN EMPEROR PENGUIN! EMPERORS DON'T HAVE A CREST. THAT'S A ROCKHOPPER OR SOME OTHER EUDYPTES!
PLUS, EMPERORS OUTRANK KINGS!
THAT'S AT LEAST TEN TIMES STUPIDER THAN MY T-SHIRT.
EMPEROR PENGUIN
KING OF ICE CREAM

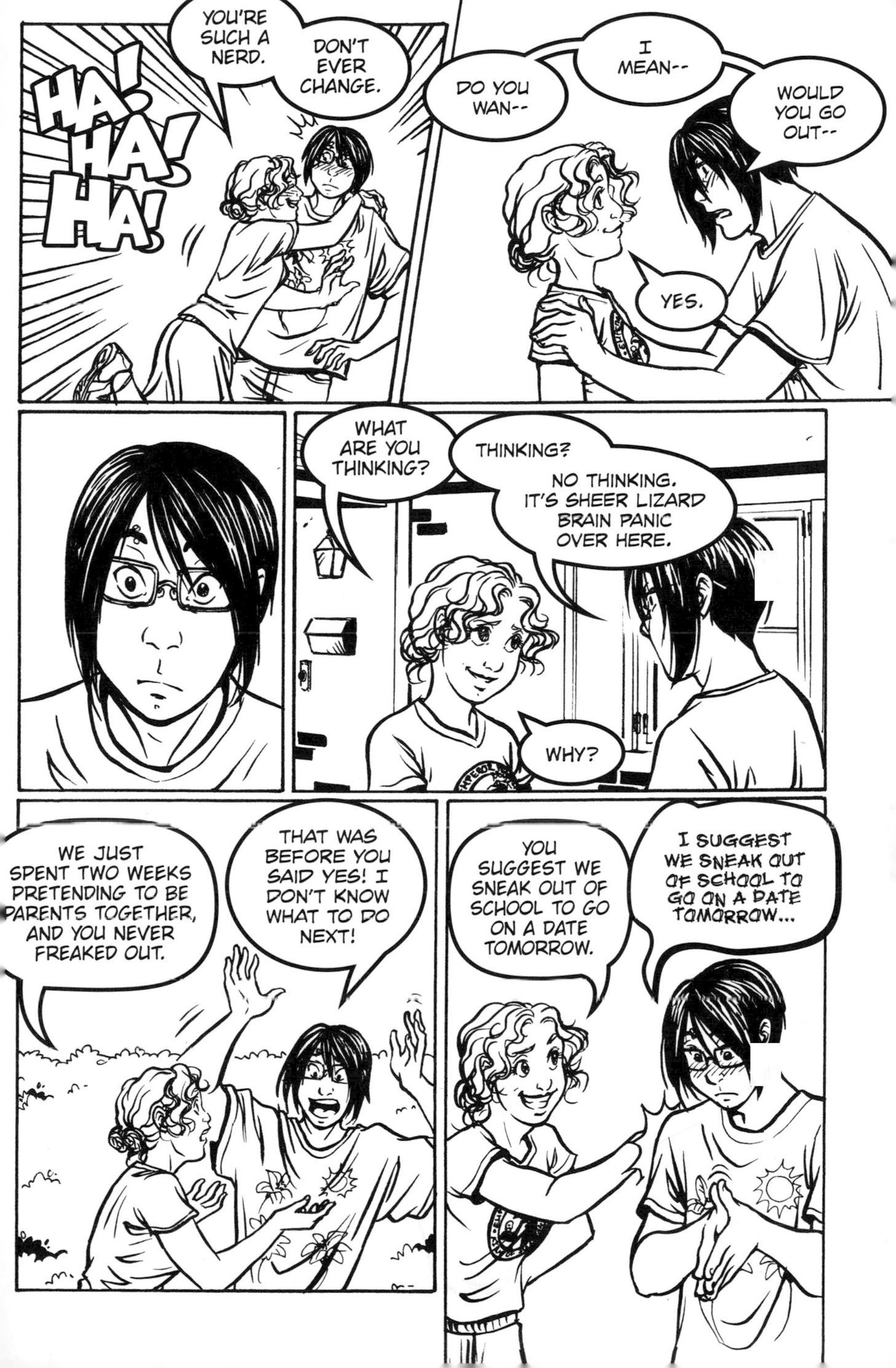
YOU'RE SUCH A NERD.
DON'T EVER CHANGE.
HA! HA! HA!
DO YOU WAN--
I MEAN--
WOULD YOU GO OUT--
YES.
WHAT ARE YOU THINKING?
THINKING?
NO THINKING. IT'S SHEER LIZARD BRAIN PANIC OVER HERE.
WHY?
WE JUST SPENT TWO WEEKS PRETENDING TO BE PARENTS TOGETHER, AND YOU NEVER FREAKED OUT.
THAT WAS BEFORE YOU SAID YES! I DON'T KNOW WHAT TO DO NEXT!
YOU SUGGEST WE SNEAK OUT OF SCHOOL TO GO ON A DATE TOMORROW.
I SUGGEST WE SNEAK OUT OF SCHOOL TO GO ON A DATE TOMORROW...

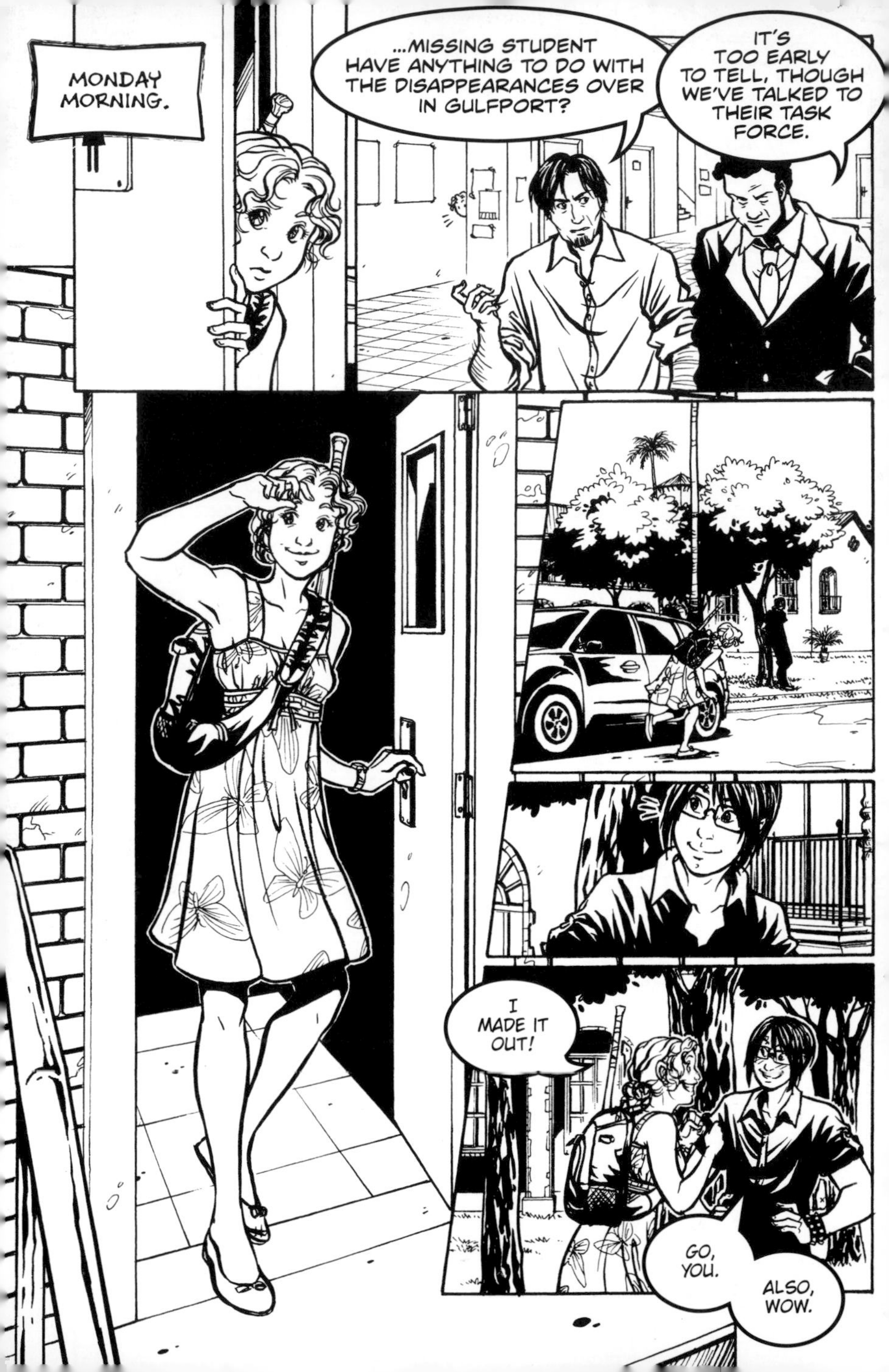
MONDAY MORNING.
...MISSING STUDENT HAVE ANYTHING TO DO WITH THE DISAPPEARANCES OVER IN GULFPORT?
IT'S TOO EARLY TO TELL, THOUGH WE'VE TALKED TO THEIR TASK FORCE.
I MADE IT OUT!
GO, YOU.
ALSO, WOW.

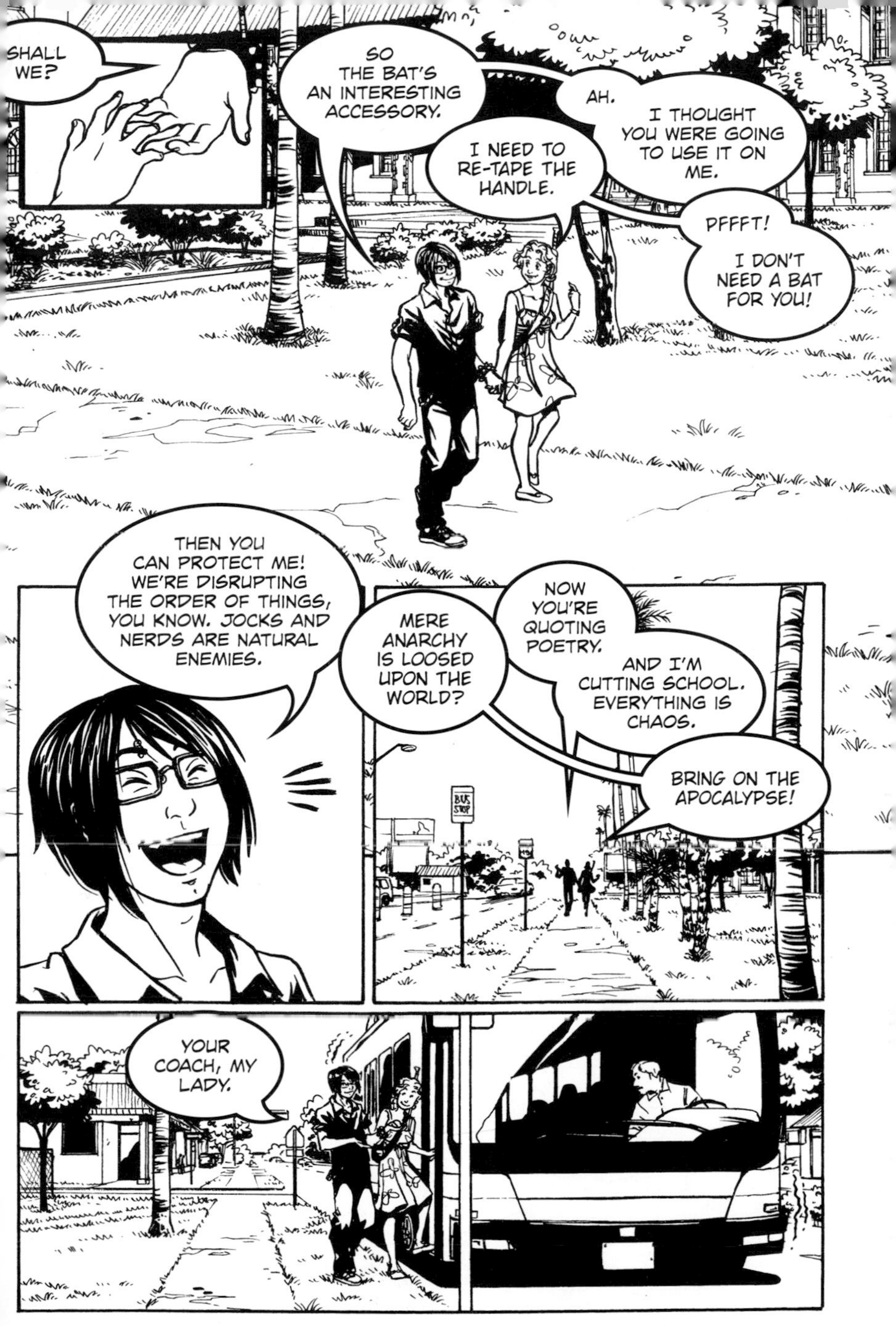
SHALL WE?
SO THE BAT'S AN INTERESTING ACCESSORY.
I NEED TO RE-TAPE THE HANDLE.
AH.
I THOUGHT YOU WERE GOING TO USE IT ON ME.
PFFFT!
I DON'T NEED A BAT FOR YOU!
THEN YOU CAN PROTECT ME! WE'RE DISRUPTING THE ORDER OF THINGS, YOU KNOW. JOCKS AND NERDS ARE NATURAL ENEMIES.
MERE ANARCHY IS LOOSED UPON THE WORLD?
NOW YOU'RE QUOTING POETRY.
AND I'M CUTTING SCHOOL. EVERYTHING IS CHAOS.
BRING ON THE APOCALYPSE!
BUS STOP
YOUR COACH, MY LADY.

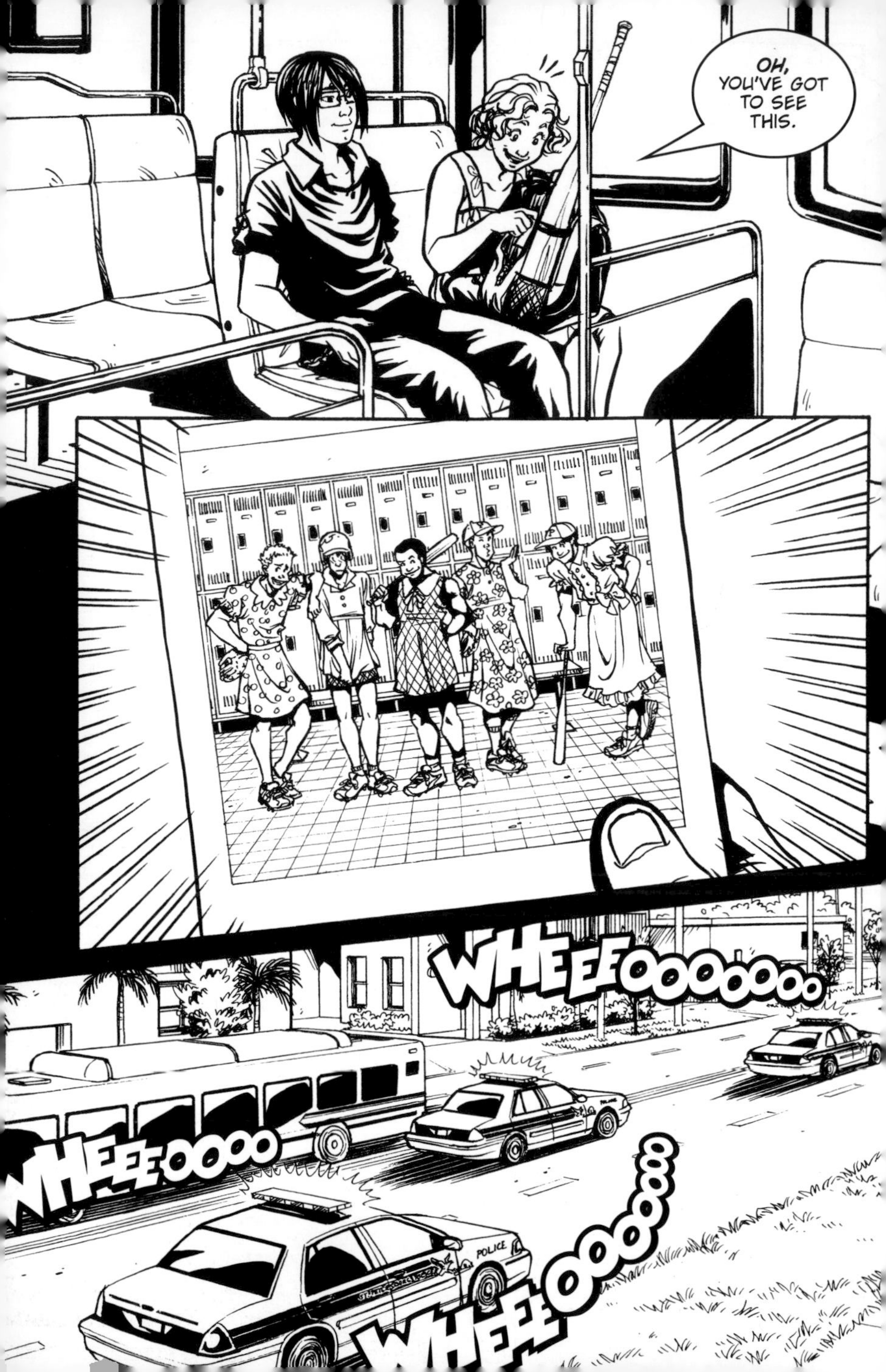
OH, YOU'VE GOT TO SEE THIS.
WHEEEOOOOOOO.
WHEEEOOOO
WHEEEOOOOOO
POLICE

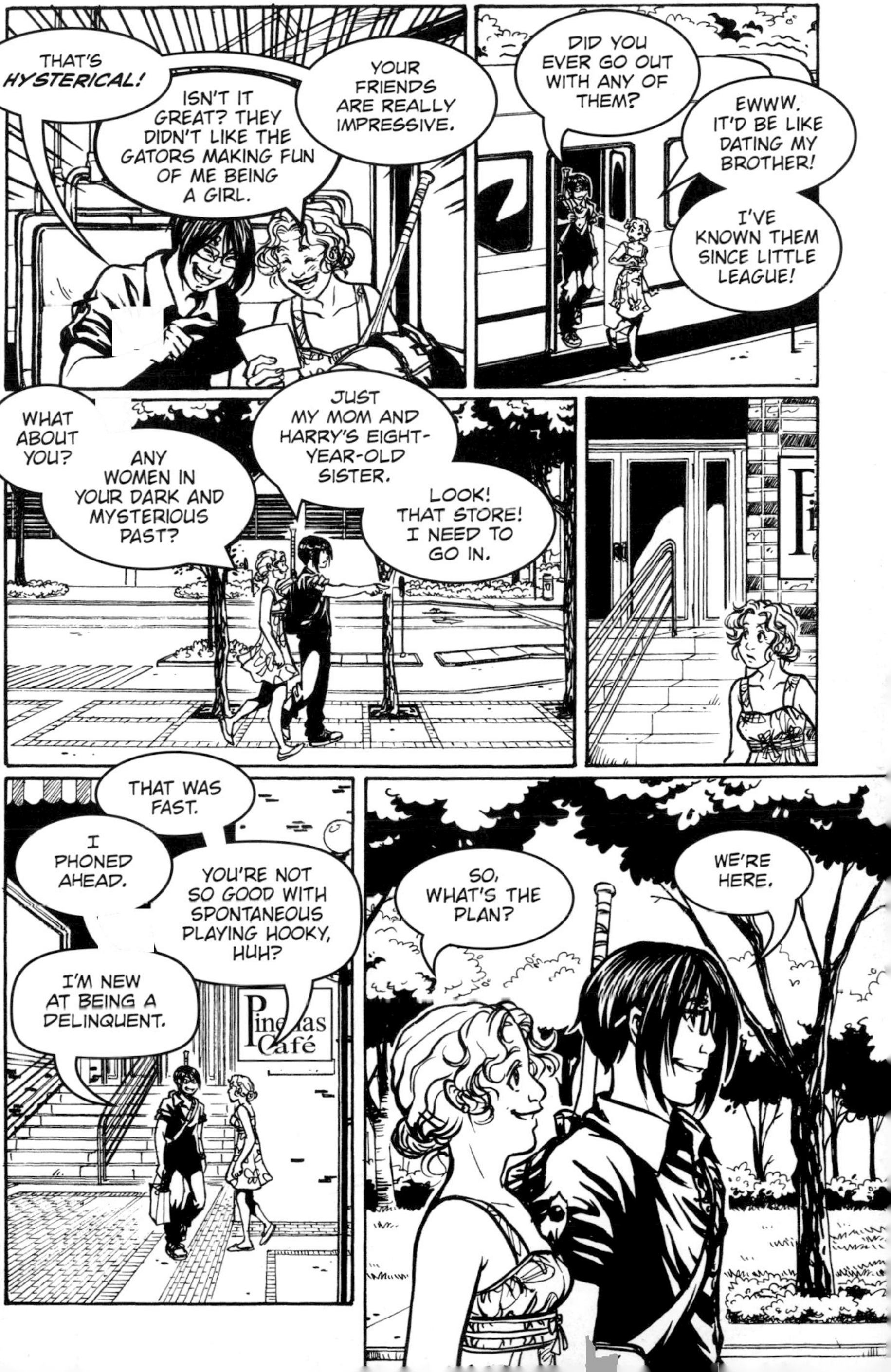
THAT'S HYSTERICAL!
ISN'T IT GREAT? THEY DIDN'T LIKE THE GATORS MAKING FUN OF ME BEING A GIRL.
YOUR FRIENDS ARE REALLY IMPRESSIVE.
DID YOU EVER GO OUT WITH ANY OF THEM?
EWWW. IT'D BE LIKE DATING MY BROTHER!
I'VE KNOWN THEM SINCE LITTLE LEAGUE!
WHAT ABOUT YOU?
ANY WOMEN IN YOUR DARK AND MYSTERIOUS PAST?
JUST MY MOM AND HARRY'S EIGHT-YEAR-OLD SISTER.
LOOK! THAT STORE! I NEED TO GO IN.
THAT WAS FAST.
I PHONED AHEAD.
YOU'RE NOT SO GOOD WITH SPONTANEOUS PLAYING HOOKY, HUH?
I'M NEW AT BEING A DELINQUENT.
Pinellas Café
SO, WHAT'S THE PLAN?
WE'RE HERE.

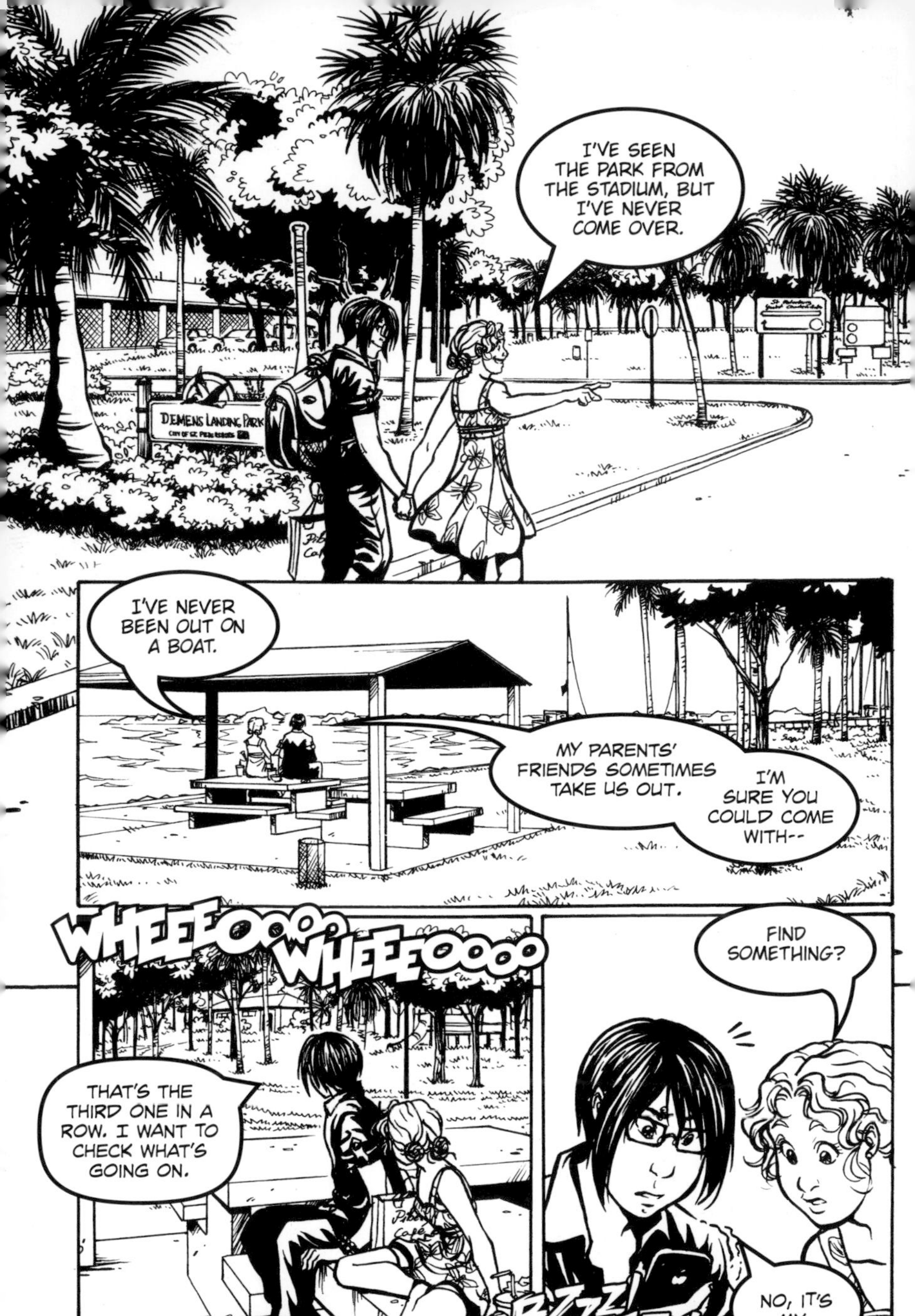
DEMENS LANDING PARK
I'VE SEEN THE PARK FROM THE STADIUM, BUT I'VE NEVER COME OVER.
I'VE NEVER BEEN OUT ON A BOAT.
MY PARENTS' FRIENDS SOMETIMES TAKE US OUT.
I'M SURE YOU COULD COME WITH--
WHEEEOooo WHEEEOOOO
THAT'S THE THIRD ONE IN A ROW. I WANT TO CHECK WHAT'S GOING ON.
FIND SOMETHING?
NO, IT'S MY--
BZZZ BZZZ!

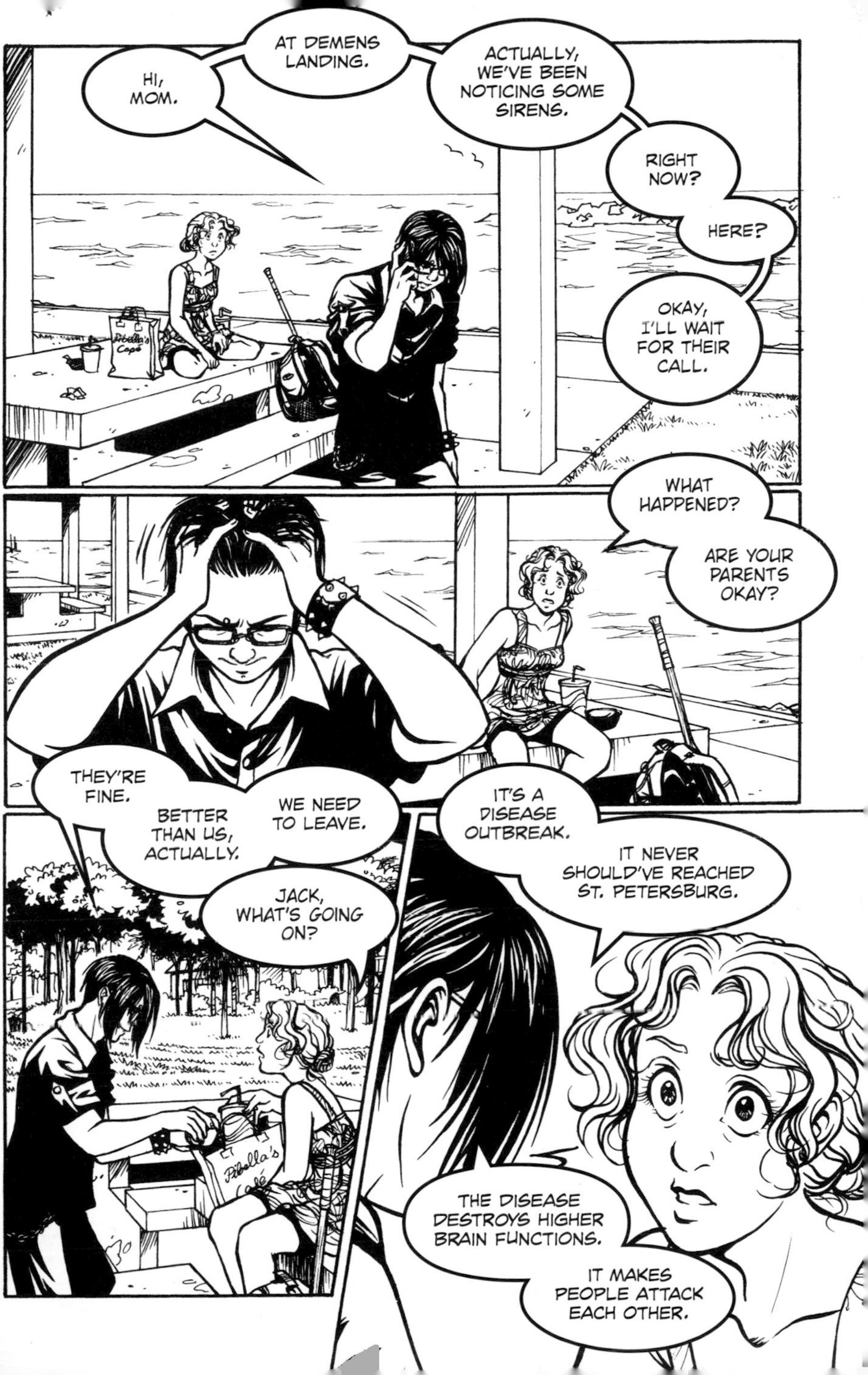
HI, MOM.
AT DEMENS LANDING.
ACTUALLY, WE'VE BEEN NOTICING SOME SIRENS.
RIGHT NOW?
HERE?
OKAY, I'LL WAIT FOR THEIR CALL.
Pibella's Café
WHAT HAPPENED?
ARE YOUR PARENTS OKAY?
THEY'RE FINE.
BETTER THAN US, ACTUALLY.
WE NEED TO LEAVE.
JACK, WHAT'S GOING ON?
IT'S A DISEASE OUTBREAK.
IT NEVER SHOULD'VE REACHED ST. PETERSBURG.
Pibella's Café
THE DISEASE DESTROYS HIGHER BRAIN FUNCTIONS.
IT MAKES PEOPLE ATTACK EACH OTHER.

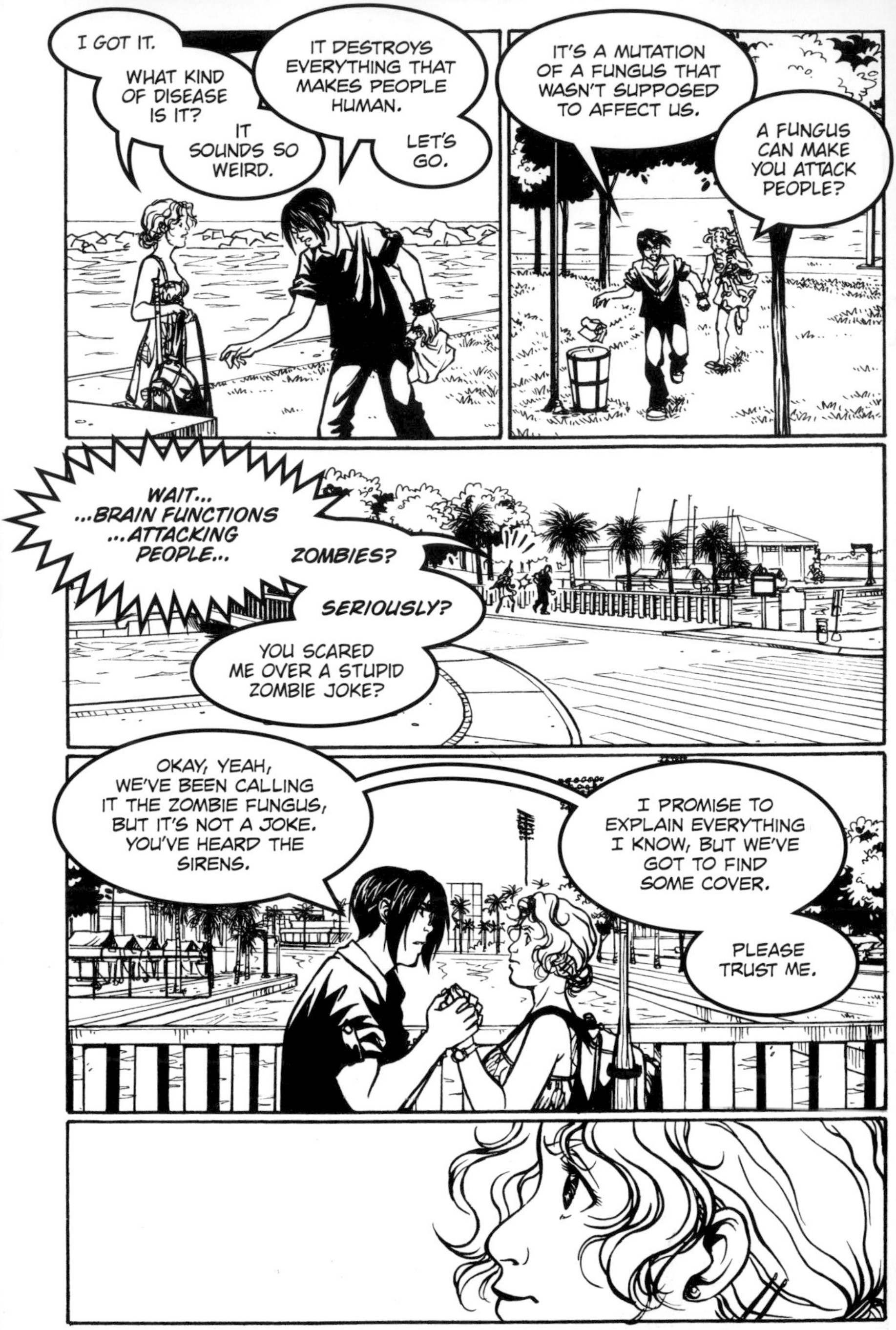
I GOT IT.
WHAT KIND OF DISEASE IS IT?
IT SOUNDS SO WEIRD.
IT DESTROYS EVERYTHING THAT MAKES PEOPLE HUMAN.
LET'S GO.
IT'S A MUTATION OF A FUNGUS THAT WASN'T SUPPOSED TO AFFECT US.
A FUNGUS CAN MAKE YOU ATTACK PEOPLE?
WAIT... ...BRAIN FUNCTIONS ...ATTACKING PEOPLE...
ZOMBIES?
SERIOUSLY?
YOU SCARED ME OVER A STUPID ZOMBIE JOKE?
OKAY, YEAH, WE'VE BEEN CALLING IT THE ZOMBIE FUNGUS, BUT IT'S NOT A JOKE. YOU'VE HEARD THE SIRENS.
I PROMISE TO EXPLAIN EVERYTHING I KNOW, BUT WE'VE GOT TO FIND SOME COVER.
PLEASE TRUST ME.

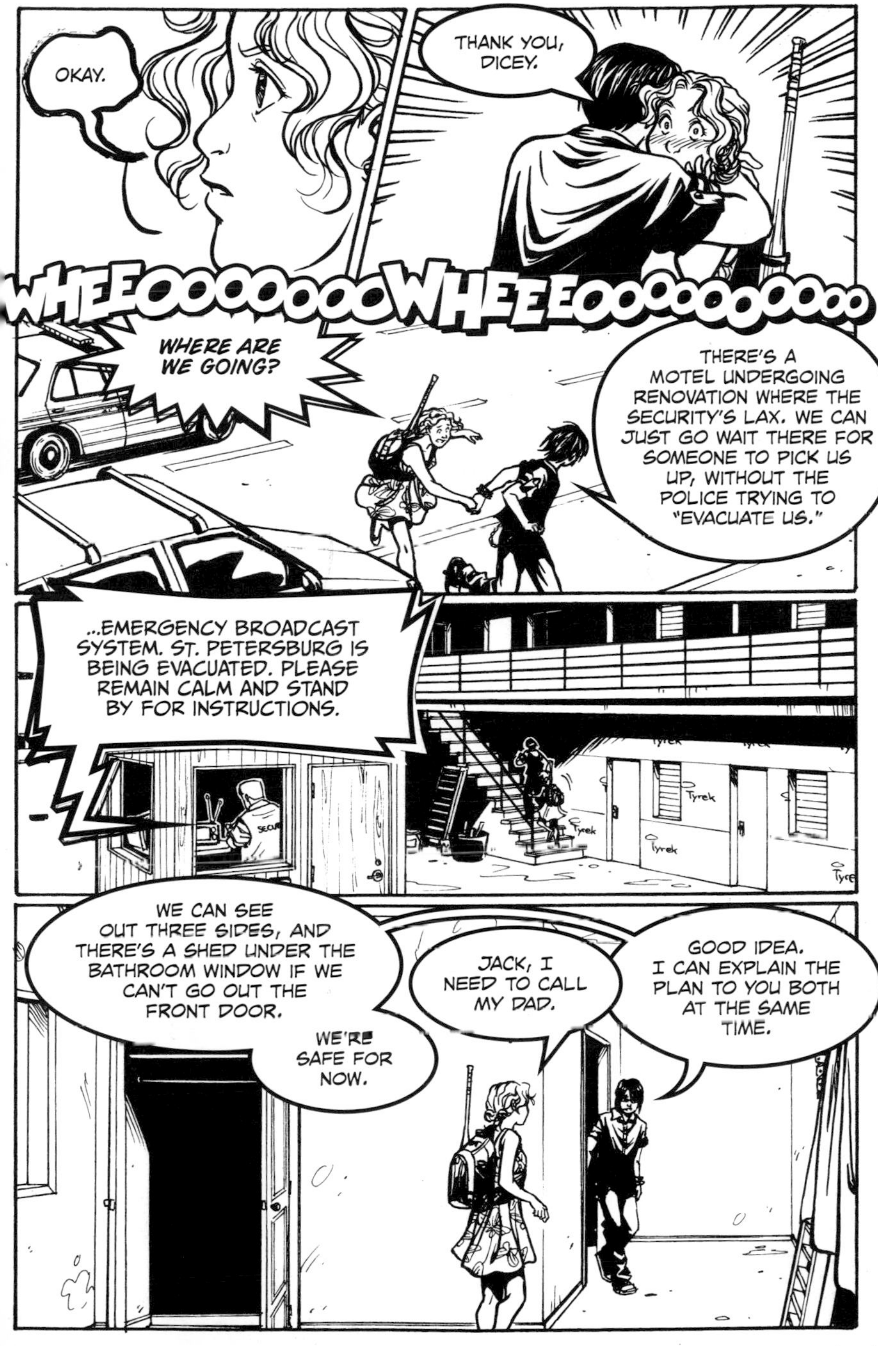
OKAY.
THANK YOU, DICEY.
WHEEOOOOOOOWHEEEOOOOOOOOOO
WHERE ARE WE GOING?
THERE'S A MOTEL UNDERGOING RENOVATION WHERE THE SECURITY'S LAX. WE CAN JUST GO WAIT THERE FOR SOMEONE TO PICK US UP, WITHOUT THE POLICE TRYING TO "EVACUATE US."
...EMERGENCY BROADCAST SYSTEM. ST. PETERSBURG IS BEING EVACUATED. PLEASE REMAIN CALM AND STAND BY FOR INSTRUCTIONS.
Tyrek
Tyrek
Tyrek
WE CAN SEE OUT THREE SIDES, AND THERE'S A SHED UNDER THE BATHROOM WINDOW IF WE CAN'T GO OUT THE FRONT DOOR.
WE'RE SAFE FOR NOW.
JACK, I NEED TO CALL MY DAD.
GOOD IDEA. I CAN EXPLAIN THE PLAN TO YOU BOTH AT THE SAME TIME.

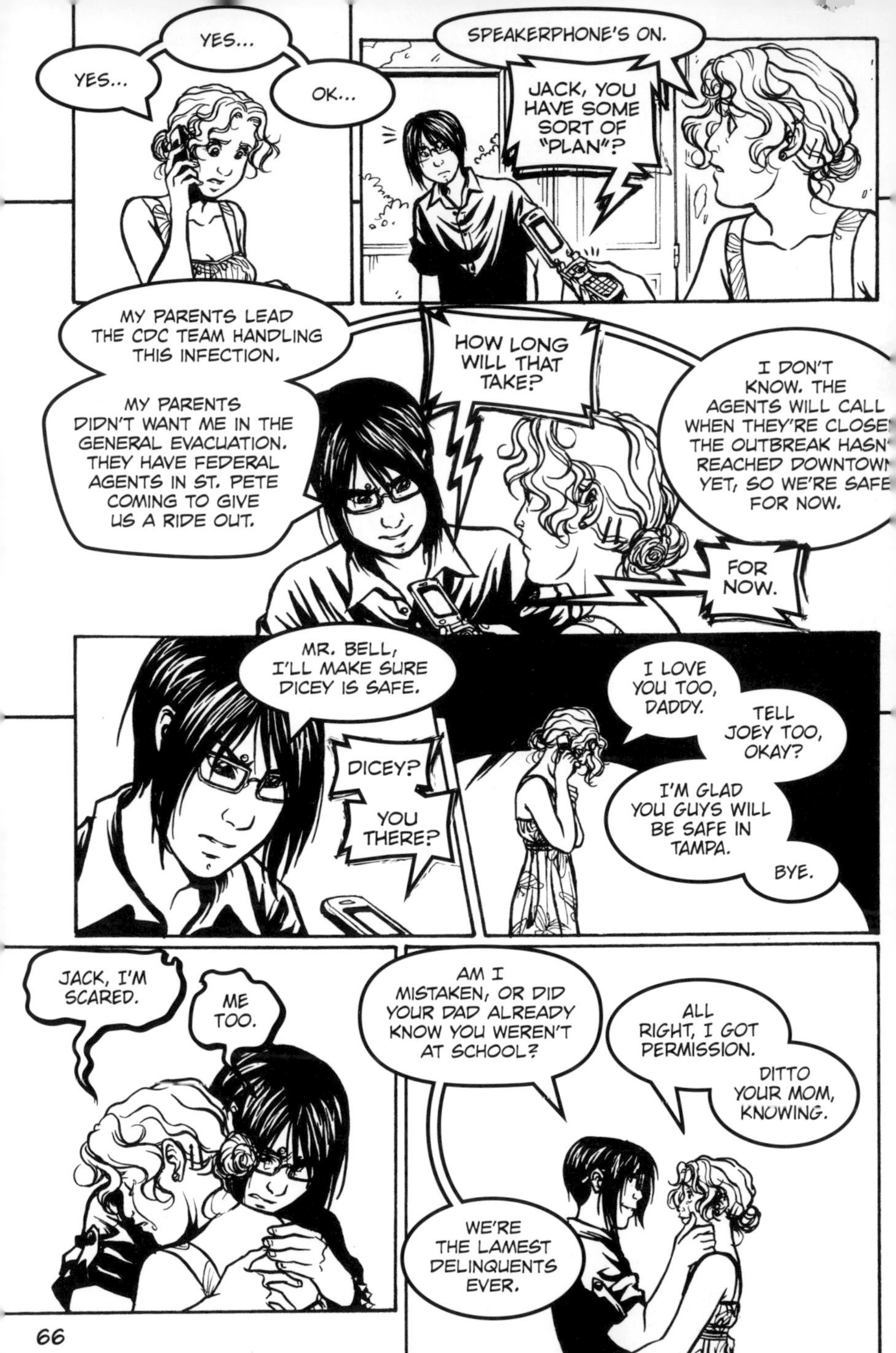
YES...
YES...
OK...
SPEAKERPHONE'S ON.
JACK, YOU HAVE SOME SORT OF "PLAN"?
MY PARENTS LEAD THE CDC TEAM HANDLING THIS INFECTION.
MY PARENTS DIDN'T WANT ME IN THE GENERAL EVACUATION. THEY HAVE FEDERAL AGENTS IN ST. PETE COMING TO GIVE US A RIDE OUT.
HOW LONG WILL THAT TAKE?
I DON'T KNOW. THE AGENTS WILL CALL WHEN THEY'RE CLOSE THE OUTBREAK HASN REACHED DOWNTOWN YET, SO WE'RE SAFE FOR NOW.
FOR NOW.
MR. BELL, I'LL MAKE SURE DICEY IS SAFE.
DICEY?
YOU THERE?
I LOVE YOU TOO, DADDY.
TELL JOEY TOO, OKAY?
I'M GLAD YOU GUYS WILL BE SAFE IN TAMPA.
BYE.
JACK, I'M SCARED.
ME TOO.
AM I MISTAKEN, OR DID YOUR DAD ALREADY KNOW YOU WEREN'T AT SCHOOL?
ALL RIGHT, I GOT PERMISSION.
DITTO YOUR MOM, KNOWING.
WE'RE THE LAMEST DELINQUENTS EVER.

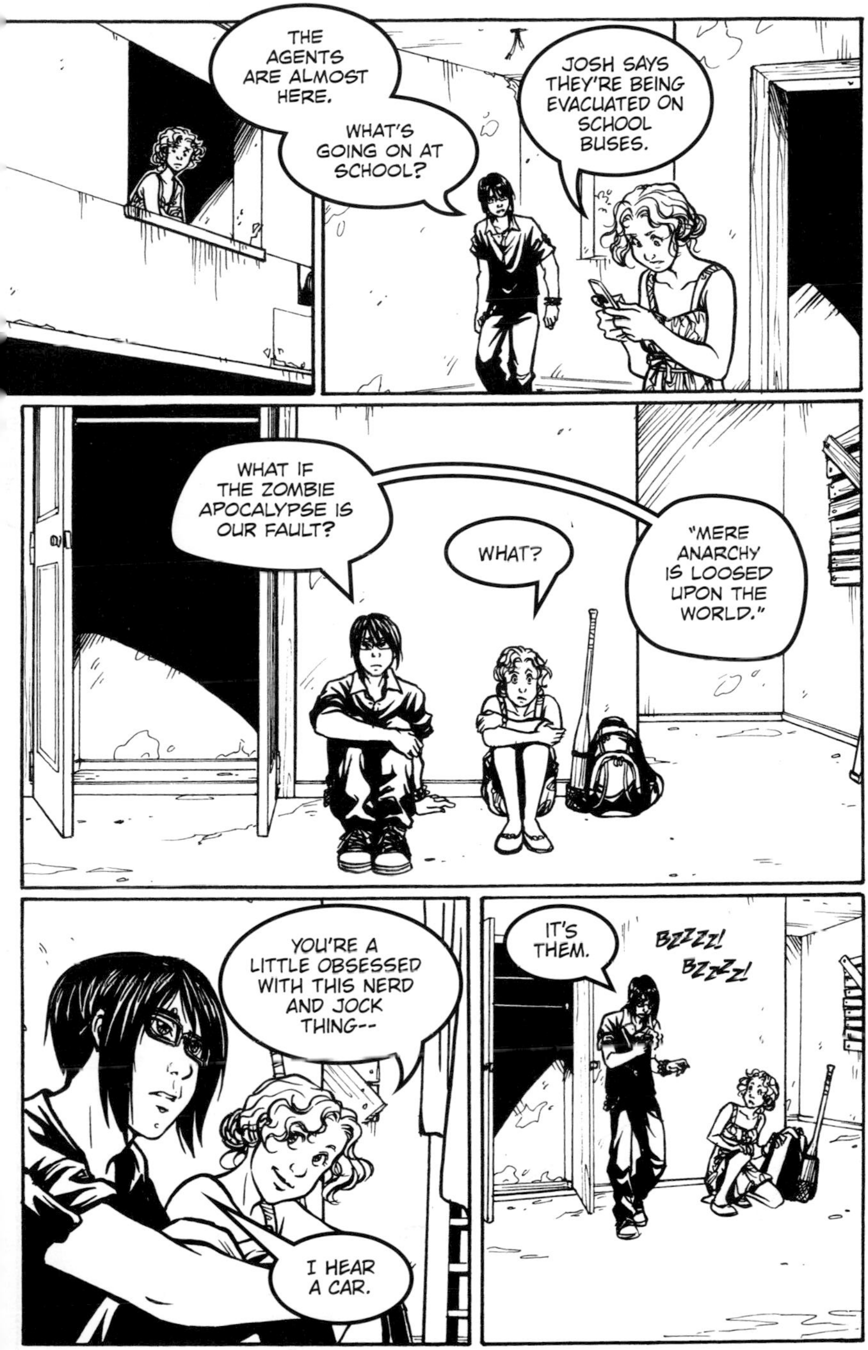
THE AGENTS ARE ALMOST HERE.
WHAT'S GOING ON AT SCHOOL?
JOSH SAYS THEY'RE BEING EVACUATED ON SCHOOL BUSES.
WHAT IF THE ZOMBIE APOCALYPSE IS OUR FAULT?
WHAT?
"MERE ANARCHY IS LOOSED UPON THE WORLD."
YOU'RE A LITTLE OBSESSED WITH THIS NERD AND JOCK THING--
I HEAR A CAR.
IT'S THEM.
BZZZZ!
BZZZZ!

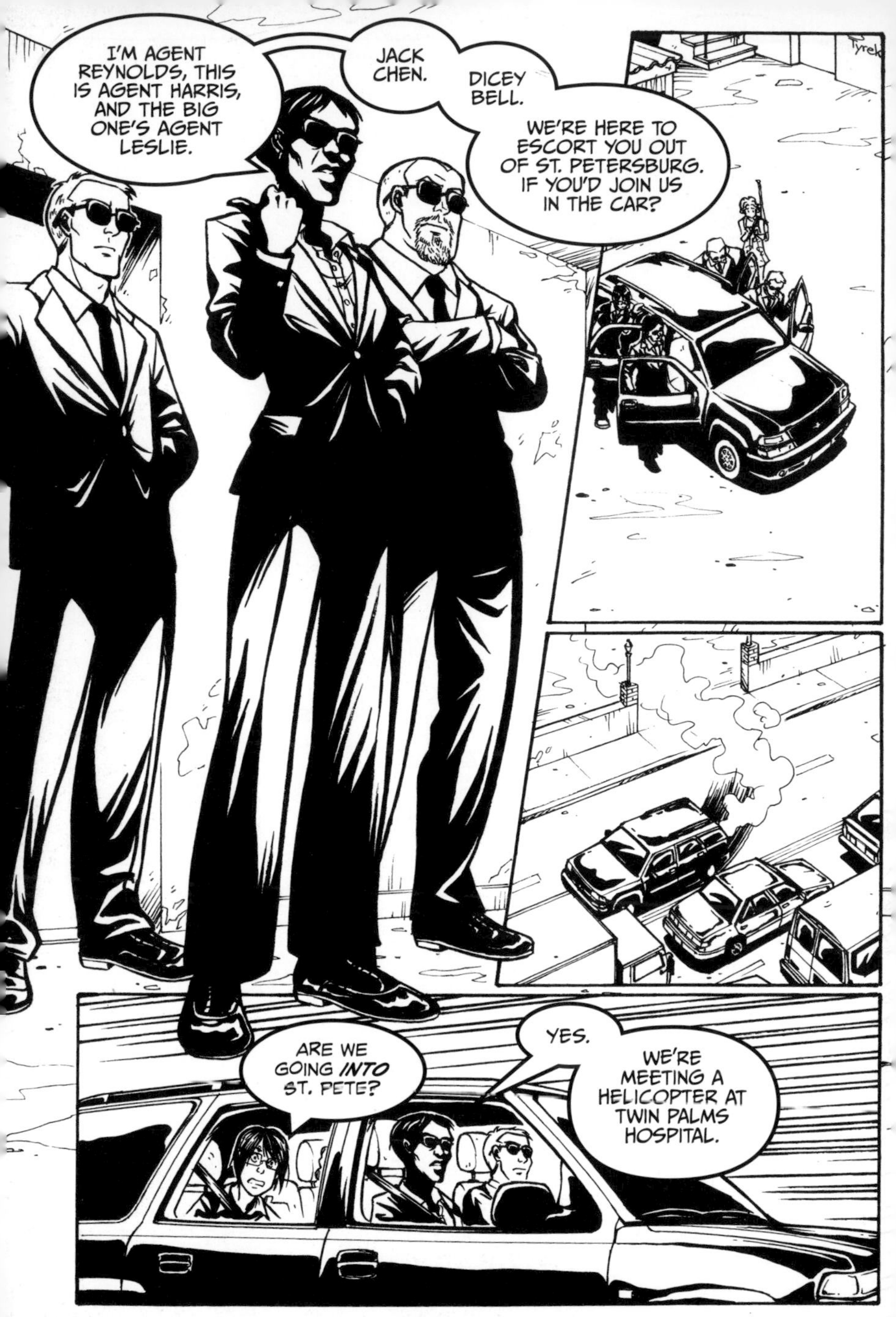
I'M AGENT REYNOLDS, THIS IS AGENT HARRIS, AND THE BIG ONE'S AGENT LESLIE.
JACK CHEN.
DICEY BELL.
WE'RE HERE TO ESCORT YOU OUT OF ST. PETERSBURG. IF YOU'D JOIN US IN THE CAR?
ARE WE GOING *INTO* ST. PETE?
YES.
WE'RE MEETING A HELICOPTER AT TWIN PALMS HOSPITAL.

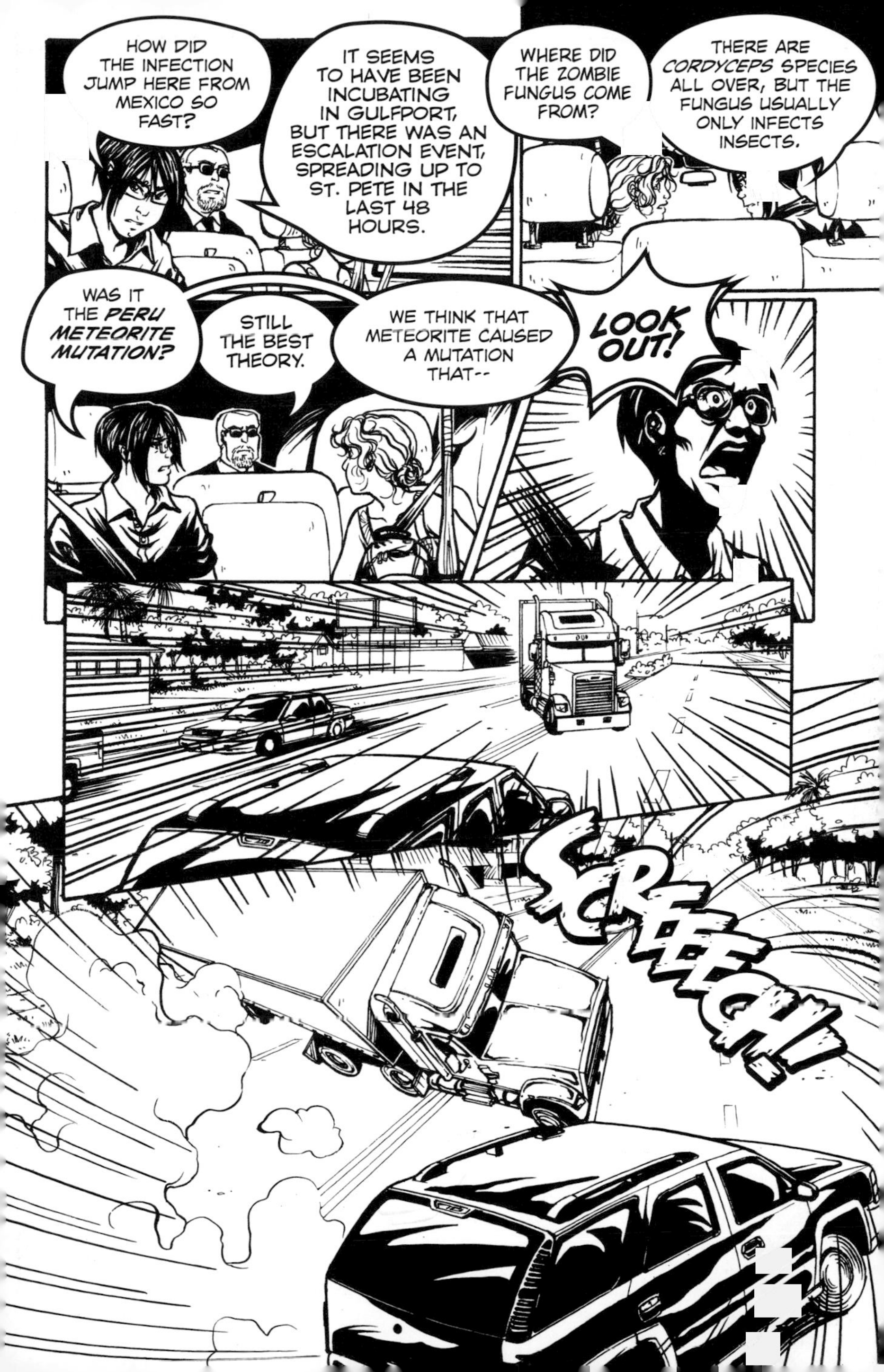
HOW DID THE INFECTION JUMP HERE FROM MEXICO SO FAST?
IT SEEMS TO HAVE BEEN INCUBATING IN GULFPORT, BUT THERE WAS AN ESCALATION EVENT, SPREADING UP TO ST. PETE IN THE LAST 48 HOURS.
WHERE DID THE ZOMBIE FUNGUS COME FROM?
THERE ARE CORDYCEPS SPECIES ALL OVER, BUT THE FUNGUS USUALLY ONLY INFECTS INSECTS.
WAS IT THE PERU METEORITE MUTATION?
STILL THE BEST THEORY.
WE THINK THAT METEORITE CAUSED A MUTATION THAT--
LOOK OUT!
SCREEECH!

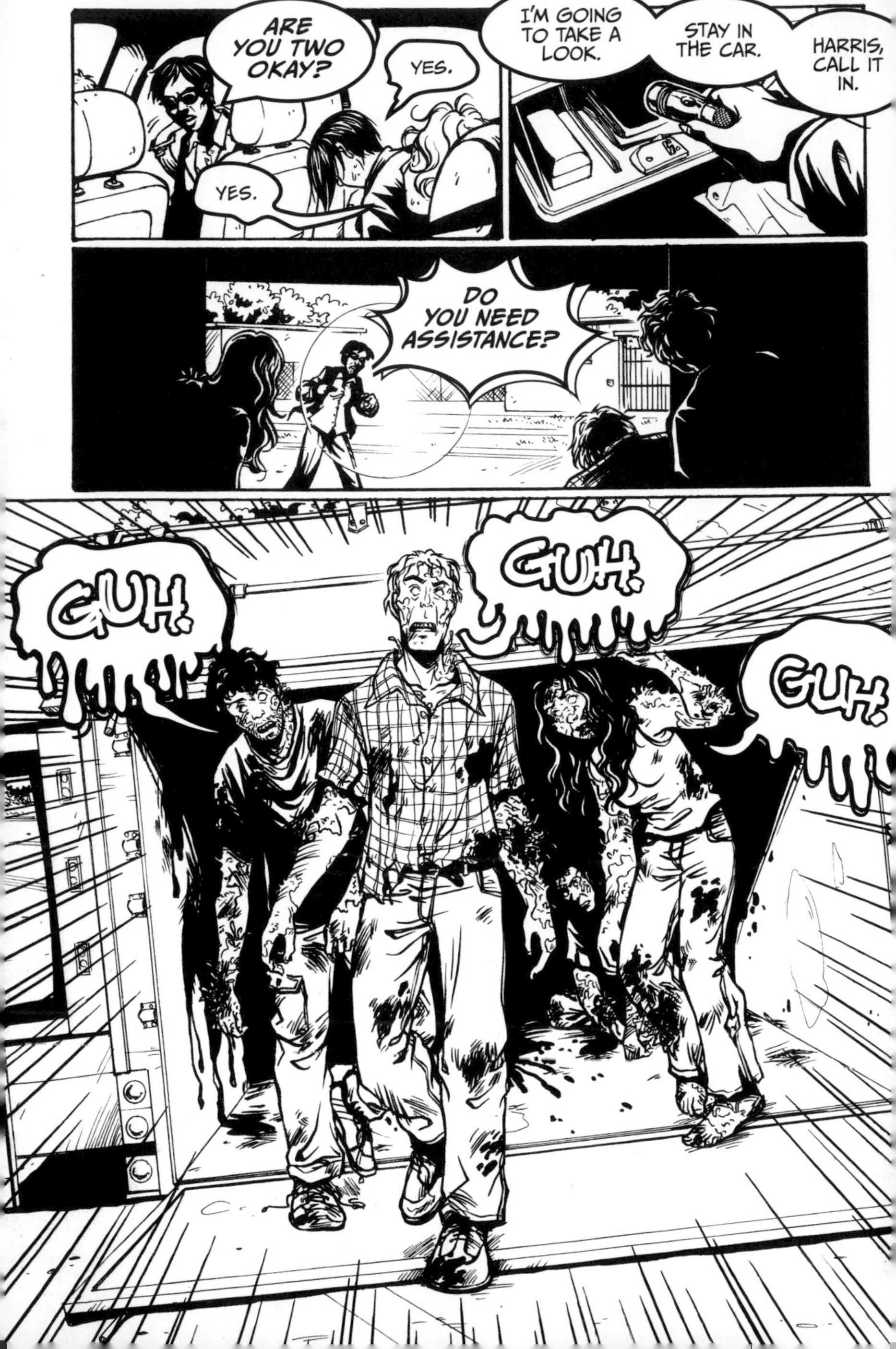
ARE YOU TWO OKAY?
YES.
YES.
I'M GOING TO TAKE A LOOK.
STAY IN THE CAR.
HARRIS, CALL IT IN.
DO YOU NEED ASSISTANCE?
GUH.
GUH.
GUH.

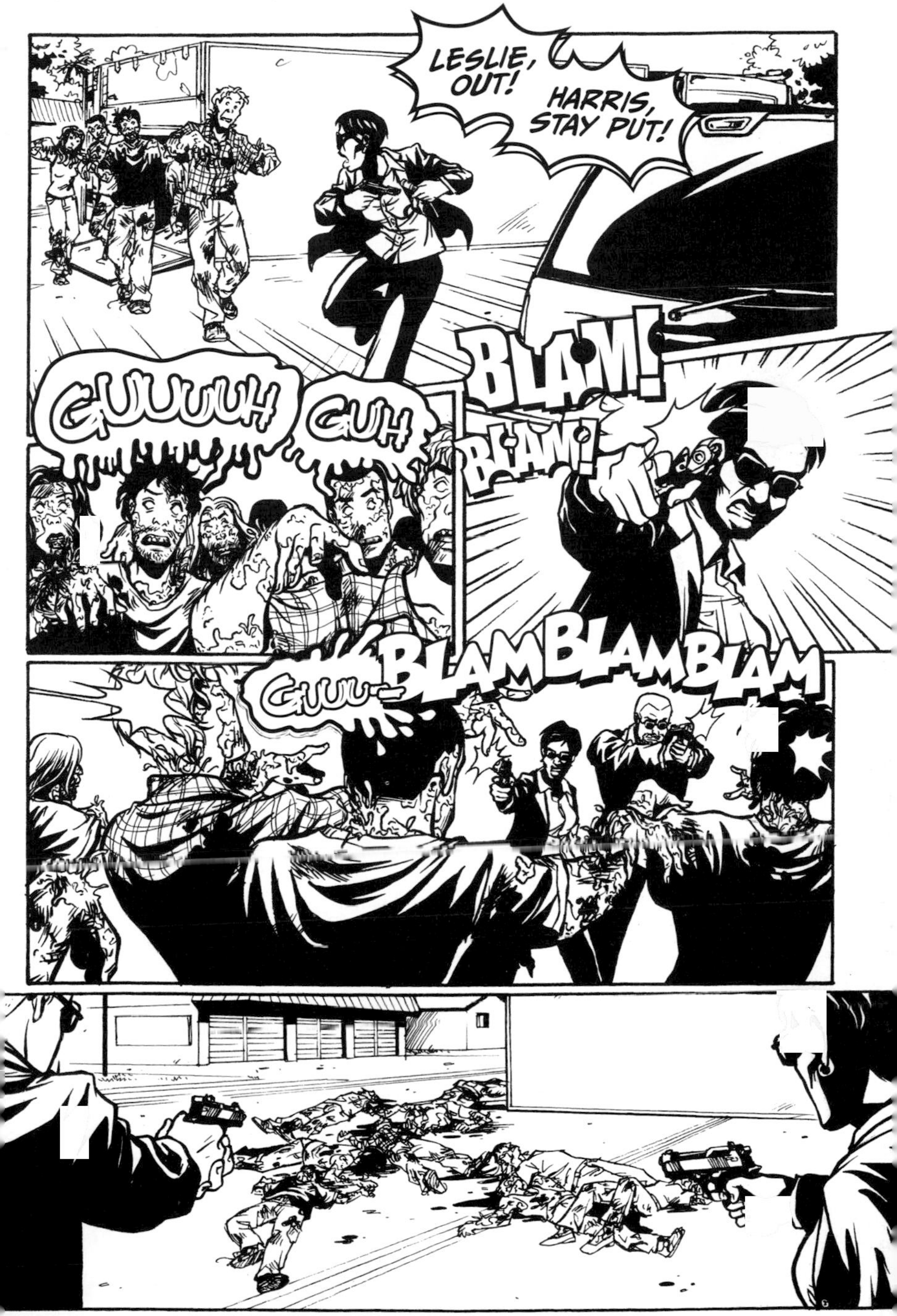
LESLIE, OUT!
HARRIS, STAY PUT!
BLAM!
BLAM!
GUUUUH
GUH
GUUU-
BLAMBLAMBLAM

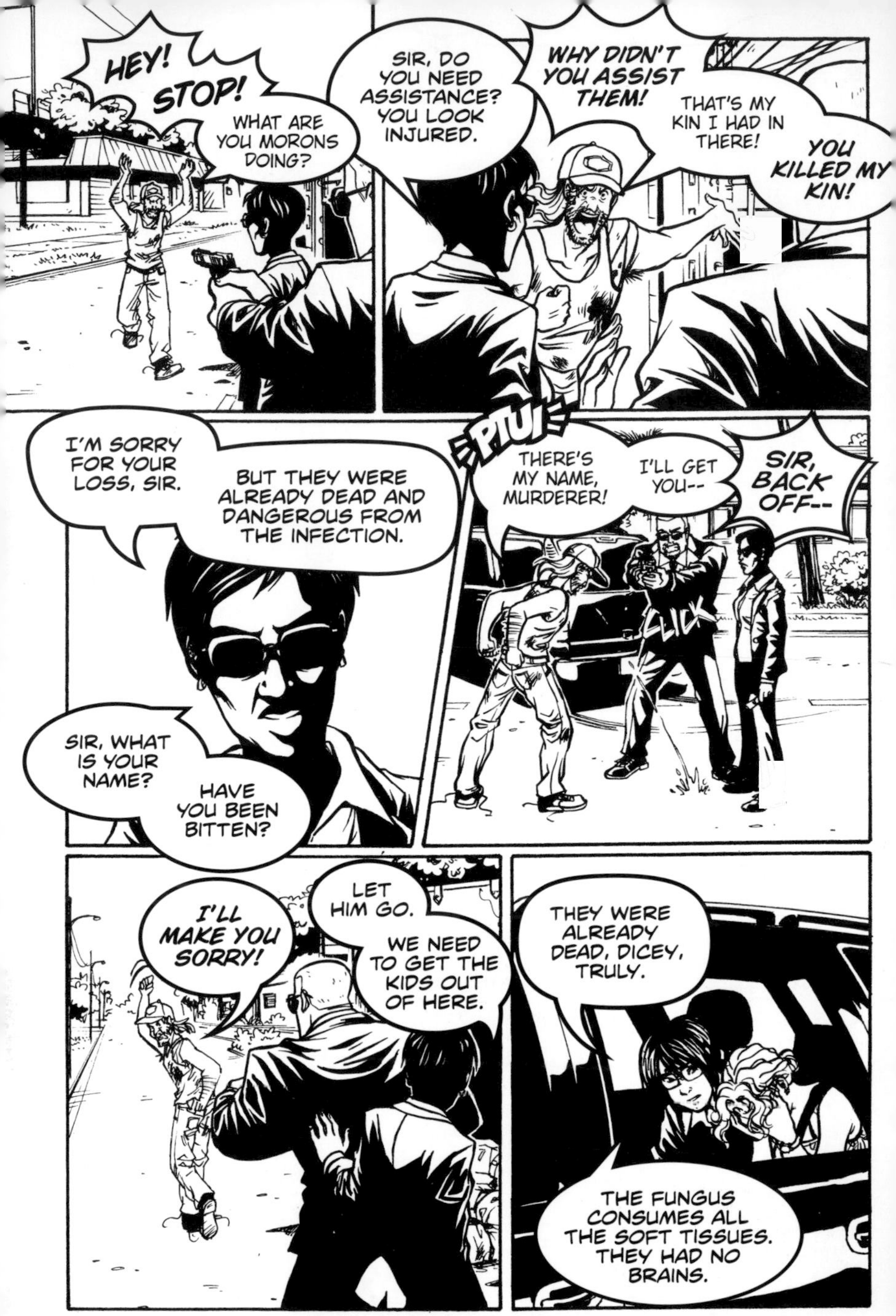
HEY! STOP!
WHAT ARE YOU MORONS DOING?
SIR, DO YOU NEED ASSISTANCE? YOU LOOK INJURED.
WHY DIDN'T YOU ASSIST THEM!
THAT'S MY KIN I HAD IN THERE!
YOU KILLED MY KIN!
I'M SORRY FOR YOUR LOSS, SIR.
BUT THEY WERE ALREADY DEAD AND DANGEROUS FROM THE INFECTION.
SIR, WHAT IS YOUR NAME?
HAVE YOU BEEN BITTEN?
PTUI
THERE'S MY NAME, MURDERER!
I'LL GET YOU--
SIR, BACK OFF--
CLICK
I'LL MAKE YOU SORRY!
LET HIM GO.
WE NEED TO GET THE KIDS OUT OF HERE.
THEY WERE ALREADY DEAD, DICEY, TRULY.
THE FUNGUS CONSUMES ALL THE SOFT TISSUES. THEY HAD NO BRAINS.

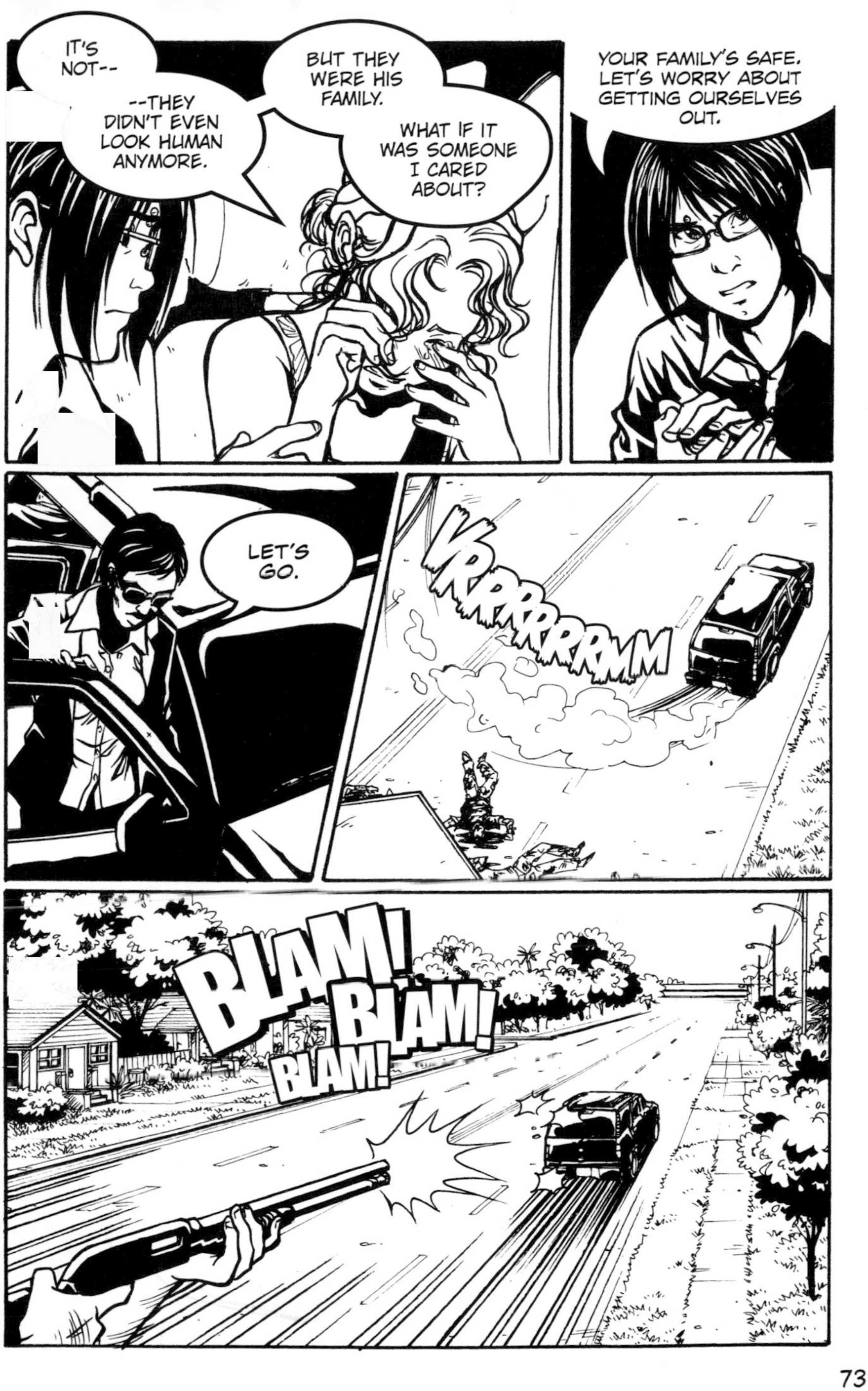
IT'S NOT--
--THEY DIDN'T EVEN LOOK HUMAN ANYMORE.
BUT THEY WERE HIS FAMILY.
WHAT IF IT WAS SOMEONE I CARED ABOUT?
YOUR FAMILY'S SAFE. LET'S WORRY ABOUT GETTING OURSELVES OUT.
LET'S GO.
VRRRRRRRMM
BLAM!
BLAM!
BLAM!

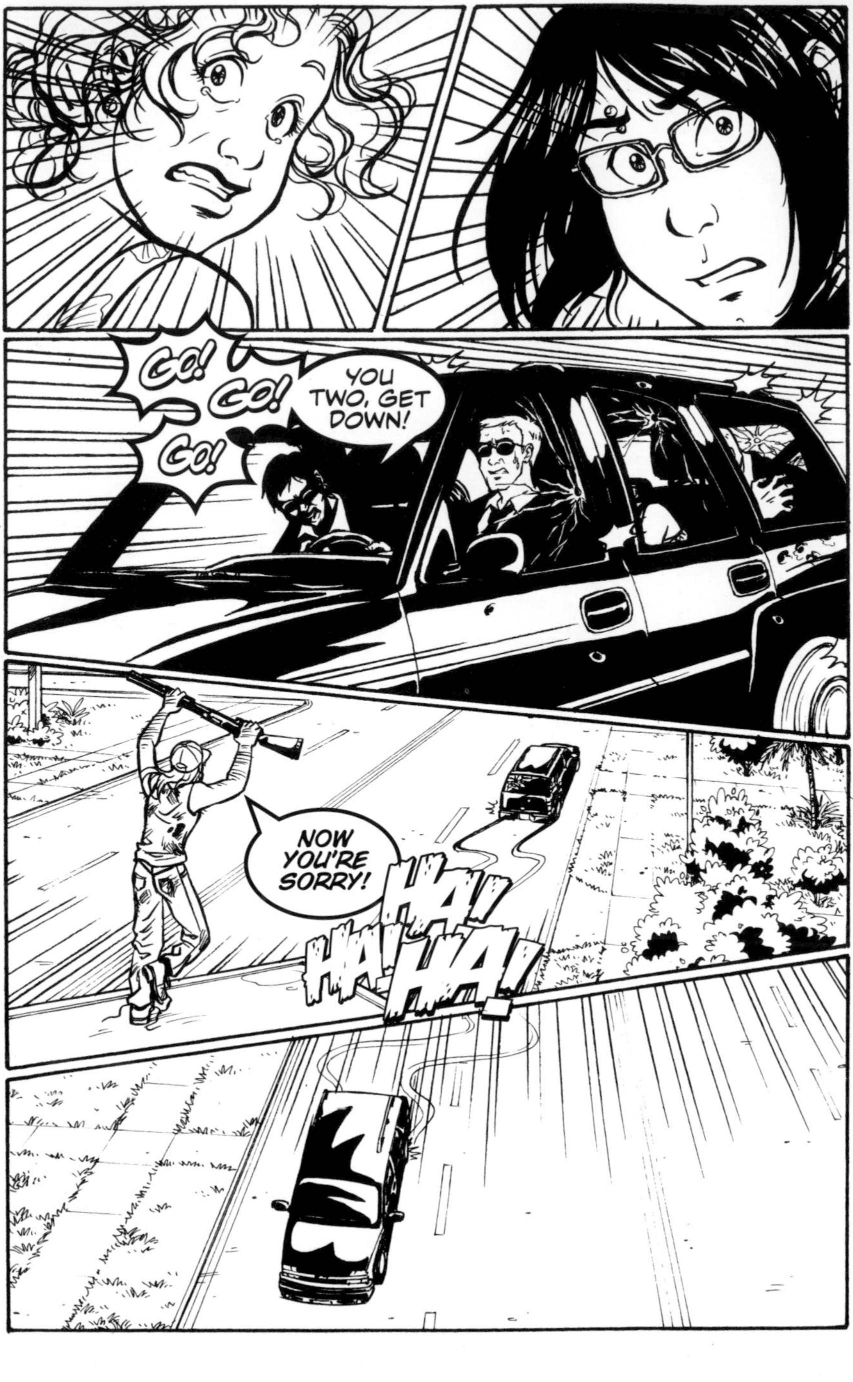
GO! GO! GO!
YOU TWO, GET DOWN!
NOW YOU'RE SORRY!
HA! HA! HA!

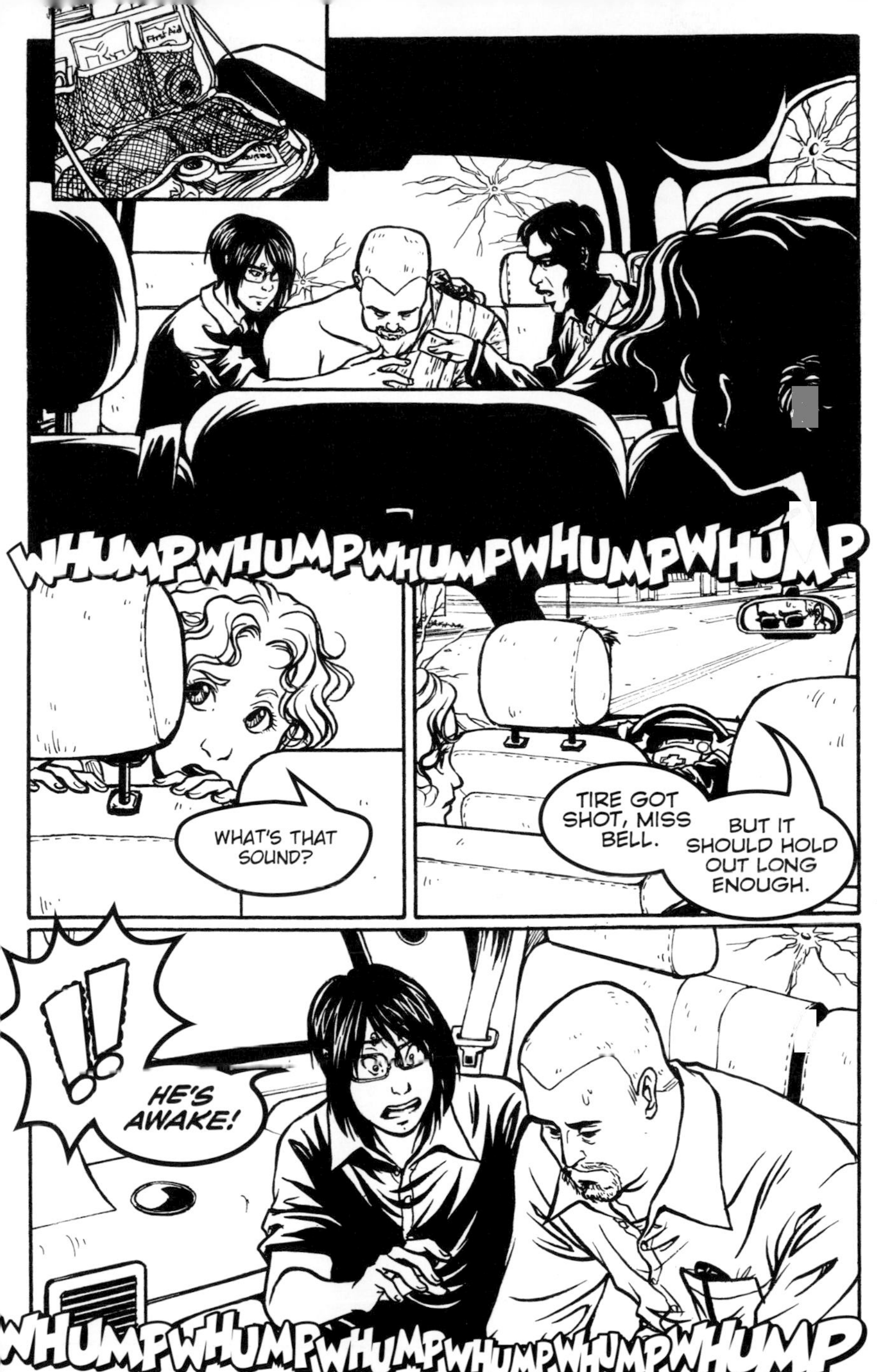
WHUMPWHUMPWHUMPWHUMPWHUMP
WHAT'S THAT SOUND?
TIRE GOT SHOT, MISS BELL.
BUT IT SHOULD HOLD OUT LONG ENOUGH.
!!
HE'S AWAKE!
WHUMPWHUMPWHUMPWHUMPWHUMPWHUMP

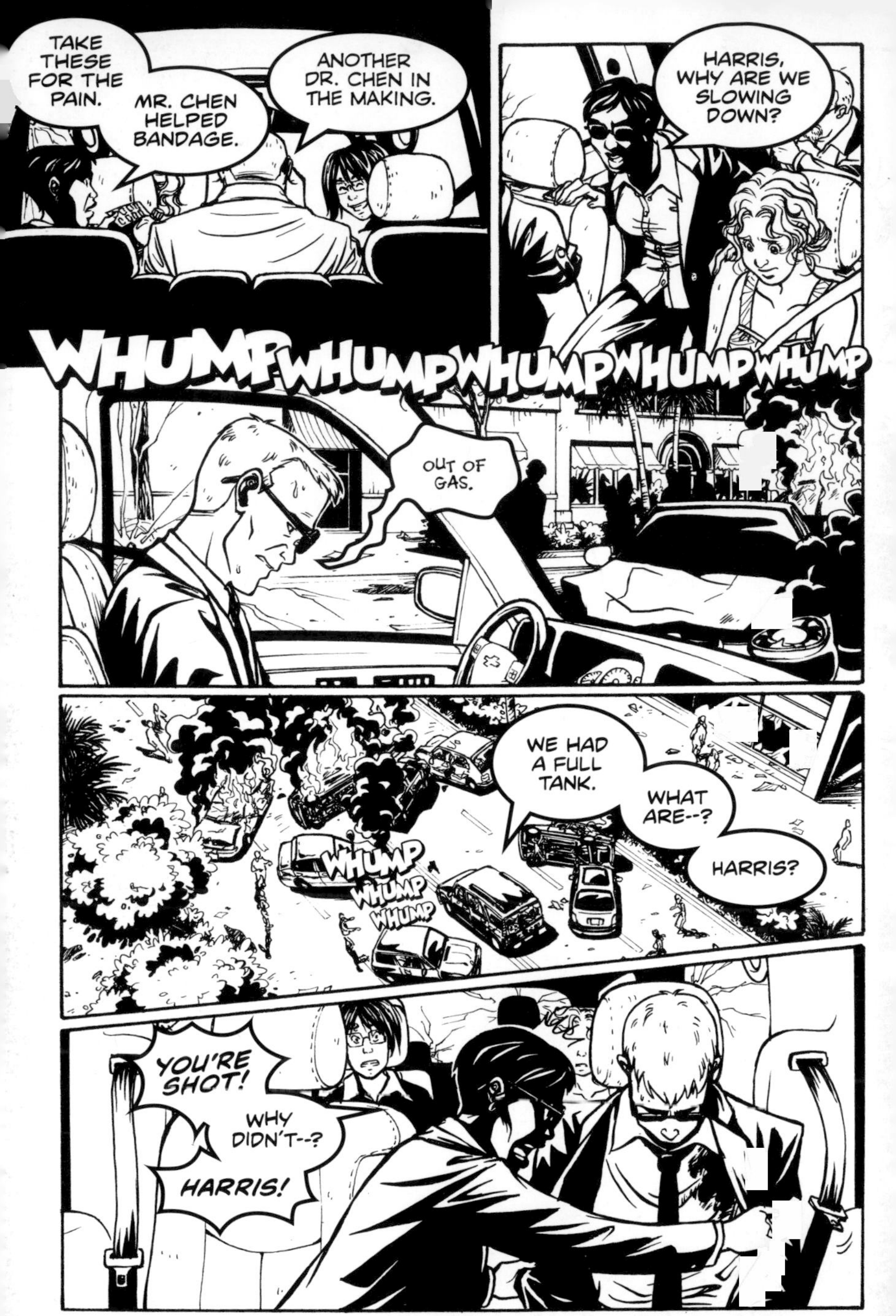
TAKE THESE FOR THE PAIN.
MR. CHEN HELPED BANDAGE.
ANOTHER DR. CHEN IN THE MAKING.
HARRIS, WHY ARE WE SLOWING DOWN?
WHUMP WHUMP WHUMP WHUMP WHUMP
OUT OF GAS.
WE HAD A FULL TANK.
WHAT ARE--?
HARRIS?
WHUMP
WHUMP
WHUMP
YOU'RE SHOT!
WHY DIDN'T--?
HARRIS!

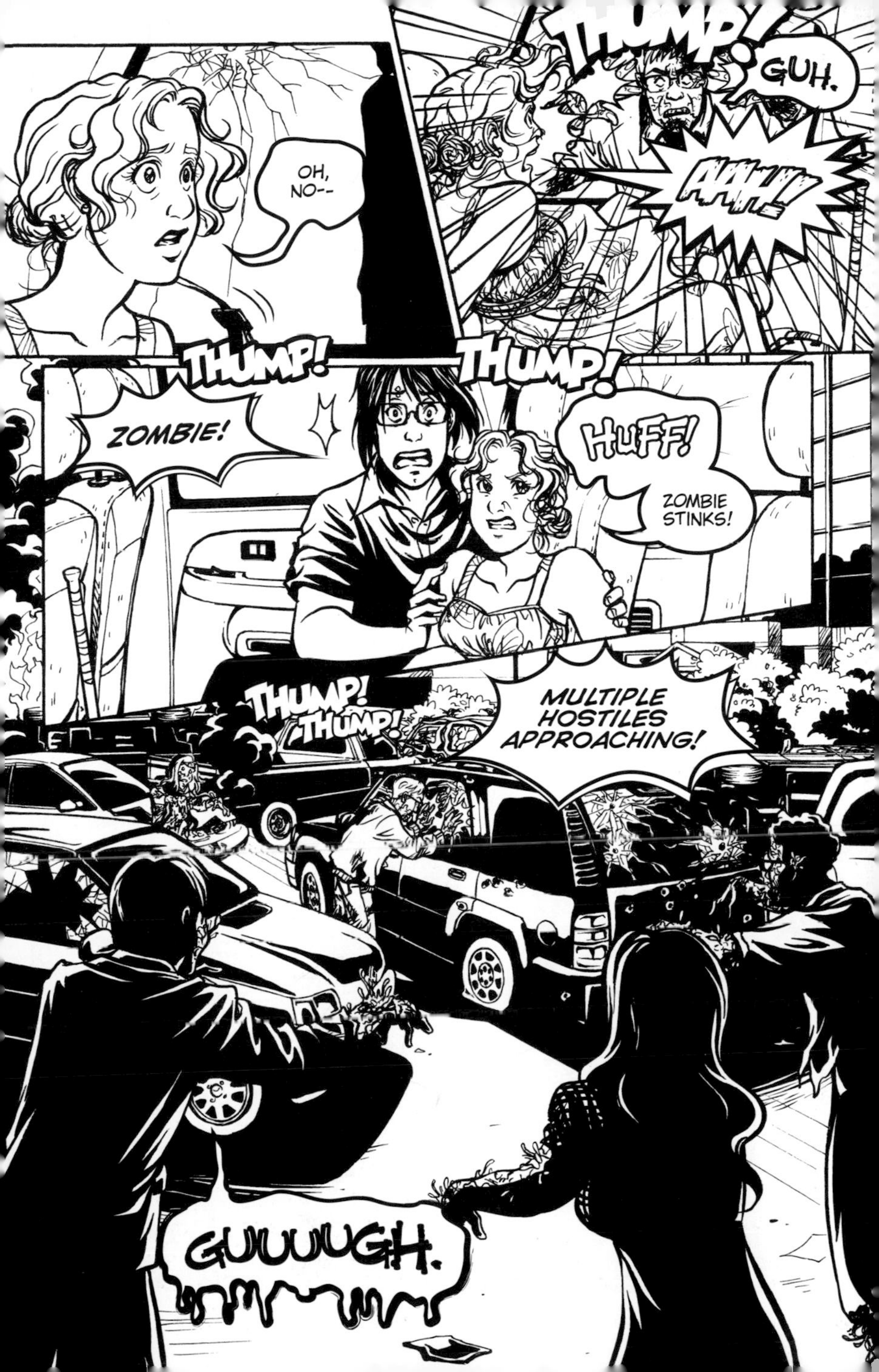
OH, NO--
THUMP!
GUH.
AAH!!
THUMP!
THUMP!
ZOMBIE!
HUFF!
ZOMBIE STINKS!
THUMP! THUMP!
MULTIPLE HOSTILES APPROACHING!
GUUUUGH.

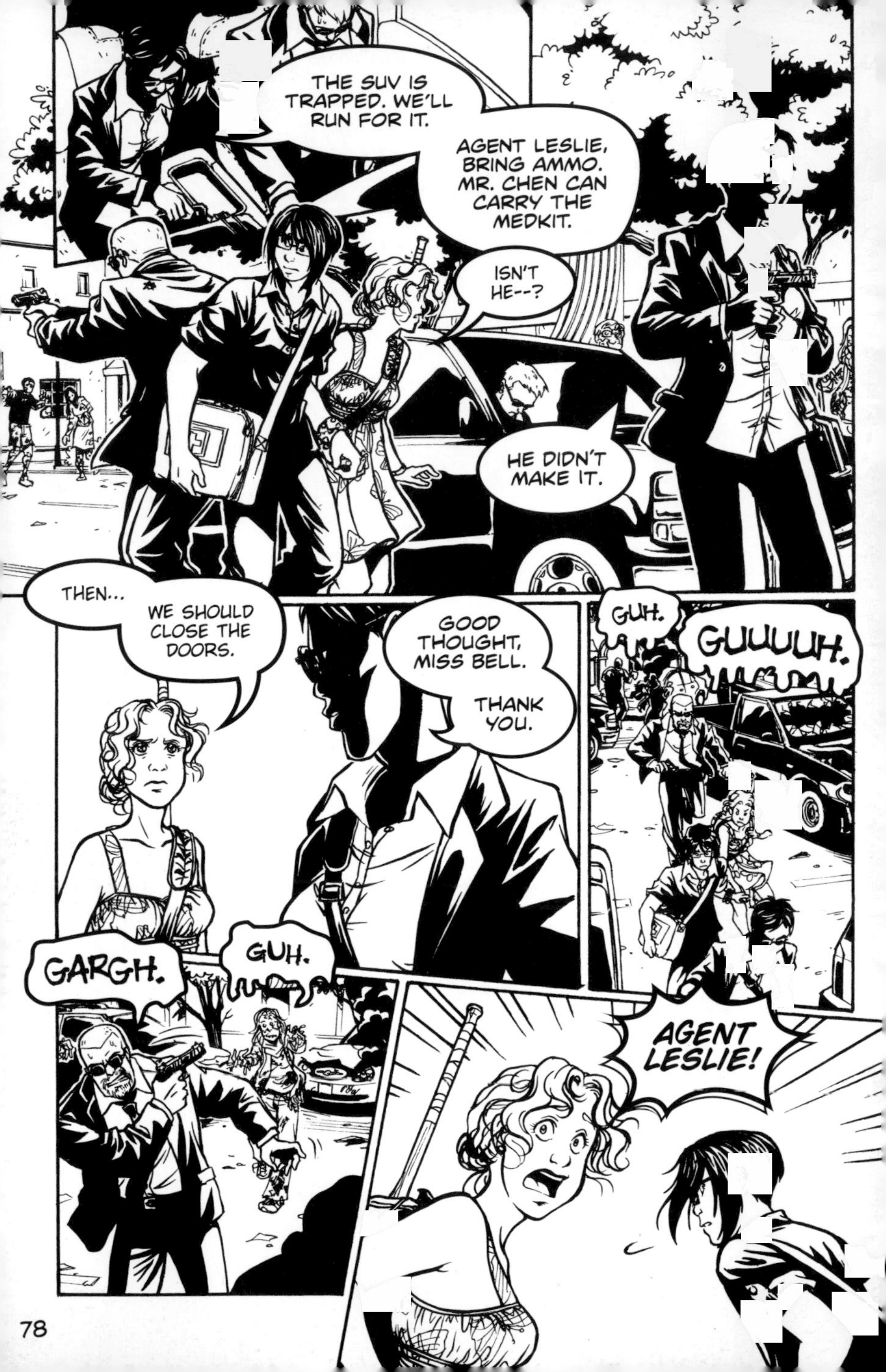
THE SUV IS TRAPPED. WE'LL RUN FOR IT.
AGENT LESLIE, BRING AMMO. MR. CHEN CAN CARRY THE MEDKIT.
ISN'T HE--?
HE DIDN'T MAKE IT.
THEN...
WE SHOULD CLOSE THE DOORS.
GOOD THOUGHT, MISS BELL.
THANK YOU.
GUH.
GUUUUH.
GARGH.
GUH.
AGENT LESLIE!

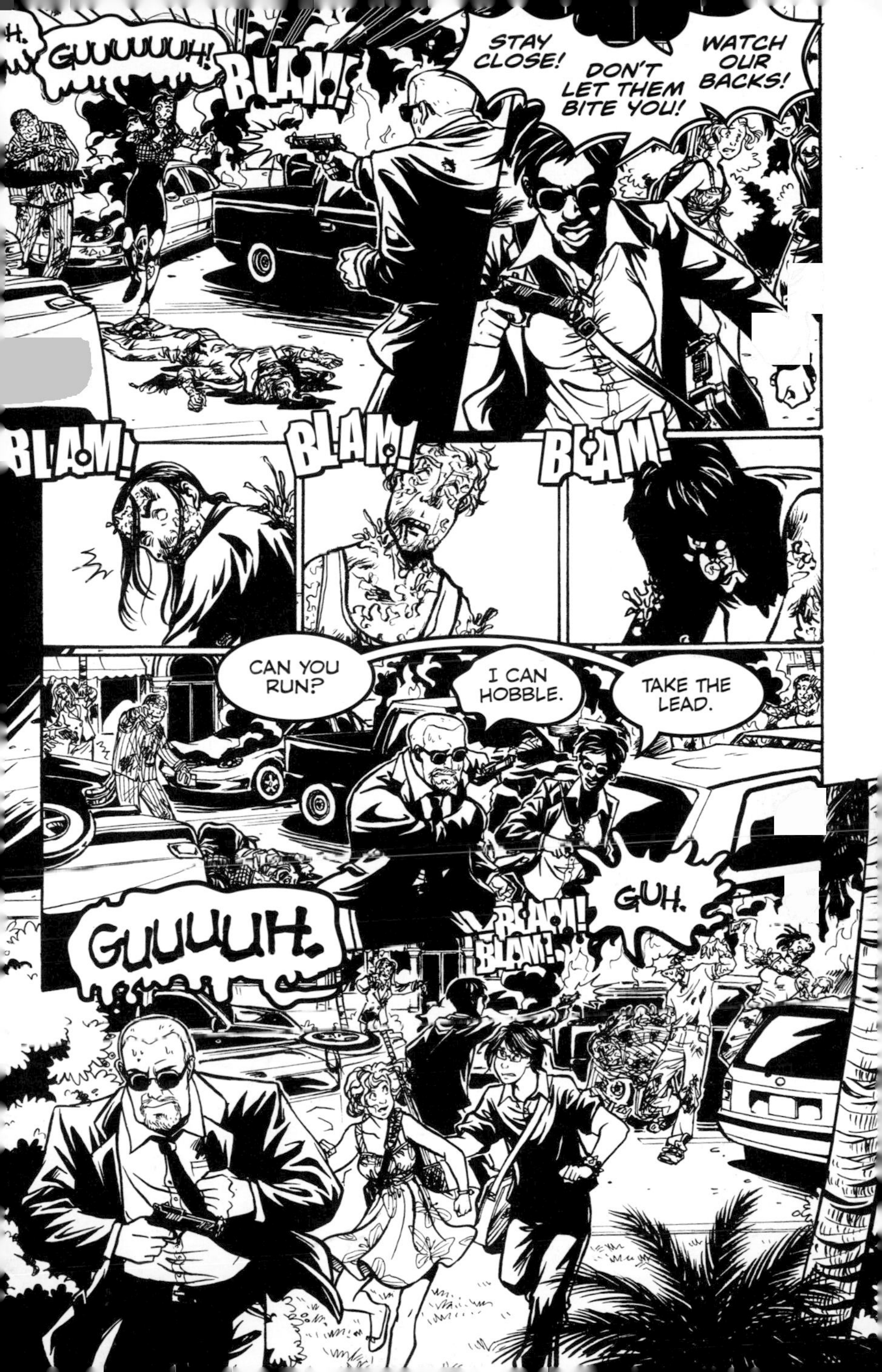
GUUUUUH!
BLAM!
STAY CLOSE!
DON'T LET THEM BITE YOU!
WATCH OUR BACKS!
BLAM!
BLAM!
BLAM!
CAN YOU RUN?
I CAN HOBBLE.
TAKE THE LEAD.
GUUUUH.
BLAM!
BLAM!
GUH.

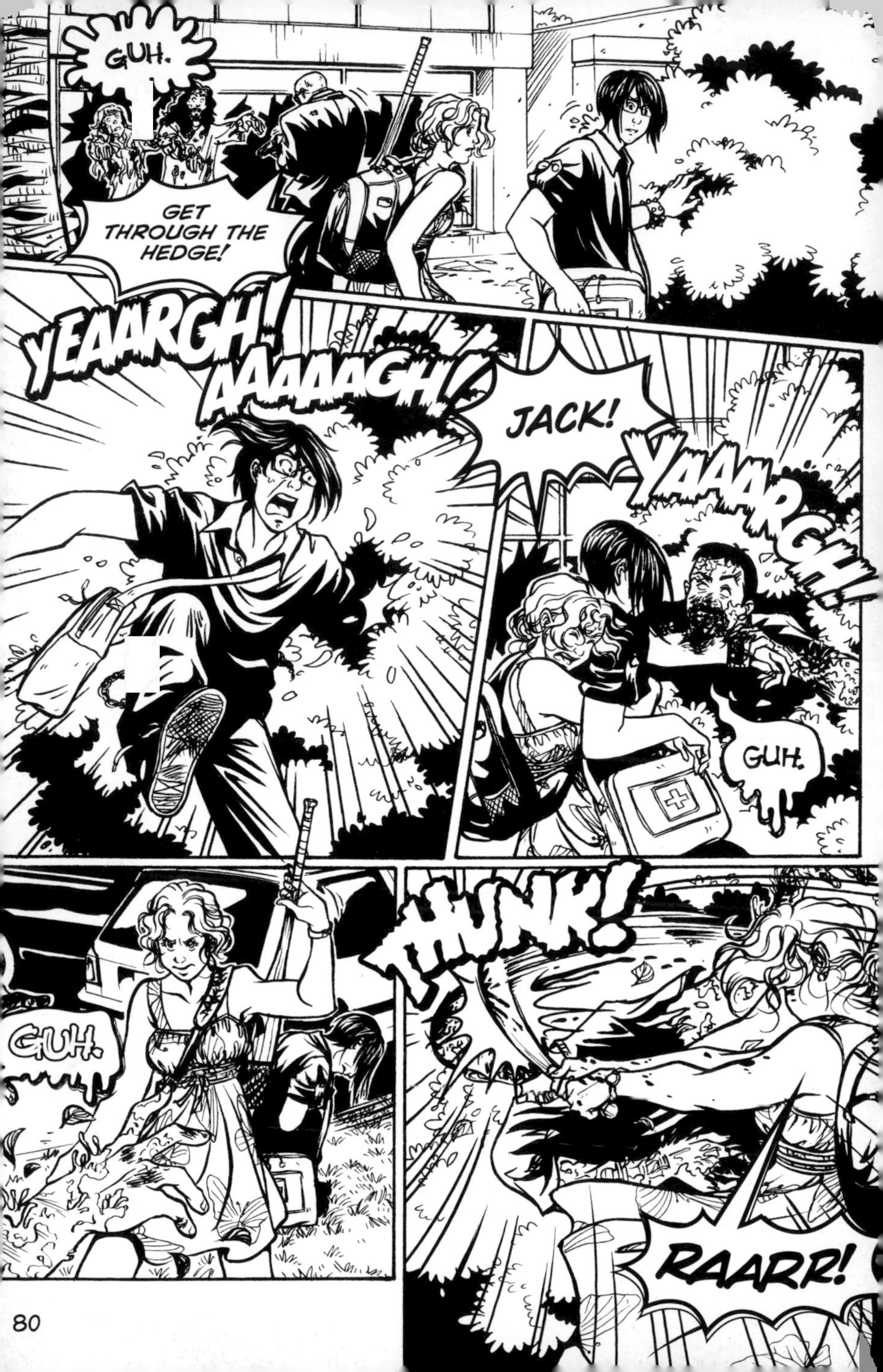
GUH.
GET THROUGH THE HEDGE!
YEAARGH!
AAAAAGH!
JACK!
YAAARGH!
GUH.
GUH.
THUNK!
RAARR!

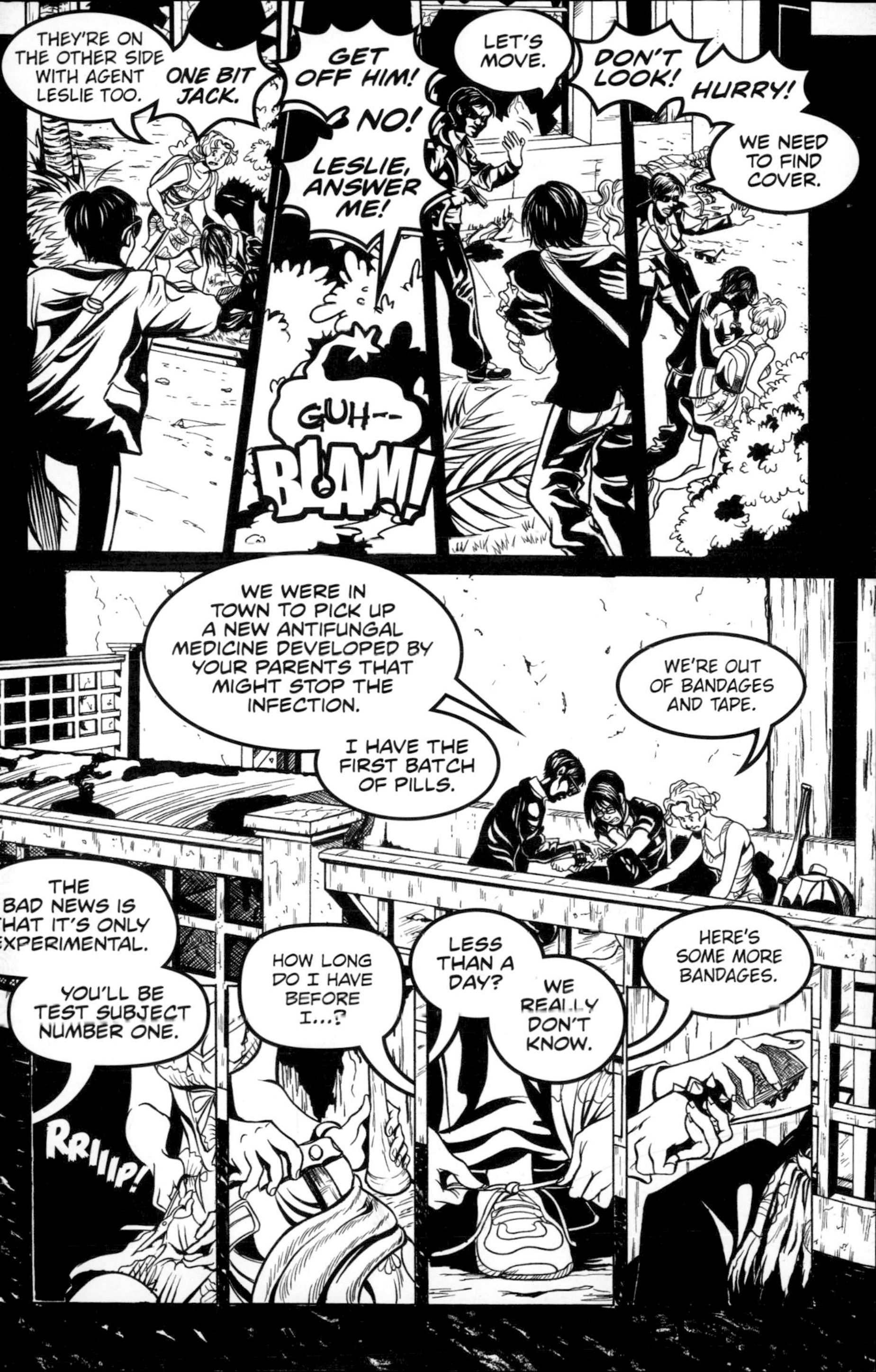
THEY'RE ON THE OTHER SIDE WITH AGENT LESLIE TOO.
ONE BIT JACK.
GET OFF HIM!
NO!
LESLIE, ANSWER ME!
GUH--
BLAM!
LET'S MOVE.
DON'T LOOK!
HURRY!
WE NEED TO FIND COVER.
WE WERE IN TOWN TO PICK UP A NEW ANTIFUNGAL MEDICINE DEVELOPED BY YOUR PARENTS THAT MIGHT STOP THE INFECTION.
I HAVE THE FIRST BATCH OF PILLS.
WE'RE OUT OF BANDAGES AND TAPE.
THE BAD NEWS IS THAT IT'S ONLY EXPERIMENTAL.
YOU'LL BE TEST SUBJECT NUMBER ONE.
RRIIIP!
HOW LONG DO I HAVE BEFORE I...?
LESS THAN A DAY?
WE REALLY DON'T KNOW.
HERE'S SOME MORE BANDAGES.

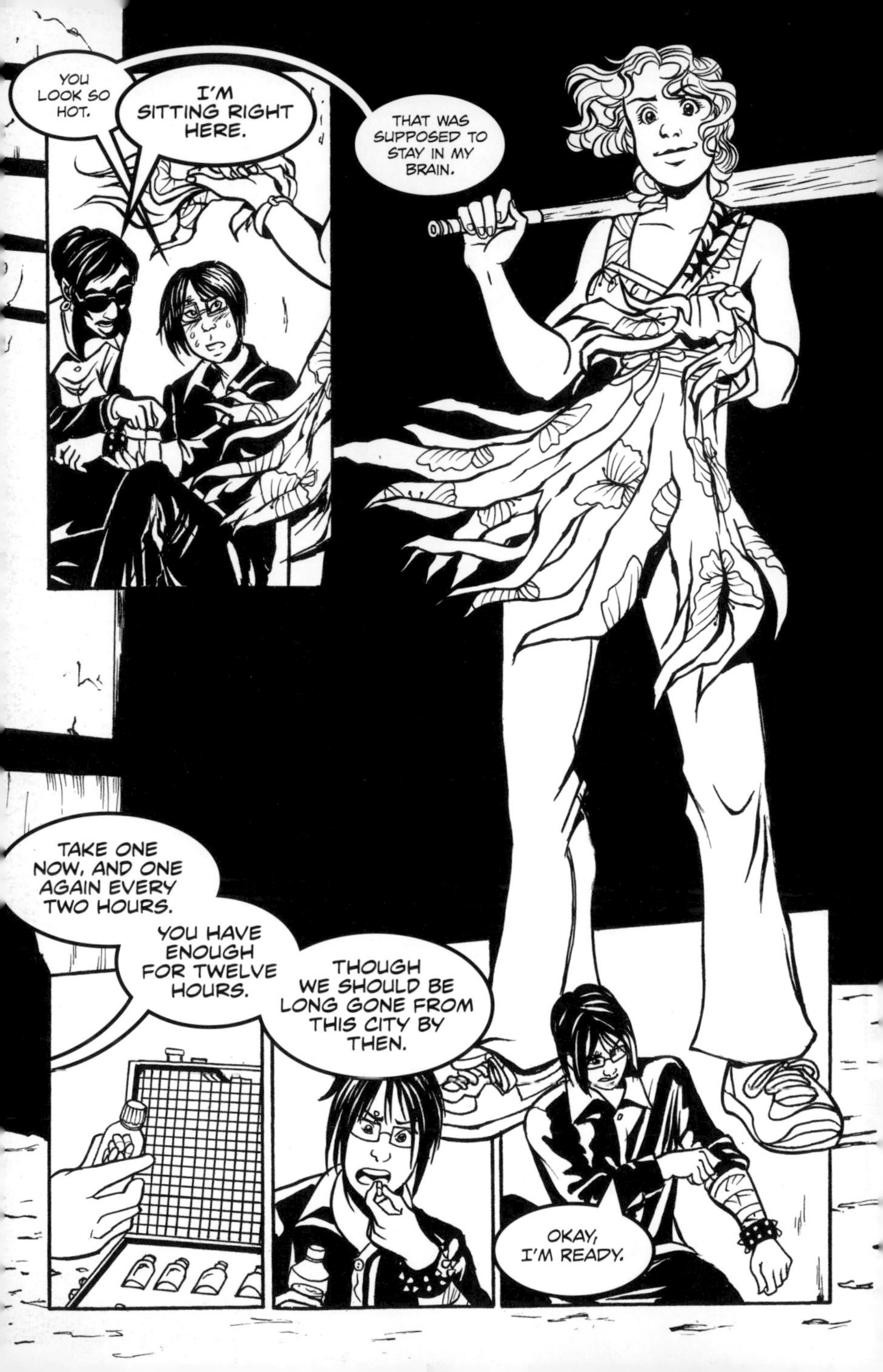
YOU LOOK SO HOT.
I'M SITTING RIGHT HERE.
THAT WAS SUPPOSED TO STAY IN MY BRAIN.
TAKE ONE NOW, AND ONE AGAIN EVERY TWO HOURS.
YOU HAVE ENOUGH FOR TWELVE HOURS.
THOUGH WE SHOULD BE LONG GONE FROM THIS CITY BY THEN.
OKAY, I'M READY.

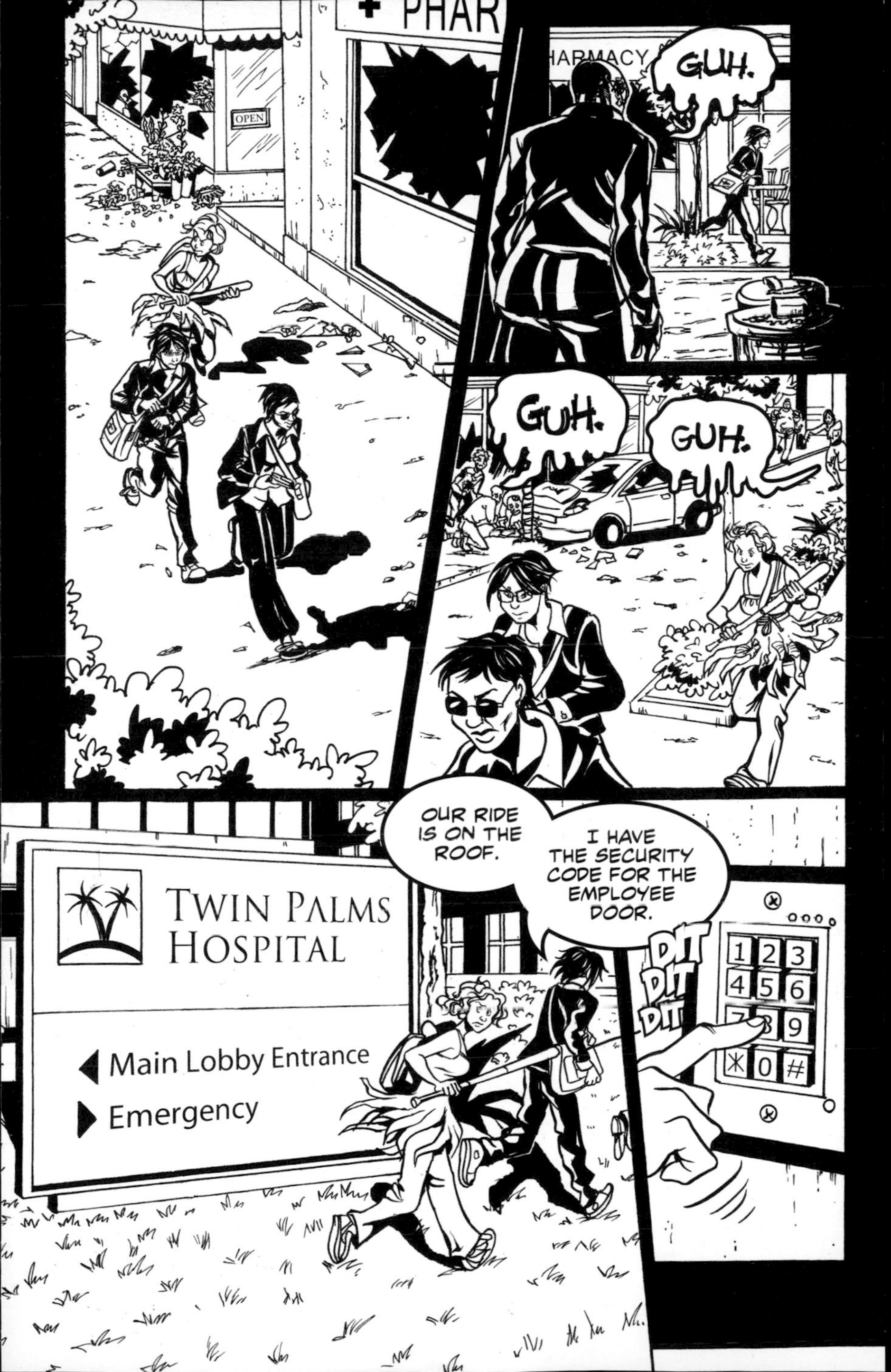
PHAR
OPEN
HARMACY
GUH.
GUH.
GUH.
OUR RIDE IS ON THE ROOF.
I HAVE THE SECURITY CODE FOR THE EMPLOYEE DOOR.
TWIN PALMS HOSPITAL
Main Lobby Entrance
Emergency
DIT
DIT
DIT
1 2 3
4 5 6
7 8 9
* 0 #

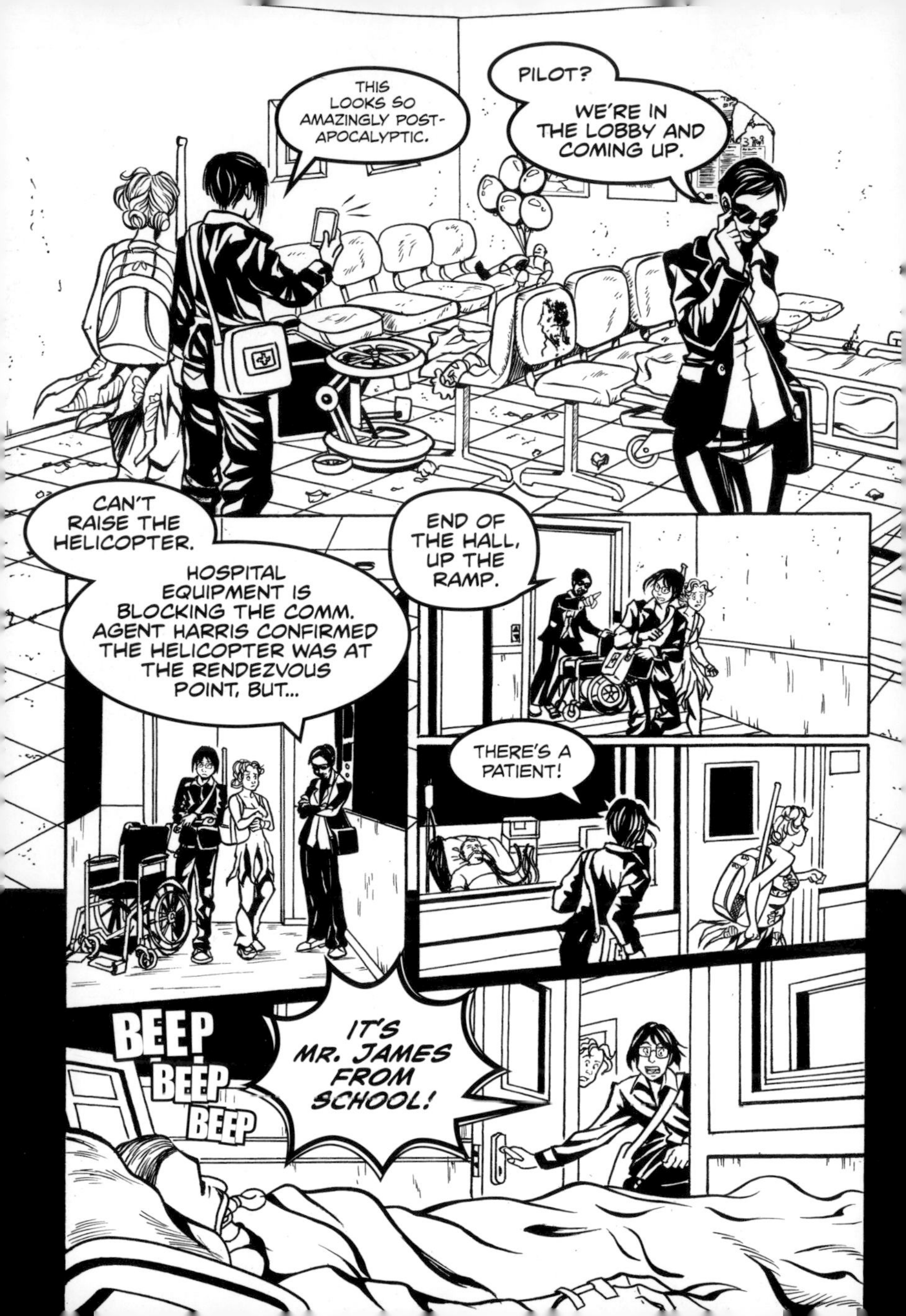
THIS LOOKS SO AMAZINGLY POST-APOCALYPTIC.
PILOT?
WE'RE IN THE LOBBY AND COMING UP.
CAN'T RAISE THE HELICOPTER.
HOSPITAL EQUIPMENT IS BLOCKING THE COMM. AGENT HARRIS CONFIRMED THE HELICOPTER WAS AT THE RENDEZVOUS POINT, BUT...
END OF THE HALL, UP THE RAMP.
THERE'S A PATIENT!
BEEP
BEEP
BEEP
IT'S MR. JAMES FROM SCHOOL!

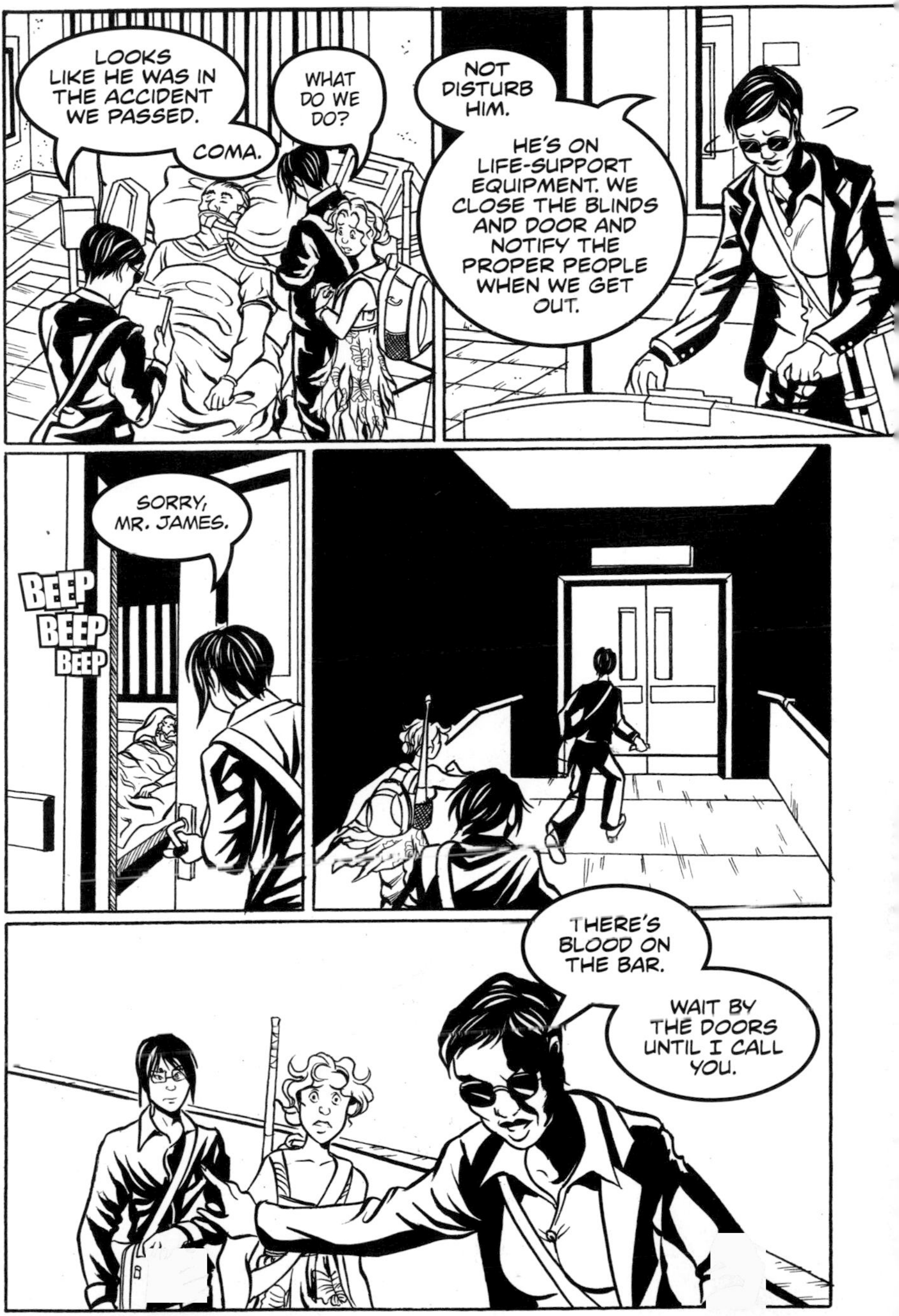
LOOKS LIKE HE WAS IN THE ACCIDENT WE PASSED.
COMA.
WHAT DO WE DO?
NOT DISTURB HIM.
HE'S ON LIFE-SUPPORT EQUIPMENT. WE CLOSE THE BLINDS AND DOOR AND NOTIFY THE PROPER PEOPLE WHEN WE GET OUT.
SORRY, MR. JAMES.
BEEP
BEEP
BEEP
THERE'S BLOOD ON THE BAR.
WAIT BY THE DOORS UNTIL I CALL YOU.

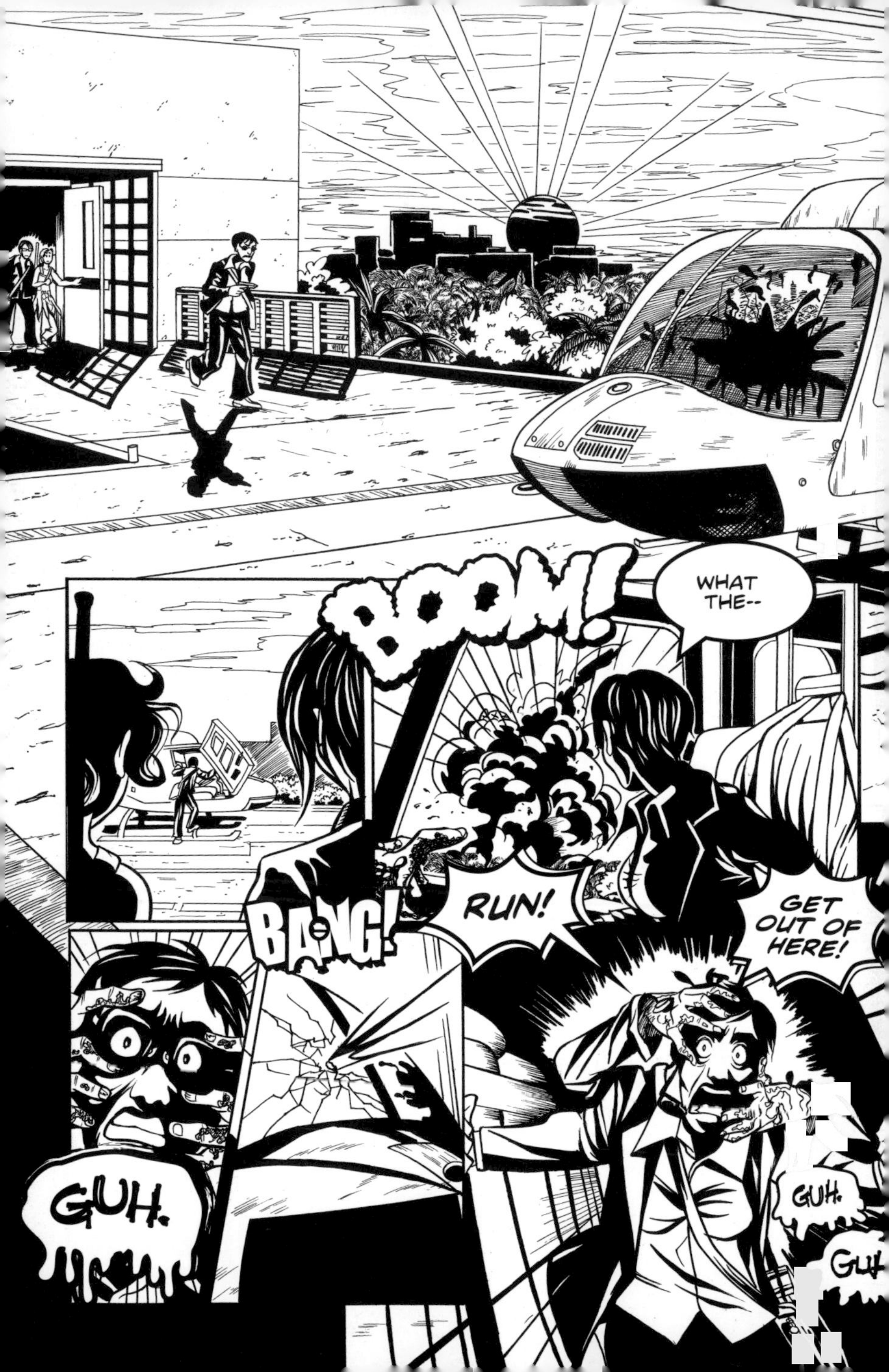
BOOM!
WHAT THE--
BANG!
RUN!
GET OUT OF HERE!
GUH.
GUH.
GUH

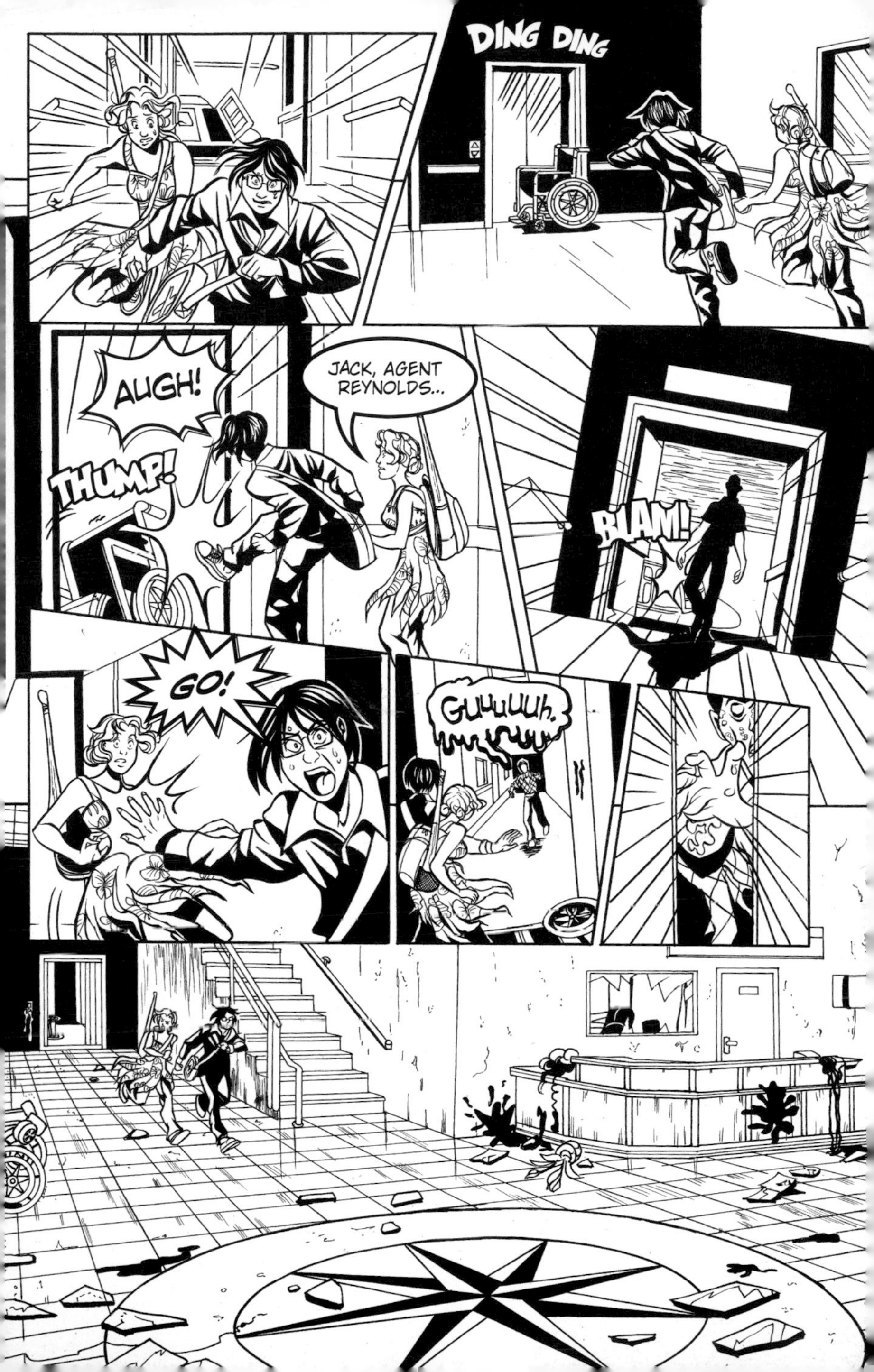
DING DING
AUGH!
THUMP!
JACK, AGENT REYNOLDS...
BLAM!
GO!
Guuuuuh.

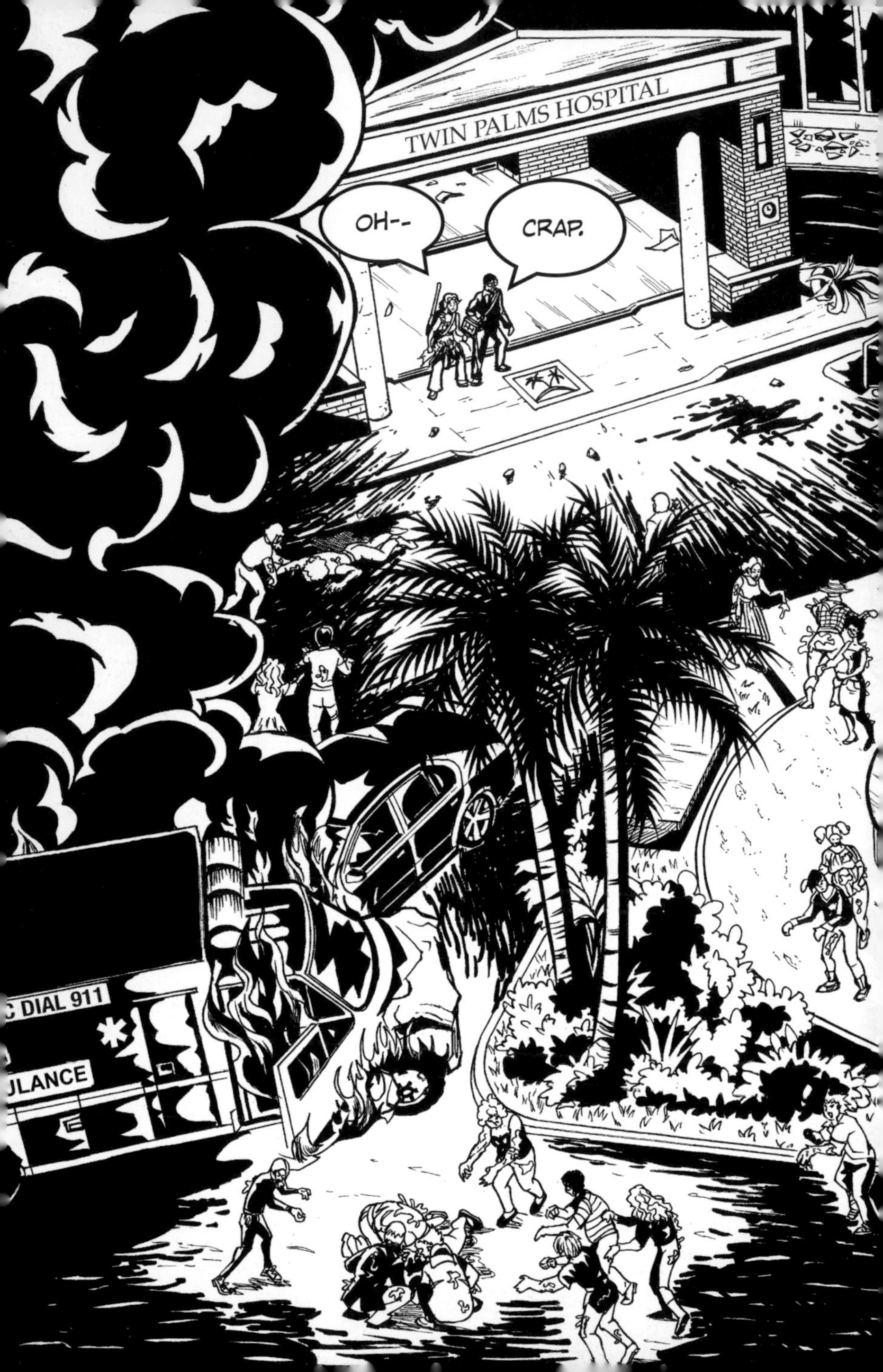
TWIN PALMS HOSPITAL
OH--
CRAP.
C DIAL 911
ULANCE

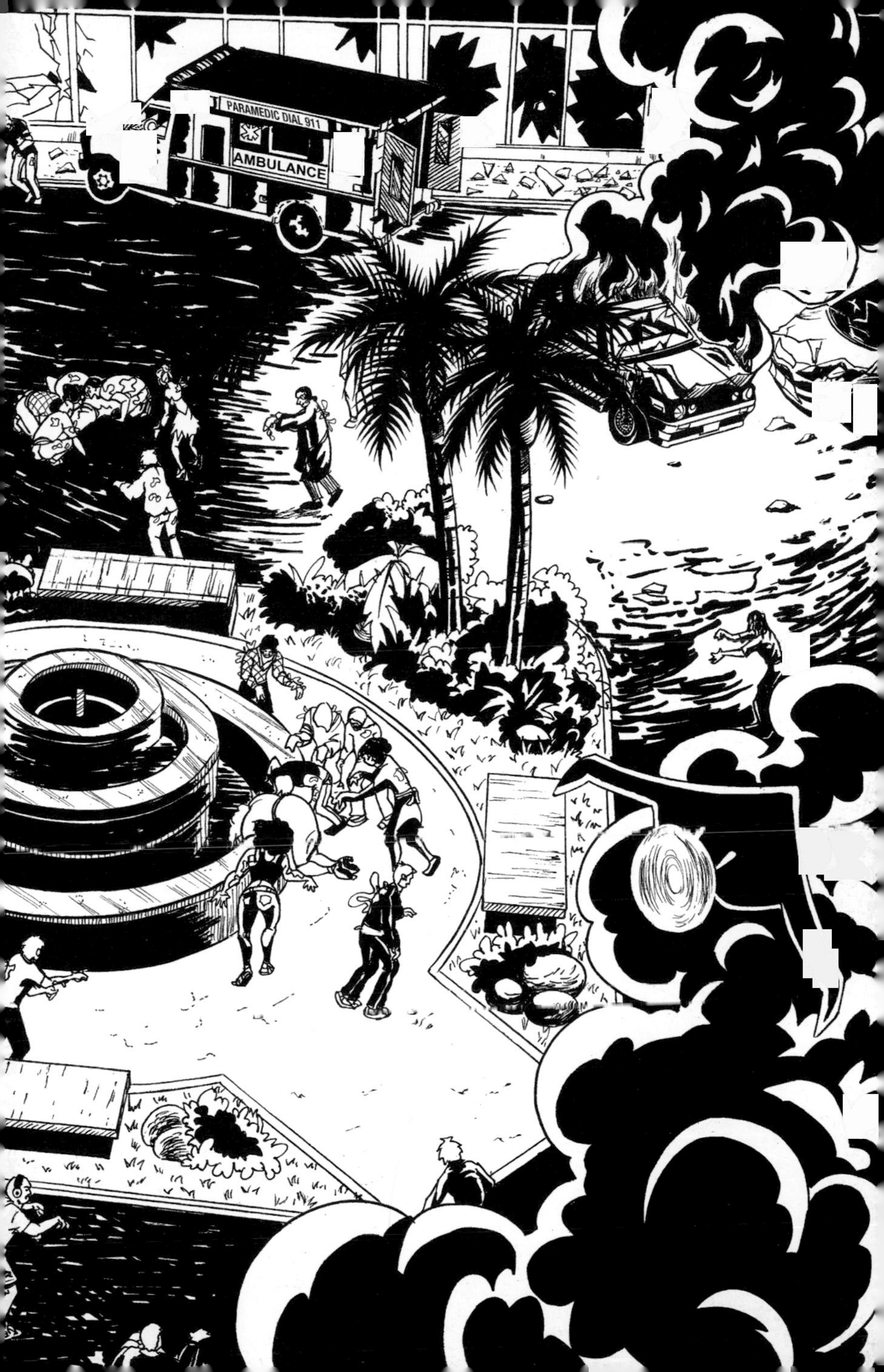
PARAMEDIC DIAL 911
AMBULANCE

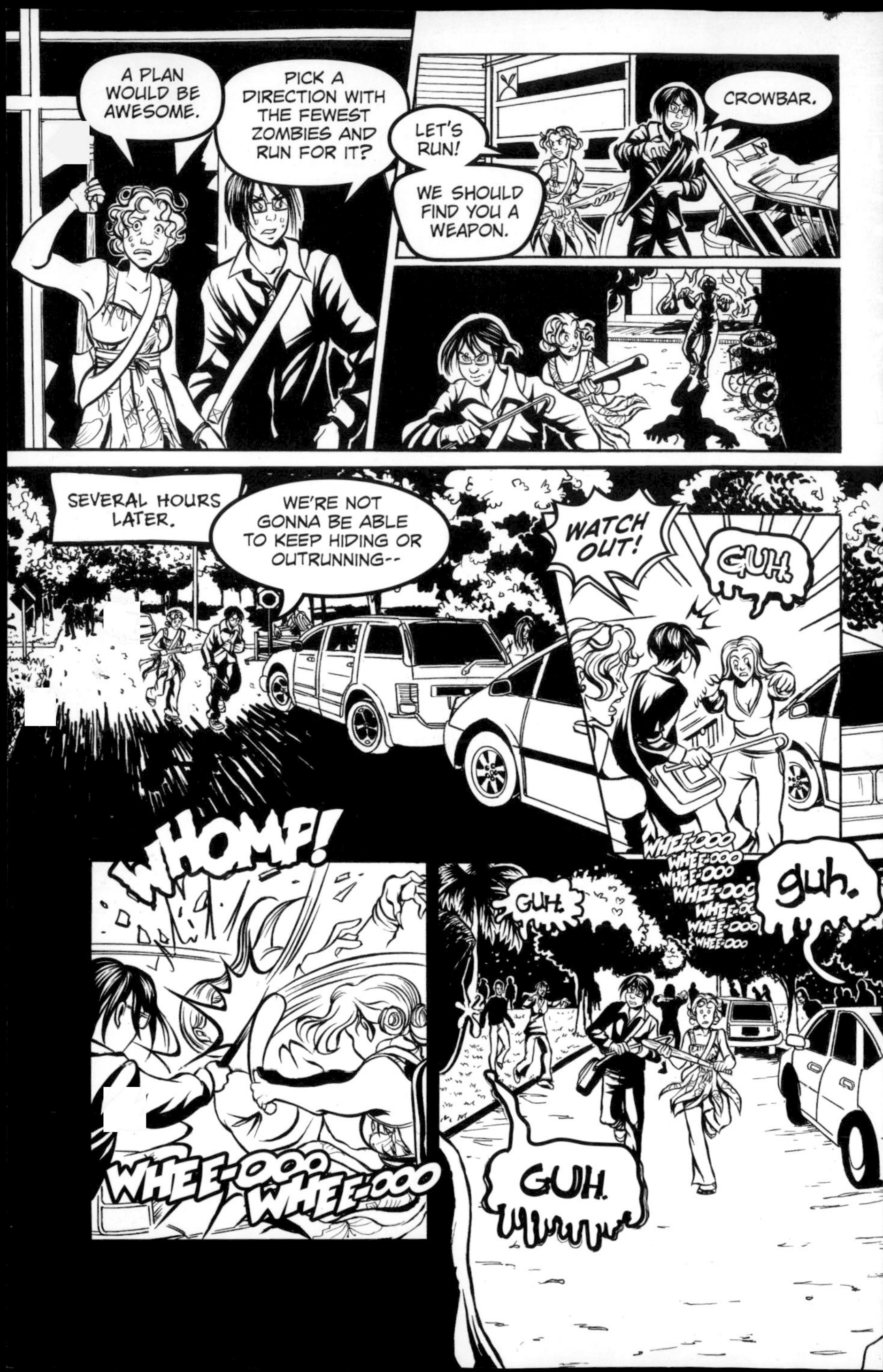
A PLAN WOULD BE AWESOME.
PICK A DIRECTION WITH THE FEWEST ZOMBIES AND RUN FOR IT?
LET'S RUN!
WE SHOULD FIND YOU A WEAPON.
CROWBAR.
SEVERAL HOURS LATER.
WE'RE NOT GONNA BE ABLE TO KEEP HIDING OR OUTRUNNING--
WATCH OUT!
GUH.
WHOMP!
WHEE-OOO WHEE-OOO
WHEE-OOO
WHEE-OOO
WHEE-OOO
WHEE-OOO
WHEE-OOO
WHEE-OOO
WHEE-OOO
GUH.
guh.
GUH.

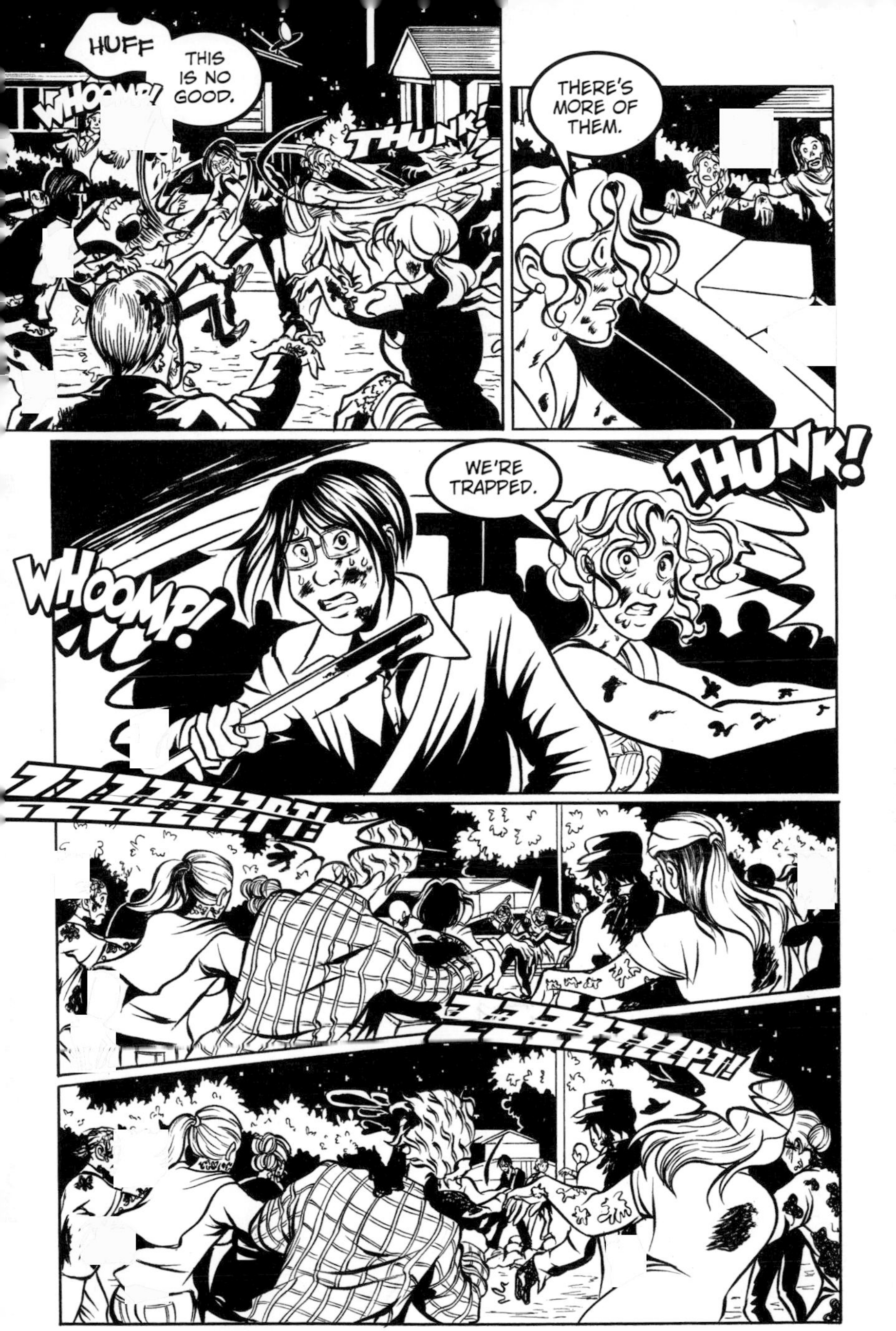
HUFF
WHOOMP!
THIS IS NO GOOD.
THUNK!
THERE'S MORE OF THEM.
WE'RE TRAPPED.
THUNK!
WHOOMP!

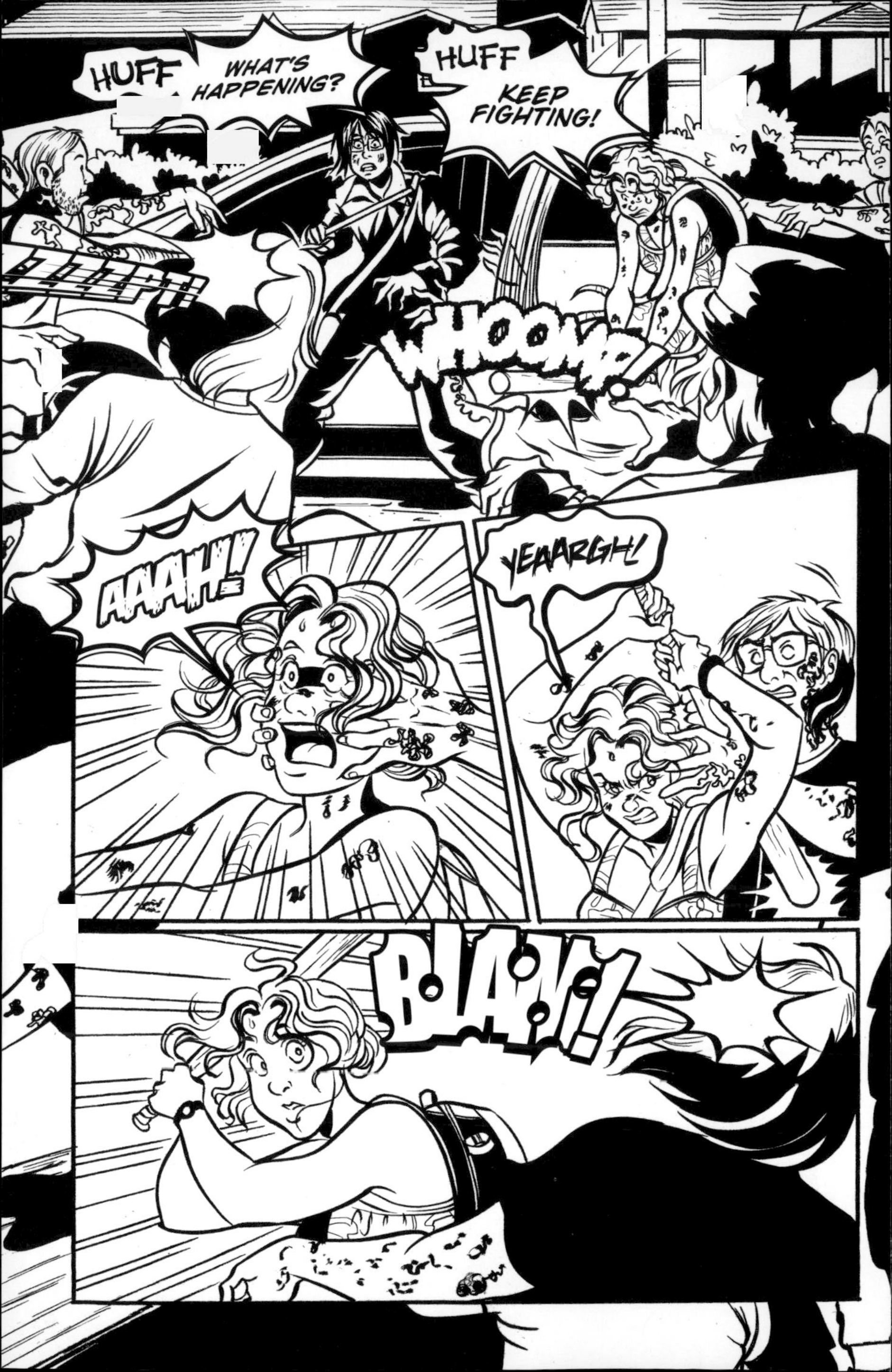
HUFF
WHAT'S HAPPENING?
HUFF
KEEP FIGHTING!
WHOOMP
AAAAH!!
YEAARGH!
BLAM!!

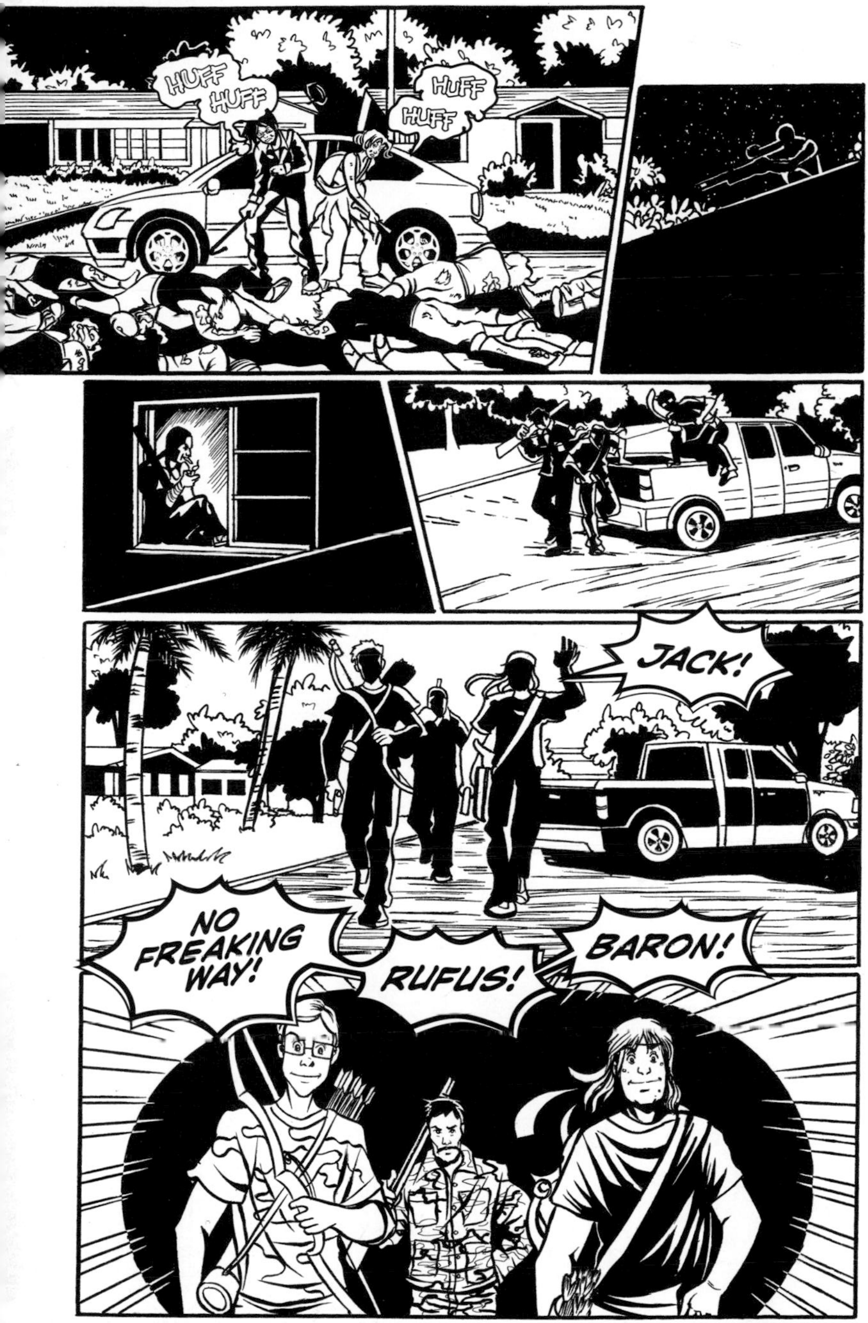
HUFF HUFF
HUFF HUFF
JACK!
NO FREAKING WAY!
RUFUS!
BARON!

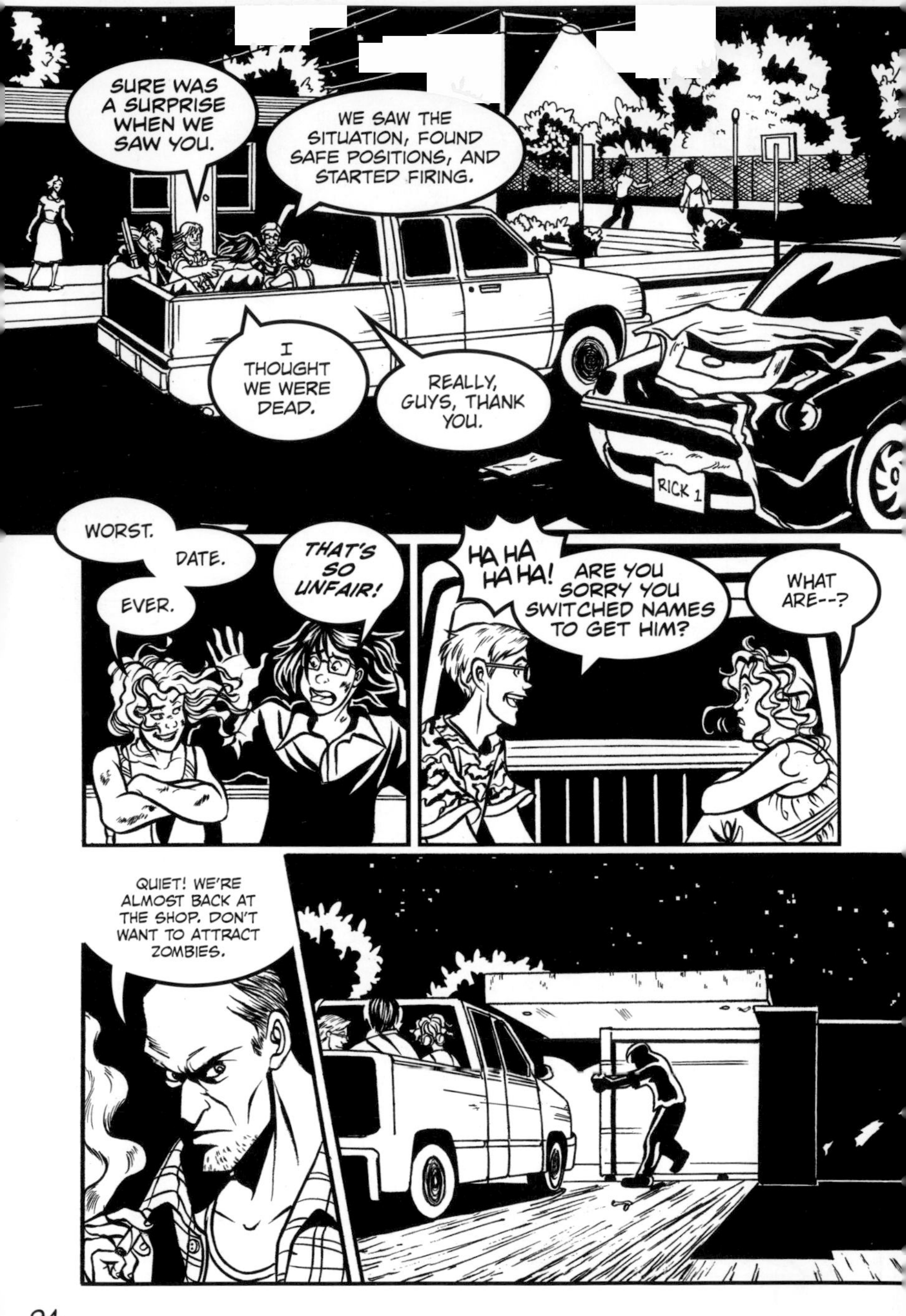

SURE WAS A SURPRISE WHEN WE SAW YOU.
WE SAW THE SITUATION, FOUND SAFE POSITIONS, AND STARTED FIRING.
I THOUGHT WE WERE DEAD.
REALLY, GUYS, THANK YOU.
RICK 1
WORST.
DATE.
EVER.
THAT'S SO UNFAIR!
HA HA HA HA!
ARE YOU SORRY YOU SWITCHED NAMES TO GET HIM?
WHAT ARE--?
QUIET! WE'RE ALMOST BACK AT THE SHOP. DON'T WANT TO ATTRACT ZOMBIES.

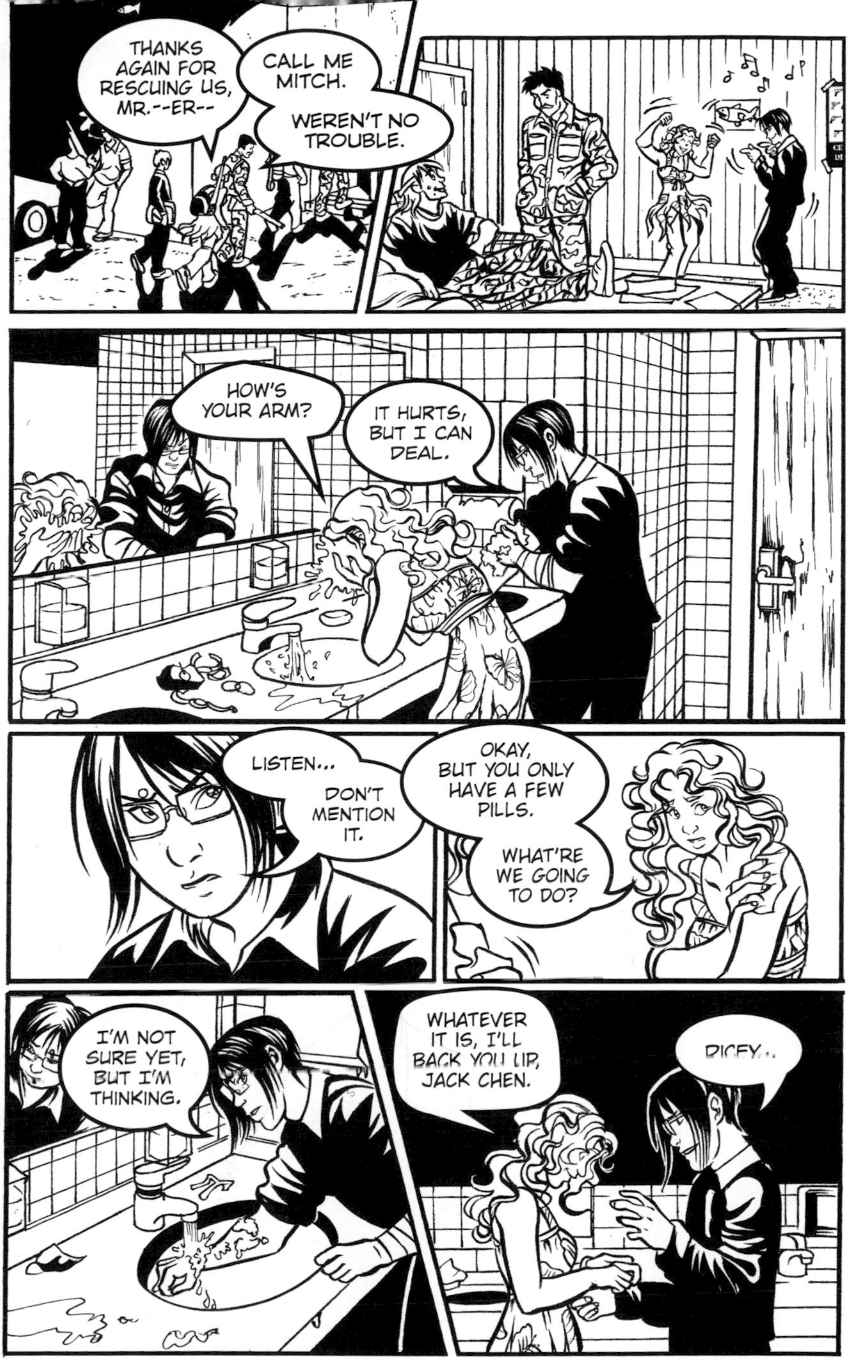

THANKS AGAIN FOR RESCUING US, MR.--ER--
CALL ME MITCH.
WEREN'T NO TROUBLE.
HOW'S YOUR ARM?
IT HURTS, BUT I CAN DEAL.
LISTEN...
DON'T MENTION IT.
OKAY, BUT YOU ONLY HAVE A FEW PILLS.
WHAT'RE WE GOING TO DO?
I'M NOT SURE YET, BUT I'M THINKING.
WHATEVER IT IS, I'LL BACK YOU UP, JACK CHEN.
DICEY...

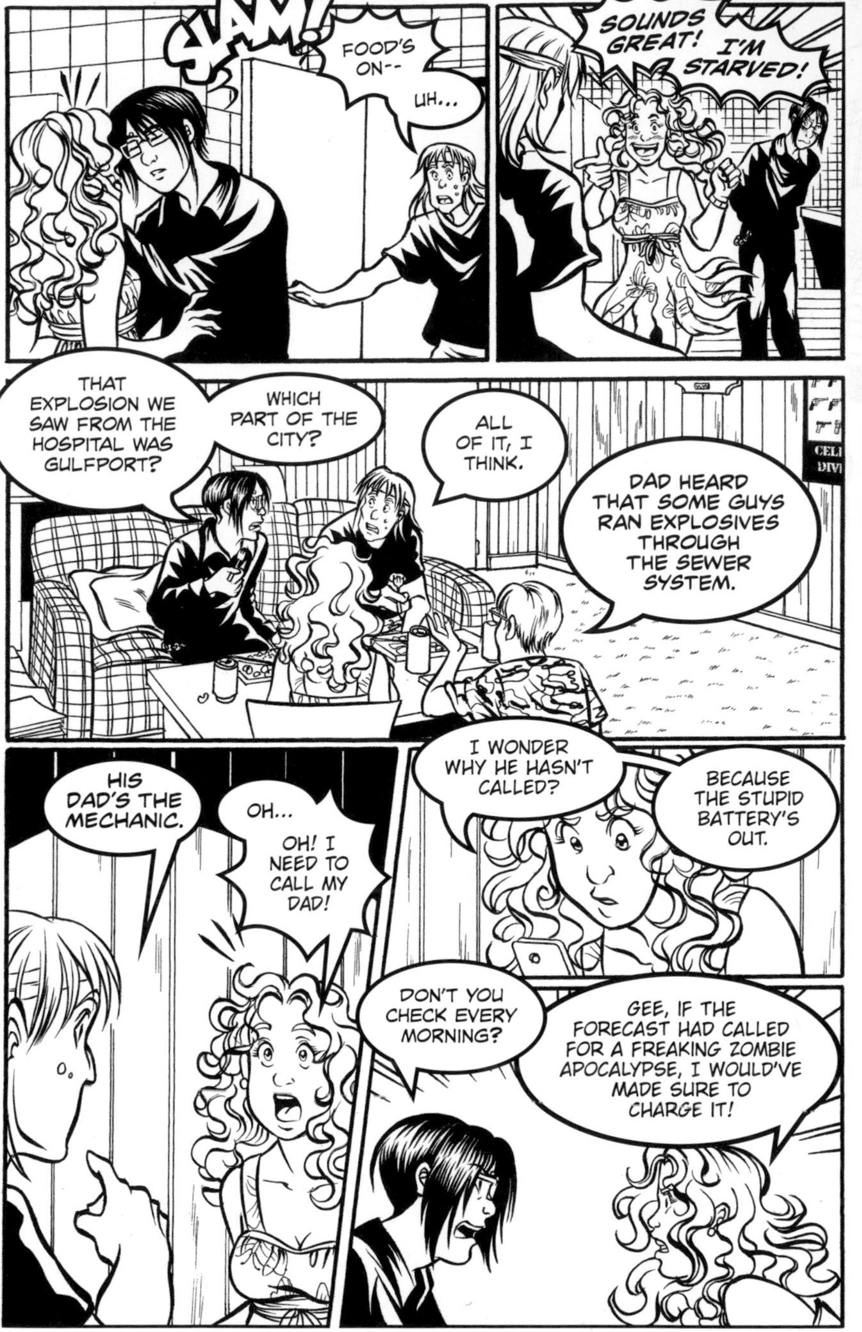
SLAM!
FOOD'S ON--
UH...
SOUNDS GREAT! I'M STARVED!
THAT EXPLOSION WE SAW FROM THE HOSPITAL WAS GULFPORT?
WHICH PART OF THE CITY?
ALL OF IT, I THINK.
DAD HEARD THAT SOME GUYS RAN EXPLOSIVES THROUGH THE SEWER SYSTEM.
HIS DAD'S THE MECHANIC.
OH...
OH! I NEED TO CALL MY DAD!
I WONDER WHY HE HASN'T CALLED?
BECAUSE THE STUPID BATTERY'S OUT.
DON'T YOU CHECK EVERY MORNING?
GEE, IF THE FORECAST HAD CALLED FOR A FREAKING ZOMBIE APOCALYPSE, I WOULD'VE MADE SURE TO CHARGE IT!

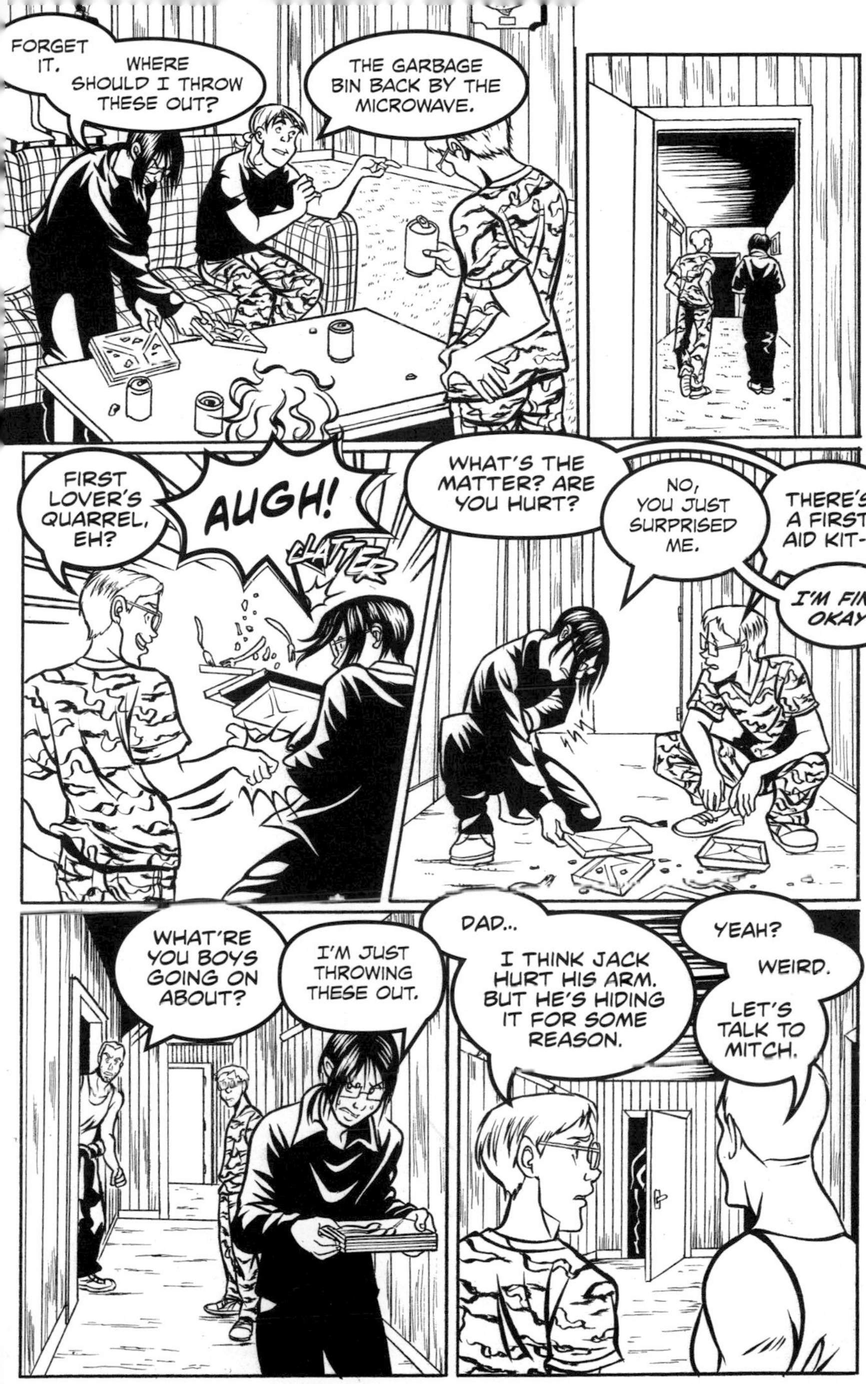
FORGET IT. WHERE SHOULD I THROW THESE OUT?
THE GARBAGE BIN BACK BY THE MICROWAVE.
FIRST LOVER'S QUARREL, EH?
AUGH!
CLATTER
WHAT'S THE MATTER? ARE YOU HURT?
NO, YOU JUST SURPRISED ME.
THERE'S A FIRST AID KIT--
I'M FINE, OKAY!
WHAT'RE YOU BOYS GOING ON ABOUT?
I'M JUST THROWING THESE OUT.
DAD...
I THINK JACK HURT HIS ARM. BUT HE'S HIDING IT FOR SOME REASON.
YEAH?
WEIRD.
LET'S TALK TO MITCH.

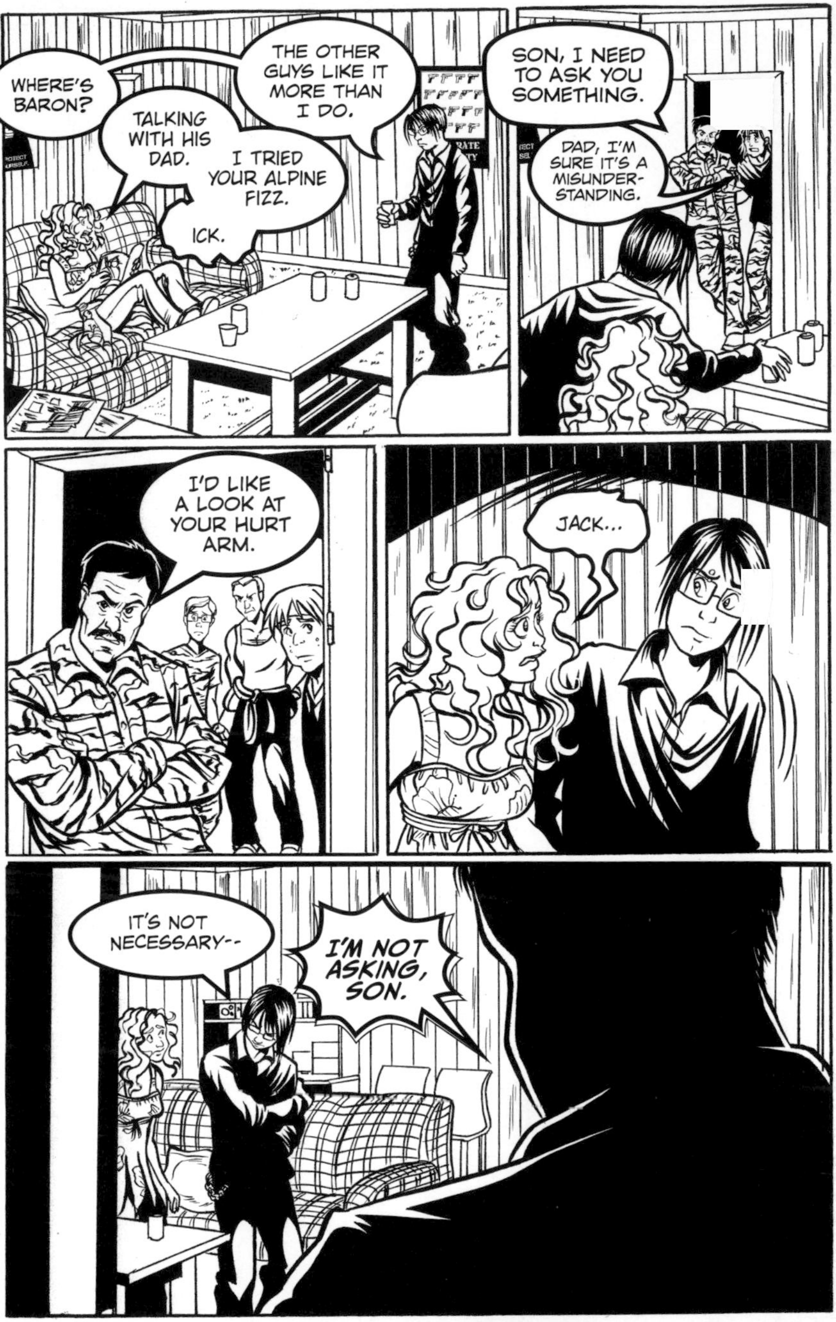
WHERE'S BARON?
TALKING WITH HIS DAD.
I TRIED YOUR ALPINE FIZZ.
ICK.
THE OTHER GUYS LIKE IT MORE THAN I DO.
SON, I NEED TO ASK YOU SOMETHING.
DAD, I'M SURE IT'S A MISUNDER-STANDING.
I'D LIKE A LOOK AT YOUR HURT ARM.
JACK...
IT'S NOT NECESSARY--
I'M NOT ASKING, SON.

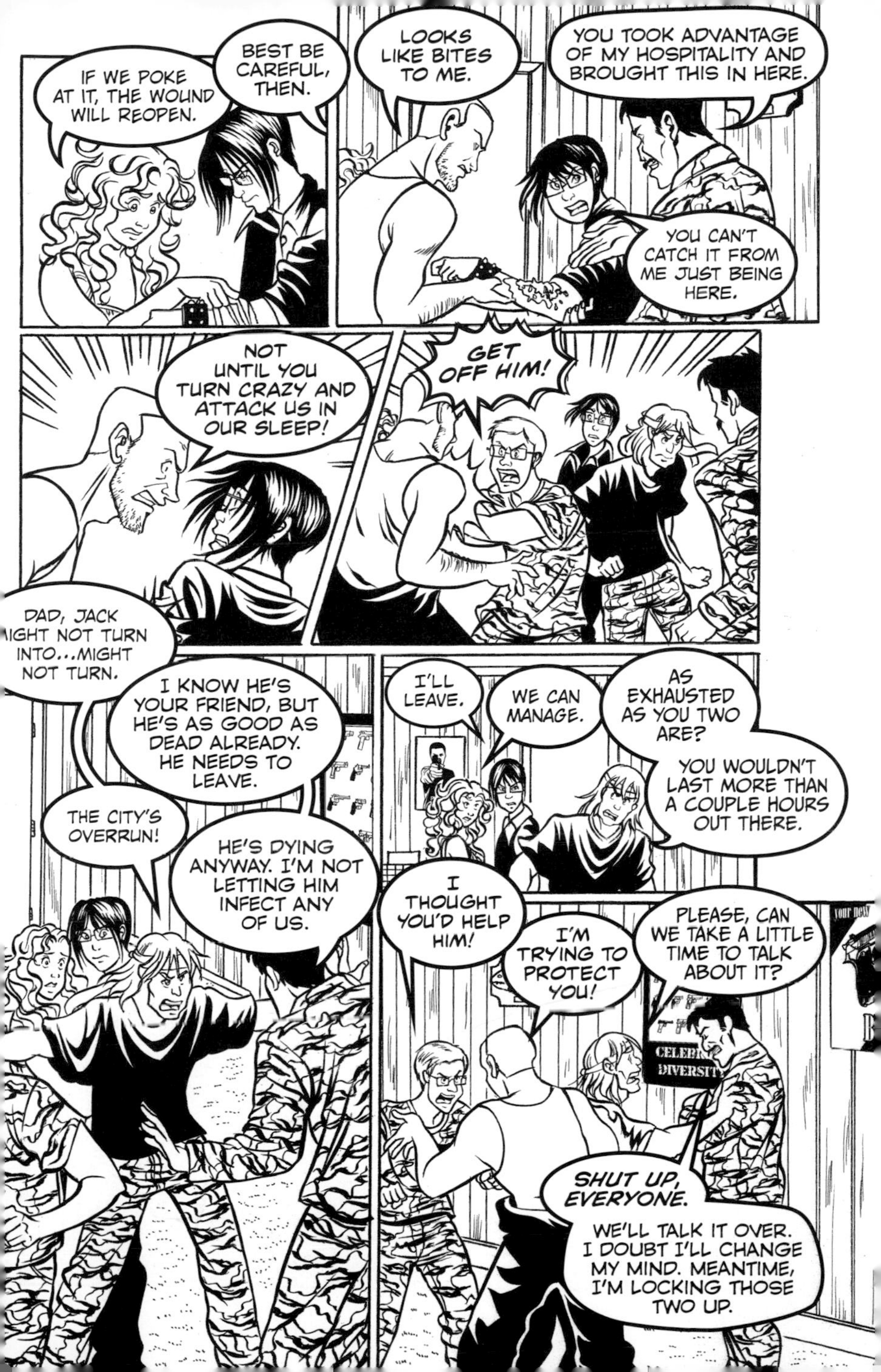
IF WE POKE AT IT, THE WOUND WILL REOPEN.
BEST BE CAREFUL, THEN.
LOOKS LIKE BITES TO ME.
YOU TOOK ADVANTAGE OF MY HOSPITALITY AND BROUGHT THIS IN HERE.
YOU CAN'T CATCH IT FROM ME JUST BEING HERE.
NOT UNTIL YOU TURN CRAZY AND ATTACK US IN OUR SLEEP!
GET OFF HIM!
DAD, JACK MIGHT NOT TURN INTO...MIGHT NOT TURN.
I KNOW HE'S YOUR FRIEND, BUT HE'S AS GOOD AS DEAD ALREADY. HE NEEDS TO LEAVE.
THE CITY'S OVERRUN!
HE'S DYING ANYWAY. I'M NOT LETTING HIM INFECT ANY OF US.
I'LL LEAVE.
WE CAN MANAGE.
AS EXHAUSTED AS YOU TWO ARE?
YOU WOULDN'T LAST MORE THAN A COUPLE HOURS OUT THERE.
I THOUGHT YOU'D HELP HIM!
I'M TRYING TO PROTECT YOU!
PLEASE, CAN WE TAKE A LITTLE TIME TO TALK ABOUT IT?
SHUT UP, EVERYONE.
WE'LL TALK IT OVER. I DOUBT I'LL CHANGE MY MIND. MEANTIME, I'M LOCKING THOSE TWO UP.

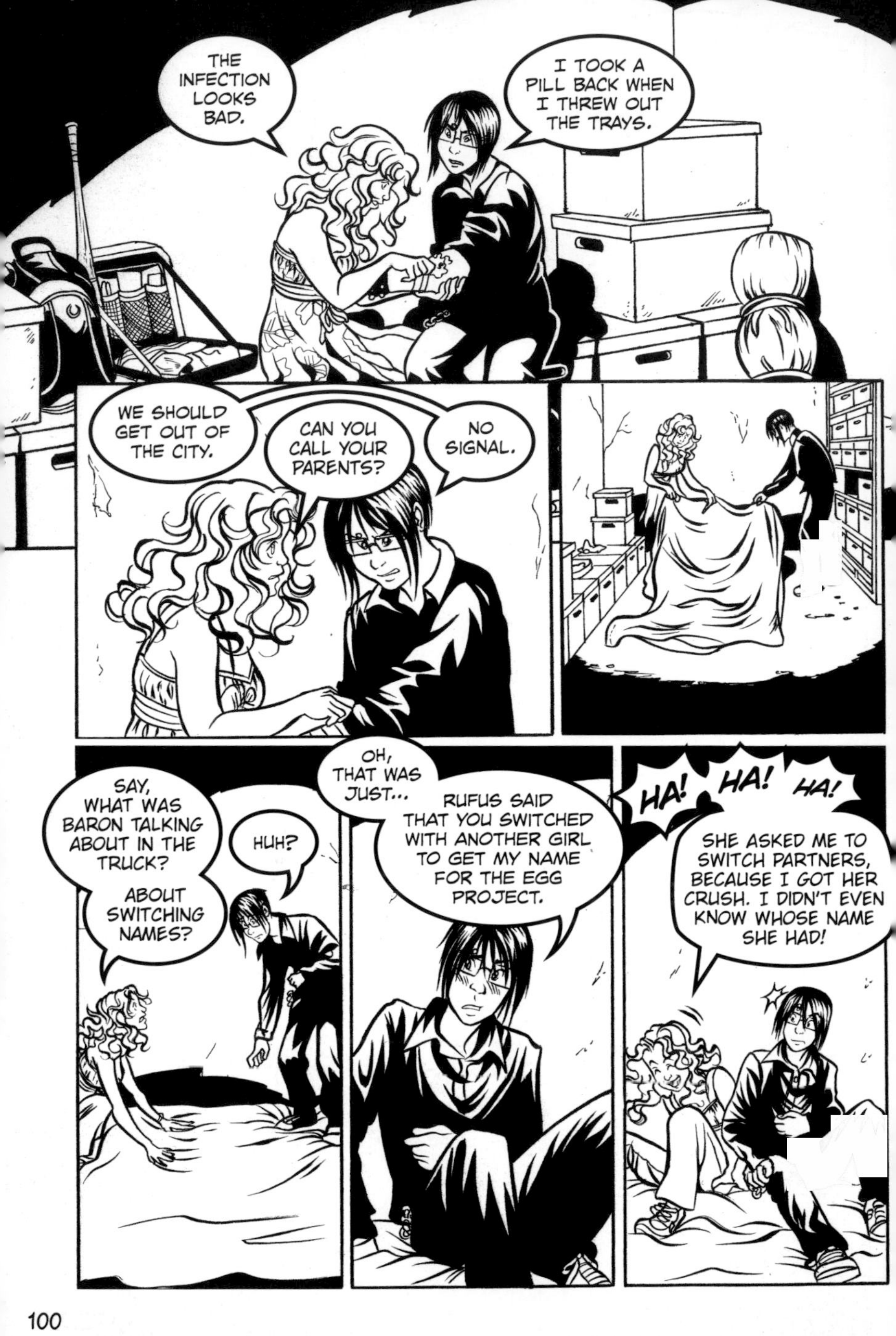
THE INFECTION LOOKS BAD.
I TOOK A PILL BACK WHEN I THREW OUT THE TRAYS.
WE SHOULD GET OUT OF THE CITY.
CAN YOU CALL YOUR PARENTS?
NO SIGNAL.
SAY, WHAT WAS BARON TALKING ABOUT IN THE TRUCK?
ABOUT SWITCHING NAMES?
HUH?
OH, THAT WAS JUST...
RUFUS SAID THAT YOU SWITCHED WITH ANOTHER GIRL TO GET MY NAME FOR THE EGG PROJECT.
HA! HA! HA!
SHE ASKED ME TO SWITCH PARTNERS, BECAUSE I GOT HER CRUSH. I DIDN'T EVEN KNOW WHOSE NAME SHE HAD!

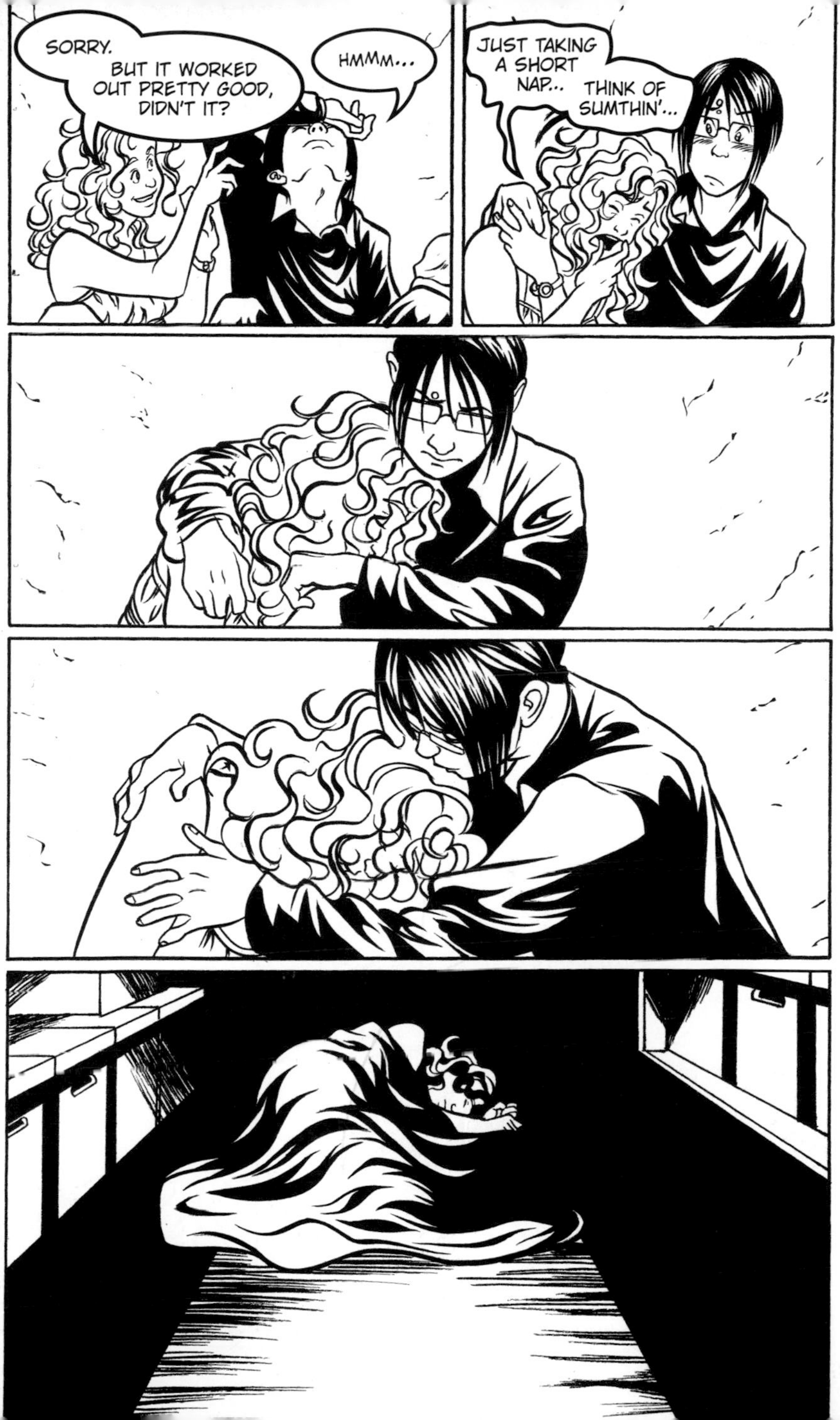
SORRY.
BUT IT WORKED OUT PRETTY GOOD, DIDN'T IT?
HMMM...
JUST TAKING A SHORT NAP...
THINK OF SUMTHIN'...

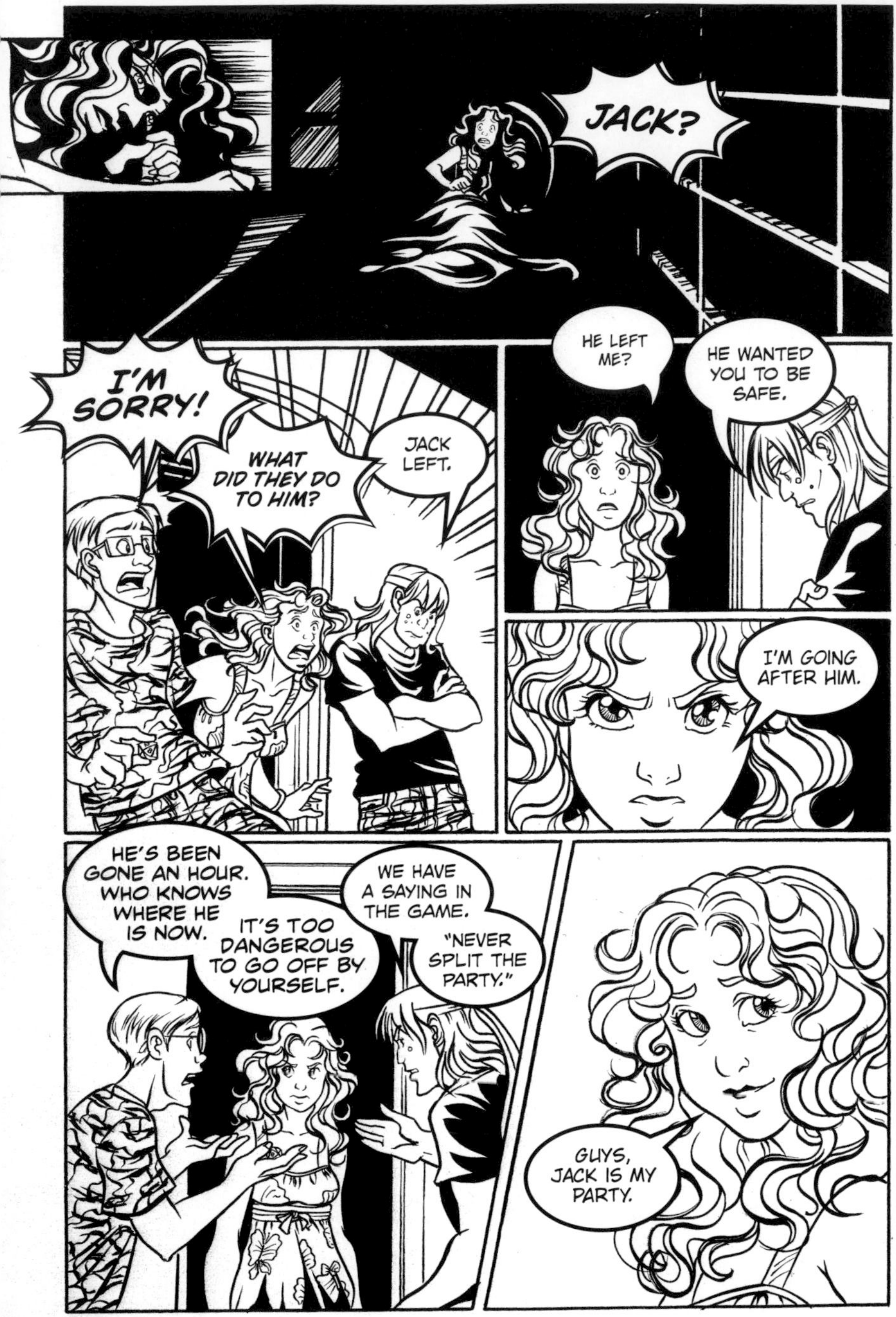
JACK?
I'M SORRY!
WHAT DID THEY DO TO HIM?
JACK LEFT.
HE LEFT ME?
HE WANTED YOU TO BE SAFE.
I'M GOING AFTER HIM.
HE'S BEEN GONE AN HOUR. WHO KNOWS WHERE HE IS NOW.
IT'S TOO DANGEROUS TO GO OFF BY YOURSELF.
WE HAVE A SAYING IN THE GAME.
"NEVER SPLIT THE PARTY."
GUYS, JACK IS MY PARTY.

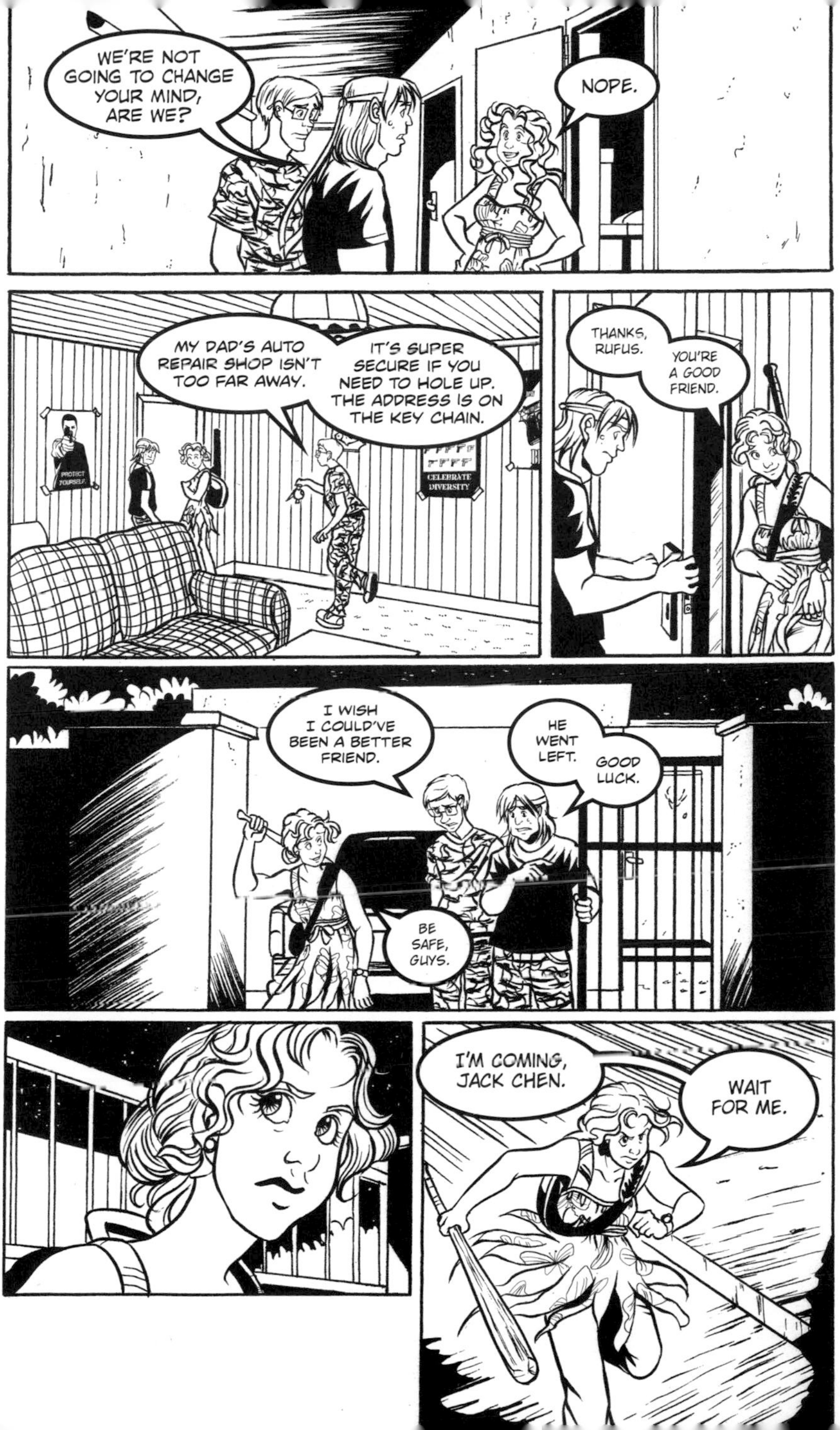
WE'RE NOT GOING TO CHANGE YOUR MIND, ARE WE?
NOPE.
PROTECT YOURSELF.
MY DAD'S AUTO REPAIR SHOP ISN'T TOO FAR AWAY.
IT'S SUPER SECURE IF YOU NEED TO HOLE UP. THE ADDRESS IS ON THE KEY CHAIN.
CELEBRATE DIVERSITY
THANKS, RUFUS.
YOU'RE A GOOD FRIEND.
I WISH I COULD'VE BEEN A BETTER FRIEND.
HE WENT LEFT.
GOOD LUCK.
BE SAFE, GUYS.
I'M COMING, JACK CHEN.
WAIT FOR ME.

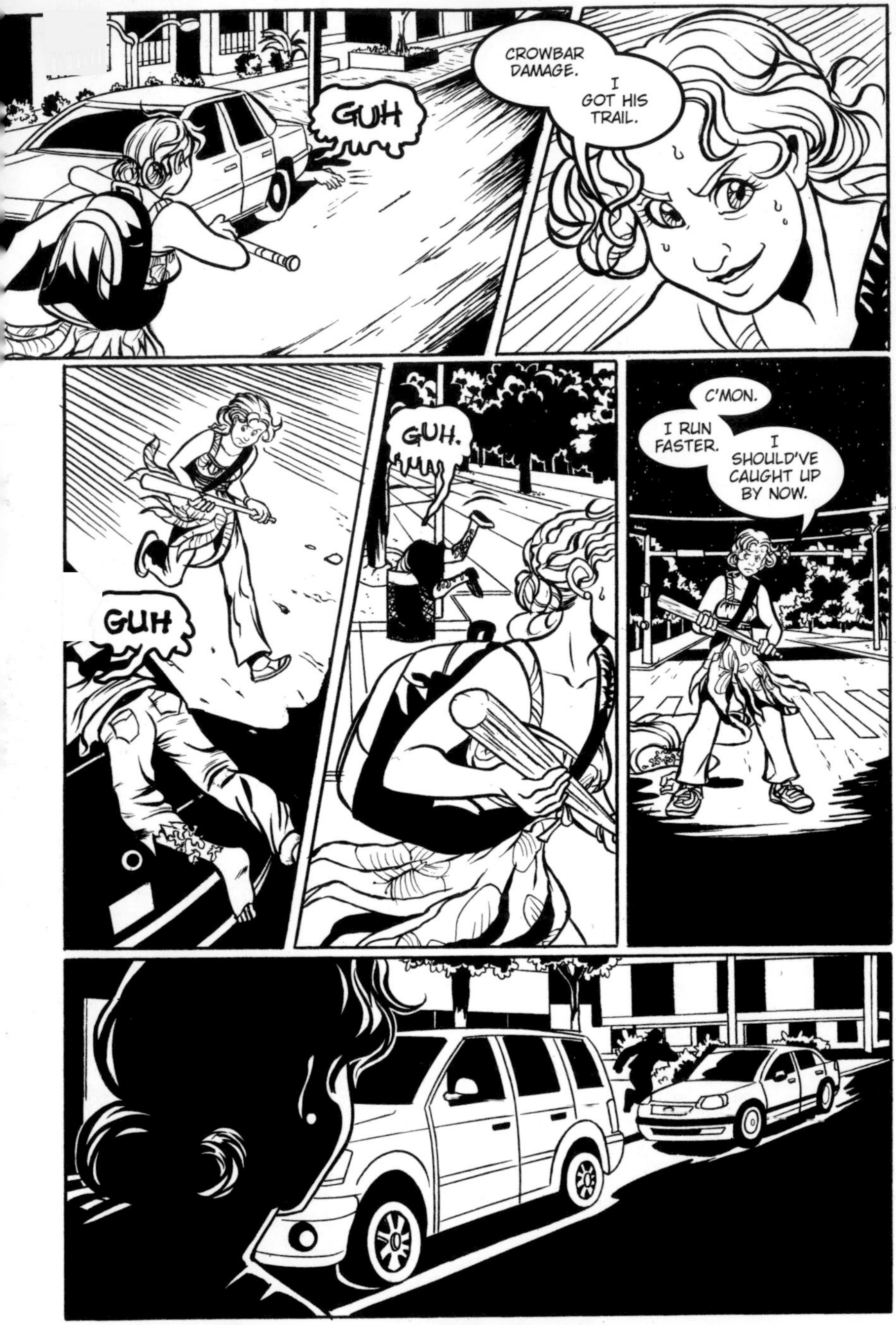
GUH
CROWBAR DAMAGE.
I GOT HIS TRAIL.
GUH
GUH.
C'MON.
I RUN FASTER.
I SHOULD'VE CAUGHT UP BY NOW.

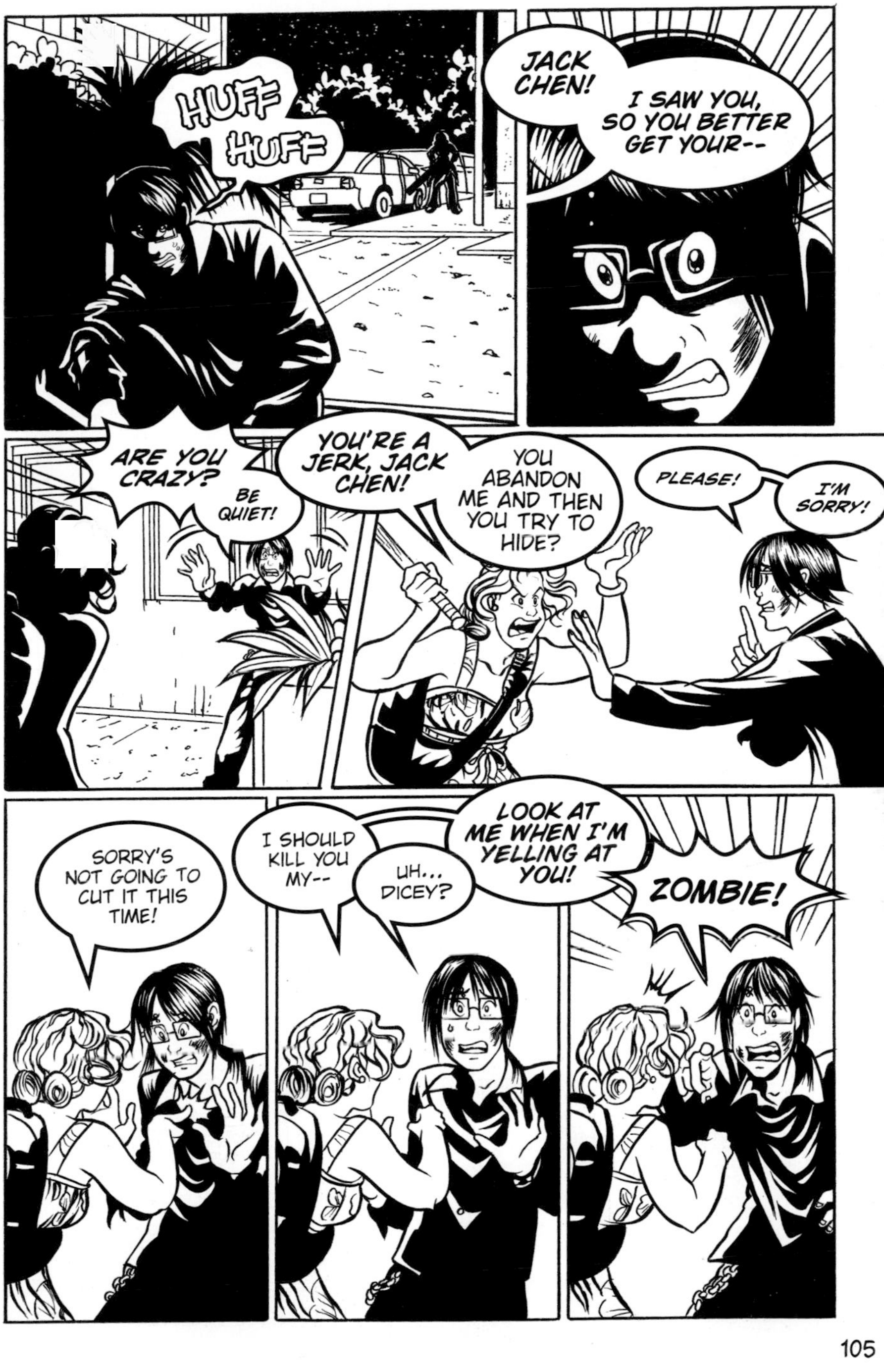
HUFF
HUFF
JACK CHEN!
I SAW YOU, SO YOU BETTER GET YOUR--
ARE YOU CRAZY?
BE QUIET!
YOU'RE A JERK, JACK CHEN!
YOU ABANDON ME AND THEN YOU TRY TO HIDE?
PLEASE!
I'M SORRY!
SORRY'S NOT GOING TO CUT IT THIS TIME!
I SHOULD KILL YOU MY--
UH... DICEY?
LOOK AT ME WHEN I'M YELLING AT YOU!
ZOMBIE!

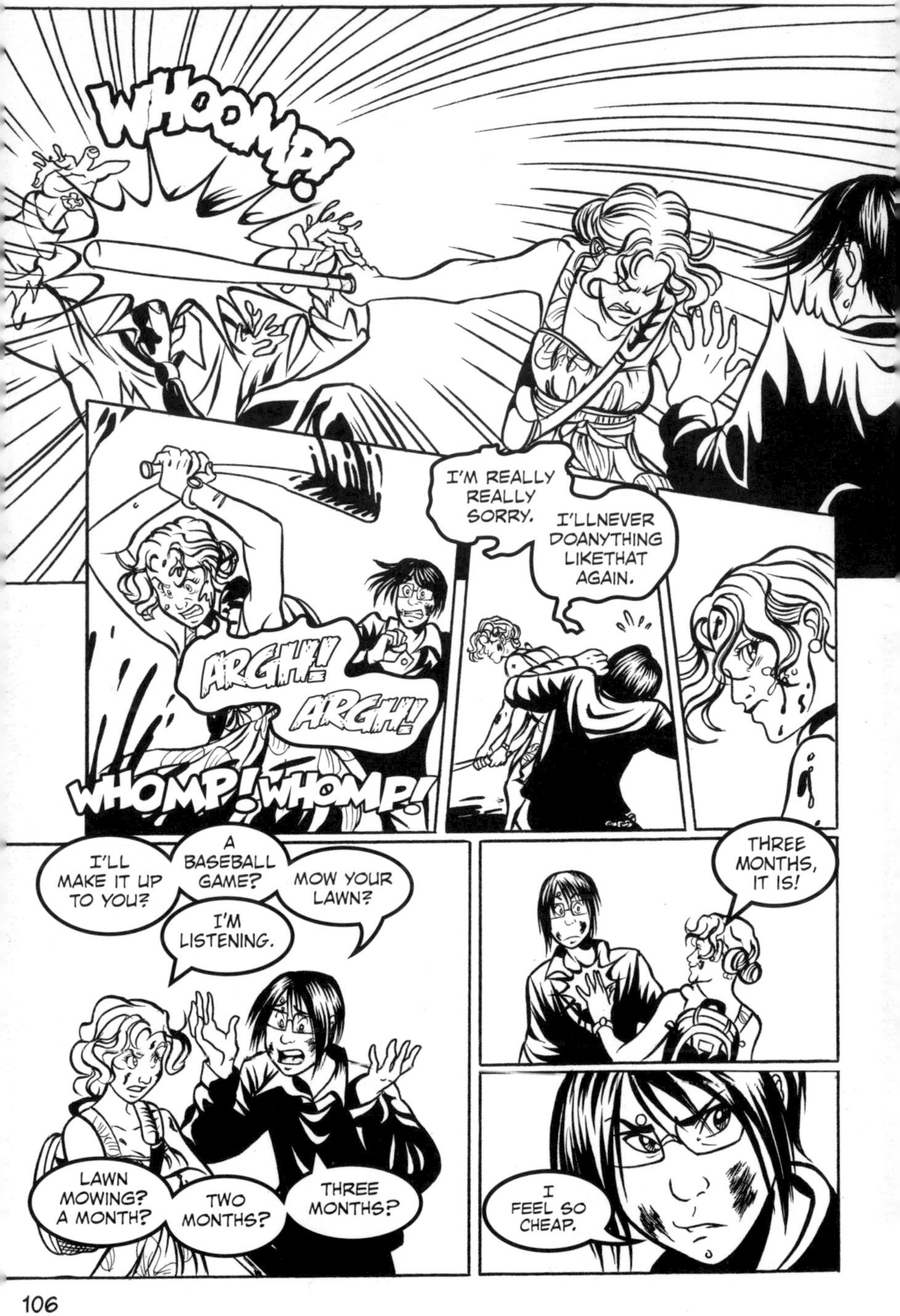
WHOOMP!
I'M REALLY REALLY SORRY.
I'LLNEVER DOANYTHING LIKETHAT AGAIN.
ARGH! ARGH!
WHOMP! WHOMP!
I'LL MAKE IT UP TO YOU?
A BASEBALL GAME?
MOW YOUR LAWN?
I'M LISTENING.
LAWN MOWING? A MONTH?
TWO MONTHS?
THREE MONTHS?
THREE MONTHS, IT IS!
I FEEL SO CHEAP.

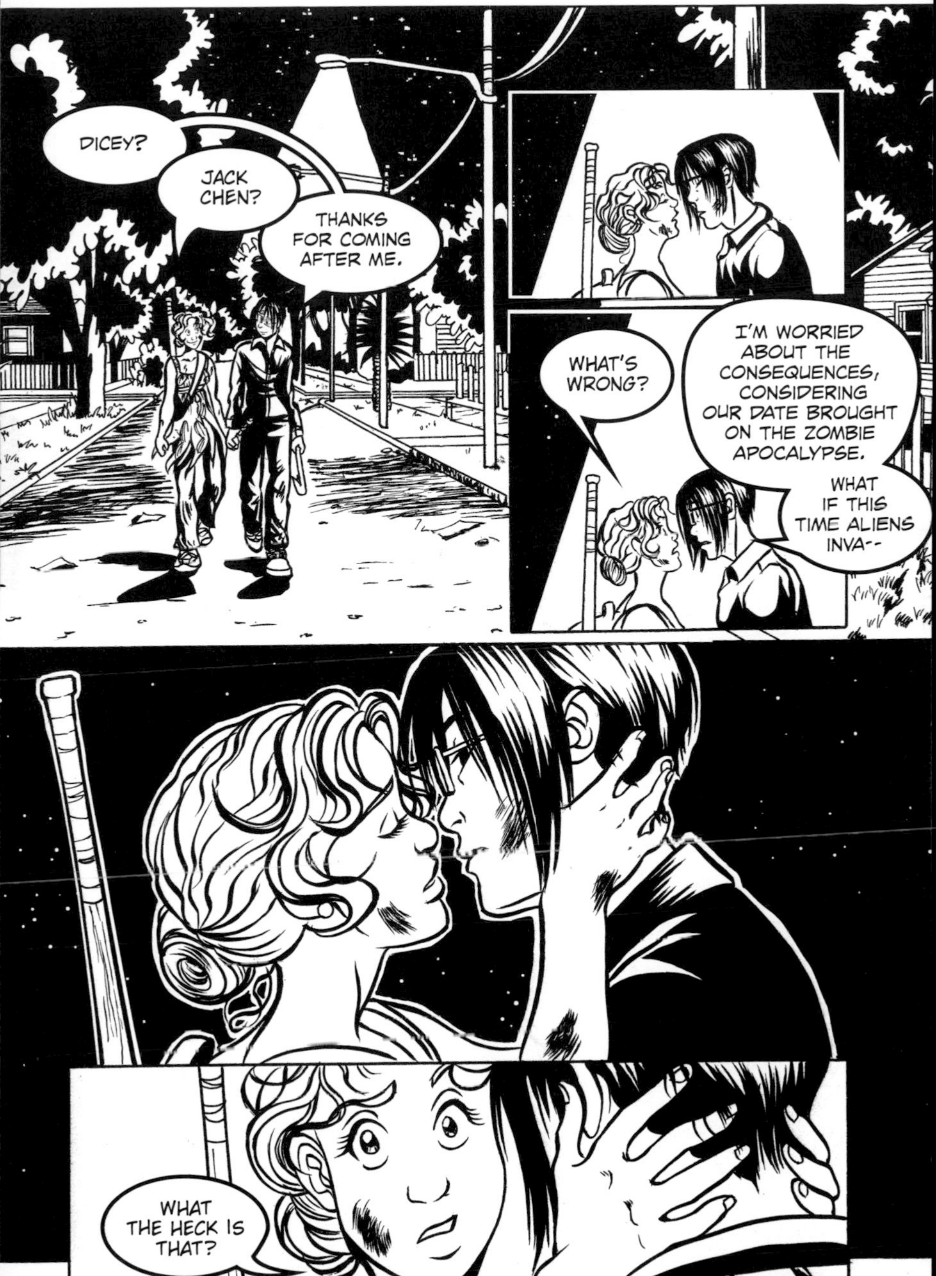
DICEY?
JACK CHEN?
THANKS FOR COMING AFTER ME.
WHAT'S WRONG?
I'M WORRIED ABOUT THE CONSEQUENCES, CONSIDERING OUR DATE BROUGHT ON THE ZOMBIE APOCALYPSE.
WHAT IF THIS TIME ALIENS INVA--
WHAT THE HECK IS THAT?

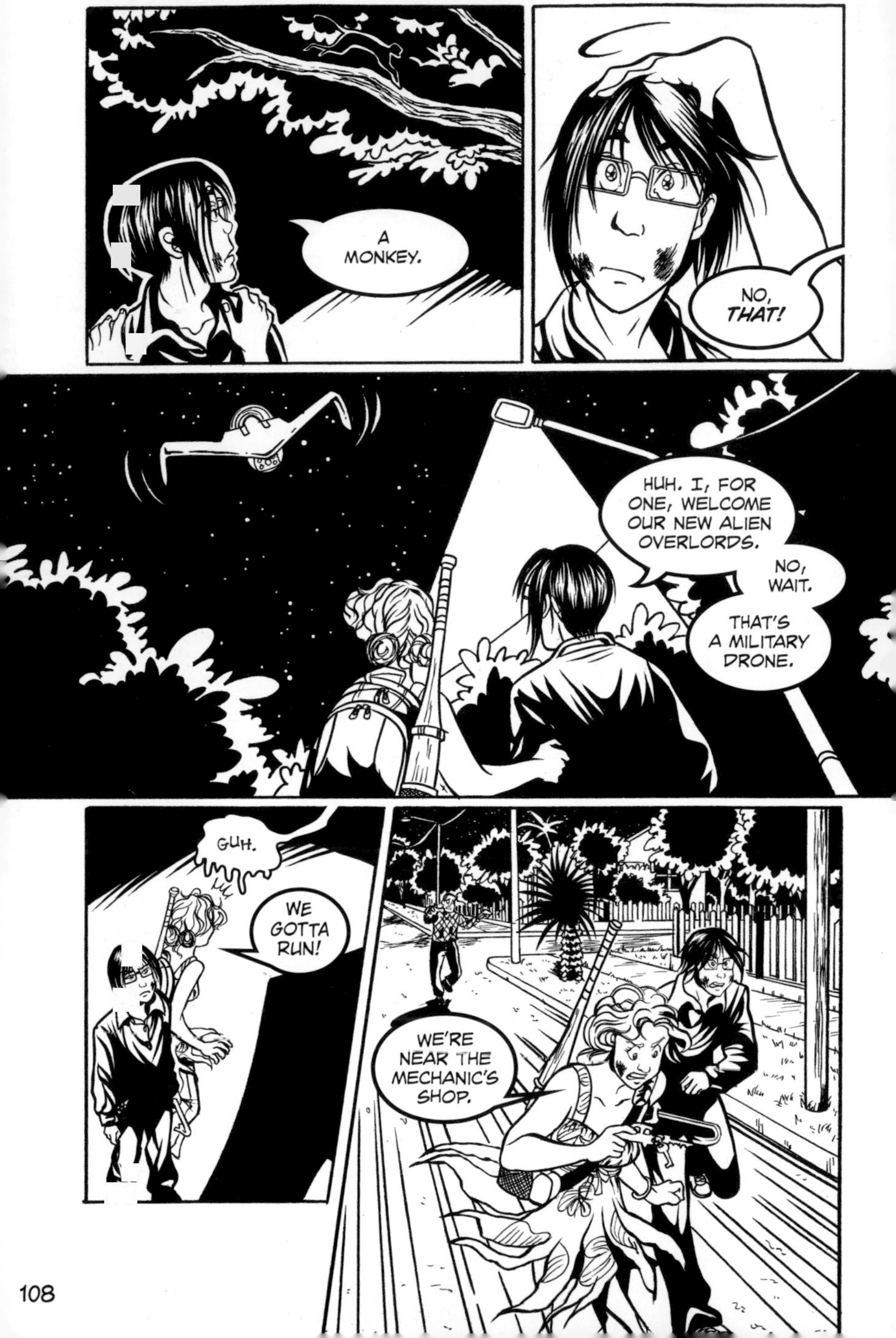
A MONKEY.
NO, THAT!
HUH. I, FOR ONE, WELCOME OUR NEW ALIEN OVERLORDS.
NO, WAIT.
THAT'S A MILITARY DRONE.
GUH.
WE GOTTA RUN!
WE'RE NEAR THE MECHANIC'S SHOP.

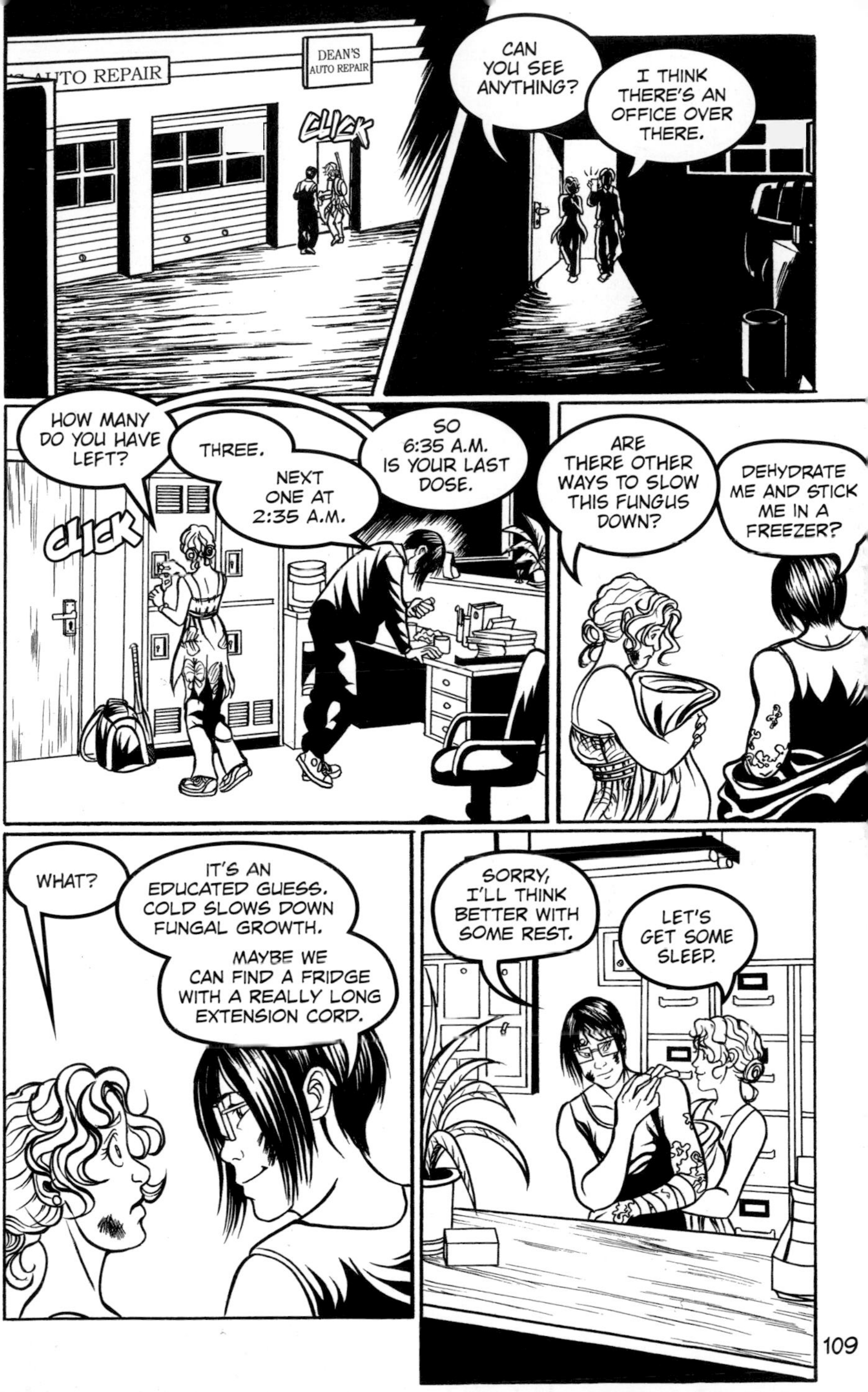
DEAN'S AUTO REPAIR
'S AUTO REPAIR
DEAN'S AUTO REPAIR
CLICK
CAN YOU SEE ANYTHING?
I THINK THERE'S AN OFFICE OVER THERE.
HOW MANY DO YOU HAVE LEFT?
THREE.
NEXT ONE AT 2:35 A.M.
SO 6:35 A.M. IS YOUR LAST DOSE.
CLICK
ARE THERE OTHER WAYS TO SLOW THIS FUNGUS DOWN?
DEHYDRATE ME AND STICK ME IN A FREEZER?
WHAT?
IT'S AN EDUCATED GUESS. COLD SLOWS DOWN FUNGAL GROWTH.
MAYBE WE CAN FIND A FRIDGE WITH A REALLY LONG EXTENSION CORD.
SORRY, I'LL THINK BETTER WITH SOME REST.
LET'S GET SOME SLEEP.

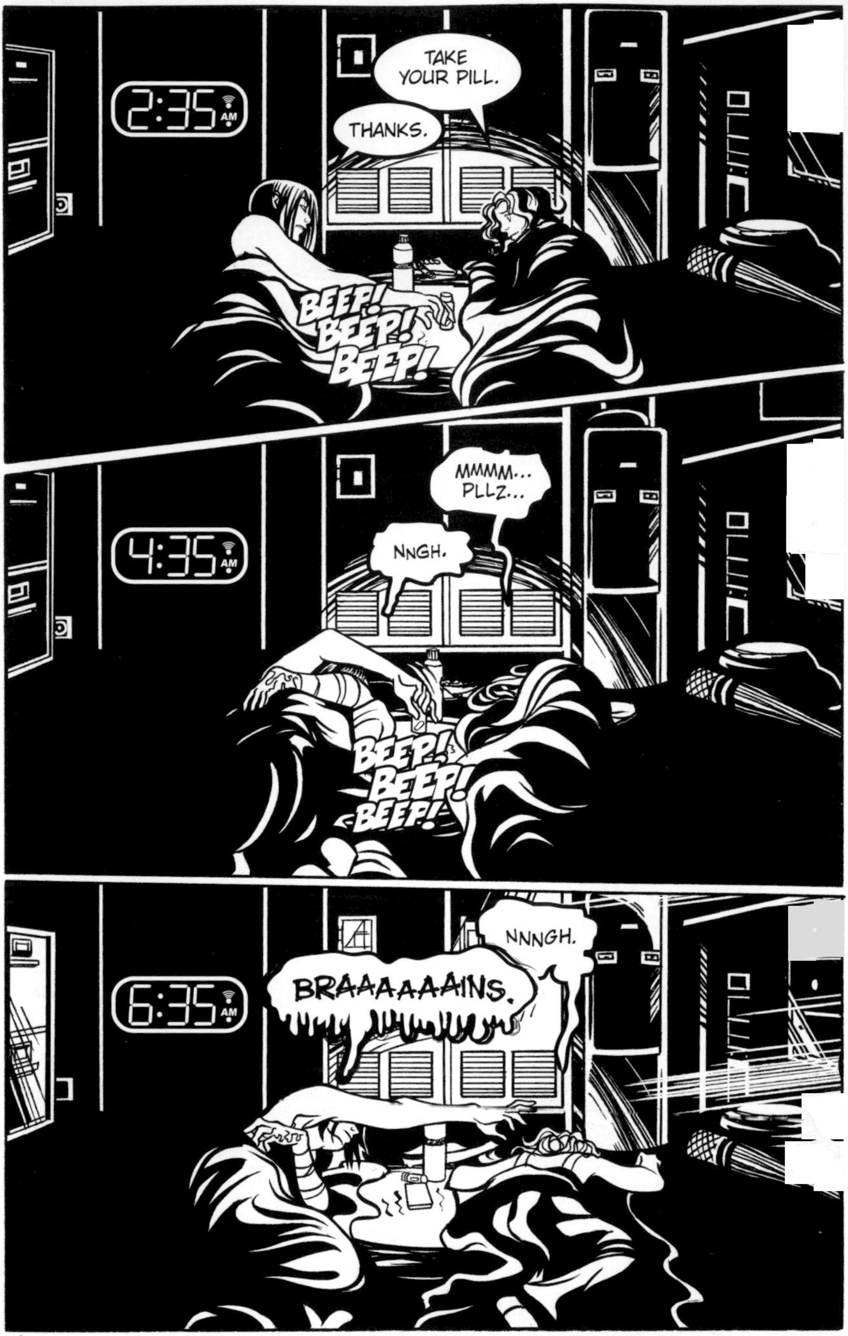
2:35 AM
TAKE YOUR PILL.
THANKS.
BEEP! BEEP! BEEP!
4:35 AM
MMMM... PLLZ...
NNGH.
BEEP! BEEP! BEEP!
6:35 AM
NNNGH.
BRAAAAAAINS.

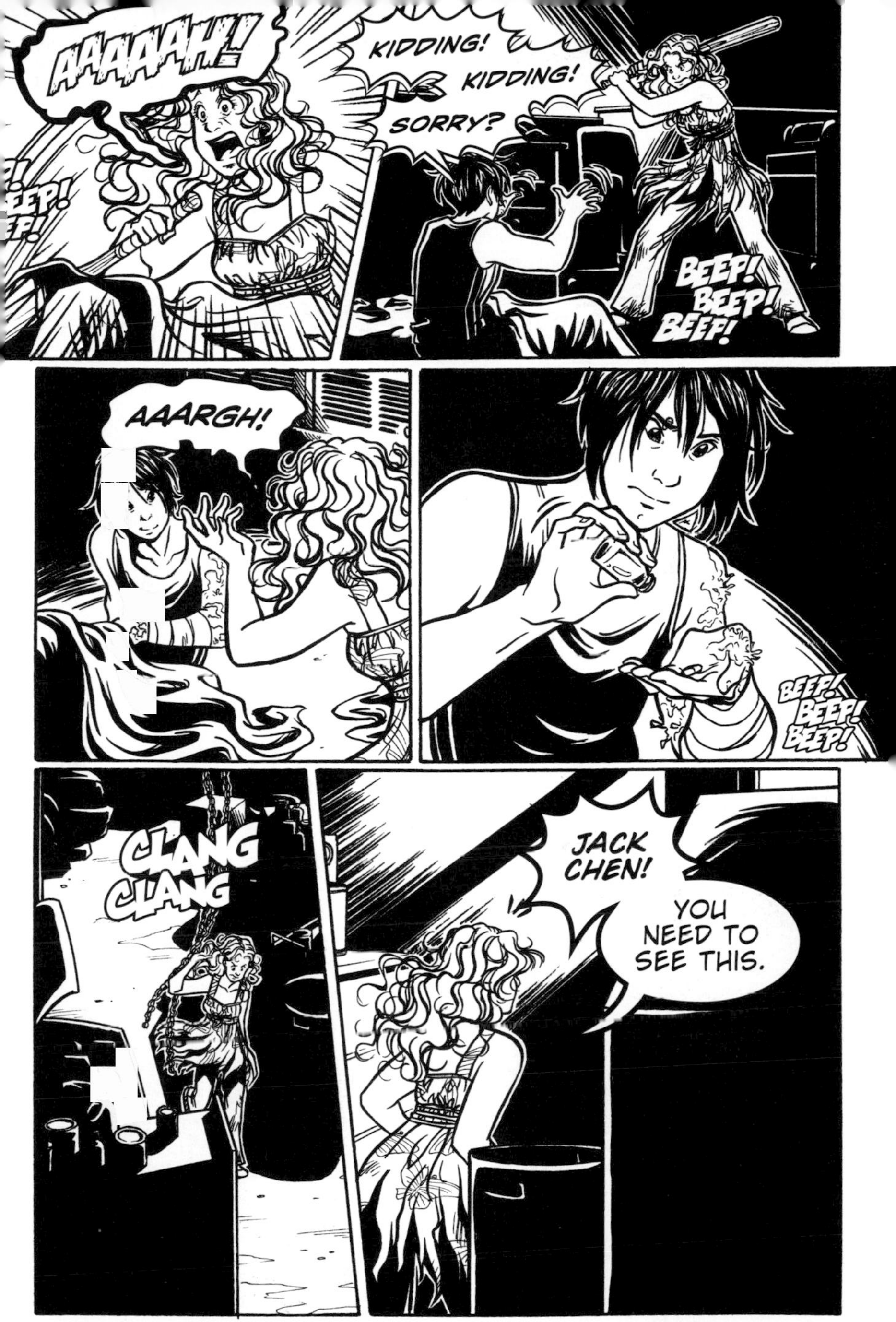
AAAAAH!!
BEEP!
BEEP!
KIDDING! KIDDING!
SORRY?
BEEP! BEEP! BEEP!
AAARGH!
BEEP! BEEP! BEEP!
CLANG CLANG
JACK CHEN!
YOU NEED TO SEE THIS.

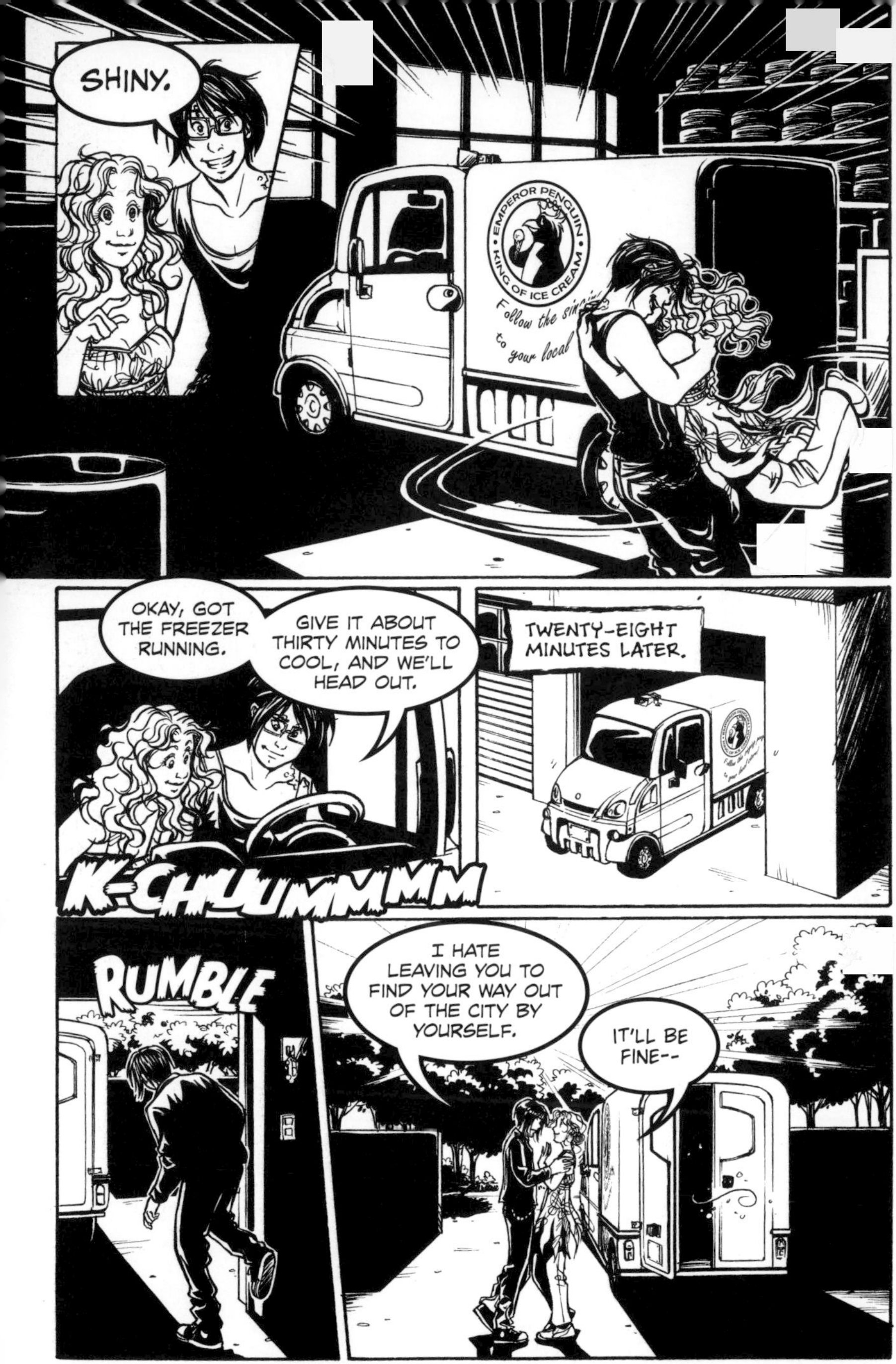
SHINY.
EMPEROR PENGUIN
KING OF ICE CREAM
OKAY, GOT THE FREEZER RUNNING.
GIVE IT ABOUT THIRTY MINUTES TO COOL, AND WE'LL HEAD OUT.
TWENTY-EIGHT MINUTES LATER.
K-CHUUMMMM
RUMBLE
I HATE LEAVING YOU TO FIND YOUR WAY OUT OF THE CITY BY YOURSELF.
IT'LL BE FINE--

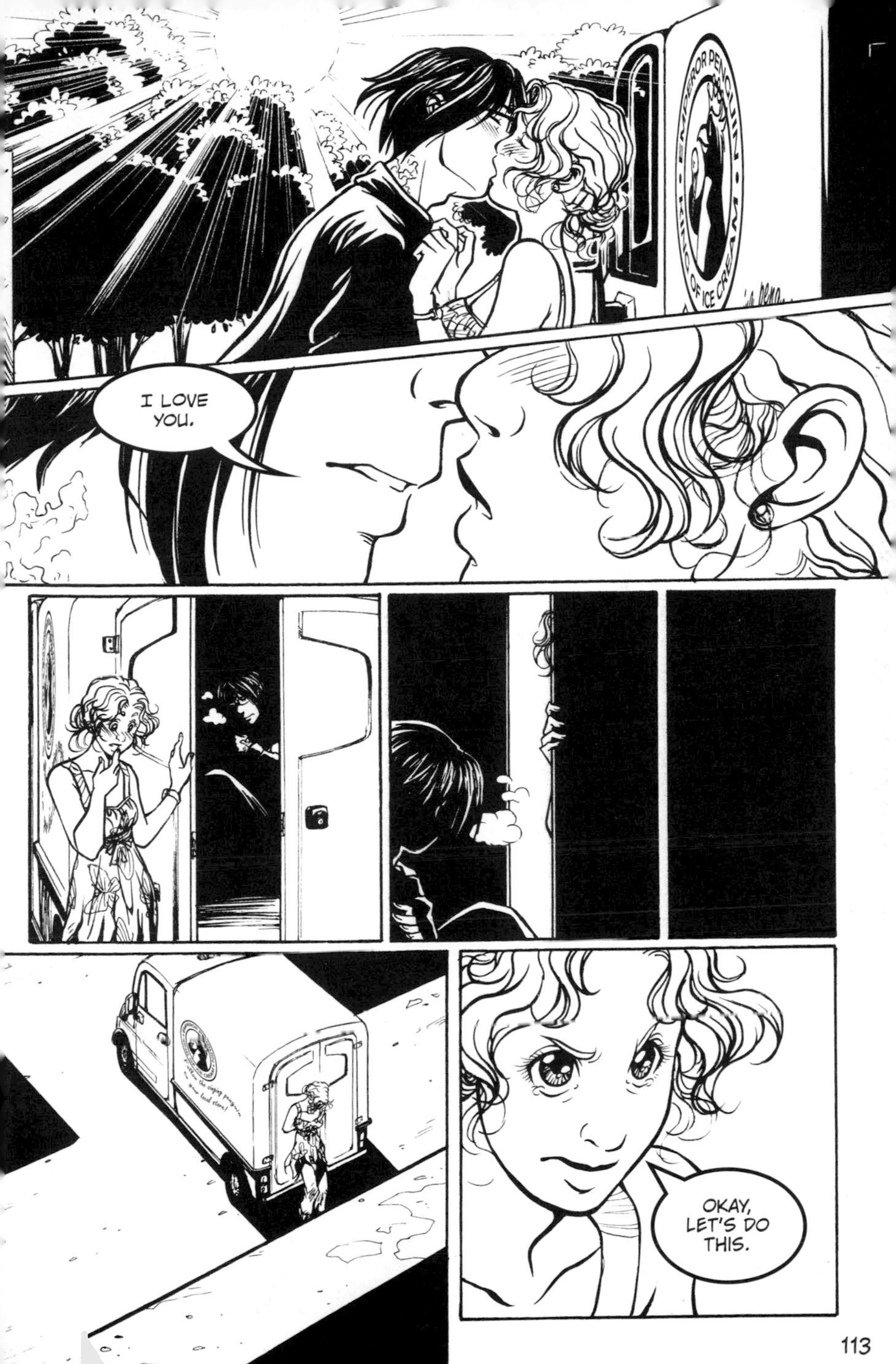
EMPEROR PENGUIN
KING OF ICE CREAM
I LOVE YOU.
OKAY, LET'S DO THIS.

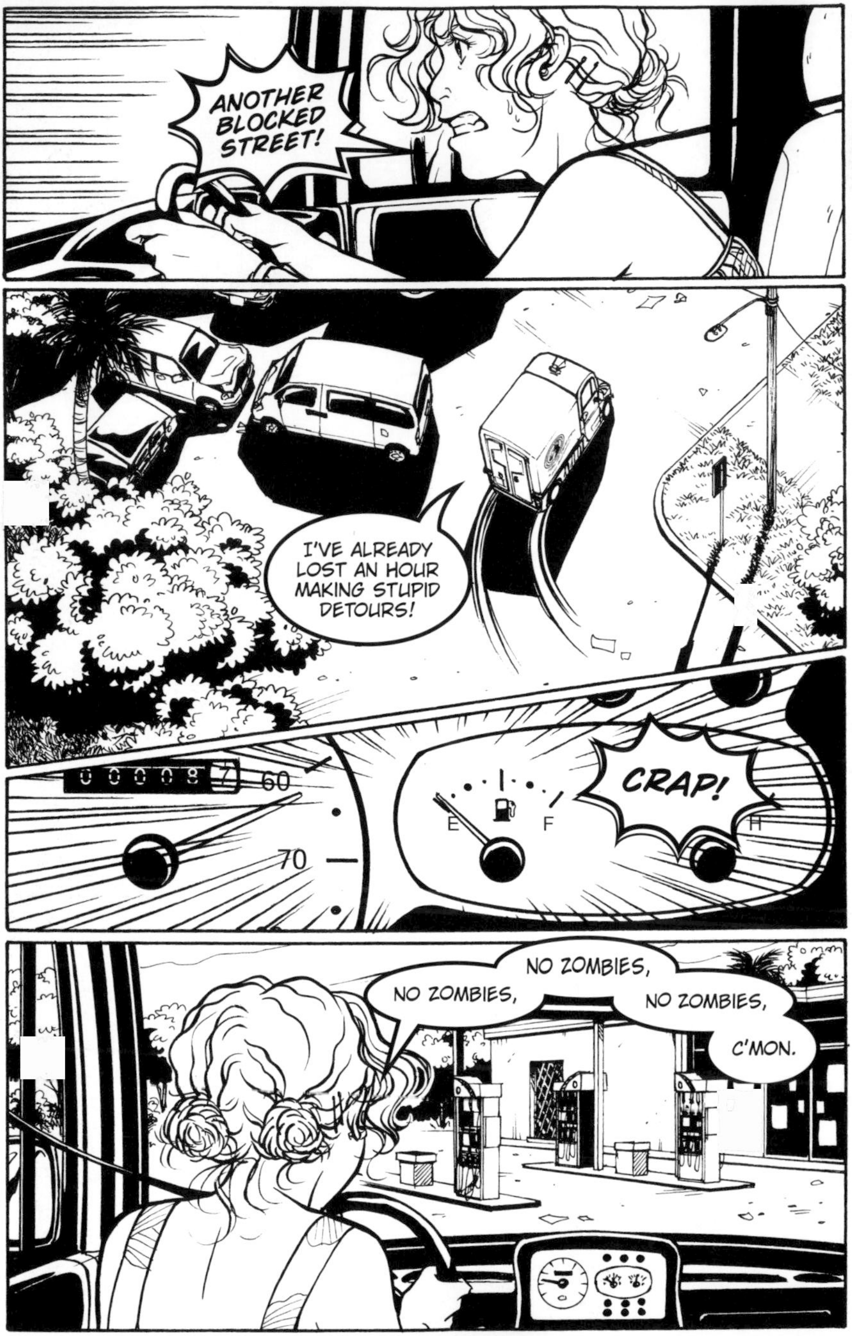
ANOTHER BLOCKED STREET!
I'VE ALREADY LOST AN HOUR MAKING STUPID DETOURS!
60
70
E
F
H
CRAP!
NO ZOMBIES,
NO ZOMBIES,
NO ZOMBIES,
C'MON.

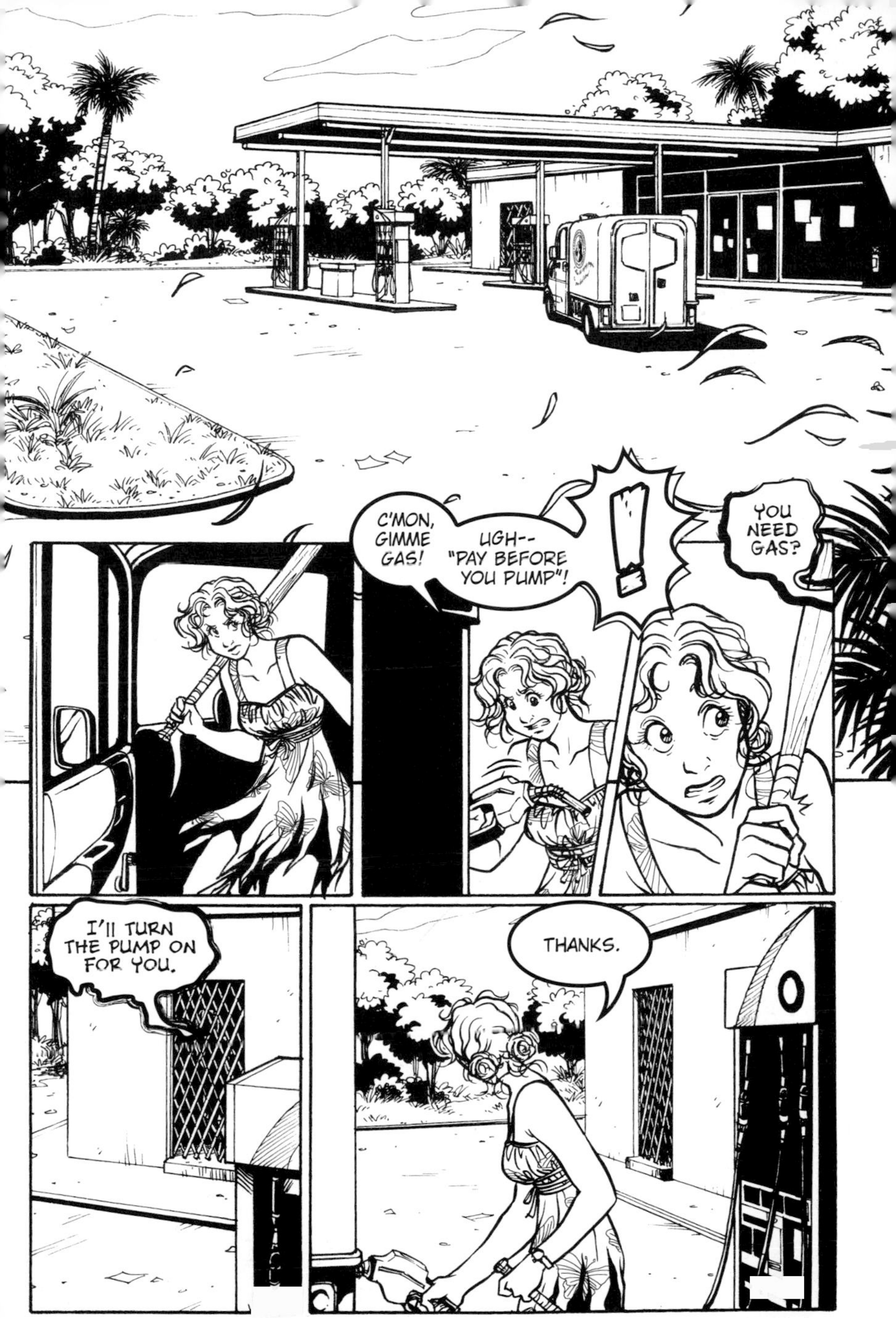
C'MON, GIMME GAS!
UGH-- "PAY BEFORE YOU PUMP"!
!
YOU NEED GAS?
I'll TURN THE PUMP ON FOR YOU.
THANKS.

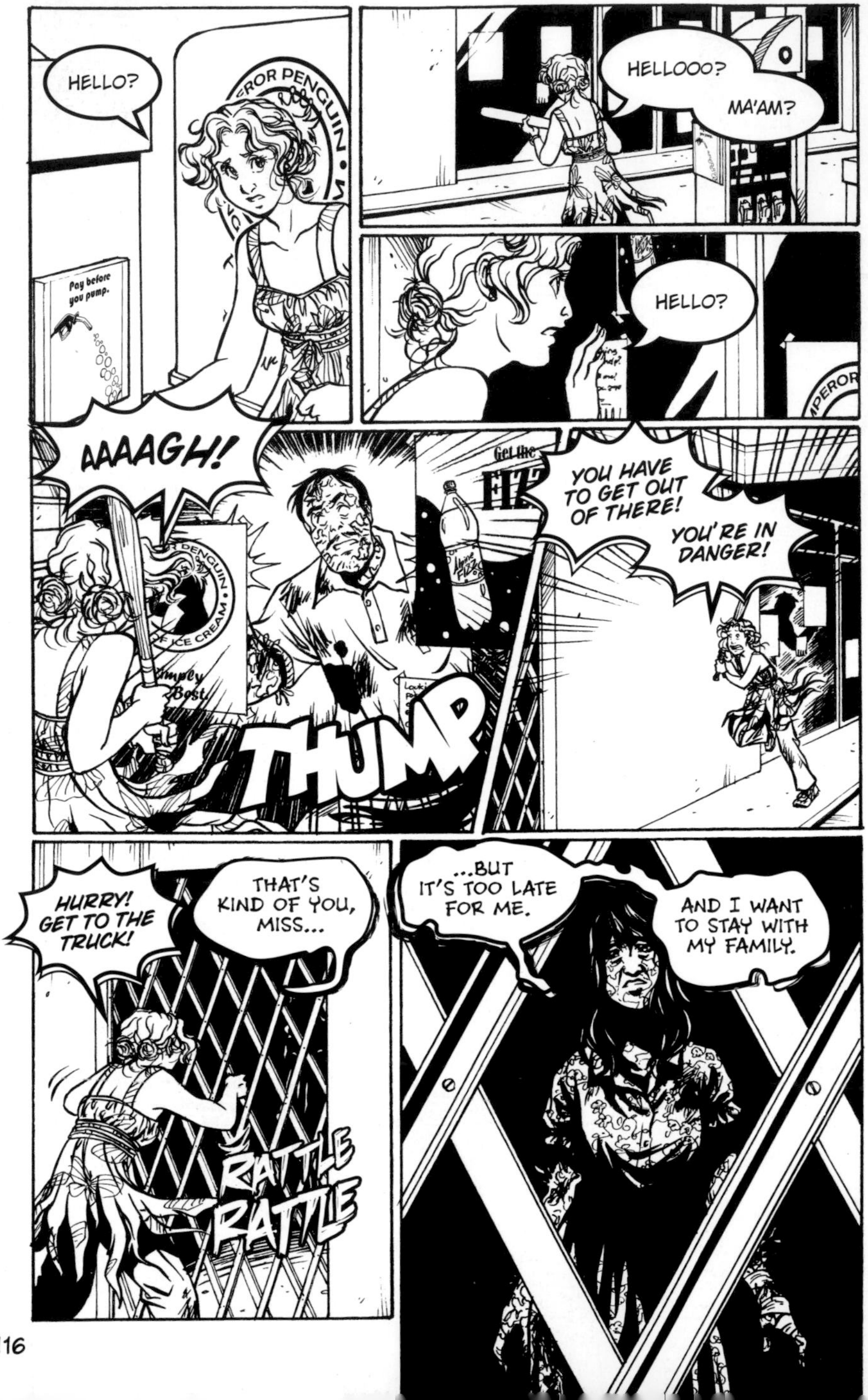
HELLO?
HELLOOO?
MA'AM?
HELLO?
AAAAGH!
THUMP
YOU HAVE TO GET OUT OF THERE!
YOU'RE IN DANGER!
HURRY! GET TO THE TRUCK!
THAT'S KIND OF YOU, MISS...
RATTLE RATTLE
...BUT IT'S TOO LATE FOR ME.
AND I WANT TO STAY WITH MY FAMILY.

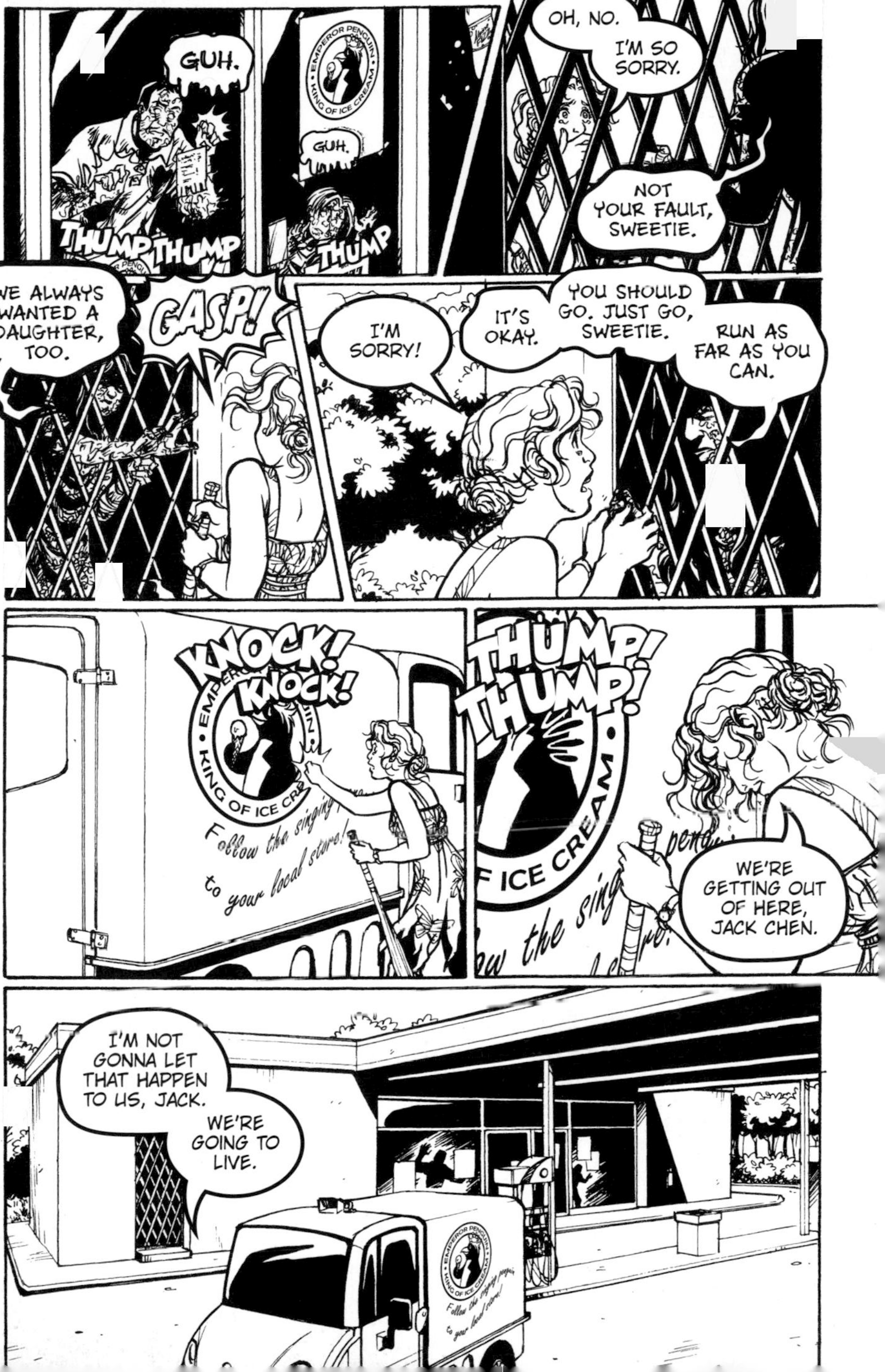
GUH.
EMPEROR PENGUIN
KING OF ICE CREAM
GUH.
THUMP THUMP
THUMP
OH, NO.
I'M SO SORRY.
NOT YOUR FAULT, SWEETIE.
WE ALWAYS WANTED A DAUGHTER, TOO.
GASP!
I'M SORRY!
IT'S OKAY.
YOU SHOULD GO. JUST GO, SWEETIE.
RUN AS FAR AS YOU CAN.
KNOCK! KNOCK!
KING OF ICE CREAM
to your local store!
THUMP! THUMP!
WE'RE GETTING OUT OF HERE, JACK CHEN.
I'M NOT GONNA LET THAT HAPPEN TO US, JACK.
WE'RE GOING TO LIVE.
EMPEROR PENGUIN
KING OF ICE CREAM

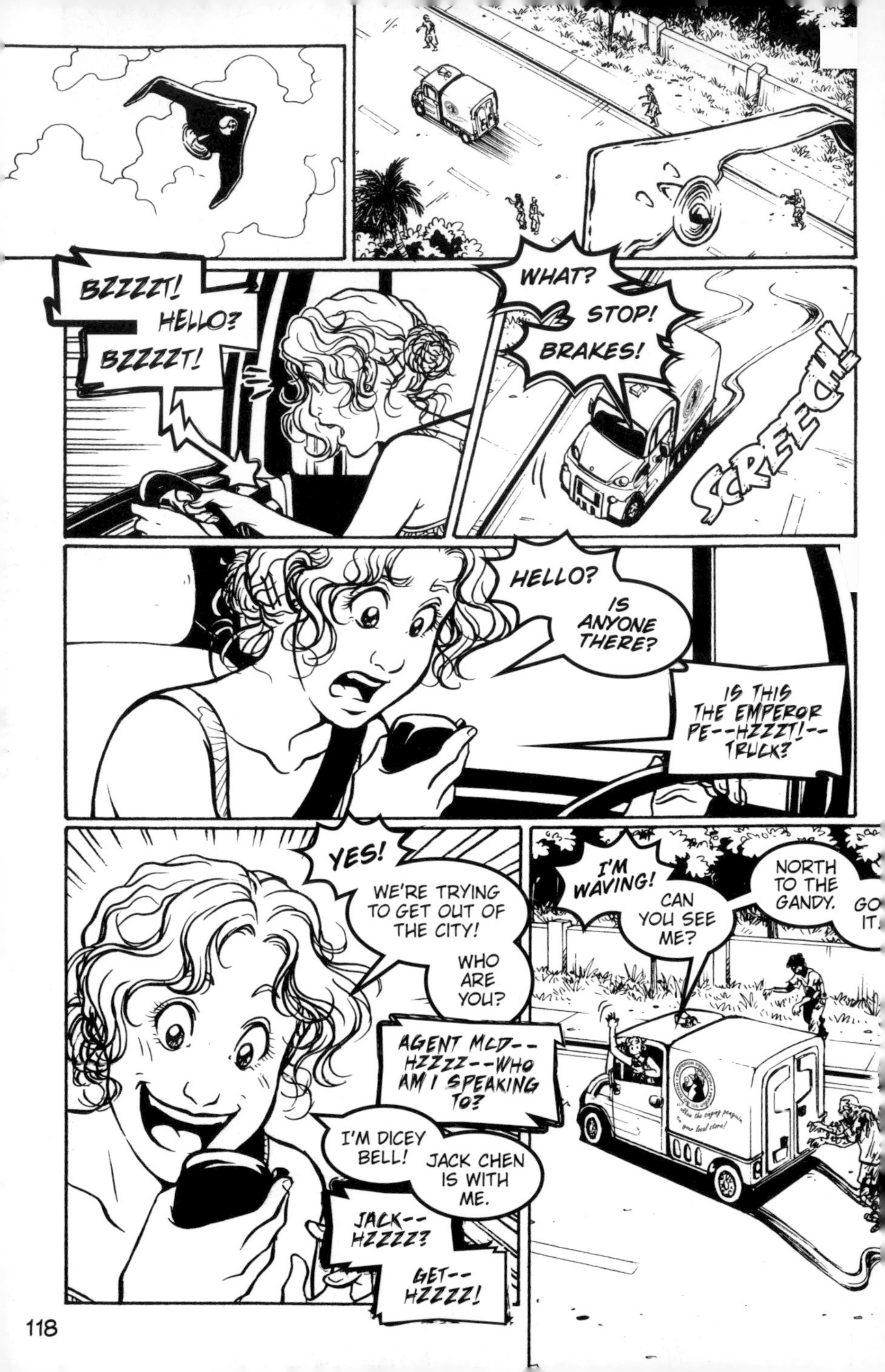
BZZZZT!
HELLO?
BZZZZT!
WHAT?
STOP!
BRAKES!
SCREECH!
HELLO?
IS ANYONE THERE?
IS THIS THE EMPEROR PE--HZZZT!--TRUCK?
YES!
WE'RE TRYING TO GET OUT OF THE CITY!
WHO ARE YOU?
AGENT MCD--HZZZZ--WHO AM I SPEAKING TO?
I'M DICEY BELL!
JACK CHEN IS WITH ME.
JACK--HZZZZ?
GET--HZZZZ!
I'M WAVING!
CAN YOU SEE ME?
NORTH TO THE GANDY.

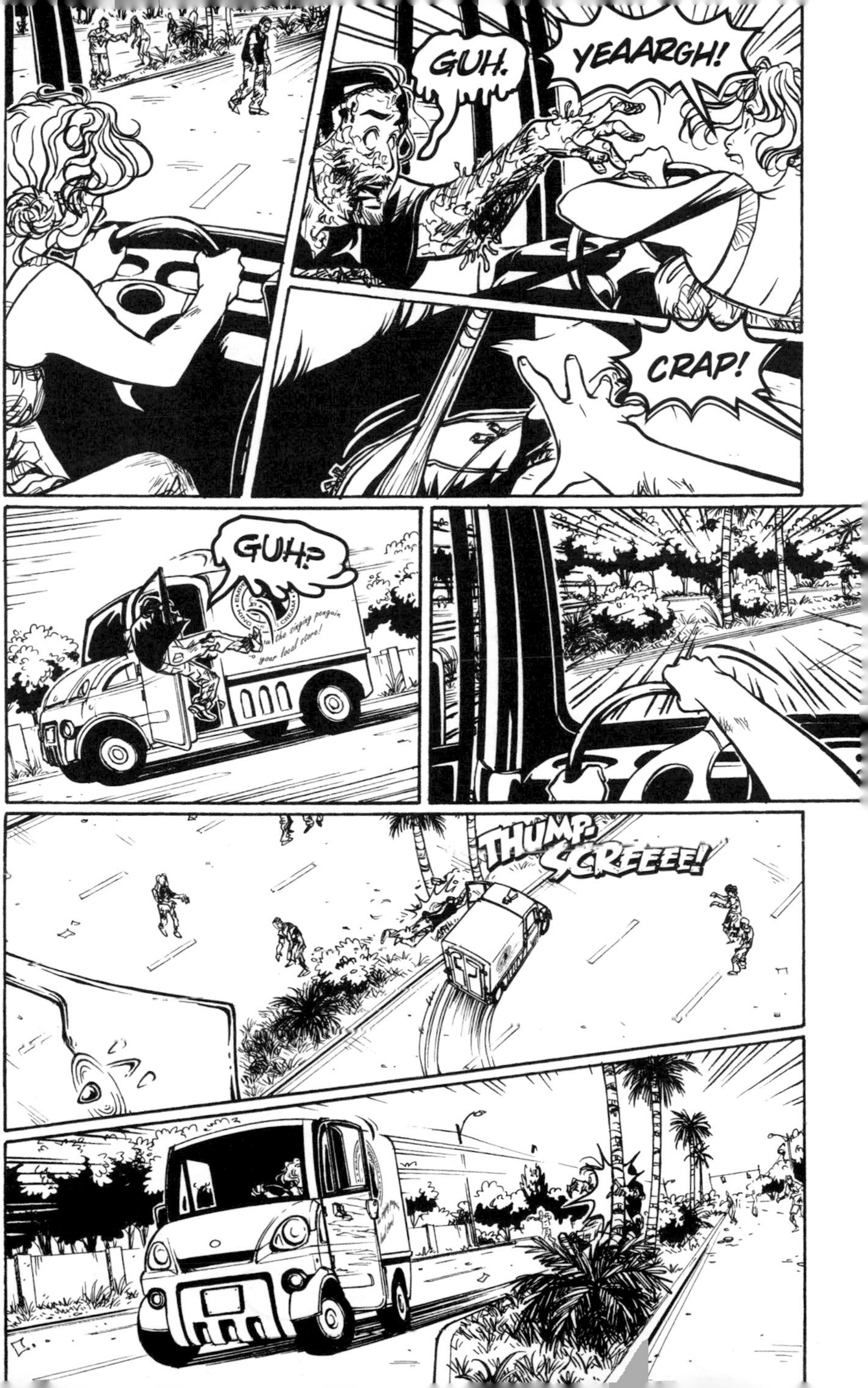
GUH.
YEAARGH!
CRAP!
GUH?
EMPEROR KING ICE CREAM
the singing penguin
your local store!
THUMP.
SCREEEE!

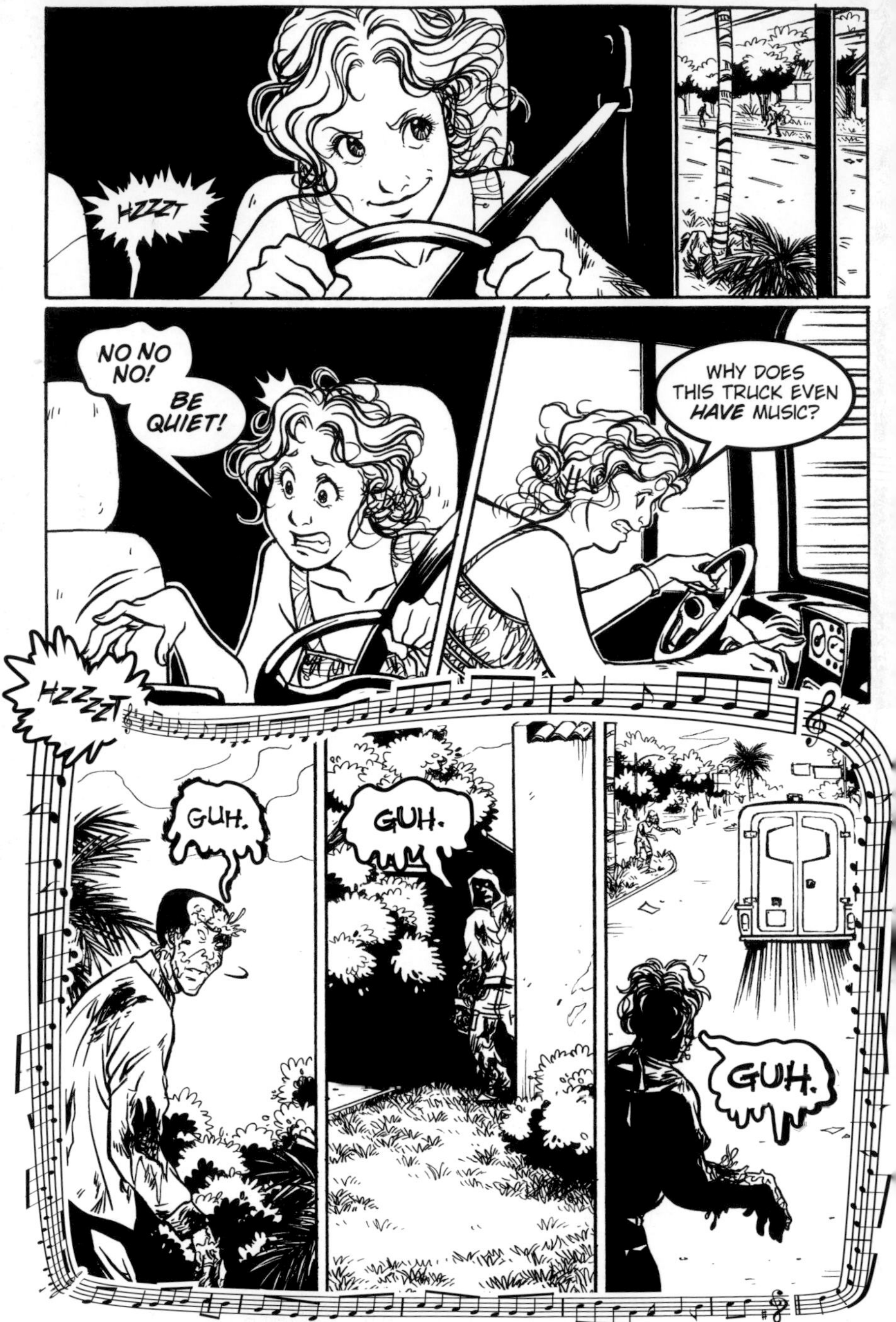
HZZZT
NO NO NO!
BE QUIET!
WHY DOES THIS TRUCK EVEN HAVE MUSIC?
HZZZZT
GUH.
GUH.
GUH.

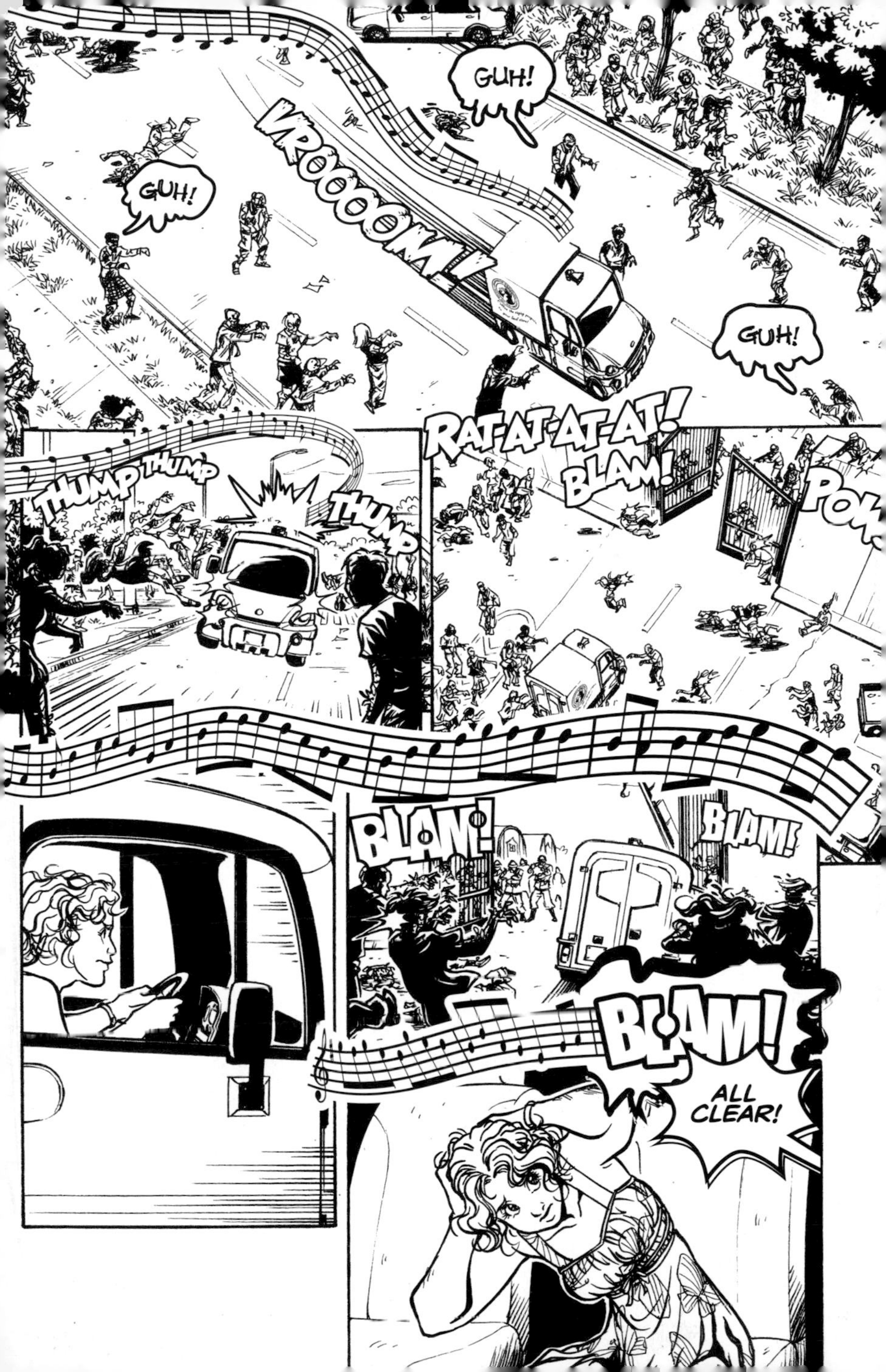

GUH!
VROOOOOM!
GUH!
GUH!
THUMP THUMP
THUMP
RAT-AT-AT-AT!
BLAM!
POW
BLAM!
BLAM!
BLAM!
ALL CLEAR!

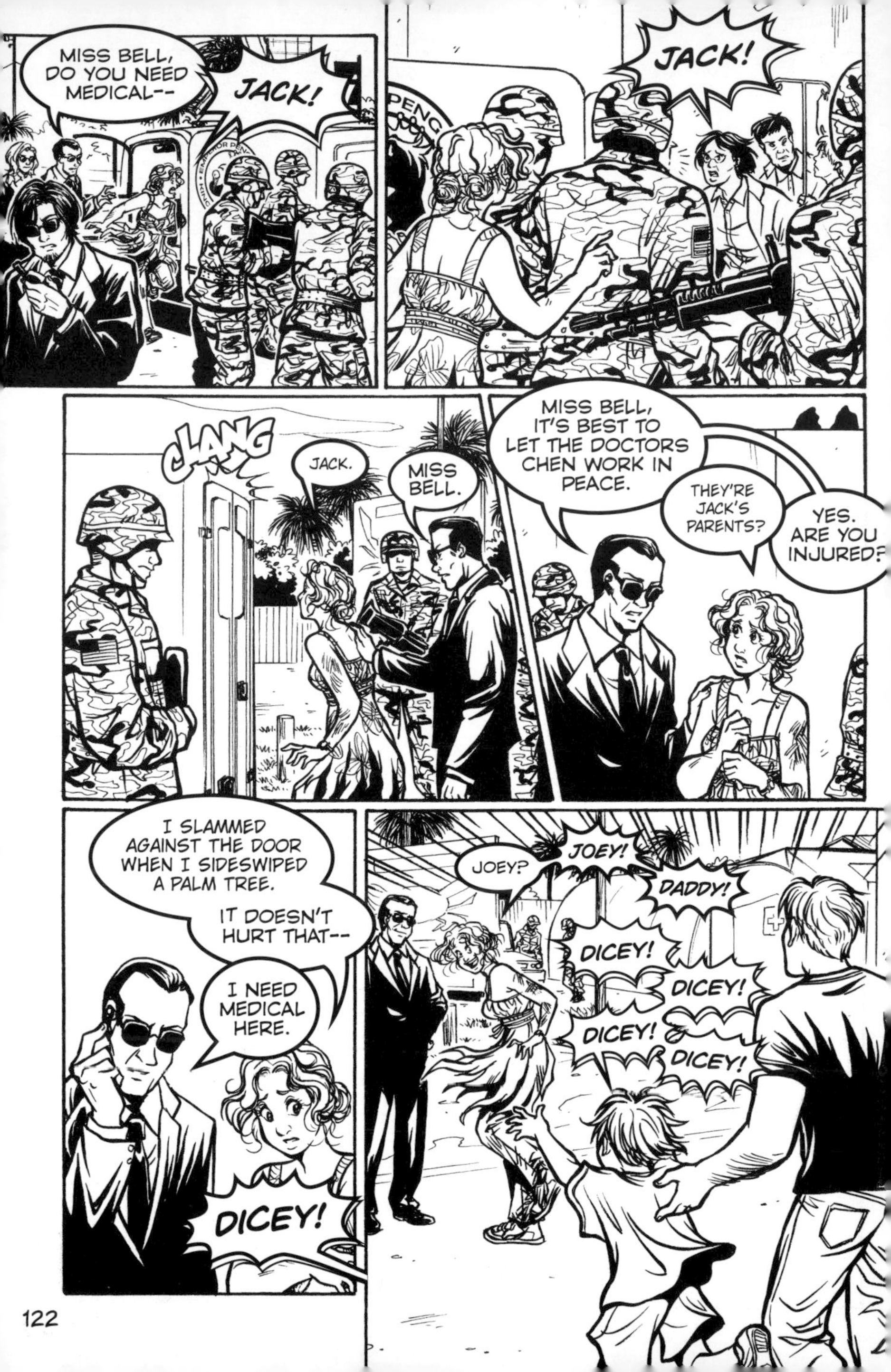
MISS BELL, DO YOU NEED MEDICAL--
JACK!
JACK!
CLANG
JACK.
MISS BELL.
MISS BELL, IT'S BEST TO LET THE DOCTORS CHEN WORK IN PEACE.
THEY'RE JACK'S PARENTS?
YES. ARE YOU INJURED?
I SLAMMED AGAINST THE DOOR WHEN I SIDESWIPED A PALM TREE.
IT DOESN'T HURT THAT--
I NEED MEDICAL HERE.
DICEY!
JOEY?
JOEY!
DADDY!
DICEY!
DICEY!
DICEY!
DICEY!

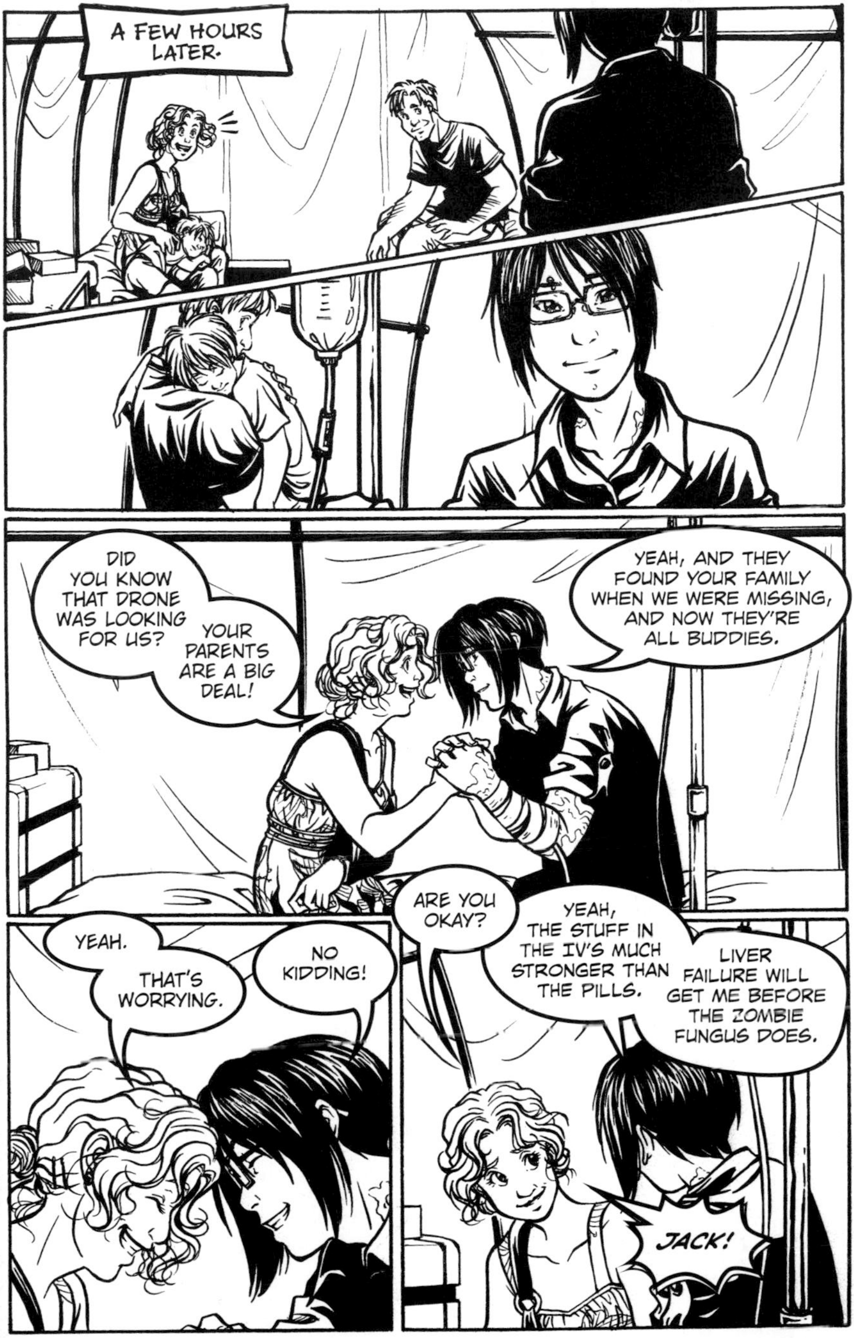
A FEW HOURS LATER.
DID YOU KNOW THAT DRONE WAS LOOKING FOR US?
YOUR PARENTS ARE A BIG DEAL!
YEAH, AND THEY FOUND YOUR FAMILY WHEN WE WERE MISSING, AND NOW THEY'RE ALL BUDDIES.
YEAH.
THAT'S WORRYING.
NO KIDDING!
ARE YOU OKAY?
YEAH, THE STUFF IN THE IV'S MUCH STRONGER THAN THE PILLS.
LIVER FAILURE WILL GET ME BEFORE THE ZOMBIE FUNGUS DOES.
JACK!

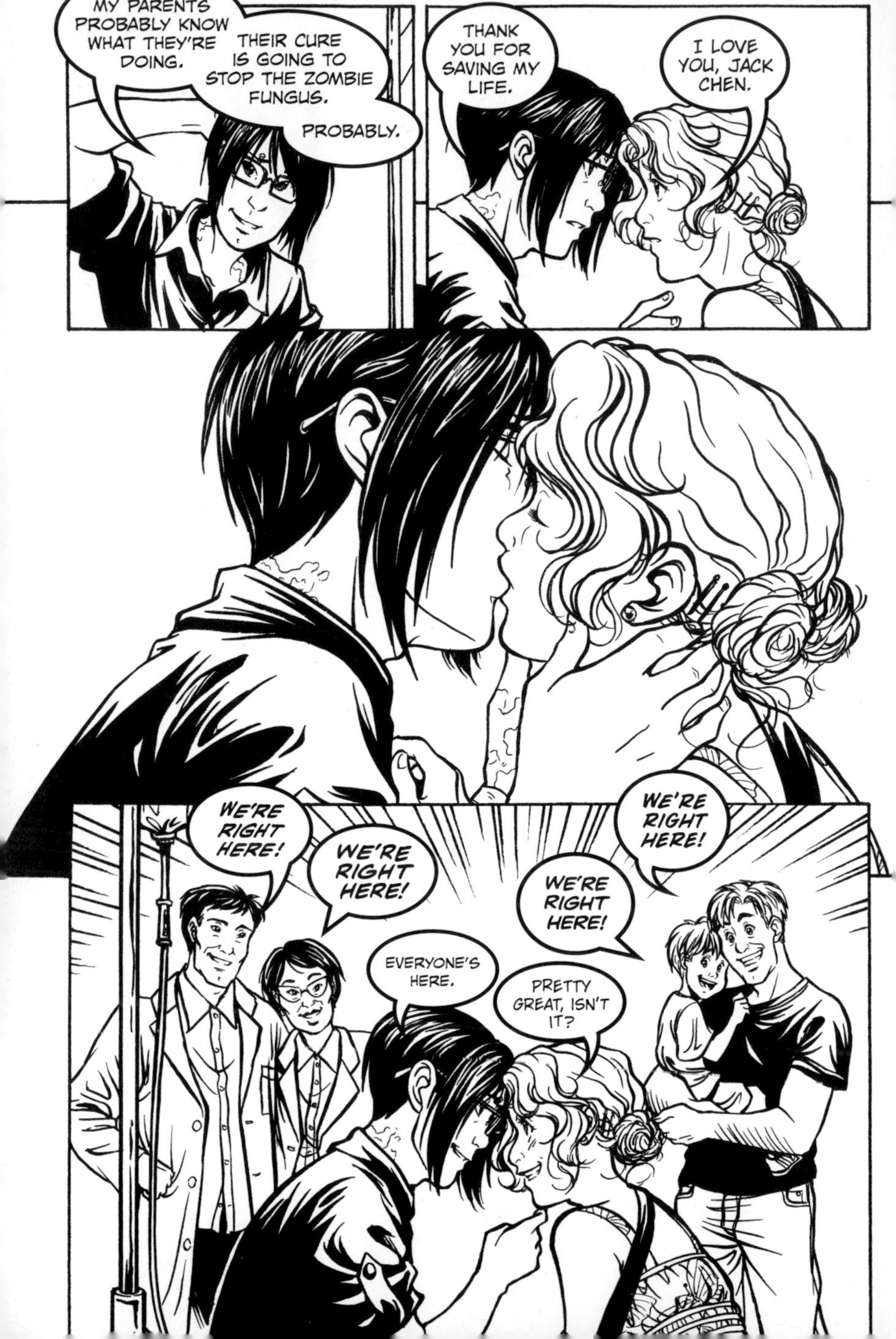
MY PARENTS PROBABLY KNOW WHAT THEY'RE DOING.
THEIR CURE IS GOING TO STOP THE ZOMBIE FUNGUS.
PROBABLY.
THANK YOU FOR SAVING MY LIFE.
I LOVE YOU, JACK CHEN.
WE'RE RIGHT HERE!
WE'RE RIGHT HERE!
WE'RE RIGHT HERE!
WE'RE RIGHT HERE!
EVERYONE'S HERE.
PRETTY GREAT, ISN'T IT?

PELICAN POST
ST. PETERSBURG HIGH SCHOOL

Transcript of a live chat with Dicey Bell and Jack Chen. Six months after the zombie apocalypse, the heroes from St. Pete answer readers' questions.

IHEARTCHEESE: Has your life changed since you got famous?

DICEY: Not really. The military cleaned up St. Pete pretty fast. It's a little weird to be doing normal senior year stuff, I guess.

JACK: There's the free ice cream.

DICEY: Oh, yeah! Emperor Penguin said we could have free ice cream for a year! That's pretty awesome.

JACK: They already regret it. Dicey could out-eat an elephant.

JACK: Dicey has her bat, so I'm just going to change that to: her athletic, svelte figure seems immune to thousands of calories of ice cream.

PARKER09: is it tru ur dating?? ++++romantic!!!

DICEY: I'm too busy eating ice cream to date.

TENNISFAN7: Jack, what was it like to be infected by the zombie fungus? Any leftover side effects?

DICEY: The brain damage seems permanent.

JACK: I'm fine! The fungus never reached my brain. And yes, we're dating!

TRUFFLEBUNNY: How could a fungus turn Jack into a zombie?

JACK: I am not a zombie.

JACK: *Cordyceps* fungus attacks insects all the time. It takes over the little insect brain and makes the bug climb out on a tree branch where the fungus spores can spread a lot more easily. In the mutation that attacked humans, the spores were concentrated in the mouth. So it turned out that the mutation spread best through bites.

DICEY: Spores in the mouth.

DICEY: You didn't tell me that.

JACK: But it didn't spread through kissing. I guess.

TRUFFLEBUNNY: Should I stop eating mushrooms?

JACK: You can keep eating mushrooms. My family used to cook with dried *Cordyceps* all the time, just like any other tasty fungus.

DICEY: You didn't tell me that.

SPARKLESRHOT: So what's it like dating a zombie?

DICEY: There's a difference between a zombie and a high school boy? Well, when you get a zombie's attention, you know that it'll stick with you, at least until it can eat your brains. Regular guys are more fickle.

JACK: I AM NOT A ZOMBIE!

Category: Interviews, Chat Transcripts
Tags: apocalypse, brains, cordyceps, dating, eating, fungus, zombies

PRINT | E-MAIL | SHARE | CHIRP

ARTIST'S SKETCHBOOK

DISEÑO DE PERSONAJES

Para diseñar los personajes el autor me envía una descripción de ellos en la que me tengo que basar. No tanto el aspecto físico—ése se describe rápidamente, y a no ser que haya detalles importantes (p. ej. piercings o tatuajes) no hace falta más. A veces los autores me nombran a actores como ejemplo de cómo se imaginan los rasgos generales de sus personajes, cosa que resulta muy útil.

Pero sobre todo quiero conocer el carácter del personaje, sus aficiones, su forma de ser . . . Todo ello puede influir en el diseño.

Normalmente, la cara del personaje queda bastante definida desde el primer boceto, ya que si no me gusta, lo borro y lo modifico. Aún así muchas veces vuelvo al primer boceto.

Supongo que como tantas veces en la vida, la primera impresión es la que se queda.

CHARACTER DESIGN

To design the characters, the author sent me a description of them to work from. Not so much the physical side—that can be described quickly, and unless there are important details (for example, piercings or tattoos), that's all that's needed. Sometimes authors name actors as examples of how they imagine the general features of their characters, which is very useful.

But above all, I want to know the personalities of the characters, their hobbies, their way of life.... All this can influence the design.

Normally, the character's face is pretty clear from the first sketch. If I don't like it, I erase it and modify it. But, many times I return to my first sketch.

I guess, as is so often true in life, it's the first impression that matters most.

—Janina

ABOUT THE AUTHOR
AND THE ARTIST

EVONNE TSANG is a native New Yorker who attended high school in zombie-apocalypse epicenter St. Petersburg, Florida, before returning to the Northeast to earn a BA in English with a minor in creative writing from New York University. At NYU she was editor in chief of the science fiction and fantasy magazine. Her previous book for Graphic Universe™ was Twisted Journeys® #12, *Kung Fu Masters*.

JANINA GÖRRISSEN was born in Frankenthal, Germany, and studied comic arts in Barcelona, Spain. Her works include the shojo manga *Kairi* (published in France by Les Humanoïdes Associés) and *Black is for Beginnings* from Flux. Her website is jgoerrissen.com.